Hawkins. Something's wrong. Meet me at Caitano and Deverick's quarters."

Closing that connection, she then said, "Corsi to Poynter, emergency site-to-site transport. Deck four, section nine."

She materialized a few meters down the corridor from the room, taking off at a sprint toward the door. When she got there, she buzzed it. There was no answer.

"Computer, security override. Priority one. Access code Corsi Gamma Three Two Two."

The door slid aside to a brightly lit room. "Caitano?" she called.

She heard the turbolift doors slide open down the hall. Vance Hawkins, Lauoc Soan, and Rennan Konya walked toward her, concern in Hawkins's dark features.

"No answer at the door," she said. "I've got a bad feeling about this."

Hand on her phaser, Corsi followed Hawkins through the door and into the quarters' small sitting room. Caitano and Deverick had somehow managed to luck into one of the two-room quarters that had been added during the ship's refit, so it wasn't until she reached the bedroom that she saw it. Caitano lay facedown on the floor, a trail of dark blood working its way from his left ear down the side of his face. She reached down and checked his neck for a pulse.

Nothing.

No.

STAR TREK®

CORPS OF ENGINEERS

WOUNDS

Ilsa J. Bick, Keith R.A. DeCandido,
John J. Ordover, Terri Osborne, Cory Rushton

Based upon STAR TREK® and STAR TREK: THE NEXT
GENERATION® created by Gene Roddenberry and
STAR TREK: DEEP SPACE NINE® created by
Rick Berman & Michael Piller

POCKET BOOKS
New York   London   Toronto   Sydney   Coroticus III

Pocket Books
A Division of Simon & Schuster, Inc.
1230 Avenue of the Americas
New York, NY 10020

First Pocket Books trade paperback edition October 2008

POCKET and colophon are registered trademarks of Simon & Schuster, Inc.

For information about special discounts for bulk purchases, please contact Simon & Schuster Special Sales at 1-800-456-6798 or business@simonandschuster.com.

Manufactured in the United States of America

10 9 8 7 6 5 4 3 2 1

ISBN-13: 978-1-4165-8909-9
ISBN-10:   1-4165-8909-0

These titles were previously published individually in eBook format by Pocket Books.

CONTENTS

Historian's Note

The six stories in this volume all take place between *Ferengi-nar: Satisfaction is Not Guaranteed* and *The Dominion: Olympus Descending*, the two short novels in W*orlds of Star Trek: Deep Space Nine* Volume 3.

MALEFICTORUM

Terri Osborne

For my grandfather, Charles Edward Haznedl Senior, and for my little buddy Mitters. Take care of each other.

CHAPTER

1

The first thing Lieutenant Commander Domenica Corsi did when the mess hall doors opened was drop to the deck on one knee.

The second thing she did was draw her phaser.

Before she could figure out exactly what had flown through the doors at eye level, it changed shape, morphing until a winged yellow ball about the size of her head floated in the air before her, complete with a strange, almost cartoonlike smiling face on its surface. The idea of Dominion incursion crossed her mind, but she quickly dismissed it.

It wasn't their style.

Why do I have a feeling Fabe's got something to do with this?

"Sorry, Dom," Fabian Stevens's contrite voice said from behind her. "It kind of got away from me there."

I like him, but I swear I'm going to have to kill him.

She holstered her phaser. "Kind of?" Brushing back a strand of blond hair, she turned on him, fully prepared to read him the riot act for losing a dangerous device on her ship. He, of all people, should have known better.

She stopped cold at the sight of an elaborate contraption

sitting on top of his head. Black goggles rested on his fore-head, with red, yellow, and blue leads running back to oddly shaped earpieces. Tiny red lights at the edges of the goggles' faceplate suggested that the device was still working. The only thing missing was a laser, but she was sure he probably had one in there somewhere. To her, it looked more like a truly unfortunate attempt at a Borg disguise than anything else. Corsi gestured at the contraption. *"What* is on your head?"

A Cheshire-cat smile spread across Fabian Stevens's face, and a mischievous glint she knew all too well lit his brown eyes.

Why do I suddenly get the feeling I'm going to regret asking that?

"A little idea I had," he said, gesturing with gloves that were covered in the same red, yellow, and blue leads. "I was reading over some of the reports from Project *Voyager.* Do you know they've got a mobile emitter for their EMH? Then I remembered this report about an experimental control interface that Commander La Forge tried out a few years ago. It plugged right into the implants for this VISOR unit that the commander used to have. Ended up acting almost like an old-fashioned virtual reality unit, but this actually allowed him to control an experimental probe. He was able to guide it through the upper levels of a gas giant with this interface and directly interpret the data. Okay, yeah, the research was abandoned when the war broke out, but it's still a useful concept. Of course, I had to completely redesign it to work on someone that had no sensory implants, but it occurred to me that if we could combine those two ideas, we'd have—"

"Something with some very interesting possible uses," Corsi interjected. Her mind began to work over the various potential options, and liked what it saw.

Stevens nodded, his voice taking on that tone that she had long since learned to associate with engineers when they were on a roll. "Took me a while to figure out how the mobile emitter worked, and I'm still not sure I managed to get everything. I mean, come on, reverse-engineering technology from the future? I love a challenge, but according to their reports, this thing's got twenty-ninth-century technology built into it, and

Voyager's engineer has a very weird way of keeping her notes. It wasn't easy, but I finally figured it out. Adding antigrav circuitry would make it too bulky to be practical. Wait a minute." The look in his eyes told her he'd had an idea. He walked back into the mess hall, placing the headset goggles on the table beside him and taking off a pair of gloves as he sat and began working on a padd. Surprisingly, his short dark hair wasn't mussed from the headgear. *Neat trick.*

"Fabe? Why aren't you working on this in the hololab?"

"Had to eat sometime," he said with a shrug, as though there were any other answer.

She turned back toward the flying yellow ball, which was still staring at her with that inane, childlike grin. The idea certainly had a lot of potential, she couldn't deny that. A mobile hologram that they could control from the bridge of the *da Vinci*—that could look like anything or anyone—was nothing short of tactical genius. Holograms as distractions were easy, child's play, even, but a hologram that could take an active offensive stance was something else.

Then there were the intelligence-gathering possibilities. The old saying "If I could only be a fly on the wall for that meeting" would take on a whole new meaning. It would almost be like having a Dominion shape-shifter working on their side. *Starfleet Intelligence would probably love to get their hands on something like this.*

"Can this thing project something that can carry a weapon, too?"

The only answer Corsi got was the chirp of her combadge. *"Commander Corsi?"* She'd never heard fear in quite that manner; it filled Ken Caitano's voice.

"Caitano? What is it?"

Silence answered.

"Caitano?"

A rock began to form in the pit of her stomach. Caitano was third-generation Starfleet, with commendations for valor during the Dominion War. It had only been two days ago that he'd saved the ship during the fight with the Silgov. The idea that something had struck him with that level of fear didn't set well. "Computer, location of Crewperson Caitano."

"Crewperson Caitano is in his quarters."

Unable to dismiss the sense of urgency that was crawling up her spine, she hit her combadge, "Corsi to Hawkins. Something's wrong. Meet me at Caitano and Deverick's quarters."

Closing that connection, she then said, "Corsi to Poynter, emergency site-to-site transport. Deck four, section nine."

She materialized a few meters down the corridor from the room, taking off at a sprint toward the door. When she got there, she buzzed the door. There was no answer.

"Computer, security override. Priority one. Access code Corsi Gamma Three Two Two."

The door slid aside to reveal a brightly lit room. "Caitano?" she called.

She heard the turbolift doors slide open down the hall. Vance Hawkins, Lauoc Soan, and Rennan Konya walked toward her, concern in Hawkins's dark features.

"No answer at the door," she said. "I've got a bad feeling about this."

Hand on her phaser, Corsi followed Hawkins through the door and into the quarters' small sitting room. Caitano and Deverick had somehow managed to luck into one of the two-room quarters that had been added during the ship's refit, so it wasn't until she reached the bedroom that she saw it. Caitano lay facedown on the floor, a trail of dark blood working its way from his left ear down the side of his face. She reached down and checked his neck for a pulse.

Nothing.

No.

Her fingertips registered one very faint beat.

She hit her combadge hard enough that it was sure to leave a bruise. "Corsi to sickbay, incoming wounded. Medical emergency. Poynter, beam Caitano directly to sickbay and then don't let anyone use it without letting me know." She'd have to get permission to lock the transporters down, but that would do for the moment. "Konya, go down there, too. If he so much as breathes a word, I want to know about it. Use the security channel."

Laura Poynter was nothing if not prompt. Before Corsi could finish talking, the shimmer of the transporter formed around Caitano's body and he disappeared, leaving behind a tiny patch of blood-soaked carpet. The Betazoid Konya was already out the door.

"Lauoc, set up in the corridor. Not even Captain Gold gets in here without my permission, understood?"

"Yes, sir," the diminutive Bajoran replied.

While Hawkins worked on getting a set of holographic pictures of the scene, she walked back to the archway and stood between the bedroom and the small sitting room. What she needed at that moment was a single visual sweep.

The layout of the place was typical of the general redesign for two-person crew quarters that the ship had received after its near-destruction at Galvan VI—sure, she'd seen smaller apartments on Earth, but this was still more livable than some of the ships Corsi had been on in her day. The bedroom had two beds that had been fixed into opposite corners from the archway. Caitano's was to her right, against the room's exterior wall. Deverick's bed sat in much the same position, but against the interior wall. Each bed had an accompanying nightstand, and a narrow shelf for personal effects ran down the length of both the interior and exterior walls. The shelf near Deverick's bed held two small starship models. In what space he had between the shelf and the room's window, Caitano had placed scattered pictures, a couple of padds, knickknacks, and something else. "Is that what I think it is?" she asked, pointing toward the shelf.

Hawkins followed her finger, getting an image of the shelf while he was at it. Both black eyebrows raised. "Looks like a bar of gold-pressed latinum," he said. "Wonder how he got that?"

"He has a weird fascination for the Ferengi markets," Corsi said. "Wong was talking to him about it the other day in the mess hall. One of his stocks probably did well. What I wonder is what the hell he thinks putting it on display like that is going to get him."

"Maybe we should ask Deverick?"

Corsi made a mental note to do just that while she inspected the rest of the shelf's contents. She recognized the friendly eyes, long face, and aquiline nose of Caitano's father in three framed pictures that were perched near the head of the bed. One looked like a snapshot from the younger man's graduation. His father's arm was wrapped around his shoulder, and both generations looked as though it were the happiest day of their lives. An older woman with features similar to, but more robust than, the younger Caitano's—Corsi automatically presumed she was his mother, although she'd only ever met the professor and his son—was on his other side. She hoped Dr. Lense could work one of her miracles and keep Caitano alive. She didn't like the idea of having to inform his parents.

Forcing her attention back to where the body had fallen, something struck her as odd. "How'd he call for help?"

"Huh?"

She turned toward Hawkins. "He called me for help. Something scared him."

"Intruder?"

Corsi shook her head and gestured toward the overturned glass about ten centimeters from where Caitano's head had been. "Do you see any sign of a struggle? The glass isn't even broken." She ran her tricorder over it. "And according to these readings, all that was in it was water."

Her immediate suspicion was that he might have stumbled and fallen on something, but when she looked around the foot of the bed, there was nothing that could have served as such an impediment. No slippers of any sort were in the room. When they checked the closets near the bathroom, they found that his shoes were arranged in an orderly manner on the floor. The sheet and blanket were folded back on the bed in a nice, almost too-neat manner. Two other padds sat on the bed, apparently put aside when he'd gotten up to get the glass of water. She couldn't see anything that he might have tripped over. She even knelt down and checked under the bed. It, too, was empty. *He couldn't have tripped over his own two feet, could he? It still doesn't explain what scared him like that.*

"What do you think, boss?" Hawkins asked from the other room.

Corsi shook her head as she stood. "It looks like he was reading, got up to get a glass of water, and then collapsed when he came back to bed. I don't think he was close enough to the table to hit his head." She leaned down, taking a closer look at the bed stand. Running her tricorder over it just to be sure, she said, "I don't see blood or signs of impact. If it wasn't a fall, what was it? What scared him?"

Could he have had an aneurysm? Could an aneurysm actually bleed out through the ear like that? Something's not right here.

Corsi stood and pulled out her tricorder. "Have Konya pull all the footage from the security cameras in this area. I'm going to need your help pulling a DNA trace off of *everything*."

Hawkins nodded. "Got it."

She tapped her combadge, not wanting to give the news she was about to give, and wishing she had more to explain it than instinct. Protocols were protocols, however. "Computer, access security channel one. Security to the bridge."

Commander Sonya Gomez, the *da Vinci's* first officer and head of the S.C.E. contingent stationed on the ship, responded. *"Yes, Commander?"*

"I'd like to put a lockdown on the transporters, Commander."

She could hear the confusion in Gomez's voice. *"Why?"*

"Caitano has been taken to sickbay. I have reason to believe he might have been attacked."

"Attacked? What makes you say that?"

Corsi's lips pursed. "I don't see anything that makes me think it was a suicide attempt, and there are no signs of an accident. He called me for help. Unless the doctor tells me a medical condition could have done this, I don't see any another option."

After a long pause, Gomez said, *"Transporters are disabled. Any suspects?"*

"None yet, but we're really just getting started down here."

"I'll let the captain know. Any word on recovery?"

Before she could open her mouth to say that she didn't know, Hawkins stuck his head through the bedroom archway. His dark skin had an ashen tone, and dread was in his eyes. "Dr. Lense just said he was DOA. She's starting the autopsy now."

Corsi's head fell forward. She swallowed hard, trying to

force the emotion out of her voice. "Yes, Commander. I was just informed that he was dead on arrival."

After a long pause, Gomez said, *"I'm sorry, Domenica."*

Corsi's voice hardened. "I'm going to start an empirical reconstruction, Commander. Until I see evidence to convince me it isn't, we're treating this as a homicide."

CHAPTER
2

Corsi reached back and pulled her blond hair into a tighter chignon. *Professional, must keep it professional. It doesn't matter that your old mentor's son died on your ship.*

Keep telling yourself that, Core-Breach, and you might believe it.

"Connection established. Channel secured."

The sharp eyes of Professor Agosto Caitano stared at her from the viewscreen. There were a few more lines in his face, and there was more salt in his salt-and-pepper hair, but he still looked as distinguished as she remembered. *"Domenica? Is something wrong?"* he asked, his usually convivial voice taking a more cautious tone. *"They pulled me out of a class."*

"I'm sorry, Professor," she began, schooling her features to be as emotionless as she could manage. "There's been an incident here that concerns Ken."

A grim smile crossed the elder Caitano's face. *"You sound like some of his teachers in grade school. What happened?"*

Corsi licked her lips. No words came to her that would make this any easier. "Professor, sir, I'm not sure how to tell you this other than to just tell you. I'm very sorry to have to say this, but Ken has died."

The professor's face fell. He took a few deep breaths. Finally, in a shaky voice, he said, *"What happened?"*

"I'm afraid I can't answer that right now. The investigation is still at the classified stage."

He slowly nodded. *"I—I understand. If someone did this to him, you'll find him. I know you will."*

I hope so, sir. Somehow, she managed to say, "I'll do my best," instead. "Professor, I hate to say it, but while I've got you on the comm, I'd like to ask you a couple of questions, if I may."

"Anything I can do to help."

"We don't have any concrete proof that he was attacked, but I have to investigate that possibility all the same." She took a deep breath of her own. "Is there anything that's happened recently that might have made someone want to get back at you or Ken for any reason? Someone who might have killed him as revenge?"

His eyes went distant for a few seconds, and then snapped back. *"I don't know of anyone, Domenica. The last few months have been nothing but classes and remodeling our house. It has all gone smoothly. I'll talk to Angelina. If she knows anything that might help—"*

"Thank you, Professor. As soon as I can tell you what happened, I will."

"Computer, initiate program Corsi Twenty-two."

"Program initiated. You may enter when ready."

The hololab doors slid open on Caitano and Deverick's quarters, precisely as they'd been when Hawkins had taken the crime scene images just a day before.

Okay, Corsi, time to figure out what you missed.

"Now, access all log files from the crew quarters. Go back twenty-four hours. Replicator logs, personal logs, entry/exit logs, medical logs, whatever is available. Correlate those and extrapolate a re-creation of the events that transpired in this cabin. Begin with Caitano returning from his duty shift yesterday."

"*Accessing.*"

While it worked, she took the time to further inspect the scene. As there was no actual evidence to contaminate, she picked up the bar of gold-pressed latinum and turned it over in her hands. As latinum was a liquid in its natural state, it was usually encased in gold whenever it was used in commerce. Her eye went over every curve, every recess of the ornately sculpted gold casing, looking for the maker's mark—that one signature that would tell her where the bar was manufactured.

Where is it?

That alone was suspicious. No maker's mark usually meant one of two things: either it had been stolen, and the mark filed off to keep it from being traced, or it was counterfeit.

And counterfeit bars of gold-pressed latinum were few and far between. How could Caitano have come across it?

"Corsi to Hawkins," she said, tapping her combadge.

"*Yes, Commander?*"

"I want some more scans done on the bar of latinum. I've got reason to believe it might be counterfeit."

"*Will do. Anything else?*"

"Not yet, Corsi out."

What's taking the computer so long to correlate that information?

As though it had read her mind, the computer finally said, "*Extrapolated sequence of events is not comprehensive.*"

She looked around the room once again. It was time to test a theory. "That's okay. Computer, run program."

The room's virtual doors slid aside, and Caitano walked through. There were no signs of a holographic representation of Deverick. Not surprising, considering that he had been on his way to his duty shift at the time.

Caitano walked over to the replicator and put in his request for dinner, instructing the machine to wait thirty minutes before executing. He then proceeded to walk toward the small doorway to the bathroom. It slid closed behind him. After a few moments of silence, the sonic shower began running.

Okay, we checked the sonic shower for malfunction. Nothing. The autopsy report said there was indication of brain tissue in the blood. Lense thought something ruptured his eardrums, and then vibrated his brain to the point of resonance. If it wasn't the sonic shower, what was it?

"Computer, speed up re-creation to twice normal speed."

"Working."

The shower stopped, and the holographic Caitano walked at an almost comical pace out of the bathroom and over to the replicator. He ate dinner, then went into the bedroom and changed into the bedclothes he'd been found wearing. The computer must have used the autopsy report and figured he pulled out the bedclothes when he opened the drawer.

He reached over, grabbed a padd from his shelf, and began thumbing through the contents. *That looks like the one that had the Ferengi business journals on it.*

But, if it's coming up in the log, that means the padd accessed the computer for an update at one point.

He put that padd down and grabbed a second, putting a pillow between his back and the wall as he settled in to read. She watched as his eyes scanned each page, until he finally began rubbing his right temple.

That one looks like the padd that had the novel on it.

"Computer, resume normal speed," she said, watching like a hawk for any indication of what might have caused the vibration in his brain. She couldn't hear or see anything unusual.

That was when he put the padd down, folded the covers back and got out of bed. He walked into the living room, and went right to the replicator. "Two aspirins and water," he said. Strain was obvious in his voice.

Aspirin? Why not just get something from sickbay?

He gulped down the pills, and lifted the glass to his lips. Slowly, he walked back toward the bed. When he was even with the foot of the bed, he fell to his knees. The glass slipped from his hand.

"Need help," he whispered. His voice was growing weak as he said, "Commander Corsi?"

How did the computer know he was trying to reach me and not thinking out loud?

She heard her own voice saying, *"Caitano? What is it?"*

He fell to the floor. From her vantage point at the foot of Deverick's bed, she could see a faint trickle of blood begin to form at his ear.

"Caitano?"

Knowing that he'd lost the battle had been one thing, but the thought that he might have lost it while she was talking to him tore at her insides. She hadn't seen or heard anything out of the ordinary before Caitano got up to get the aspirin. Corsi tried to force that feeling into a corner to deal with later, realizing that even being able to see it happen, she still wasn't sure what caused the death.

CHAPTER
3

"How's it going, boss?" Vance Hawkins said as he walked into the security office.

Corsi barely looked up from the readouts on her viewscreen. "Not good. The re-creation gave me a couple of leads, but nothing that looks like it could have caused the vibrations that Lense thinks happened."

Hawkins slid into the chair opposite Corsi's narrow desk. "You're kidding."

Shaking her head, she said, "He had a headache, got up, ordered aspirin from the replicator, and collapsed on the way back to his bed. It's like something that nobody could hear or see caused his brain to start shaking and then burst about a thousand blood vessels at the same time. Our illustrious CMO has never even heard of something like that happening before, let alone seen it. *Please* tell me you had better luck."

Hawkins's dark fingers ran over the padd in his hand. "You were right. The latinum was a counterfeit, but the scans of the two padds on the bed show that they're both standard-issue. As for the DNA traces, both padds had traces we couldn't localize."

That was unusual. There were only two ways that a DNA trace wouldn't be identifiable. One would be if it were from a species that they hadn't catalogued yet. The other would be if the creature that left them had been wearing something that hampered its ability to leave traces, like wearing gloves to keep from leaving fingerprints had been in the days before it was discovered that some alien races didn't have fingerprints to leave behind. "What about the counterfeit latinum?"

"Besides human, there were traces of Ferengi, Cardassian, and Bajoran DNA. There were also three other traces that we couldn't match."

Corsi raised a blond eyebrow. "Three others?" Pressing the control to get a secure channel, she said, "Corsi to Lense."

"Yes, Domenica?"

"I'm sending Hawkins down to you with three pieces that we need examined. We've got DNA traces that aren't coming up in the database. I need to know if they're for new species, or if someone's trying to mask traces."

"Understood."

"Um, hi," a tentative voice said from behind Hawkins. "You wanted to see me, Commander?"

Signing off with Lense, Corsi saw Ted Deverick standing in her office doorway, his eyes riveted to the floor in front of his feet. His short, sandy blond hair was rumpled, as though he'd just gotten out of bed. He shifted his weight from one spindly leg to the other. She'd only seen him a couple of times since he'd come on board, but he'd looked better. "How're you doing, Deverick?" she asked, genuine concern in her voice. "Settling in to the new quarters?"

A bitter smile tried to work its way onto his face. "About as good as can be expected, I guess. Thank you for moving me."

"When was the last time you slept?" Hawkins asked. Corsi couldn't help but wonder if he'd also noticed the exhaustion in the young crewman's eyes.

"Night before last. I keep wondering if what got Ken was really meant for me."

That piqued Corsi's interest. She gestured for him to sit down. "Do either of you have any enemies who might try something like this?"

Deverick sank into the other chair that faced Corsi's desk. "Not that I know of," he said. "I mean, I knew Ken pretty well from the *Musgrave,* but we'd both only been there about a year when we got transferred."

"What about before the transfer? Did he take any vacations?"

Deverick shook his head. "Are you kidding? He was saving everything he could to retire on Risa. He didn't leave the ship that often. I think the last time either one of us left before the transfer was an away mission near the Badlands. They actually found the *Manning* floating dead near a massive tachyon eddy. We got sent in on salvage."

Corsi and Hawkins exchanged a look. She remembered something in her history class about that being one of the first ships lost in the Badlands almost fifty years ago. Starfleet had always assumed that all hands had gone down with the ship. A derelict, however, brought in a whole new level of possible causes, up to and including possible influence by the aliens that lived in the Bajoran wormhole. "Nothing strange happened while you were in the Badlands? Did you see any signs that he might have been sick?"

"No, ma'am. Nothing," Deverick replied. "He was always making sure he was healthy. He went in for a checkup every six months, whether he needed to or not. He was in the gym every day. He always made sure he ate right. I bet he was probably in better shape than Captain Dayrit."

Corsi's lips pursed. That certainly jibed with what she'd learned from the files sent over from the *Musgrave.*

"Did he ever talk about anyone being mad at him? Someone who might have had a vendetta against him?"

Deverick shook his head.

Corsi cursed to herself. *If there were no known enemies, and no foreign objects to point to, what was it?*

Hawkins leaned forward. "Ted, did you ever touch his padds, or maybe his bar of latinum?"

The younger man's expression turned even graver. "He almost broke one of my ships once. After that, we agreed that he wouldn't touch anything of mine, and I wouldn't touch anything of his."

"Those ships mean a lot to you?" Corsi asked.

Deverick nodded. "I'm an engineer, Commander. Building and fixing ships is what I do. There's a model of the *Constitution*-class *Defiant* at home that I built when I was twelve. I built both the *Grayson* and the *Commonwealth*."

"The which?" Hawkins asked.

The young man turned sharp eyes on her deputy. "The two models in my quarters. They're old pre-Federation explorer ships." With a halfheartedly proud smile, he added, "My great-great-grandfather helped design the *Grayson*."

"You don't happen to know why he kept the bar of latinum on his shelf, do you?"

Deverick shook his head. "No, ma'am."

Corsi leaned back in her chair, sure this discussion was going nowhere. Deverick's file was about as empty as deep space—no reprimands, no warnings, nothing. She didn't even see a note for his and Caitano's bickering over the models. *If it didn't get out of hand when his precious models were nearly broken, could Caitano have actually provoked him to an attack? Could he have done a time-delay attack so he might look innocent?*

Ultimately, all she could do was sigh. Too many questions, and too few answers. "Hawkins, get the evidence down to Lense. And see what she has on the glass, okay?"

CHAPTER
4

As Corsi keyed the lock to her quarters, she was beginning to give a modicum of credence to the notion of a vast conspiracy by the universe in general to keep her from finding the murder weapon. She had finally settled on three possible candidates, but no idea how it could have been done. None of the tests that had been run on either of the padds or the latinum showed any signs of something that could have caused vibrations in Caitano's brain or a rupture of his eardrums.

As the door slid closed behind her, the corner of the wooden box that contained her family's heirloom fire axe caught Corsi's eye as it peeked out from beneath the bed. She couldn't help but think it was almost taunting her, sticking its tongue out like a spoiled child.

She tried to look away from it, but it would only be a few seconds before it filled her vision once again. Taking a deep breath, she reached down and dragged the case from its usual home, setting it on the foot of the bed so it could stare at her properly.

What would her father think? The last time she'd seen Aldo Corsi, they'd made some sort of peace, but she still wondered how stable that peace was in reality.

"Domenica? You okay?" Lense's voice asked.

Corsi turned to find her roommate standing in the doorway, a level of concern in the doctor's expression that she couldn't recall seeing outside of sickbay.

"Yeah," she said, her eyes going back to the axe. "I just need to know—"

"What killed Caitano?"

Corsi shook her head. "No. Well, yeah, eventually, but that's not it."

She heard Lense sit down, judging by the distance, on her own bed. "Then what is it?"

Corsi opened her mouth to speak, but for a few moments no words came. How could she explain it to Lense when she couldn't even explain it to herself? Finally, she said, "I don't know."

"You need to know something, but you don't know what that something is?"

Corsi pinched the bridge of her nose between her right index finger and thumb. "I don't know how to explain it."

"Try me," Lense said. "I'm not a counselor, but . . ."

"I'd be dead about five times over now if you were," Corsi said, an edge of sarcasm in her voice. She didn't want to think about the way things might have gone over the years if the *da Vinci* had had a lesser CMO. Elizabeth Lense had saved her life, as well as the lives of her staff, on more than one occasion. Corsi had long ago discovered that having such an accomplished medic on the ship made doing her own job that much easier. She didn't worry about bumps and bruises when she was on a mission, because she knew that Lense could fix just about any problem she might be able to come back with, so long as that problem wasn't someone being dead.

Lense sighed. "Okay, direct questions it is. How about telling me why you're staring at that axe like it's going to do a trick?"

"I'm getting tired of dead ends," Corsi reluctantly said. "I don't know any more about how he died than I did when I walked into his quarters. Well, I do, but it's not useful."

She could have sworn she heard the doctor laugh. She

moved her eyes from the axe long enough to see a wry smile on her roommate's features. "What's so funny?"

"Domenica, in all of the time I've known you, I've never seen you run out of options."

Corsi raised an eyebrow. "Who said I'm out of options? I just tested every one I thought of already and have no likely scenarios. There wasn't any evidence that he tripped on anything. He didn't have a medical condition that would cause him to suddenly collapse. There weren't any incurable blood disorders involved. So why? How could he still have enough of his wits about him to clearly call for help before he died if his brain was coming apart?"

Lense shrugged. "Trust me, I'm just as frustrated as you are. His blood chemistry was otherwise perfectly normal."

"So, if he wasn't drugged, there wasn't a struggle, and he didn't trip, then what?" Corsi's stare returned to the axe.

Lense sighed, and then said, "What we need is a change of subject. Sometimes that helps me think. You know, you never did tell me what's so important about this thing."

"Huh?"

"What's so important about an axe? It seems pretty impersonal to be a family heirloom."

Corsi leaned back in her chair, reluctantly thankful for the change in subject. She had to admit, the doctor had a point. She'd only met two or three other people over the years who carried heirlooms with them, and those pieces had been things like ancient jewelry or quilts that had been made by their great-great-grandmothers back wherever home was.

"You're right," Corsi said, rubbing a hand over her face in an attempt to clear the mental cobwebs. "It was an ancestor of my father's. He was a firefighter back in New York at the start of the twenty-first century. He got killed in the line of duty during a terrorist attack on the city. Remember when the Breen attacked San Francisco during the war? From what I've read, it was like that."

A cloud crossed Lense's features.

Corsi winced. "Sorry. I forgot you've got family there."

"It's okay. Thankfully, I didn't lose anyone. Go on. What happened?"

"He was responding to the site of the attack when the building he was in came down around him. All that was left of him was what they could find back at his firehouse. They used to give a firefighter's badge to his next of kin, but his was never found. Yeah, it may not be the most personal family heirloom, but it's all they could do at the time."

The corners of Elizabeth Lense's eyes pinched. After everything they'd been through in recent years, far more close calls than even Corsi cared to remember, she could only guess that the doctor was imagining the same thing she had from time to time—what Starfleet would give *their* next-of-kin.

"The terrorists used things people saw every day against them, so what their victims thought nothing of became weapons."

They hid things inside everyday items . . . so standard security measures wouldn't see them. Wait a minute. What if there's something inside one of the padds? We would have spotted it on the scans, wouldn't we?

Not if it had a masking signal.

Corsi's eyes shot open. She was about to slap her combadge and contact Commander Gomez when a comm came through. *"Hawkins to Corsi. We've got another body."*

CHAPTER
5

Corsi was really getting sick of the harsh, sharp smell of death forcing its way into her life. Deverick's body stared up accusingly. She cursed to herself, convinced that she should have been able to stop this one. They had the padds in custody. How could one of them have gotten out?

Maybe it isn't the padds after all?

The evidence, what little there was of it, was just as inconclusive as it had been for Caitano. No fibers out of place. No unusual dust. Nothing remotely of use. The only major difference with the body seemed to be that this time, he'd ended up on his back instead of facedown. Corsi took little time pointing out a trail of blood that led from the victim's ears. "From what you said you found in Caitano's autopsy, looks like the same thing."

"That would be a logical assumption," Lense said from beside her. The doctor had followed her from their quarters the second the call from Hawkins had come in.

Lense pulled out her own tricorder and began scanning the body. "Creatine kinase levels are normal. Save for blood type, these readings are virtually identical to what I found on

Caitano. It's even picking up the same percentage of brain tissue in the blood."

Corsi couldn't believe her ears. *"Identical?* That shouldn't be possible. There are too many variables involved for it to come out identical."

Lense held out the tricorder, and Corsi immediately inspected the readings. The tricorder was only able to do a few of the exams, but a bare-bones toxicology reading, pathology scans, even scans of the blood trails from his ears—scan after scan, it was all the same. "At least now we've got a signature on the murder weapon," was all she could manage.

Corsi visually scanned the area around the body. It looked remarkably like the scenario she'd found Caitano in, only transposed to the new quarters' sitting room: body on the floor near the sofa, glass of a clear liquid on the table near his head—she presumed it was water, but aimed her tricorder at it, just to be safe.

It was precisely as it appeared—water.

Damn. With the glass Caitano had, that's about the only other consistency between the crime scenes.

She checked the closets and dressers, but came up empty. The replicators showed that he'd requested a homeopathic headache remedy. She called up the chemical composition that had been programmed into the replicator. Both the pattern on that and the one on the aspirin Caitano had called for checked out as having nothing added.

One detail jumped out at her, though. "Where's the padd?"

"Padd?" Lense asked.

"Yeah. The padd. If what I was thinking before is right, it might be the key here." As soon as Hawkins had scans of the room for the official record, Corsi began going over the room. Between a pillow and blanket on the sofa, she found the object of her search. "Here it is. Hawkins?"

"Yeah, boss?"

"Get this to Commander Gomez. Run a DNA trace while you're at it. I want to know what the difference is between this one and the ones we've got in custody."

Hawkins nodded, and gingerly took the padd. "Anything else?"

That was when it struck her. "Yeah. Take a DNA trace on the glass. Compare it to the one from Caitano's murder and standard replicator settings. Have the chemical compositions double-checked on both glasses. I want to make sure the replicators aren't lying to us."

"You got it," Hawkins said.

"What are you thinking?" Lense asked.

Corsi tried to figure out an appropriate way to phrase the thoughts in her head. She gestured for Lense to follow her into the corridor. "Remember how I was saying that the terrorists used everyday things as weapons?"

The doctor nodded. A glimmer of understanding quickly followed. "You think whoever did this used something we wouldn't notice?"

"That's exactly what I think."

"But, what is it? Domenica, I don't know of anything that could do this kind of damage that isn't something we could easily pick up on a simple scan. Whatever this is, it's something new. The only drug I found in Caitano's body was the aspirin, and so far I don't see any difference here, either. I don't think whatever did this was delivered in the glass."

Corsi slowly shook her head. "I'm not so sure, either. I've got a feeling it's got something to do with the padds. So far, it's the only other connection between the two deaths. We need to examine that padd." Tapping her combadge, she said, "Corsi to Gomez."

"*Yes, Commander?*"

"Has Mr. Hawkins reported to you yet?"

"*He just got here. What's up?*"

She took a deep breath. "Doctor Lense and I need your help. Could you meet us in the hololab as soon as you have a chance?"

CHAPTER
6

The look on Sonya Gomez's face couldn't have been more incredulous. "The *padds?*"

Corsi set the two padds recovered from Caitano's bed, as well as the padd she'd found at Deverick's crime scene, on the workbench between them. "Whoever did this is using our own equipment against us."

"Our own equipment?"

Corsi tried to keep the frustration out of her voice. *You're the only one who's taken counterterrorism training. Don't forget that.* "It's an old terrorist ploy. If they use things that we take for granted, they can plant the bomb in the center of town and nobody will give it a second look." She pointed at one of Caitano's padds. "Commander, Hawkins scanned this one three times and found nothing unusual about it. I even scanned it once myself, but it was the same reading. If I'm right, somebody wants it that way."

Gomez picked up the device and began giving it a closer inspection. She retrieved a sonic screwdriver from the nearest tool kit. Grabbing the unit that had the novel Caitano had been reading, she got to work. Her eyes widened when she cracked the padd's case open on two bits of electronics that obviously hadn't been part of the padd's original design. "How'd the scanners miss this much tampering? That's got to be the smallest emitter array I've ever seen. That looks almost like an acoustic amplifier. Bounce the acoustic signal off of this, and you can focus it like a phaser beam. You know, I'll bet that's designed to fool any scanner into thinking the padd's just a plain, off-the-shelf unit," Gomez said in the same tone that Corsi had heard from Stevens—she was rolling, and nobody with any sense should interrupt. "I wonder what the other thing's for." Her voice trailed off as she resumed staring down into the guts of the altered padd. She stared intently at the small piece of obsidian circuitry that sat beside the emitter. "Have you told Captain Gold yet?" she muttered.

Corsi shook her head. "There was nothing new to report until now. How long before you think you'll know what the other emitter does?"

Gomez shrugged. "Don't know. A day, maybe? Caitano got this on Deep Space 9, right?"

Corsi nodded. "Best we can tell. I'm already working on the message for Captain Kira and Lieutenant Ro. If my hunch is right—"

"Yeah, a padd with that novel on it came through Quark's place last month," Ro Laren said, her brow furrowing into ridges that matched those on the bridge of her Bajoran nose. *"He told me it was some bestseller in the Gamma Quadrant."*

"That's their cover story," Corsi replied. "The crew here believes it was designed to pass scanner detection, because we'd never think to look at a padd. Who'd tamper with that?"

Ro shook her head. *"I know it's probably not worth much, Commander, but we should have thought to look at it more closely. At least half of the grandfathered militia members were in the resistance. The odds are good somebody tried a stunt like this once."*

Corsi leaned back in her office chair, staring at Deep Space 9's security chief. Dark eyes that had seemed pretty happy when they'd begun the conversation now looked haunted—the eyes of someone who was going to be feeling some serious guilt when the conversation ended. Corsi couldn't say that she blamed her, really. In her shoes, she probably would have felt the same. If she didn't figure out who used the padds to kill Caitano and Deverick, she was pretty damned sure she'd feel the same.

"Do you know if he has a paper trail on the device?" Corsi asked.

Ro shook her head again. *"No, but I will by the time you arrive. I suppose you'll want to talk to Quark about it?"*

Corsi thought about that for a moment. She would definitely have to question the Ferengi on the transaction, but something as simple as Bajor's recently finalized Federation membership would throw more than just a spanner into the works. Quark's Bar had become the Ferengi embassy. She realized, with a depressing turn of her stomach, that this would require questioning an ambassador, possibly even in his own embassy, where he could pretty much call all of the shots.

Her lips pursed. She didn't like that one bit.

"We may want to get him out of the bar to do it," Corsi said. "Questioning him inside the embassy could raise all kinds of diplomatic problems."

Ro's eyes rolled. *"Especially since he also happens to be the brother of the Grand Nagus. What a time for fatherhood to make Rom grow a spine."*

Corsi shook her head. "From what Nog said, he's always been protective of Quark."

The ends of Ro's lips turned up. *"That protection works both ways. Those two have been to hell and back together. He held the guns on a couple of Jem'Hadar guards to get Rom out of jail during the Dominion occupation. Who knows what Rom might do in return? Although, I just don't see Rom going ballistic."*

A thin smile spread across Corsi's face as she thought of something. "On second thought, a little 'interview' in the bar might prove handy. He won't want to cause a scene in front of the customers."

"*True,*" Ro replied, one dark eyebrow raised. "*Bad for business.*"

"Let me work on a strategy here," Corsi said. "We'll be there in about another day."

CHAPTER
7

"Commander Corsi, do you have a moment?"

Corsi looked up from Gomez's latest report on the padds with weary eyes. Standing in the doorway to her office was P8 Blue, the ship's pill-bug-shaped Nasat structural engineer. "Pattie," as she had come to be known, held out a padd in one clawed hand. "Captain Gold said that you are looking at the padds that had been owned by or come in contact with Caitano or Deverick?"

"Yeah, why do you ask?"

Pattie reached forward, placing the padd on the desk. "Caitano donated a copy of a novel to the ship's library and then checked it out to my padd. He thought I might enjoy it."

"Did you?"

Pattie held out her arms. If she'd had visible shoulders, Corsi suspected Pattie would have shrugged. "The translation from its native language was rough at best. I am sure if the translation had not been required, it might have worked better. It isn't a bad story, kind of fun, actually. But as it is, I don't believe it would be nearly as successful in the Alpha Quadrant as Caitano thought."

Wait a minute. Corsi's overworked brain stopped in its tracks. *If he uploaded it before he read it, he wouldn't have known something was up.* "Computer, pull up the contents of the ship's fiction library, sort by date of donation. Route the results to my viewscreen."

"Working."

Her screen flickered, and was quickly filled with a listing of most of the major fiction works the Alpha Quadrant's authors had to offer. The most recent donation, however, was from Caitano. The same title had been on the padd they'd recovered from the sofa when Deverick died, and the padd that Caitano had been reading when he died. "Computer, give me the details on the book titled *Tafock Navar Relal.*"

"Donated by Crewperson Kenneth Caitano. Author: Unknown. Genre: Suspense fiction."

"Author unknown? If it was a Gamma Quadrant bestseller, why didn't he know who the author was?" Corsi looked up at Pattie. "Did you really read this?"

"Yes," the Nasat replied, concern edging her voice. "Is that a problem, Commander?"

"Well," Corsi said dryly, "you're still alive."

A tinkling that Corsi had come to know as nervous laughter came from Pattie. "Very funny, Commander."

"I'm serious. I don't know why I didn't see it before now, but both Caitano and Deverick had this file on the padds that were near them when they died. Computer, did anyone else check this file out besides P8 Blue?"

"Crewperson Theodore Deverick."

Corsi let out a breath she didn't realize she'd been holding. "Computer, this file is a security risk. Put it under Security Quarantine Alpha. Access only to myself, Chief Petty Officer Hawkins, Commander Gomez, and Captain Gold."

As soon as the computer confirmed the quarantine, she pressed the comm button on her desk. "Corsi to Gomez."

"Yes, Commander?"

"Are you still in the hololab? We've got a new lead."

CHAPTER
8

"How're we doing?" Captain David Gold said as he strode through the doors into the hololab. He made his way around the two unused workbenches and over to the one where Gomez had more small tools than Corsi had ever seen scattered across the surface. Even though he only came up to Corsi's nose, Corsi knew better than to dodge anything with him. She'd trust the man with her life if it came down to it, and on occasion it had. It wasn't anything she'd ever admit to anyone, but there were times when she hoped to have that sharp a mind when she was old enough to have great-grandchildren.

Provided I survive this and live long enough to have children. I did not *just have that thought.*

Shaking it off, she said, "We believe we may finally have the murder weapon, and it's a mean one."

That seemed to pique Gold's interest. One gray eyebrow rose. "Really? What have you got?"

"The padd," Gomez said, pulling herself out of the hunched position she'd been in for the last several minutes. "There's an emitter array that lets the thing pass scanner detection. We'd have had to crack the thing open to know it had been altered."

"So, what does it do when it passes detection?"

Gomez brushed a strand of black hair out of her face, using the needlelike probe in her hand to point at the complex bit of circuitry that sat beside the emitter array. "See this? It's designed to learn the species of whoever is holding the padd. We're still trying to figure out exactly how it interacts, but we know it works with something else in the padd's programming. To the best I've been able to determine, it's set to generate different results for each species. I've got a feeling that those results modulate the frequency of the sound that it produces, but I haven't been able to prove it yet. This piece here allows it to be focused."

"A focused beam of sound?" Gold asked. "I thought those were weapons that were left behind centuries ago?"

Corsi shook her head. "They were developed about four hundred years ago, sir, but they're still no less effective than a sword or a knife."

Gomez pressed a touchpad, and the monitor to her left flickered to life. Line after line of text scrolled by. "Wow."

"What?" Gold and Corsi asked in unison.

Gomez held up one long finger. "Give me a second." She reached over and pressed a control that slowed the scrolling. "Those results that the other array generates? It looks like they *do* control another program on the padd."

Corsi leaned over Gomez's shoulder, trying to read the lines of gibberish that were scrolling by on the monitor. "How can you tell?"

Gomez pointed at a line on the screen. "I can't read the exact language, but these look like very basic 'if–then' subroutine structures. Look at this—" The engineer's fingers ran over several lines of programming, all of which held an identical character structure.

"You're right," Corsi said. "That line's in each subroutine. Should we call Faulwell to see what the characters mean?" As the resident linguist, Bart Faulwell loved alien languages. Corsi wasn't sure she wanted to unleash this particular one on him, though. *Anthony would kill me if Faulwell ended up dead.*

"What about Soloman?" she asked. It wasn't out of the

question that the Bynar computer specialist might find something they couldn't.

"That may not be a good idea, either," Gomez said. "If he plugs into this programming, I'm not sure what it could do to him."

"We already know what it does to humans," Corsi said.

Gold wagged a finger at Corsi. "She's got a point, Gomez. The last thing I need right now is to break in another first officer."

Corsi shuddered at the thought of Mor glasch Tev as first officer, hoping the reaction had gone unnoticed. While she had no doubt that he hadn't been involved in this—she was certain that he was arrogant enough to brag about how he'd developed the technology if he'd been even remotely involved—the thought of the irritating Tellarite being in a position of greater authority made her begin to seriously consider a transfer. In an effort to cover her reaction, she said, "But if it's the extra equipment that actually does the damage, wouldn't the array give it the pitch modulation?"

Gomez stared at the now-stagnant lines of programming on the monitor. After a few seconds, she dropped the small probe onto the table. "You may be right. I'm guessing the program only triggers the equipment. The problem is, all I really can do is guess." Sonya reached up to tap her combadge, but Corsi stopped her.

"Wait a minute. Before we do this, we should open the other padds. If it needed this additional equipment to kill Caitano, how'd it kill Deverick? Both he and Pattie had copies of the file downloaded to their padds. Those came directly from Starfleet, not the Gamma Quadrant. How'd it kill Deverick if it didn't have the extra equipment? For that matter, why is Pattie still alive?"

Gomez reached over and grabbed the padd that had been found on Deverick's sofa. "Let's find out." Once she cracked the case, Corsi was beginning to wish she hadn't. The same set of equipment stared at them from the inside of the case of Deverick's padd.

There's only one way I know of that that could work.

Gomez opened Pattie's padd.

Corsi stared, speechless, at the third padd. While she watched, a third tiny device was forming inside the padd's case.

"Nanites," Gomez whispered. "The original brought nanites with it so it can replicate. Pattie's probably alive because she finished the novel before the nanites finished the emitter in her padd." Her eyes widened as a thought struck. "Wait a minute. He uploaded it to the library? Computer, call up the cross section on computer core processor one-seven-six. I want to see element zero-one-hundred to zero-two-hundred. Route it to the monitor at this workbench."

The monitor in question flickered, and the image of what looked to Corsi to be a wounded circuit appeared. Tiny dots flickered over the damage like an infestation of ants.

"Is that what I think it is, Gomez?" Gold asked.

"Yes, sir. They're in the system," Gomez said, her tone hardening. "Captain, we had nanites infest the computer core when I was on the *Enterprise*. Problem was that then, they were sentient, so it tied our hands on how to deal with them. If we can prove that these nanites aren't sentient, it's a simple matter of using the gamma pulse generators on the computer core. Whoever programmed these things probably gave them a single-minded goal."

"Agreed," Corsi said, "it's not a good idea to let the creatures making your weapon work think for themselves. If they figured out what they were doing, they might not do their jobs."

Gold pulled a stool over from a nearby workbench. "So, if we start at the beginning, we need to figure out if they're intelligent. Can their programming tell us that?"

Gomez nodded. "To an extent. We can at least find out if there's any adaptability written into it." Grabbing a pair of microtweezers, she reached into Pattie's padd, and after a few seconds of poking around, lifted the closed tweezers out of the unit. "Computer, please place a microscanner on the table behind me."

The unit in question appeared on the workbench. Gomez turned around, placed the tweezers' contents on a watch glass and slipped it under the viewer. "Good, I got a few of them.

Computer, can you extract the programming from the nanites on the slide and route it to my monitor?"

"*Accessing.*"

The monitor that had held the image of the computer core flickered again, and then showed a stream of ones and zeroes. Gomez leaned forward. "Computer, translate the coding."

Midstream, the numbers became letters. Corsi shook her head. "I don't know what we're looking for here. Is it programmed to adapt, or not?"

After a few moments' silence, Gomez said, "No. It looks single-minded. From what I can see here, it looks like it's programmed to activate when it's first called, then seek out the power source and build its equipment off of that." She quickly took a small, sealable container and slipped the slide into it.

A bad thought picked that moment to appear at the back of Corsi's mind. "We should warn engineering, if these things decide to go for the warp core . . ."

Gomez did just that, and then went back to the monitor. "It looks like they're programmed to shut themselves down."

"So they're acting like computers executing their programs," Gold said with a shake of his head. "What about consciousness? Self-awareness?"

"If they were self-aware," Gomez began, "wouldn't they stay active when their job was done? If they've evolved outside their programming, then should a shutdown subroutine even engage?"

"Good question," Gold said. "If the programming tells it to die, and it listens to that programming, can it be self-aware?"

Gomez reached with the microtweezers into Caitano's padd and picked up something. She placed it onto another slide and stuck it on the microscanner. After a few seconds of observing them, she said, "These are inert. They've shut down."

Gold's expression grew serious. "Gomez, Corsi, do whatever you need to do to get these things off my ship."

"Yes, sir," Gomez and Corsi replied in unison.

"Gomez to Conlon, flood the computer core. Use the gamma pulse generators."

"*Aye, Commander.*"

Closing that connection, she then tapped her combadge and said, "Gomez to Soloman."

"Yes, Commander?" the Bynar's typically flat voice asked.

"Could you join us in the hololab, please? We have a problem that could use your expertise."

"Of course, Commander. I'll be right there."

Before the captain could suggest it, Corsi quickly called sickbay to get a medic to the lab. An instinct she had long since learned to trust was screaming that something was going to go wrong.

"You said it generates different results for different species. Any idea on what triggers it?" Gold asked.

Corsi leaned against the workbench. "That's the big question."

The hololab doors slid aside with a soft whoosh, and the tiny Bynar walked in. He bowed his slightly oversized head toward Captain Gold. "Captain. You requested my assistance, Commander?"

"Yes, Soloman," Gomez replied, a weary smile working its way onto her features. "What we know is that we've got a program in this padd looks like it's calling on something else. We have an idea of what file it's calling on, but we need your help to find out precisely what this thing's designed to do."

Soloman stepped over to the workbench. "Of course," he said.

Gomez put a hand over the opened padd. "Be careful," she said. "We've got evidence that this program is designed to be a weapon. There are nanites involved."

The Bynar took a step back from the workbench. He turned wide eyes on Corsi. "Nanites? Do you believe this is what killed Caitano and Deverick?"

Corsi sighed. "We can't guarantee it won't do anything to you, too," she said. "There's a medical team coming. You don't have to do this if you don't want to."

Soloman's eyes bounced between Corsi and Gomez for a long time. Finally, he took a long look at Captain Gold and nodded. "I'll do it."

"Well," the captain began, "I'll get out of your way. Let me know what you find out."

"Will do, sir," Gomez replied.

Almost as though on cue, the hololab doors opened for Elizabeth Lense. She quickly nodded to the captain as their paths crossed. Once the doors were closed behind him, she asked, "What's up?" Her eyes went to Soloman. "Why do I have a feeling you're about to do something stupid, and you've called me down for the inevitable moment when it all goes to hell?"

Corsi half-smiled. "Because you've been on this ship long enough to figure out how things always go?"

Gomez shot Corsi a look. "Because Soloman has agreed to help us figure out something that relates to the software on the padd."

Placing a medkit on the table, Lense pulled out her tricorder and pointed it at the Bynar. "If he so much as twitches the wrong way, I'm putting a stop to this."

Corsi watched carefully as Gomez turned the padd over to Soloman.

"This is the file we're looking at," Sonya said, using the probe to point to the right line on the monitor. "I can tell it's calling something else in the file structure, but I can't tell what it's meant to do beyond that."

Soloman nodded once. "I will determine that, Commander."

Before any of the three women could get another word out, the high-pitched chatter of a Bynar communicating with a computer began. The lines on the monitor scrolled by faster than Corsi could keep up. Soloman's reedlike fingers worked over the opened padd, moving with a speed that she wouldn't have thought possible if she hadn't seen it herself.

What felt like a few minutes later, the Bynar noticeably swayed. Lense and Gomez simultaneously reached forward, steadying his tiny body. Both his hands and the computer chatter stopped simultaneously.

"Thank you, Commander. I can tell you that it is designed to affect the display of a particular electronic file. I believe that file is entitled *Tafock Navar Relal*. It takes the readings from the padd's added sensors and uses that to produce a focused ultraso—"

Soloman collapsed to the floor in a heap. Gomez looked down in shock as her hands held nothing but air. "Soloman?"

Lense's tricorder kept running as she checked him over. Relief filled her voice as she said, "He's okay. Looks like it overloaded part of his short-term memory. He's going to have a pounding headache when he wakes up, but that I can treat."

Corsi allowed herself to pay attention to what was on the monitor on the workbench. "He was in the middle of saying it generated something when he collapsed. Ultrasonics?"

Gomez looked as though the light had gone off in her head at about the same time. "Sonic bullets. So hyperfocused that you don't hear anything unless you're the target, and if you're the target . . ."

"It all depends on what result they want," Corsi finished. "They can either give you a migraine, or turn your internal organs to goo. That works for humans; what about other species?"

"Different races react differently to different things," Lense replied, looking up from her perch over Soloman's still-prone body. "Whoever dreamed this thing up probably knew that. If it's lethal to humans, I really don't want to expose anyone else to it if I don't have to."

Gomez slid off her stool and walked over to a less-cluttered area of the lab. "Computer," she said. "Access the medical database and prepare to generate test representations of the auditory and neural pathways of every Federation species."

"Working."

A small, featureless, roughly humanoid shape appeared in the corner. It was gray, and its surface was smooth, but Corsi could make out attempts at two arms, two legs, and a head. "What's that?"

Gomez folded her arms across her chest. "It's the base pattern that the computer is working from. I intend to test this thing to see every possible output."

CHAPTER
9

Corsi strode into the dissonant cacophony that was Quark's Bar both anticipating and dreading what she had to do. It looked just like she remembered it: bar full of people of many different species, dabo tables in full spin, drinks and food free-flowing—for a reasonable price, of course. The enormous yellow and orange Cardassian glasswork that she'd learned had always stood in the rear of the bar still glowed, lending its odd shading to the various complexions that filled the bar.

The crowd was just what she wanted. There was no way Quark would risk making a scene in front of so many customers. She'd never actually interrogated an ambassador before, but she had interrogated Ferengi. Getting the slippery businessmen to divulge anything they didn't want to without offering monetary gain was usually just as difficult as it sounded.

No sooner was she through the door than a tall, lithe Orion female almost clothed in a diaphanous white dress whose hem barely passed her hips greeted her. An aroma of cinnamon followed, strong enough to plow its way through the general smell of the mass of people, as well as their respective dinners and drinks. Her flaming red hair was pulled up on her head, ornately braided strands dangling around her slender green neck. "Welcome to Quark's," she said, her voice perfectly balanced between loud enough to be heard over the gambling patrons and not loud enough to be yelling.

"Hello, Treir," Corsi said, matching her for volume. Judging by the woman's reaction, she hadn't expected the newcomer to know who she was. Corsi smiled. "One Hundred Ninety-fourth Rule of Acquisition. It's always good business to know your customers before they walk in the door."

The Orion frowned. "Let me guess. You're here to see Quark."

"Got it in one. If the ambassador isn't available, let him know he's interfering in a Starfleet investigation. His government might not like that too much."

Was that a snort of derision, or did one of the dabo tables give out? "That would require the ambassador liking his government. I take it you haven't heard—"

"About the problems he's had with the Grand Nagus? Or about the fact that the Grand Nagus's first clerk owes him a favor? Or are you talking about the fake Grisellan icons?"

One red eyebrow rose. "You're well-informed," she said, having the decency to sound surprised.

"Just knowing my customer."

Before Treir could say another word, the nearly slavering Ferengi ambassador appeared behind her. "Welcome to Quark's," he said, the tone in his voice far more of a "Can I show you my collection of Risean art?" than a real welcome. "It's always nice to have our Starfleet friends pay us a visit. Treir, has our guest asked for anything to drink?"

"No," the Orion said.

"Well, the couple at table three have. Could you take the order to them?"

Treir glared at the Ferengi before walking off.

"I'm here on business, Ambassador," Corsi said as she pulled Caitano's altered padd out of her shoulder bag. "Does this look familiar?"

The Ferengi's oversized lobes perked. "Business, you say? Well . . ."

She didn't like the way his voice had trailed off. "Look, we can do this the easy way, or we can do it the long, obnoxious, diplomatic-red-tape way. Either way, it doesn't change the fact that I've got two dead bodies on my ship because of this thing."

Quark turned a shade of green that Corsi couldn't recall ever seeing in nature. "Two dead bodies?" he asked, his eyes widening.

Corsi forced herself not to smile. Quark's reputation preceded him by several parsecs, and he knew it. Fortunately, she knew that he knew it. If Ro Laren was right, the fact that Quark essentially acted as a fence in the trade of an illegal weapon would be enough to throw diplomatic relations between Ferenginar and the Federation into a tizzy. Add the deaths of two Federation citizens as a result of that trade, and Corsi didn't even want to think of the kind of problems Federation President Zife would give Grand Nagus Rom. Diplomatic immunity only extended so far.

Still, trafficking in weapons was something that Quark should have known better than to attempt. He already had one charge on his record, and Corsi figured there were probably far more instances that never made it to the filing stage.

A glimmer of dread seeped into the Ferengi's features. Corsi didn't have to turn around to figure out who must have been standing behind her. Everything was going precisely as they'd planned. "How are we doing, Quark?" The congeniality in Captain Kira's voice sounded forced. "I trust you're not giving our guest any trouble?"

"Captain," Quark said, his smooth tone firmly in place and accompanied by what Corsi suspected was an all-too-usual *This isn't what you think it is* grin. "Of course not. As a representative of the Ferengi government, it would be—"

"Keep your lies consistent. Rule of Acquisition Number Sixty," Corsi said, raising one blond eyebrow. "I wouldn't expect anything less from the Ferengi ambassador."

"You know the Rules?" Kira asked, stepping up beside her. The Bajoran had her arms crossed over her chest, and her chin-length red hair blended with the command-track red on the neck of her uniform.

"It's a hobby," Corsi said with a shrug. "The ambassador

was about to tell me where he obtained this particular piece of technology that he sold to one of my staff."

"That's a padd," Kira said, her voice flat. "Quark, what are you doing selling Federation technology?"

The Ferengi pointed one finger at them. "Ah, but that's a specially-modified *reader*, Captain, enhanced to allow all of the nuances and sensory input from a very special book to be experienced. It's extremely popular in the Gamma Quadrant. Aren't the modifications the property of the person who designed them?"

Corsi tried to resist the urge to slug him. Instead, she held out her clenched fist and opened it over the bar, showing him the sensors and emitters Gomez had removed from the device. "You want to give the designer of this thing back his property, then? You're telling me that you knew this thing had been modified, yet you sold it anyway? Did you bother to check to see what these little trinkets do? They're specifically designed to *kill people*." She took great pains to enunciate the last two words as though she were talking to a two-year-old. "We tested it. Whoever designed this thing doesn't care what species you are. It adjusts itself for every known species. You're playing right into the hands of whoever let this thing loose."

She could have sworn a bead of sweat formed on the Ferengi's oversized forehead. In the corner of her eye, she caught sight of a smile on Captain Kira's features.

Ro had mentioned that there was a certain amount of history between the captain and the bartender-turned-ambassador, but from the look on Kira's face, "history" didn't seem to quite cover it. She was enjoying watching Quark squirm. "Where'd it come from, Quark?" Kira asked. "Don't make me have to start an interstellar incident. You linked this thing to the station's computers. Nog found nanites in the computer core. That makes it a danger to the station."

Corsi could recognize a cue when she heard one. "A representative of the Ferengi government fencing weapons disguised as Federation technology? You're in big trouble, Quark. Tell us who sold it to you, and maybe we'll believe you didn't know what you were doing when you resold it."

The Ferengi's eyes bounced back and forth between her and

Kira. "I—I—I want to talk to Ro," he said, furtively wringing his hands.

Corsi somehow managed not to roll her eyes. *Of course he does.*

Kira, however, took a step forward. In a tone that broached no question, she said, "Ro can't help you on this one, Quark. Any investigation she does will be immediately suspect. She couldn't possibly clear you without being accused of conspiracy. Two people have died because of what you sold. How many more, Quark?"

The Ferengi composed himself, staring her in the eyes. "Those people didn't die from reading a book."

"I've got a chief medical officer who would disagree with you on that," Corsi said. "Where'd it come from?"

Quark's eyes anxiously shot back and forth between Corsi and Kira.

"Quark. . . . Ambassador," Corsi began, "tell us where it came from, and the report the Federation Council reads will tell them you didn't know what you were doing when you sold it." She wasn't sure if she could even make such a deal, but if it got the Ferengi to cooperate, he never needed to know that. "You can tell me who it is, or we can go through your records and find out ourselves."

After a long moment in which Corsi began to believe he might make them get a warrant, Quark said, "It was a Wadi. That trader that came through here a couple of weeks ago. Tellow. He's the one that sold it to me."

Corsi smiled. *Well, confirms the paper trail. Ro's suspicion that this one wasn't forged was right.*

"They went back through the wormhole," Kira said. "We should have their flight plan on file."

"Wouldn't happen to have a DNA sample, would you?" Corsi asked.

"I'll check with Dr. Bashir. If we have anything, it's yours."

CHAPTER
10

"*We'll have a high-security cell ready when you get back. Are you sure you don't want the* Defiant *as backup, Captain?*" Kira asked from the *da Vinci*'s main viewscreen. "*You're not exactly a fighting vessel, and the* Defiant*'s got far more Gamma Quadrant experience.*"

David Gold leaned back in his chair. "Thanks, Captain, but if what the ambassador told us is true, that would be like taking a howitzer into Casablanca. If you could keep her on standby in case I'm wrong, though . . ."

Corsi could see the confusion in Captain Kira's eyes. The Bajoran opened her mouth to ask, but seemed to think better of it. "*You've got it, Captain. I'll have Commander Vaughn take care of it.*"

Gold gave her a curt nod. "Thanks. We'll see you when we get back."

"Course laid in, sir," Songmin Wong said, turning from his seat at conn.

The viewscreen image changed to the slowly receding docking ring of Deep Space 9. "Wong," Gold began, "take us in."

The ship sailed around the station, and made a bank toward an empty area of space. While Corsi watched, the swirling maelstrom of blue and white energy bursts that comprised the wormhole's mouth flashed into existence, and the ship was dragged inside.

Corded strands of blue-white energy filled the viewscreen, slowly oscillating in time with the shaking the ship was experiencing. *I don't even want to think about a ride like this in Dad's ship. The cargo would be liquefied by the time he got to the other side.*

When the wormhole finally deposited them in the Gamma Quadrant, she allowed her hands to let go of the railing beside the tactical console. "How long before we reach the Kar-telos System?" she asked.

"Couple of days, Commander," Wong replied.

Gold turned his chair toward Corsi. "Did the captain send us the Wadi DNA sample?"

Corsi nodded. "Lense is trying to see how it compares to the other trace she couldn't identify."

"Keep on it."

Elizabeth Lense didn't look happy. That could only have meant one thing.

"What did you find?" Corsi asked, fighting the urge to yawn. It had been twenty-eight hours since the discovery that enhanced sonic bullets had killed Caitano and Deverick, and Corsi hadn't had a wink of sleep. It was as though her body's clock had turned somersaults. When she was off duty, her brain wouldn't shut down. It would keep trying to go over every little nuance of the evidence, flailing to see the answer to one question: *Why?* When Lense had contacted her in the security office, Corsi had been dangerously close to falling asleep at her desk.

"Well," Lense began, pointing toward a display in her lab, "the Wadi DNA came up positive. It wasn't the same person that gave the sample, but it was consistent. I've also managed to figure out what species the other DNA trace on Caitano's padd might be from."

Corsi closed her eyes, a well of dread forming in her stomach. "What?"

"Whoever did this masked themselves very well. I only got a partial trace, but there were chromosomes present consistent with Vorta DNA."

That was a word Corsi had hoped never to hear again. "Vorta?"

Lense nodded. "I can't tell you which Vorta it is, but there are a couple of specific nucleotide sequences that we've only found in their DNA."

"Okay," Corsi began, "there aren't any Vorta in the Alpha Quadrant that we can't account for. Since the file that the nanites were attached to is supposedly a Gamma Quadrant bestseller, then could it be from anywhere else?"

Lense shook her head. "I don't think so."

"Then where is the little Vorta hiding, and does he have any Jem'Hadar still loyal to him?" Corsi hit her combadge. "Computer, secure channel. Corsi to Captain Gold."

After a few moments' silence, presumably while he got to a private location to take the comm, Gold replied, *"Yes, Corsi?"*

Corsi's mind scrambled to try to think of a good way to put what she had to say. "Captain, we have a lead."

"Good work," Gold replied. *"Who?"*

"Not quite, sir," Lense said. "More like a 'which species.' I found masked traces of Vorta DNA on the padd."

"Vorta?" Gold's voice tightened. *"I'll inform Starfleet Command. If this is the first wave of a new Dominion attack—"*

"Captain," Lense said, "please make sure they're aware that every species in the Federation is vulnerable. All this thing needs is a bodily orifice to allow the waves to enter. The Strata might be safe, but I'm not sure anyone else will be."

CHAPTER
11

When they beamed down outside the seedy little bar that the Wadi trader reportedly had been headed to from Deep Space 9, Corsi immediately wanted a shower. The place looked as though it had been carved out of the asteroid, and now the asteroid was seriously considering reclamation. A thin layer of reddish-brown dust seemed to coat everything in the area, including her nostrils. If it hadn't been for the aroma of dirt and grime, the mixture of sweat and sickly-sweet perfumes that assaulted her senses as she and Hawkins walked through the door might have sickened her.

She counted nine small tables scattered throughout the bar, but only two had patrons. At the table nearest her sat a large bipedal creature with an elongated snout, stubby claws in place of fingers, and tiny ears at the top of its black-furred head. It bore more of a resemblance to a two-meter-tall wombat than any other humanoid she'd ever seen. A bowl of something wriggling sat before it. Corsi wasn't sure she wanted to know precisely what it was, but what little she saw as the creature scooped the contents into its mouth immediately sent her appetite packing.

In the back of the bar, behind two scantily clad red-haired Bajoran females, sat a heavyset male with long black hair pulled back from his face. A large, ornate pattern was either tattooed or painted—at that distance, she couldn't quite tell—in dark blue on his forehead. The two Bajoran women were pawing his gold-accented blue tunic. From the descriptions Captain Kira had sent along with the flight plan, she figured this was Tellow.

Hawkins followed her into the bar, a look of distaste on his features. "Sure we've got the right place, boss?"

"Go home, Starfleeter," the bartender—a tall, muscular humanoid with rust-red skin, a dark pewter-toned bodysuit that came up in a hood over his forehead, and metallic face paint on his cheeks—said. "Get back through the anomaly where you belong. You got no power here."

Dosi, Corsi thought. *Bad attitude toward the Federation, and no problem with forwarding a Dominion agenda. Think we've got the right place.*

"Not until I talk to Tellow."

The Dosi's bright orange lip curled up in a sneer. "What do you want with Tellow?"

Before she could answer, the two Bajoran women came up and began pawing over Hawkins. One purred into his ear, while the other curled around him like a snake. The conflicted look on her deputy's face said he couldn't figure out whether to enjoy the attention, or shoo the women away.

Considering that he and Carol Abramowitz had been seeing each other since Teneb, Corsi immediately began wondering how much this might be worth on the blackmail market. That thought was short-lived as she realized the situation for what it was—a distraction. She immediately turned to the heavyset man who had been in the company of the two women. He was sliding his way out from behind the table and toward a back door. *Why do they always run?*

"Hawkins," Corsi said, fighting the urge to laugh at the man's pained expression, "keep an eye on your new friends, will you? I'm going to go have a little chat."

She slipped easily between the tables, getting through the back door and into what appeared to be the empty—but just as grimy—kitchen a few seconds after the Wadi. A clattering sounded from her right as a tray full of metal plates fell to the floor.

"Don't bother, Tellow!" she yelled. "I've got people covering the landing bays. You won't get anywhere."

A growl emanated from the other side of the kitchen. Finally, Tellow rose from his hiding place behind a pantry. On any other humanoid, the unpleasant twist to his lips would have been far more disquieting. "What do you want, Starfleet?" he asked, his deep, raspy voice nearly a snarl.

"You know, it doesn't look good when you run."

Corsi took a step closer to the Wadi. A flash of light near his wrist caught her attention. She quickly drew her phaser. "Drop the weapon." When he did nothing more than stare at her, she made a show of adjusting a setting. "You can be put in the brig quietly, or I can shoot you and drag you there. Your choice."

Tellow reached toward his wrist, pulling out a small blade. It fell to the floor with a clatter. "What do you want?"

The phaser didn't waver. "All of it."

The Wadi reached under his tunic, pulling out a small pistol.

Corsi raised an eyebrow questioningly. She really didn't like the idea of patting the sweating behemoth down, but when Tellow didn't reach for any other weapons, she didn't see any other choice. "Hands up," she said, gesturing with the phaser. The Wadi finally succumbed. When she was satisfied that he was, in fact, unarmed, she grabbed his gun from the floor. Securing his right arm behind his back, she led him out into the bar . . .

. . . where she was faced with a sight that sucked the wind right out of her sails. Hawkins had both of his Bajoran "assailants" sitting in chairs in one corner, his phaser warily trained on them. *Damn. The blackmail potential on that was priceless.*

Corsi leaned on Tellow's arm, pushing him forward. "Now, why run like that? I just want to ask you a few questions. Running like that might make me think you had something to hide."

Tellow's dark head shook. "No. I don't deal with Starfleeters."

A thin smile spread across Corsi's lips. She pushed the Wadi against the nearest wall, allowing him to turn around. When he could see her face, and his own pistol pointed directly at his chest, she put on her best predatory expression. "No, but you do deal with Ferengi."

Something resembling a growl came from Tellow's throat.

Unabated, she continued, "And that Ferengi, he deals with Starfleeters. One of the things he traded was a weapon— a weapon he says you sold to him, and a weapon we found traces of Wadi DNA on."

"I don't know anything about a weapon or a Ferengi."

"Do you know anything about Betazoids?" she asked, a thin smile spreading on her features.

Tellow's eyes widened. "Federation law—"

"That weapon you sold was directly responsible for the deaths of two of my crew," she said. "Do you think I have any problems with stretching Federation law until you can reach through it to get whoever's responsible?"

"Commander," Hawkins said, "are you sure about this? The captain—"

"I don't care what the captain thinks!" she shot back. The look in her deputy's eyes said he'd picked up on what she was doing. *Good cop, bad cop, Hawkins. Good cop, bad cop.* "We're dealing with a threat to Federation security here. We do whatever it takes. If that requires getting our resident Betazoid to pull the name of the guy that created the device out of this worthless bum's head, that's what it takes."

She hoped Hawkins wouldn't blow it by mentioning that Rennan Konya was too low-level a telepath for such a thing, and he didn't disappoint. He looked appropriately chastised as he quickly nodded. "Okay, boss. Sure you don't want me to talk to him?"

It was tempting to let him loose, as the sharp briny smell coming from the Wadi was getting worse. *When was the last time this guy had a bath? Those two women must have had their senses of smell removed.* Finally, she shook her head. "Now," she began, "are we going to play nice, or do I get to shoot you?"

Tellow's eyes bounced back and forth between Hawkins and Corsi for a few moments.

"Or," she said, intentionally sounding as though she'd just gotten the idea, "my friend here could do something to your lovely ladies that might make them, shall we say, a little less profitable?"

When she glanced over at Hawkins, she was pleased to see something bordering on a menacing expression on his features.

"Nothing life threatening, of course," she added. "Just enough to cut into your profit margin."

The Wadi's eyes narrowed, sizing her up. "You would not. Starfleeters—"

"Give it up," she flatly said. "I have no qualms about killing you and getting the information out of your ship's computer. Matter of fact, I'm beginning to like the idea. It would save me some time. I've got a job to do here, Tellow, and you're only in my way. Now, let's dump the formalities and get down to business." Resisting the urge to find a vat of soap and douse the Wadi, she leaned in closer. "Are you going to tell me what I want to know?"

CHAPTER
12

"We're looking for a Vorta named Luaran," Corsi said as she walked into the conference room and slid into her usual chair. "She set up shop in the Dominion's old subspace relay station at Callinon VII. Reportedly, the Dominion abandoned it after the retreat, and she's taken over. It was described as 'lightly secured' in the reports. Something tells me that's changed."

Seated to her left, Fabian Stevens blanched. "Luaran?"

"Yes."

Stevens leaned forward, turning his gaze to the man seated at the head of the table. "Captain, recommend calling in the *Defiant* to meet us there."

Gold perched his elbows on the armrests, steepling his fingers at his chin. "I'll consider it, Stevens. How is she operating outside of Dominion space?"

"Not sure yet, sir," Corsi replied. "I'm looking into the possibility that we may have a defective clone."

One gray eyebrow rose. "Defective?" Gold asked. "The Dominion's primary goal was to take over the Alpha Quadrant. Getting rid of the indigenous species only helps that cause. How does that make her defective?"

"According to our new friend down in the brig, she's working entirely without Jem'Hadar. If I add to that the fact that she's working in a facility the Dominion abandoned, then I come up with the theory that she's operating independently. Vorta aren't capable of doing that on a long-term basis, and she'd have to have been at this for a while to get the padd perfected."

"Or gotten damned lucky," Gold said.

"Sir," Stevens began, "if we've got another Luaran on our hands, she could prove even more dangerous than the Weyouns. The last Luaran clone that we know about led the occupation of Betazed."

"I'm aware of that, Stevens." Turning to Sonya Gomez— seated just to his right—Gold said, "Make sure Starfleet Command knows this may be isolated. I've got a feeling Corsi's right, and this is a defective clone. The Dominion may not know this Luaran is out there."

Elizabeth Lense shifted positions in her chair. "I did get traces of Vorta DNA off the padd Caitano was reading when he died, but I didn't get a hit. Then again, I only searched for living Vorta . . ."

Before they could get any further, Songmin Wong's voice came over the comm. *Bridge to Captain Gold. We've arrived at the Callinon System.*

Corsi stared at the viewscreen. As gas giants went, Callinon VII was pretty run-of-the-mill—swirling oranges, purples, and reds mixed with some white for effect. *It looks almost like Jupiter, but without the spot.* She studied the readouts as they approached. It was a small system, but it was apparent that some cataclysm had caused at least two of Callinon VII's moons to either collide or self-destruct, as a small band of asteroids formed a string of pearls around the gas giant's equator. No sooner did that thought cross her mind than a tiny speck floated in front of one of the planet's white bands. *There you are.* "Captain, bearing zero-zero-one mark five." Checking a readout, Corsi added, "Looks like it's in a geostationary orbit over the planet." She hit the control that sent the coordinates to the conn station.

"Take us in, Wong," Gold said. "Slow and easy. Haznedl, scan for booby traps. Corsi, Stevens, keep an eye on it."

Ensign Susan Haznedl's hands worked the ops controls. "Aye, sir. No sign at this—"

Bolts of phaser fire began to streak across the viewscreen. The ship shook as one struck home.

"Phaser cannon, sir," Lieutenant Anthony Shabalala said. "Localizing it now."

"Evasive maneuvers, Wong. Damage report."

"Minimal hull damage decks seven through ten. No reports of injury," Haznedl said. "Sir, incoming fire is originating on two asteroids in geostationary orbit approximately one hundred kilometers away from our target."

The ship banked to starboard as a portion of the shields began to glow brightly. The phaser cannons were doing a fine job of draining their shields. At the rate they were being hit, Corsi didn't think they'd last much longer.

"Phaser source localized, Captain. Two sources. One bearing three-three-zero mark one-five. The other at bearing three-nine mark five," Haznedl said. "Routing coordinates to tactical now."

Gold leaned back in his chair. "Take them out, Shabalala."

One nick-of-the-time evasive maneuver from Wong later, the ship's targeting sensors got a lock. "Quantum torpedoes away," Shabalala said.

They watched as the two torpedoes streaked away from the ship, finding their targets with relative efficiency. "Targets destroyed, sir," Haznedl said. "Shields at eighty-five percent and holding."

"Keep an eye out for more," Gold said, his eyes on the viewscreen. "Something tells me these aren't the only upgrades Luaran's made to this place. Wong, take us back in, but this time, come in from above. I want to see if her defensive capabilities were thought out in three dimensions."

"Aye, sir," Wong said.

The two defensive stations had been buried in the asteroid

belt, and it wasn't outside the realm of possibility that there were more such stations. Corsi had to admit, though, it was a good approach. Coming in on the Z-axis might throw anyone—or anything—at those stations off their game.

Wong executed an almost perfect vertical approach. Corsi grabbed the railing once again, expecting another round of phaser fire as they neared the station. What they got, however, was something different.

"Captain," Shabalala said, "we've got incoming. Two photon torpedoes. Scratch that. Picking up two *quantum* torpedoes."

"Shoot them down, Shabalala."

"I'm trying, sir. Something's keeping the phasers from getting a lock. Going to visual."

Corsi's eyes went to the viewscreen. The gap between the ship and torpedoes was closing alarmingly fast.

Before Gold could get another warning out, phaser fire flew toward the torpedoes, destroying them on the first shot. As the explosions cleared on the viewscreen, Corsi allowed herself to breathe again.

They continued on toward the array. When they were within ten thousand kilometers, tiny flickers of light began coming from the facility's communication dishes. "Shabalala—" Gold began, a warning tone to his voice.

"Already on it, sir. It appears to be light reflecting off the arrays, but I'm not sure where it's coming from," he replied. "No sign of any more incoming fire."

Could it be this easy?

Corsi scanned the readings herself. There really was no sign of more incoming fire. *Either this Luaran is the luckiest Vorta still alive, or the most shortsighted.* Something occurred to her. "Sir, she's got phaser cannons protecting the logical approach vector, and saved the quantum torpedoes for the Z-axis vector. If she doesn't have Dominion backing, she can't have a lot of either one. With the geostationary orbit, she's got the planet pretty much covering the rear approach. That covers most of the possible incoming trajectories. Thing is, what happens if they get past the phaser cannons and torpedoes? What's the close-range line of defense?"

That was the point where something started to hit the shields like rainfall. *What the—?*

"Small-missile fire, sir," Shabalala called out from tactical. "The shields are now at eighty percent."

The ship banked hard to port as Wong began more evasive maneuvers.

"Divert power to the shields," Gold said.

"In process, Captain. Ventral shielding now at one hundred five percent," Shabalala reported. "Count twenty-five incoming projectiles."

"Can you get a lock, Shabalala?"

"Working on it, sir."

The display on the main viewer was shimmering like a diamond as the impacts began to register. The missiles were mostly concentrating on the ventral portion of the ship, but as she watched, one seemed to be heading directly for them. Intellectually, she knew she wasn't at risk. It was aiming for a tiny camera mounted somewhere on the hull, not the bridge. Still, that didn't stop Corsi from flinching when the viewscreen lit up like a Roman candle as the missile impacted.

"We're down to a dozen incoming, sir," Lieutenant Shabalala said. "Phasers locking on now."

In the most rapid-fire succession of shots Corsi had ever seen outside of handheld phasers, Shabalala took out each of the dozen remaining missiles. A deep scan revealed there were no more incoming projectiles behind them.

"Guess that answers my question," Corsi mused aloud. On the viewscreen, the Y-shaped, disc-covered "wings" of the array, meeting at its circular hub, greeted them. The hub bore a slight resemblance to the operations center of Deep Space 9, approximately three or four floors of what she guessed were computer routers, transmitters, transceivers, and other equipment. She was already trying to look into the windows to see what was there. For a station that was reportedly unmanned, there were a lot of interior lights. *The lights are on, but is anybody home?*

"Captain, should I put an away team together?"

"Not until we get a good look around down there, Corsi," Gold replied. "Is there any sign of shielding in place?"

"Nothing we can't interfere with, Captain," Shabalala said, confidence in his voice.

A wide smile spread across Corsi's lips. "Then I have just the man for the job, sir."

CHAPTER
13

Fabian Stevens carried a small device into the conference room. On his head was the same control headpiece she'd seen on him a few days before. "You wanted to see me, sir?"

Gold, Corsi, and Gomez all looked up from their positions at the conference table. Gold was the first to stand. "Excellent, Stevens. Corsi here thinks she might have a use for your new toy."

Stevens raised one dark eyebrow. "She does?"

"Yup," Corsi said, pulling herself out of her chair. "This is the perfect situation to test your advance scout, Fabe."

His eyes bounced among her, Gomez, and the captain. "Well, I'm not sure it's ready for a field test yet, but if you want it, she's yours, Captain. Where should I go to control it?"

Gold's eyes dropped to the unit in Stevens's hands. "That's where we have a problem."

Corsi slipped on the headpiece, adjusting it so the earpieces and goggles fit. She slipped a glove on each hand, feeling the wires that ran down her arms and to each sensory conduit. *Commander La Forge must have had it easy if all they had to do was plug into his sensory inputs.*

"How're you doing, Dom?" Stevens's voice sounded in her ear. She knew he was irritated about the captain wanting her to pilot the thing on its maiden voyage, but she couldn't deny the validity of his statement that if she were to lead the away team, it made the most sense for her to pilot the virtual reality scout. It certainly would save her time if they had to get to a safe location in a hurry.

"Okay," Corsi replied, sounding a lot more confident than she felt. "Get in position and hook me up."

She heard the muffled sounds of activity, then Fabian's voice returned in her ear.

"The mobile emitter is in position. Activating the remote sensors," Stevens said. *"Initiating interface now. Feeding sensory inputs to the control system now."*

A dusky blur filled her vision, slowly sharpening into a visual of a small, well-lit room. She was surprised when a slight burst of air hit her nose. There was a sharp cleanliness to it that suggested the recirculators had been recently replaced. Consoles lined the walls, each appearing to have a different function. Tiny beeps and other electronic sounds were soft in her ears. She only knew a little bit of the written Dominion language, but it looked like there was a console for the airlock right near the emitter's location. Just beyond that console was a window, where she could see one of the array's three wings. A few kilometers off the end of the wing sat the *da Vinci* in a parking orbit.

"Do you see anything?" Fabian's voice asked in her ear.

"Yeah. There are consoles all over the place. The monitors are displaying what looks like Dominion text. I think the one next to me controls the airlock."

Her entire visual field lowered, until she felt as though she were lying on the floor of the room. "Fabe? What's going on?"

"I've adjusted the holo-configuration. You're now configured for a small gecko."

"A gecko? What are you, nuts?"

"Yes, Dom. A gecko. They have something that'll help the

emitter hide that doesn't require antigrav circuits to work. The setae on their hands and feet will let them walk on the walls. Hopefully, the small size of the projection will keep it hidden longer."

It took her a couple of seconds to get acclimated to maneuvering the device, but she managed to get it positioned high up on the wall near the airlock door. There was enough space between the ceiling and the top of the window to use it as a temporary resting place. She moved around the upper edges of the walls, navigating the corridors with relative ease. There were a few gaps in the consoles that looked big enough for a humanoid to hide behind in a firefight, if necessary.

"Fabe," she said, "are we getting a map of this?"

"Yes. Just keep going, Dom."

When she reached what appeared to be a central command structure, she stopped. A ring of consoles surrounded one workstation, each more complex than anything Corsi had seen in the other corridors. There was a Vorta standing by the central workstation, studying displays. There didn't appear to be any alarm bells going off, which both mystified and encouraged Corsi. The Vorta reached a long, slender hand over the controls, an arch expression on her features. Her eyes were rimmed in kohl, and her short black hair only served to make her look paler. The purple of her lips blended with the purple trim on her otherwise green jumpsuit.

"Luaran," Corsi whispered.

"She's there with you?" Stevens asked.

"Yes. I don't think she—"

Before she could finish, the Vorta pulled out a plasma rifle and aimed it straight at the emitter.

"Fabe, she's got a gun."

"Take the gear off, Dom. If she—"

Before he could finish, Luaran fired. The last thing Corsi saw in the goggles was the mobile emitter exploding.

CHAPTER
14

Corsi's eyes *hurt,* and the glare from the penlight for Sonya Gomez's headset camera wasn't making it any better.

"Watch that thing, Commander. The last thing we need is one of us with retina burn."

The commander adjusted the tiny penlight perched over her right ear. "Sorry, Domenica. Didn't realize it was that bright. Last check. Can you get this, Bart? Okay? Good. I'm shutting down for transport."

Corsi, Hawkins, and Rennan Konya formed a circle around Sonya Gomez as they prepared to beam down to the array, phasers at the ready. There was no doubt in her mind that Luaran not only knew they were out there to get her, but that they were coming in. Just to be safe, she slid a second phaser into the waistband of her uniform pants, placing it at the small of her back under her jacket. Much to her approval, Konya and Hawkins both did the same.

No sooner did they beam down than alarms went off. *How'd they miss the mobile emitter?* She fought the urge to put her hands to her ears. It sounded almost as though the alarms were going off inside her skull.

A device that looked distressingly like a larger version of one of the pieces Gomez had found in Caitano's padd was mounted in one corner of the ceiling. One phaser blast later, the ringing in her skull subsided. When she was able to actually think again, Corsi quickly pinpointed their location. "Come on," she said, pointing down the corridor to her right. "The central control room is this way. Hawkins, take point."

They got three meters before he ran headfirst into a security field.

"I got it," Gomez said, flipping the switch at her waist. The penlight once again shone like a beacon, illuminating the console that Gomez was studying. "Bart, can you see anything?"

Corsi heard an occasional sound of acknowledgment come from the first officer, as well as the sounds of her tools at work, and gestured for Konya and Hawkins to take defensive positions around the engineer while she worked. "I didn't see any guards before," Corsi said, staring back down the corridor they'd come from, "but that doesn't mean there aren't any here. Keep your eyes open."

At that point, a phaser blast grazed her arm. She lowered to her knee, mostly to protect Gomez, but also to hopefully get the shooter to damage the array's own equipment. Konya had found one of the gaps on the other side of the corridor, his phaser at the ready as he ducked behind the console. *For a low-level telepath, at least he can read people. Let's hope that extends to Jem'Hadar.*

Corsi looked up, hoping there might be some indication of what was coming toward them. A lone Jem'Hadar came down the corridor, a snarl like she hadn't seen since the war curling his scaly lips.

Corsi adjusted her phaser to its highest setting, narrowed the beam, and took aim. She caught the Jem'Hadar once in the chest, but not before he got off another shot. That shot impacted the ceiling, taking out a row of lights.

Everything dimmed, until finally a dull light mixed with the smoke of the exploding circuits all around them. The beam of Gomez's lamp shone in the corner of her eye, and the lights from the central command center radiated a glow that she could see all around. Still, the shadow of the Jem'Hadar grew larger.

Corsi and Konya exhanged glances in the dirty light, and then both stood and began firing at the Jem'Hadar. They each got three shots off before the sound of the security field falling made it to Corsi's ears.

A fourth shot from Konya finally felled the Jem'Hadar.

"Command—"

Hawkins's alarm call was interrupted by the sound of a plasma rifle firing, and Gomez shouting in surprise.

Corsi and Konya turned to find Hawkins facedown across Gomez's outstretched legs, a burn from the plasma rifle visible over half of his thigh as he tried to push himself back up . . .

. . . and Luaran standing on the other side of the opening, the plasma rifle in her long-fingered hands and aimed at Gomez. "Drop the weapons," she said, her voice arch.

Hawkins pushed himself off of Gomez's legs, shaking his head slowly. Corsi was surprised to see that Gomez had already flipped off the camera's overly bright penlight.

Luaran lowered the rifle and took aim. "I can shoot the other leg, human." Raising her eyes to Corsi and Konya, she said, "Drop the weapons."

Corsi slowly bent down and put the phaser on the floor, gesturing for Konya to do the same. *Wait until the time's right, Rennan. Wait until the time's right.* Konya followed suit, and had enough sense to not draw his backup weapon. Hawkins was already disarmed of his primary weapon. From her angle, Corsi couldn't see his backup. Gomez slid slowly out from under the console, her eyes warily on the Vorta as she stood up.

"Can I help my deputy stand up?" Corsi asked. "Otherwise he's just going to lie here and bleed on your floor."

Just turn around, Luaran. Just turn around.

"No," the Vorta said, disdain filling her voice. "Let him die. He can be the first casualty of the new war."

Great, Corsi thought. *We've got a nut job Vorta who wants to restart the war. I really hate being right sometimes.*

She glanced down at Hawkins, giving him a quick "sit tight" look.

"This way," Luaran said, gesturing toward central control. "After you."

Konya took the lead, followed by Gomez and then Corsi. She hated the feeling of the plasma rifle at her back. "New war, huh?" Corsi said. "Hoping to lead the battle with your little acoustic weapon?"

"Ah, so it's been used, has it? That would explain why there's a Federation starship sitting outside."

"Yes," Gomez said, beginning to turn her head to the left. "Where'd you get the nanites?"

"That would be for me to know and you to . . . not know, human."

"Really?" Before she could take another step, Gomez finished the turn and flipped the switch on her belt that controlled the camera's light. Corsi ducked, just in time for the beam to hit Luaran full in the eyes. In the time it took her to stand up, backup phaser in hand, it was already over. The Vorta crumpled to the ground in a heap, a phaser burn still smoking on her back.

Gomez turned the light off, and when her eyes adjusted, Corsi saw Hawkins propped up on his right elbow, his backup phaser in his left hand. Tapping her combadge, she said, "Corsi to *da Vinci*. Beam Hawkins to sickbay and send over some backup. We've eliminated the Vorta threat and need to secure the facility." Before Laura Poynter could execute the command, Corsi said, "Nice work, Hawkins. Nice work."

As soon as he was gone, she turned to Gomez. "Let's hope she only had the one Jem'Hadar. Commander, is that link still working? We need to figure out what those consoles in there do."

CHAPTER
15

"*What's the word on the computers, Gomez?*" Captain Gold asked.

Sonya Gomez looked up from the console, keeping the penlight aimed at the ceiling. "Working on it, Captain," she replied. "We're downloading the data and should have them ready to go in about an hour."

Corsi checked the security sensors one last time. *Looks like they were calibrated to only pick up intruders with enough mass to be a threat. Might even have been able to have the hologram do a human projection and it wouldn't have picked it up.*

That reminds me.

She began visually scanning the upper edges of the central command chamber, looking for signs of the charring from the plasma rifle. She finally found it, directly over the subspace relay controls. A smattering of charred parts were scattered over the top of the unit. Corsi gathered them up in one hand, and shoved them into a small shoulder bag she'd had sent over from the *da Vinci*.

"What's that, Commander?" Gomez asked, looking up so her light hit the scorched spot on the wall.

"Parts of Fabe's little toy," Corsi replied. "It would have worked if Luaran hadn't shot it. Figured I should bring it back for a fitting burial in space."

Gomez chuckled.

"What's so funny?" Corsi asked.

"Bart. He says now Fabian may finally shut up about you co-opting his experiment."

Corsi glowered at the camera over Gomez's right ear. "Yeah, right. Faulwell, tell Stevens he can kiss my entire ass. No, he might actually enjoy that. Never mind. I'll be happy to pay him back for that when I get back to the ship. Have you figured out whether or not she's got more of those things out there?"

Gomez looked back down at the consoles that surrounded her. She reached toward one with her left hand, working a few controls. "I can't find any more references to it in the database. Looks like the one that we got was the prototype. Tellow's ship didn't show any sign of any copies being made."

Corsi looked around the small control chamber. "All of this, just to create one stealth weapon? What about test subjects? She couldn't have sent that thing out without testing it on someone first."

"With the gravitational field of a gas giant to work with? I'm guessing that she's dumped all of the bodies into the planet's atmosphere."

Clambering down from the console, Corsi said, "What about the nanites?"

Gomez smiled. "Already got it covered. I've shunted them all into one portion of the computers' drive. There should be enough for them to chew on in there to last a week or two. That's enough time to take care of them."

"So, what do we do with nonsentient nanites that are programmed to build weapons?"

Gomez shrugged. "We'll think of something." Something on the display seemed to catch her attention.

"What?" Corsi asked.

"She did get lucky, didn't she?"

That only served to confuse her more. "What? How?"

"The book."

Corsi walked around to look at the console. "Just looks like a bunch of cryptic symbols to me. What's Faulwell say?"

"He says it's a development log. Apparently Luaran spent months looking for something she could attach the weapon to, and wasn't able to move forward until *Tafock Navar Relal* became popular and traffic started coming back into the Gamma Quadrant through the wormhole."

Corsi stared at the display. "We got all of them; DS9 is purging the nanites from its system, and they have no record of the program being downloaded to anyone. The Wadi ship and the *Musgrave* both came up clean. We've purged it from our system. The three padds that actually contained the thing are in custody. I think we've got all of them."

Gomez raised her head, a wide smile on her face. "Nice work."

EPILOGUE

"*In nomine Patris et Filii, et Spiritus Sancti,*" the priest intoned.

In unison, everyone around her said, "Amen."

Domenica Corsi stood by the open grave, her head bowed as the casket was lowered. *Rest in peace, Ken. Wherever you are.*

Once the gathered crowd started to break up, she turned and walked slowly toward the well-worn terra-cotta cobblestones that formed a path through the ancient Sienese cemetery. Captain Gold took up step beside her, a somber expression on his features, highlighted by the all white of his dress uniform. She didn't want to consider what the gray-and-white version she wore was doing for her appearance.

"Do you hate these things as much as I do, Captain?" she asked.

The exhaustion was evident in his voice. "Maybe more." After everything that had happened on Deep Space 9 after stopping Luaran, two funerals on top of it was almost too taxing.

"Domenica!"

Corsi turned to find Angelina Caitano ambling toward her, a sad smile on her tear-streaked, robust features. "Domenica," she began, lifting the black mourning veil that covered her face. "You and your captain will eat with us tonight, yes?"

"I'm sorry, Mrs. Caitano," she began, "I wish we could have brought him back sooner, but we got caught up in a crisis on Deep Space 9. We really should get back to the ship. We still need to—"

"Bah!" the elder woman said, throwing her chubby hands toward the sky. "That can wait until tomorrow. My Agosto says good things about you. You found the person who killed our Kenny. You both are family now. So, you come home with us and you eat. Those Starfleet meals cannot be as good as our family's marinara." Angelina's sad smile was suddenly filled with pride. "A recipe that has been passed down for six centuries must have something right, yes?"

Corsi felt a lump begin to form in her throat. "How can you—? I mean, your son—"

"Died?" Mrs. Caitano asked. "Yes. This is true. The world, however, it continues. We must move on." She stepped delicately over the cobblestones, trying to avoid the gaps with the slender heels of her shoes. "The funeral—that is where we mourn the death. After that, we find ways to continue with life. Family is the best tradition. We gather. We eat. We talk. We celebrate the life."

Corsi swallowed hard. "Good tradition."

Angelina smoothed the full skirt of her black dress down with her hands. "I have thought so, too."

After the dire histrionics of the Deverick family on the loss of their only child, Corsi was almost grateful for the approach the Caitano family took. She could remember a time when the family on the *da Vinci* had taken a similar approach to their losses at Galvan VI, and a similar celebration of life in a backyard in New York. A glance at Captain Gold revealed a small, melancholy smile on the captain's face. She couldn't help but wonder if he was remembering that same gathering. "Mrs. Caitano?"

"Yes, Domenica?"

"May I ask you something about Ken? There was something

we found in his quarters that didn't make sense to me, but ended up not being related to what happened. It's still bugging me, though."

Angelina folded her hands over her ample belly. "Of course, my dear. What is it you want to know?"

"There was a counterfeit bar of gold-pressed latinum in his quarters. We never did figure out where it came from."

"He still brings that with him?" Angelina began to laugh.

Corsi and Gold exchanged a look. "Yes," she replied. "It was on a shelf in his quarters when he died. We weren't sure if it was connected to his death. There was nothing about it in his official file."

Professor Agosto Caitano chose that moment to walk up. He wrapped an arm around his wife's shoulders and pulled her close. "That's because he got it when he was thirteen years old. He helped one of the local policemen figure out something for an investigation, and the officer gave that to him as a reward."

"Some reward," Corsi dryly said.

"Yes," Agosto replied with a solemn expression. "I wish we could have done more to help you find Ken's killer, Domenica." He reached out with his free hand, placing it on her arm. "I do want you to know that we're very grateful for what you've done. I am proud that one of my students stopped such an insidious terrorist weapon. If my son had to lay down his life, it is good that it helped to stop that Vorta."

Corsi's stomach twisted. She would have preferred the gratitude for keeping Caitano from ever getting the padd in the first place. However, she forced a sad smile onto her face. If it would help them get some closure, she'd play along.

Ken, wherever you are, I promise. This won't happen again. You opened our eyes, and we're going to keep watching.

"Now," Agosto said, releasing her arm long enough to gently pat it. "We go eat."

LOST TIME

Ilsa J. Bick

"Lost time is never found again."
—Benjamin Franklin

CHAPTER
1

"Here comes the second front, here it *comes!*" yelped a Bajoran lieutenant. The woman was new and was at the science station. Captain Kira Nerys didn't remember her name and now wished she could because the woman looked good and scared. Her blond hair was matted to her forehead, and her skin had an oily sheen of perspiration that slicked her cheeks and the underside of her jaw. She was sweating so much she looked basted. "Captain, it's—it's bigger, this one's much—!"

Deep Space 9 jerked, quick and sharp and with a violence that reminded Kira of the way a very large, very strong Talmuna swordfish fought a line, yanking and snapping back and forth, trying to shake itself free. Something shorted in a shower of sparks, and Kira caught the odor of ozone and seared metal. There was a loud metallic groan as the station bucked, and in the next instant, the ululating shrill of an alarm klaxon spiked its way into Kira's brain.

"Someone shut that thing *off!* You'd have to be brain-dead not to know we're in trouble!" Another jolt threw her off balance, and she stumbled, flailed, searched for a handhold, her nails scrabbling against smooth duranium. She missed, her

right temple smacked solid plasticine, and she went down,
hard, right on the point of her chin, snapping her head back,
driving her teeth into her tongue. Pain exploded in her mouth
and jagged into the space behind her right eye, scorching a
path through her brain. Hot bile crowded into the back of her
throat, mixed with the blood filling her mouth with a taste like
wet rust, and Kira gagged, coughed out a crimson spray, and
fought back the urge to vomit.

She felt a hand on her right shoulder and then someone
was hauling her up, bracing her as she swayed; she tried to
pass out but, mercifully, failed.

"You still with us?" Commander Elias Vaughn: voice pinch-
ing with anxiety, hazel eyes searching her face. When he gently
pressed the edge of his left thumb to the corner of her mouth,
it came away smeared with black blood. "My God. Nerys?"

"I'm fine," Kira lied. She was woozy and hurt, but she
thought the fact that her tongue still worked was a good thing.
Something thick and sticky dribbled over her eyebrow. She
put a shaky hand to her forehead, felt the wet. Smelled the
copper edge of her blood.

Got to hang on. . . . Impatient now, she pulled herself up,
squared her shoulders and shrugged her way out of Vaughn's
grip. He looked hesitant but then nodded and moved back to
rerouting traffic away from the station. Kira turned to Ezri
Dax, monitoring internal systems. "How's everyone else? What
about the station?"

Dax said something about Ro's security people confining
folks to their quarters, and the infirmary getting swamped and
Bashir sure picking a hell of a time to be off-station. Someone
else rattled off a series of damage reports (all of them bad) and
while Kira registered this and digested the information, her
mind snagged on a staccato, slightly nasal chant. The chant
was more pure sound than song: a spiked line that, nevertheless, flowed straight and true like the principal root of a
complicated fugue.

The sound came from the Bynar, Soloman, communing
with DS9's main computer. Kira had heard someone say that
he'd found the sound soothing, but it set Kira's teeth on edge.

Kira snapped her head around to Vaughn—too fast, as it

happened, because she was rewarded with another wave of vertigo. She blinked back from the edge of unconsciousness. *Come on, don't lose it now, Nerys.* "Vaughn, is the *da Vinci* away?"

"Just in time." Vaughn spared a glance from his systems' boards. "I've locked down all the docking pylons and issued a general warning to reroute out of the system. There are a few freighters—empty, thank God—willing to help evacuate the station."

"If we have to. Give them our thanks, then tell them to stand by—or to bow out if they have to. It's no crime to stay alive." She looked over at the Bajoran lieutenant. "Time to next distortion wave."

"Impossible to predict, Captain." The lieutenant input data, squinted at her screen, then shook her head. "It's just . . . *random.* The only thing I can tell for certain is that the shock waves are getting stronger."

"Uh-hunh," said Kira. She glanced back at Vaughn. "What about Bajor?"

"Not good." Green-yellow light emanating from Vaughn's console played over the high planes of his bearded cheekbones and made black hollows of his eyes. His lips were so thin his mouth was a dark gash. "Ground-based stations report increased tectonic activity along the Tilar and Musilla plates. They're trying to evacuate the coastal areas, but with so little warning . . ." Vaughn didn't finish but then again, he didn't have to.

With so little warning, they'll be lucky if only a third of the coastal population drowns. And that doesn't count the mudslides, earthquakes, and Kendra Valley's lousy with fault lines. . . . Benjamin and Kasidy, Jake and Korena, the baby, they'll be right in the middle. Running out of time . . .

Her thoughts were cut by a hail and then a leisurely baritone fuzzed at the edges with static. *"Captain Kira, this is Gold. What's your status?"*

She had to smile. "I was just going to ask you the same question, Captain."

The channel fizzed, and then Kira caught the babble of background noise, a buzz of conversation, and the blats of a

computer spitting out information. Gold said something—
Koomel? Toomel?—and then came back. *"Not one of Wong's
more graceful uncouplings. A couple bumps and bruises, but
this old bucket's seen a lot worse. I'll hold together—oh, wait,
you were asking about the* ship.*"* Despite herself, Kira appreciated the levity. *"Well, the* da Vinci's *fine. We're stringing baling
wire right now. What about my people?"*

"Still in one piece, Captain." This from Sonya Gomez,
who staffed a long-range sensor with Nog. An impromptu pow-
wow: When the *da Vinci* had docked at the station following
its sojourn in the Gamma Quadrant, Dr. Lense received word
that she was one of five finalists for the prestigious Bentman
Prize. What Lense clearly *hadn't* planned on was heading off
in a runabout with Bashir at the helm because—surprise,
surprise—Bashir was a finalist, too. (Personally, Kira thought
Lense looked like she was being knifed when she got that little
bit of news.)

The *da Vinci* had been set to get under way—they'd had two
crew fatalities and needed to head to Earth for the memo-
rial services—when the first distortion waves came rippling
through Bajoran space. Gomez had beamed directly to ops
from the *da Vinci.* Nog had appeared a second later on the lift,
so impatient to get to his duty station he'd practically vaulted
the railing. Sometime in all of this, Gomez had pinned back
her shock of curly sable-colored hair, but that last jolt had
loosed a thick shank that now grazed her left cheek. Gomez
backhanded the hair with an impatient gesture. "And I think
we've got something here."

"Go," said Kira. She took the distance to the sensor station
in two strides. "What the hell's going on?"

"I don't *know* exactly," said the Ferengi, his words rocket-
ing out in spurts as if they'd piled up behind his teeth, anxious
as all hell to get out already. It was something Kira noticed
Nog did, not when he was nervous, but good and pissed off.
Nog's fingers danced over his console. "The distortion waves—
they're not sequenced or periodic in any way. They're much
more random—like someone's flipping a switch on and off,
only at irregular intervals. All I can tell is that, what these sensors say, it shouldn't be happening."

Moments like these, Kira almost wished she was Vulcan: *But it's happening, so your point?* Instead, she settled for something in between. "Except?"

"Except it is, and it's coming from Empok Nor."

"What?" Crowding in between Nog and Gomez, she double-checked their readings and then wished she hadn't. "Will someone please explain this? Never mind that we've got Empok Nor's lower core." She planted her fists into her hips and pinned Nog with a hard stare. "You said you guys tore that station apart looking for any little presents the Androssi left behind. So how did you manage to overlook something powerful enough to start cracking into space-time?"

It came out harsher than she liked, and Nog's lobes flushed purple. Abashed, Nog shook his head and Gomez opened her mouth, but it was the tiny slip of a Bynar directly across the bowl of ops and next to Vaughn who answered. "I believe I've pinpointed the problem, Captain."

"Thank the Prophets." Kira turned on her heel, ignoring the headache that was trying to leak out of her ears, and the blood-taste in her mouth. If they got out of this, she'd toss back a few painkillers and take a nice long nap. "What is it?"

"I can't say for sure what it is." The Bynar's eyes glittered, a bright cerulean blue. "But what I can say is that the reason it was overlooked was because the Androssi did what they always do. The problem was never, technically, *there.*"

There was a beat. Then, Kira said, "Say what?"

"*Well, I'm* verklempt." The *da Vinci* captain sounded about as confused as Kira felt. "*But it'd be just like Biron. They used interdimensional rifts?*"

Soloman's bald head bobbed in an emphatic nod. "Yes, sir. It's a virus, or a code, that hasn't just been encrypted, it's been hidden *within* a quantum singularity. To all outward appearances, the data has been generated *by* it."

"There's precedent, Captain," said Gomez. "The Romulans' quantum singularity drive, for example."

Vaughn frowned. "That uses a gravity well to generate power by fusing subatomic particles. They can't *hide* anything in it."

"But, in theory, you could," said Soloman. "No one has

ever done it because you can't time or predict when the code will reemerge. Similarly, retrieval is very difficult. We're accustomed to thinking of information becoming lost once this information, whether it exists as matter or energy, crosses an event horizon. Clearly, if the Romulans harness power, then information is never truly lost, it merely changes in form. Similarly, a code or command—or virus—may be stored beyond an event horizon. Either the originators of this information intended to retrieve it, or understood when it would resurface at a later time to carry out its specified functions."

Gold, on his channel: *"But there's a third possibility, right? That if the Androssi put it there, the* putzes *couldn't get it out either."*

"That is also possible."

Gomez spoke up. "The problem is the quantum foam."

Kira blinked. "The what?"

"It's not the kind of foam you're thinking of, Captain. Quantum foam is a region composed of quantum particles and micro-black holes that pop in and out of existence. The more closely you look at the fabric of space-time, the more chaotic that fabric becomes. What looks solid—a chair, a rock—becomes a morass of energy states and vibrating particles when viewed at the subatomic level. Similarly, the smaller a black hole, the greater space-time is distorted around the hole in proportion to the hole's size."

Kira pinched the ridged part of her nose between a thumb and forefinger. Her headache throbbed in time with her pulse. "Okay. But how does this explain what's going on here?"

"This quantum foam hasn't destroyed the information. Somehow the foam's interacted with the singularity in which the information was hidden. The question is, what activated the code?"

"It's impossible to answer that for certain at the moment." Soloman's smooth forehead crinkled in a frown. "To follow upon the quantum analogy, it could be coming from any of an infinite number of universes. The information—in this case, energy—is streaming as an encoded quantum datastream."

"Okay," said Kira. "So this signal, or code, or virus, or program—whatever is potentially coming from a computer in a different universe, only you can't nail down exactly what it's saying because the data represents all possibilities at once. Or the other way around: Something *here* is talking to someone out *there*." Kira looked back at Soloman. "And now because of this connection, this . . . foam's getting more agitated and the micro-black holes are expanding so that its effects are more pronounced on a macroscopic level?"

"Intermittently, yes. That's what is causing these temporal-spatial distortion waves."

"Can you shut it down?"

Soloman shook his head. "Not from DS9. I don't even know if you could properly call the datastream *here* in the first place. The datastream is *within* a contained system continually fluctuating between temporal dimensions."

Kira sighed. "Why do I have the feeling that this isn't the worst part?"

"Because it isn't, Captain." Nog was more grim than angry now. "The more information passes through that region, the more unstable it's making the surrounding space-time. Space is literally cracking. What we've felt now isn't half as bad as it's going to get."

"Ten to one, those temporal-spatial ripples are triggering Bajor's tectonic shifts," said Vaughn. "Only a matter of time before Bajor comes apart at the seams, literally. Lord knows where it will stop."

"What about the wormhole?"

"I don't see how its horizon can remain coherent," said Gomez.

"Meaning it breaks apart, too." *And, maybe, the Prophets die.* "Soloman, is there any way to stop this?"

"I would have to proceed via inference," said Soloman. "If I can't interact with the datastreams directly, I might be able to infer their content by interfacing with one of Empok Nor's nonessential systems. Something innocuous, like the turbolifts. If I can determine the *ways* in which the virus is encrypted, I'll likely be permitted to understand what's being said between the two systems and then effect change."

"A self-authorizing language," said Nog. "If we're smart enough to figure out how to read it, we'll be admitted into the system."

"Exactly. Once I'm in, then I can deactivate one system, or both."

"But if that's the wrong thing to do? You'll be choosing, Soloman," said Gomez. "You'll pick one path out of infinite possibilities. For that matter, if you squeeze yourself into a system even as an observer, that will collapse superpositions, right? It's that old paradigm, Schrödinger's Cat. So long as you don't look the cat's both alive and dead."

Gold asked, *"Are you saying we shouldn't do it, Gomez?"*

"No, I just want everyone to know the risks. The events in this other universe may actually favor the opposite, or something we can't, or don't, want to imagine." She let out a breath. "But it beats doing nothing. I'm going with Soloman's recommendation, Captain—Captains," she added with a look at Kira. "We need to get to Empok Nor."

After Gomez, Nog, and Soloman transported over to the *da Vinci,* Ezri Dax said, "All this talk about possibilities and universes . . . awfully interesting timing."

"Why?" asked Kira.

"Soloman." Pensive, Dax folded her arms across her chest. "Earlier, he asked if he could access the Orb of Time."

"You're kidding."

"Nope. It seems he's been studying the Orbs and concluded that the way an Orb emits energy is very much like a computer program. I think he also sees them as devices that access information available on the quantum level, like the Androssi use dimensional shifts. He said he wondered how the wormhole aliens manage to harness and direct the energy you need to create a time shift. I told him those were all good questions, but—"

"He didn't know about the Vedek Assembly's new restrictions on the Orbs?"

Dax shook her head. "And I tried to tell him what it was like the first time Jadzia tried studying an Orb. Not exactly a spiritual experience—but, maybe, the Dax symbiont's not receptive to spirituality. I don't know."

Now it was Kira's turn to look thoughtful. "I've never thought about spirituality like that. Spirituality is just me. I wasn't aware that a Bynar could get religion."

"Maybe communing with a computer is about as spiritual as a Bynar gets. Or maybe it's just the way a Bynar's brain is wired. You can never really know whether a god exists, or if you search for a god and construct a religion because that's the way your brain works. If you buy into that, then spirituality's as innate and natural as breathing—and not mystical at all."

"Can't disprove that one way or the other and maybe that's a good thing. Maybe we need to hope that . . ." Kira tried finding the right word but couldn't. "Maybe we just need to hope."

They looked at each other. Then Dax said, "In the end, maybe hope is all we have."

CHAPTER
2

From space, looking at Empok Nor, Gomez's first thought was: *haunted house*. In her EVA suit now, with the rasp of her breathing very loud in her ears, Gomez glanced right, left. There was something about the way Cardassian design emphasized the slash of shadows and the arch of bulkheads that made the absolute black of the abandoned station seem like a carcass. Kind of the way a bug looked flipped on its back, legs stiff, deader than a doornail. Pattie might not have appreciated the analogy, but there it was—though knowing the Nasat's sense of humor, maybe she would.

The station was a derelict with just enough auxiliary power to keep it in orbit, a rudimentary deflector system to prevent the random meteor strike—and not a drop more.

Keep expecting a couple eyes to pop out of nowhere and go booga-booga . . .

Suspended in midair, Gomez turned in a slow pirouette. The light of her wristlamp slid over bulkheads and empty computer wall panels and open-mesh grids—there and then just as quickly gone again as she spun around. A stable pocket of normal space enveloped this part of the station, including the now-empty fusion core, two-thirds of the habitat ring, and one set of docking pylons above and below, the latter onto which Vance Hawkins had eased the *Kwolek*. The other third of Empok Nor slipped in and out of temporal-spatial fissures.

The *da Vinci* had shadowed them the whole way—not just for evac if needed, but because the *da Vinci's* cargo hold was crammed with two emergency generators beamed in series from DS9. When they were ready, Hawkins would activate the *Kwolek's* transporters at the same time as Transporter Chief Poynter powered up the *da Vinci's* transporter, snag the generators' transporter patterns and do a linked transport right into the lower core. *Easy, right?*

Wrong-o. Gomez came out of her spin and pulled herself to another handhold. *Nothing about this is going to be easy. Nothing ever is.*

They rolled and tucked and pushed off in a straggly single file, like beads on a very loose string, down a pitch-black service corridor tacking toward the base of the station's midsection and the control room for the lower core: Hawkins in front with a phaser rifle, Conlon's tiny figure bobbing just ahead, and Gomez bringing up the rear. (Corsi had reluctantly remained behind at DS9. If things got dicey on the station and they had to start evacuations, Ro Laren would need all the security expertise she could find. Besides which, Gomez wasn't sure that a dangerous mission like this was such a good idea so soon after Caitano and Deverick's deaths.)

Hooking the fingers of her right hand around the metal rim of a bulkhead, Gomez pulled her body along, tucked her knees, planted her feet, and pushed. Normally, Gomez got a kick out of weightlessness. Not this time. Gomez hadn't been on the mission to retrieve Empok Nor's fusion core; she'd been on Sarindar and Kieran had taken her place and he'd said that Nog was a helluva good engineer. . . .

As always when she thought about Kieran Duffy, a wave of sadness curled and broke over her mind and body. The wave was small this time. As she got farther and farther away from Galvan VI, the crushing grief got less debilitating. She'd been able to go hours without thinking about him. She'd even gone and set a date for a vacation with Wayne Omthon on Hidalgo Station in a few days.

To some degree, that scared her. If she stopped thinking about Duffy, ceased missing him so much that the ache was physical . . . well, then, what was left?

Can't think about that now. She shoved thoughts of Duffy into a mental black box and slammed down the lid. Later, maybe, when she was alone . . .

A click in her helmet just as they reached the access hatch to the control room: *"Okay, we're in ops."* Nog. *"It's like the rest of the station. Everything's off except for the computer system. Soloman's going for access in a couple seconds."*

"Roger that. I don't suppose there's any way that Soloman would like to access this hatch down here and pop it for me."

"It's gonna be no. He won't want to interfere with things too much."

"Ask anyway."

A pause while Nog said something then came back. *"No."*

"Figures," said Conlon. The petite engineer made a face. *"It's never easy."*

"Our motto," said Gomez. "Well, one of them, anyhow. If it's easy, they don't call us. Okay, Nog, thanks. Holler soonest." Then, activating her magnetic boots, Gomez planted herself onto the deck. She unholstered her tool kit, pried open an access panel and isolated the hatch's primary circuits. Fitting a portable battery pack to her patch, Gomez flicked a switch, was rewarded with a flash of orange light, and then the hatch slid to one side.

Okay. Gomez secured the battery pack to a bulkhead just in case and walked inside. Her wristlamp punched a hole through the darkness, the light sliding over the contours of reactor panels and computer banks and then, just beyond, the silver gleam of a railing lining the drop-off: a void now, a hole in Empok Nor's heart where the core would've been. She stepped forward, poking her lamp here and there until she found the main computer console. Without knowing why, she smeared dust off the console with the flat of her left hand, then played the light over her glove and the rim of gray fringe held by electrostatic charge.

"Commander." It was Conlon at her right elbow, and Gomez turned, looked down, read understanding in her dark eyes. *"We've got work to do."*

"Right." Slapping dust from her glove, Gomez turned aside and nodded at Hawkins. "Contact the *da Vinci.* Let's get to work and then?" She huffed out a breath. "We get the hell out of here."

Nog stabbed his tricorder harder than absolutely necessary. That little dressing-down in front of the *da Vinci* crew was all kinds of fun and thank you, Captain Kira. The captain's displeasure had been like a smack right on a lobe. He'd gotten dressed down before. That wasn't it. But to have it happen in front of a crew that Nog had worked hard to prove he could do whatever engineering job they could, and light-years better? That was worse.

And talk about worse. Last time he'd set foot on Empok Nor he'd nearly gotten fried by a computerized Androssi security sentry device: a brown ball that shot arcs of electricity like a Van de Graaff generator on hormones. Time before that, the Jem'Hadar kidnapped his grandmother. Time before *that,* Garak had taken potshots. Vic told him once: *Kid, relax, third time's the charm.* Except it hadn't been a charm at all, although he had convinced the *da Vinci* crew to tow the station back and yes, he had saved DS9's butt.

Still, given all this? Nog figured he was within his rights to expect all kinds of bad stuff.

Furious, he jabbed at his tricorder, forcing his mind to concentrate on his readings and Soloman. The Bynar wasn't as hesitant as he'd been the last time. Probably more time being alone had done that for him, made him autonomous.

Yeah, and Nog still hated being alone. No *drad* music this time, though, and the Bynar was oblivious. The blue computer glow gave the Bynar an eerie, otherworldly quality, and if Nog looked closely enough, he'd probably be able to see the whiz of computer code mirrored in Soloman's eyes. Soloman was completely silent, not chittering away the way he'd done with DS9's computer but just still, staring. Intent. Something spooky was going on in the distance; Soloman was watching, and Nog wasn't a part of anything, really.

Out of the loop again. What was it he'd thought about the last time as he hung in the *Rio Grande*? Right before the *da Vinci* had shown up in the Trivas system? Yeah, he'd thought about AR-558, and about how he'd been humiliated. He'd thought about loneliness, too, and here he was, full circle, as if he were on some weird carnival ride that stopped in just exactly the same place every single time.

"Face it," he muttered, though he probably could've shouted in the Bynar's ear, Soloman looked that out of it. "Nog, you're a bad-luck magnet."

As if to prove him right, his tricorder picked that moment to sound an alarm—and Soloman screamed.

For Soloman it was glorious, but in a way that was as much about pain as pleasure. He was doing nothing, really, other than watching the stream of numbers racing across his monitor. He disengaged himself as much as he could, what a human might call free-floating attention, trying not to focus on any one parameter but merely to hover and allow the impression and the form of the datastream wash over him like cool water.

Unbidden, his thoughts tugged him to the last time he'd been privy to the same blaze of information crossing between systems: the Bynars 1011 and 1110 on Ishtar Station. Communing with the other Bynars had activated memories Soloman had suppressed. He hadn't told Lense about it. He hadn't told anyone. He'd felt it as envy and knew it now as . . . a void. Being self-contained was an asset and a curse. Communing with DS9's computer, or the *da Vinci*'s, or any of a host of other computers was like trying to snuggle up to a ghost for warmth. But there was Empok Nor's unseen twin matching it move for move, like a perfectly mirrored counterpart. Like he'd been for 111 . . .

What? Soloman's mind lurched. A tiny prickle of something close to alarm touched his mind. He'd seen something, he'd . . . Unconscious that he was doing so, Soloman leaned forward, as if to bring the numbers into better focus. A synchronization signature whizzed by, and before he knew what he was doing, because it was second nature, Soloman honed in, focused, and . . .

There! Soloman's breath caught. *No, it can't be, it can't. . . .* His head throbbed and his heart ballooned with joy and pain; without realizing he had, he snagged the signature. . . .

Stop . . .

. . . meshed, and then his thoughts . . .

Stop . . .

. . . whirled like leaves caught in a fast-flowing stream, swirling and hurtling out of control and . . .

Stopstopstop . . .

"Stop, stop, *stop!*"

Not something Soloman had said: The word, the voice was from outside, not the datastream, and Soloman pushed back, hard, forcing his mind to stay with the synchronization signature.

"STOP!"

The word tore the veil of his communion, and Soloman was jarred free with a violence that was physical. He was thrown back; even weightless, he hit hard, rebounded off the deck before getting slammed down and pinned into place. His head bounced against his helmet like a bean rattling in a tin can. His concentration blanked; the communion blacked out, and his mind was hurled, brutally, into his body, his consciousness snapping back like a stretched, elastic cord snipped in two.

Soloman stopped screaming. His throat was raw and his ears rang. When he opened his eyes, he was staring into Nog's faceplate.

"*Are you okay?*" Nog shouted even though it was perfectly silent now. "*What happened? Are you all right? What the hell happened?*"

Soloman cleared his throat. "I am fine, Lieutenant. If you would not mind getting off, please?"

"Oh." Nog rolled off, then extended a hand and helped Soloman, who'd activated his boots, clamber to his feet. *"Sorry. It's just that my tricorder registered a spike in your chip, and then you started screaming and I . . ."*

"I apologize," said Soloman, embarrassed that he'd been so public with something so very private. "It is only . . . this datastream is a search program and I found a synchronization signature. A Bynar signature."

"What? A Bynar?" Nog was goggle-eyed. *"Who?"*

"One-one-zero," said Soloman. "The person on the other end of this datastream is . . . it . . . it is I."

CHAPTER
3

"*G*ive *that to me again, Soloman.*" Gold's voice was measured and Soloman did not detect that his captain thought he had gone insane. "*A search program in a parallel timeline?*"

"Yes, Captain." Soloman and Nog were still in Empok Nor's ops. "We can agree that parallel universes and worlds within worlds contain all possible arrangements of matter, yes?"

"*I got that.*"

"Time is just a concept, a way of ordering matter in a sequence our minds can handle. There is no time. There are events that occur in a multiverse upon which we impose order."

"*That's a relief,*" said Hawkins, who'd come running as soon as Nog called for help. "*There are a couple of dates I'd like to —*"

"*Stow it,*" said Gold. An audible sigh. "*Soloman, what are you talking about here? Time travel?*"

"No, what I am saying is that the multiverse is fixed. The fact that I accessed my own synchronization signature, even for an instant, implies that I have tapped into another point in the timeline of a parallel universe. I have found myself somewhere and some*when* else. Therefore, I can commune with this 110 at another point in *his* universe and determine what it is that 110 is searching for."

"For all you know, son, that is precisely what the Androssi want you—and us—to believe. Remember, the Androssi programmed their sentry security systems to respond to our combadge codes. Anyone smart enough to design this code or whatever it is where da Vinci *has been before had to bet we'd be back when things went haywire."*

That stopped Soloman for a moment. "That is a possibility I had not considered."

"You'd better. You're proposing that you commune with . . . well, with an alien. We won't even call 110 a mirror—you. He's his own person. He represents forks in the roads you did not take and some you can't imagine."

"For that matter," Nog said, *"how do we know that the Bynars there even call themselves Bynars, or think the same way? Maybe they're the quantum computers: all things at once."* The Ferengi had recovered from his initial panic and was busily collating the information he'd stored from Soloman's foray into Empok Nor's computer. *"There may not even be a Federation. He—if it is a he—won't know what we're talking about. We've had some experience on DS9 with mirror universes—from the reports I've read, we shouldn't assume anything."*

"That may be true, Lieutenant, but we must try," said Soloman. "That 110 bears some trace of who I am, or else I would not have recognized myself, correct? This is our best option."

"Or a booby trap." This from Gomez down at the fusion core, where she and Conlon were halfway through rigging up the generators. *"Soloman, you'll be making a choice. Once you do this, we're locked in because everything will change around what you do. How do you know this is the right way?"*

"I do not. But it is a choice."

"So is not taking it."

Gold said, *"There's something else. If you've reached, well, you, and this 110 is still Bynar enough that you recognize you—he's probably bonded, right? To his own 111? And if he is, wouldn't you also have picked up her synchronization signature?"*

It was the question he had been waiting for, and he knew what he would say. There were, in fact, two questions. But Soloman knew that Captain Gold did not have enough information to ask one of them. Indeed, it would never occur to Captain Gold to ask because the Bynars of *his* universe did not possess the ability. (The ability was there: alien and utterly surreal in its intimacy.) Soloman wondered if he would feel differently about himself afterward, and decided that this was a risk he was willing to take. So, he took it.

"No," Soloman lied. "I did not."

CHAPTER
4

On red alert, the light crimson as blood, their alarm Klaxons screaming, they slammed to port and let gravity work for them. The ship spun so quickly that Bajor flashed by in a swirl of blue ocean and white clouds, and then they were roaring past the station, picking up speed, hammering on full impulse, trying to get enough distance to go to warp. A risky thing and some kind of crappy odds, pushing the *Gettysburg* nose-first toward Bajor and then angling off, using gravity as a slingshot to hurl them out of high orbit and past the station, but the ship was getting pretty banged up, and Captain David Gold was outnumbered: a *Keldon*-class warship and two *Hideki*-class ships on their tail. But if he was lucky, Bajor's gravity well would snatch at those bursts of disruptor fire, and they might just pull off this cockamamie heist.

But then McAllan shouted a warning and Gold spun in his command chair; he saw the *Keldon*-class warship coming for them on an intercept course, right between the eyes. His stomach bottomed out. "Helm, evasive maneuvers! Keep our aft shields to them!"

"Trying, Captain!" Wong's teeth were set, and the cords of

his neck bulged as if he could move the stubborn ship by wishing it so. "That last disruptor hit tagged our starboard maneuvering thrusters; they're really slow, and she's sluggish on the turn, I can't—"

Gold cut him off with a savage cut of his hand. "McAllan, what about my torpedoes?"

"Torpedoes still offline, sir!" At tactical, immediately behind Gold's command chair, McAllan's square features were set in intense concentration, his fingers flying over his weapons console. "Working to restore, but I've got phasers back!"

"Then what the hell are you waiting for, an invitation? Fire phasers!" Gold bellowed. He turned back just in time to see an emerald-green glitter, and then he was out of his chair. "Wong! Hard to port, hard—"

A series of disruptor salvoes burst over the ship's hull. The impacts were like being punched broadside in rapid fire. The *Gettysburg* bucked, shimmied; Gold felt the deck jitter, and he would've fallen if his XO hadn't snagged him.

"Damage report, Lieutenant McAllan," said his XO.

"Hull breach on decks twenty through twenty-five, Commander. Starboard shields are forty percent and our inertial dampers will not survive another salvo."

"Starboard maneuvering thrusters are out, Captain," said Wong.

A hail sliced the air. *"Captain, this is Gomez. We've got a plasma leak. I'm going to have to vent her if you want to get out of here in one piece. But you've got to move us to a more stable region of space. All that weapons fire out there, it'll touch off that plasma like—"*

"Incoming message," McAllan broke in. "Terok Nor, Captain."

"Let him cool his thrusters," said Gold. "Gomez, prepare to vent on my mark, you got that?" Then, to McAllan: "When I give the word, you touch off phasers."

"Phasers, sir? But with the plasma . . ." Then McAllan's face brightened. "Roger that, sir."

"Attaboy." Gold looked at Wong. "You clear?"

Wong was already busy inputting coordinates. "Crystal. Just give the word."

"Count on it." Gold nodded, tugged on his uniform shirt, and turned toward the viewscreen. "Onscreen."

The viewscreen shimmered; a face blurred, then coalesced into features Gold recognized. "What do you want, Garak?"

"Why, Captain Gold." Gul Garak's oily tenor undulated from the speakers. *"You astound me. Isn't it obvious? You stole something, naughty you, and now I'd like it back. You do that and I'd be ecstatic to order my ships to stand down."*

"So generous. Let me guess: In exchange for your magnanimity, I presume I'll be your guest and will be . . . convinced, in the most subtle ways you can devise, to hand over the precise location of all of Starfleet's forces in this sector, right?"

"Not only a brave captain but a mind reader as well. Ah, Gold, you are a treasure. You never fail to astound me. Not as cultured as Picard by any means, may he rest in peace, but still very charming in your way."

"I notice that your high esteem for Picard didn't exactly translate into any unwillingness to execute him."

"You wound me." Garak placed both hands over his left breast. *"When it was over, I was stricken for at least an hour. Picard was such an interesting conversationalist, too. So bookish. Not nearly the boor Dukat was—and, oh my, such language! That man did have a mouth. Assassinating Dukat was a matter of self-preservation, I assure you."*

"No doubt. I hear Dukat was pretty well off, too."

"Yes, indeed. You may rest easy that his fortune was divided fairly among his various friends. And his command, well, let us just say that I feel the weight of my responsibilities here on Terok Nor. Fortunately, Dukat's very own, very special comfort woman is quite . . . well . . . honestly, I blush."

"Spare me the details. I can't imagine the Bajorans being anything *but* hospitable and oh-so-comforting to their paid thugs."

"Captain, you cut me to the quick. You know very well that we are here at the invitation of the Bajorans. It is you who trespass. But, oh, bother the details. Let's bury the hatchet, shall we? Why don't you stand down and beam on over to Terok Nor? We'll chat over a nice snifter of Lakatian brandy: an excellent vintage, astounding nose, and the finish! To die for."

"In the words of an exceedingly bright engineer . . . up your shaft, Garak."

"*Such a consummate wit. Captain Gold, I shall very much regret killing you. It will pain me, truly.*"

"Not half as much as this will," said Gold. He turned to McAllan. "*Now.*"

On cue, McAllan cut the channel; Garak's face winked out; and Gold whirled on his heel. "Wong, show these bastards our sweet pink asses! McAllan, aft shields; give them all you've got! Gomez!"

"*On it, sir! Venting now . . . done!*"

"Fire phasers! Wong, warp three, now!"

Suddenly, the space around the *Keldon* flashed as McAllan touched off phasers into a swirl of vented plasma. The plasma pillowed into a mushrooming orange-red cloud; the *Keldon* and *Hideki*s disappeared in the fiery slurry of ignited plasma and gas, and the glare was so bright Gold blinked and looked away. In the same instant, Wong whirled the ship to starboard and the *Gettysburg* shot into warp.

"Are they away?" From his office in Terok Nor, Gul Elim Garak watched space ignite. His predominant emotion was a grudging sort of admiration. "Zotat, are they away?"

"*They're gone.*" Zotat's reply sputtered amid pops of ionization static. "*Shall we give chase?*"

"No, no." Garak raised a finger in admonishment. "Let the brave captain and his crew go. We'll be meeting them again, very soon. Take up your stations at your prearranged coordinates and signal the other vessels to do likewise. I will notify you when it is time. Garak out."

In the silence that followed, Garak raised a snifter of very old, very fine Lakatian brandy to his visitor in the chair opposite. "A toast."

"Indeed." The Androssi overseer was male and slim with a skin tone that was more gray than yellow. Unlike many of his kind, his face was clean-shaven, but his hair was a lush mane that stretched beyond his waist in a darkly amber cascade that he wore loose—again, not like others of his kind. His right and left nostrils bristled with an array of five nose rings that bespoke his position. "Isn't celebration a bit premature?"

"What, you doubt the abilities of the Bynars?"

"What I doubt is that the Bynars have the necessary skills to utilize the device to our advantage. That would be . . . unfortunate."

"But not irreparable. And if the Bynars succeed!" Garak flashed a grin that was all teeth. "Think of what we shall deliver to the Bajoran Assembly in a mere twenty hours. A treaty *and* their gods: Not even the religious caste can argue with that. I drink to your health, Overseer—and to David Gold, noble captain, patron saint of lost causes."

Garak tipped his snifter to his mouth. The nut-flavored liquor was smooth and warmed a track to his belly. Garak released a sigh of pure contentment. "Who says religion and politics don't mix?"

Still blinking away stars, Gold thumbed a tear from his left cheek. His eyes stung. "Pursuit?"

McAllan studied his boards, then shook his head. "They're not after us."

"Good. Stand down from red alert. Tell Gomez to get on that plasma leak. Wong, how long to rendezvous?"

"Three hours, forty-seven minutes, sir."

"Very well." Gold nodded at his communications officer. "Haznedl, get a message to Kira. Tell her we'll be at the rendezvous point in four hours."

"That ruse will only work once, Captain," said Gold's XO. He was about as nonplussed as Gold had ever seen him: sweating so much that the man's black hair gleamed like a skullcap. "Garak will not make the same mistake again."

"I'm kinda amazed he made it the first time. Garak doesn't make mistakes."

He was cut off by the shrill of a hail. *"Bridge, this is sickbay."* An eerie, high-pitched wail on the channel, and then the sound suddenly grew distanced and muffled, as if the person had been moved into another room. *"You've got to get down here right now."*

"Sickbay?" Gold's XO arched an eyebrow, his left. "How many casualties, Dr. Kane?"

A snort. *"Enough to keep me busy, that's for sure. But that's not why I'm calling. Captain Gold, it's the Bynars."*

Gold groaned. "Oh, no." *Damn, that would be perfect; just perfect. We go through all this and then the damn Bynars can't even commune with the thing* . . . "Are they hurt?"

"We don't know." Another voice: female, taut with urgency. *"The Bynars were communing with that device* . . . *and now 110's unresponsive."*

"Unresponsive?"

"Like in a coma, sir," said Kane.

"What?" Gold and his XO exchanged glances. "Dax, what happened?" asked Gold.

"I don't know," said Dax. *"But we've got to figure this out, and fast. The Bynars are the key to finding the wormhole, I'm sure of it. Only . . ."*

"What?"

"Well, 111 says there was somebody there, in the datastream. Captain, she's totally hysterical. She says the Bynar's a singleton, and he's got a name."

"Not a designation?" said the XO.

"No, a name; 111 said he was very specific. Only she's so upset, I can't make sense of what she's saying. But without the Bynars, Captain . . . it's over."

This was true. There was dead silence as Gold and his XO looked at one another. Then Commander Salek said, "Actually, I believe the expression is . . . we're *shtuped.*"

CHAPTER
5

He drifted the way one did in the cold vacuum of space. Soloman's first EVA had been over Byanus, and he remembered the moment he and 111 stepped from the lip of the ship. Everyone said that the first time, they expected to fall. But 110 and 111 did not; 110 recalled that the sight of their world—steel-gray oceans and dusky landmasses glimmering with yellow lozenges of light—made their heads balloon. They were at once very small and quite huge, and the feeling was so expansive they could describe it as nothing short of ecstasy.

And yet there was this now, this second chance, and it was almost more than Soloman could bear. There was no describing it, really, but it reminded him a bit of the moment immediately after stepping out into space, expecting to fall and yet not. He hovered, watching the blaze of information passing between the two Bynars—and yes, it was 110, and there, his own heart. And he studied what they were able to do with each other that went far beyond anything Bynars of his universe knew—*but how perfect; a logical extension of our abilities*—and then, he found his opportunity and dropped into the datastream.

In an instant, he was submerged. The sensation was like leaping into a whirlpool, only the water was made of light above, around, below: a cocoon of sensation that was at once totally alien and utterly familiar. He sensed two things at once: 110's instinctive flinch at his intrusion, and 111's hesitation. A slight stutter to her datastream, as if her mind had tripped.

He longed to touch her mind, but first things first. He folded himself into 110, seamlessly, not unlike an anomalous bit of code that instantly mutates. And then, he reached for her with thoughts both eager and tentative. . . .

Do not be afraid. It is I. I am 110 and yet my own person. I am . . .

But he was not fast enough. Maybe it was that he was, truly, alien. She was terrified and even as he soothed, cajoled, pleaded, she kicked back, pushed, tore away so violently that 110's mind shrieked in agony—because it was not just a datastream from which he was being ejected; it was more complicated than that; and it hurt so much, their minds bled, and they were flailing now, the way drowning men snatch at a passing twig just before they go over the falls; she was gone, winging away, leaving chaos in her wake, and he/they left behind in a strong current that pulled him/them under . . .

Do not be afraid. Come back. Please . . .

. . . into the blackness . . . into an empty . . .

Gomez squatted next to the Bynar. Swathed in the cocoon of his suit, Soloman sat, perfectly rigid. His gray-white skin was still as a waxen statue. He didn't blink. His breathing was so slow and shallow Gomez checked his suit's readings just to make sure he was still alive. She moved her gloved hand up and down in his line of sight. Soloman didn't twitch, didn't blink, didn't move. The readings scrolling on the computer panel were reflected on his faceplate and mirrored in the blue, still pool of his irises. The embedded chip on his right temple winked in a rapid staccato. "How long has he been like this?"

"About twenty minutes now." Nog nibbled the left corner of his lower lip as he studied his tricorder. "Started about three minutes into it. Like he tripped into something, or got sucked in."

"Has his buffer failed?"

"No. His neuropeptides are sky-high, like his brain is over-loaded, or multitasking: serotonin, GABA, VBC, psilosynine. I wish I knew if all that's good or bad."

"If he's not responding, I'd say that's bad." Gold's voice, at-tenuated through the intercom in ops. Gomez and Conlon had gotten life support working in this room at least, so they had removed their helmets. (Soloman's was still on, though; Gomez though it best not to disturb him.) In the background, Gomez heard Tev barking orders to reinforce *da Vinci's* stabi-lizers. Shields were up, so there was no way to beam Soloman off Empok Nor—or even know if she should. The interval be-tween distortion waves was shorter, and Nog's readings con-firmed what Gomez feared: that Soloman's interface was the trigger.

Like he's opened a gateway he can't close . . .

"It's getting pretty rough up here," said Gold. *"Tell me what you do know, and let's go from there."*

"It's like he's frozen, sir. He's still receiving input," said Nog.

"To what? This twin? Himself?"

"Yes, sir, a quantum twin," said Gomez. She was about to say more when she took a second to really think about what she'd just said. *A quantum twin . . . and if this twin is Soloman before he became unbonded, then . . .* "Oh, my God."

"What?"

She said, very carefully, "Maybe, sir, it's that he can't ter-minate the connection, or maybe . . . he doesn't want to. Or both."

A fizz of static. Then, Gold said, *"Come again?"*

"A coma?" Gold frowned across 110's body at Dax and Kane. The Bynar had been moved to a biobed, and 111 had been se-dated. "What do you mean a *coma?*"

Dr. Tori Kane was a small woman, a strawberry blonde with freckles and green-gray eyes, and a head shorter than Gomez.

She gave Gold a fierce, moderately contemptuous look: an expression that screamed *nu, what, I'm speaking Swahili?* "I mean," she said with the type of enunciation a teacher might use on an exceptionally slow student, "that 110 is unresponsive. His autonomic functions—blood pressure, pulse, respiration, temperature control—they're fine. But he won't come out of it. Or, maybe, he can't."

Salek stood at Gold's left elbow. "Do we know why, Doctor?"

"It's his chip. He's . . . latched on to something the Bynars found when they communed with that device you brought on board." Her head jerked left to a cylindrical object made of shiny metal and bristling with nasty-looking quills. "I still say this is one cockeyed plan."

To Kane's right, Dax stiffened. "It's necessary."

"Yeah, yeah." Kane waved Dax's comment away. "And I'm just the hired help."

"Kane," Gold warned.

"Fine, okay." Kane gave a noisy exhale. "Captain, for all you know the Androssi hid something inside, like a computer virus."

"Then why wasn't 111 affected?"

"Beats me. Maybe the plan was to knock out one of them. Just as effective; neither one can function without the other."

"Then why don't we just shut it down?" asked Gold.

"Because I don't know what that would do to 110, and if I understand the mission right, you need the Bynars."

This was, unfortunately, true. Gold said, "But *another* Bynar? In the datastream? How? I didn't think Bynars could exist as singletons."

"What I don't understand is how a singleton could interface with this device at all," said Dax. Her long, dark brown hair was pulled into the ponytail she habitually sported, but errant strands straggled here and there, giving her a frayed look. Backhanding hair from her forehead, she sighed, and the cuffed earring in her right lobe jingled. "For that matter, where is he?"

"Perhaps," said Salek, "this device is contaminated with something that can mimic a Bynar's neural patterns. We know that the Androssi are exceptionally skilled at developing booby traps. Although one fails to understand how sabotage equates to the capture of an unintelligent bird."

Dax ignored the Vulcan. Her eyes were that color of intense, concentrated brown that bordered on black, and now she drilled Gold with a look. "This is our last chance. The Bajor Assembly formalizes its treaty with Cardassia in less than a day. We have to find the wormhole before then. If we can't access this device with the Bynars, then we have to go back to Terok Nor and find another way."

Gold shook his head. "Not on your life, or mine for that matter. Treaties can be broken. You find this wormhole, and the religious faction is as big as you say? Then Bajor'll come around. Now either the Bynars can access these . . . these Prophets with this device, or they can't. That'd be tough from your end, but that doesn't mean we can't adapt the technology for ourselves. You'll find another way."

"But too late to be of any practical benefit." Dax pulled herself to her full height and looked down at Gold, who was shorter by half a head. "Once that treaty is formalized, then the Cardassians have every excuse to round up the religious sect, herd them into camps and out of public view. Then the Cardassians wait. Enough time passes, people forget, and then the Cardassians get rid of the religion because they won't want dissension. It will be genocide, Captain. You can't allow that to happen."

"The galaxy's full of nasty people and bad things happen all the time. Once the Bajorans formalize that treaty, Starfleet won't want to interfere in a civil dispute."

"And pray tell, what is this?" Dax swept a hand around to include the ship, the stolen device. "What, this is just us passing through? Or is it perfectly all right for the Federation to interfere before the treaty's finalized?"

Gold shrugged. "You make your opportunities. One of those diplomacy things."

"Don't you mean that the Federation sees an opportunity to develop Bajor as a resource? Uridium brings in a lot of money. Surely, I wasn't mistaken in my impressions about the Federation being strapped for resources?"

It was an open secret that the majority of the Federation's seventy member systems were resource-poor. The Federation had to expand if it was going to survive, and they'd poured much of their available resources into a fleet of starships: window-dressing and a show of force since there weren't replacements to back them up. The whole thing reminded Gold of mid-twentieth-century Earth with the A-bomb. Drop two and pretend you have a bunch more. On the other hand, the fleet would, at the very least, have a fighting chance at grabbing what planets it could. With its uridium ore and the peculiarities of a loosely worded agreement, Bajor was prime real estate: a jewel in the Cardassian crown that the Federation wouldn't mind stealing.

"Yeah, there's that. But I can imagine a universe without the Cardassians, that's for damn sure. I'd be tickled pink if the Androssi crawled back under whatever rock they came from. Hell, for that matter, I'd like to get paid more." Gold planted his fists on his hips. "Starfleet's in this because we're allies with Kira. Personally, I don't care what religion the Bajorans get; they can believe in the Tooth Fairy, for all I care. All we want is Bajor. . . ." He stopped, realizing that last remark had been a mistake.

Dax's eyes slitted. "The only reason Kira's allied with the Federation is that your record of tolerance for others is better than the Cardassians'. You actually seem to care about civil liberties. As long as we're allowed to devote ourselves to the Prophets . . ."

"You? Dax, you're a *Trill*. These aren't your people."

"That's irrelevant. I'm the only one who's ever communed with an Orb—something you cannot know or understand— and the Prophets have spoken to me. The wormhole is in Bajoran space, somewhere, perhaps in a subspace pocket, and once opened, it will remain stable. All we have to do is find it. Now whether you like it or not, the organized resistance on Bajor is a religious one. It's that simple. If Kira hadn't vouched for the Federation, you'd be out of the equation. You need *me*."

"I'd say the need is pretty damn mutual."

"Yes and no. Bajor requires what I can bring them. You

want a slice of Bajor's wealth, and we want the right to worship as we please. We want the wormhole, and the wormhole is prophecy, Captain. The *truth* is in prophecy."

Gold barked a nasty laugh. "Yeah? Well, I prophesize that we're gonna end up as a big plasma smear if we go back anywhere near Terok Nor right now without confirmation of where this wormhole really is. Now I'm glad you've gotten religion. I'm ecstatic that you've gotten the word that your Prophet buddies are waiting on you to break them out. But get this straight: We take a breather. We make repairs; we meet up with Kira. We hope that 110 there wakes up. Then we'll see."

"You mean that you'll see if furthering the Bajoran resistance's goals and those of Starfleet are the same."

"Yeah, I think I just said that."

"Look," said Kane, "I hate to interrupt this little lovefest, but we've still got a problem here. Either we figure a way to get 110 back in working order or we can kiss this mission good-bye."

"What do you suggest?"

"You ask me, 111's got to be talked into establishing a link with her bondmate, that's what. Can't Bynars, I dunno, repair each other? I mean, they're essentially computers, right? So, they worry about getting infected, but they've also got to have some repair mechanisms. Maybe 111 can reboot him, or something."

"But if you observe, Doctor, 110 is in active communication with someone else. His chip," Salek nodded at the Bynar's chip that flashed and winked, "indicates intense activity. He appears to have interfaced with someone, or some other system."

"It's a Prophet," said Dax.

"Will you give it a rest?" said Gold. "The only person who can tell us who or what it is, is 111. We—"

His combadge beeped. *"Bridge to Gold."*

He patted the channel open. "Gold."

"Incoming message from Captain Kira on the Li, *sir."*

"I'll take that in my ready room," said Gold. He nodded at Kane, turned on his heel and left, Salek a step behind.

Kane waited until the doors to sickbay hissed shut. Then she turned to Dax. "You want to talk to 111, or shall I?"

"I'll do it." Jadzia Dax's features hardened, the skin drawn tight across her mouth. "They will make contact with the Prophets—and then we'll go back to Terok Nor, and Bajor."

"Gee," said Kane. "Swell."

CHAPTER
6

"*Q*uantum twins?" Gold repeated. "*Gomez, are you saying what I think you're saying?*"

"Yes, sir," said Gomez, wishing the truth was otherwise. "I think that Soloman's not only found himself. He's found 111. That's why he was so eager to reestablish contact."

"*But eager enough to lie? Soloman's never lied.*"

"That we know of. Maybe he didn't have something worth lying about before."

"*Well, this is a hell of a thing. What do we do now? We can't just wait around. Ever since he initiated this last link, those wavefronts have increased.*"

"That follows. The channel's open now, permanently, unless we can get Soloman to break off contact."

"*Can we do that for Soloman without harming him?*"

"I doubt it. But since we haven't found anything here, we have to assume that whatever device has initiated, or is potentiating this effect, it's got to be somewhere else."

"*In this other universe?*"

"I'd say that's likely, sir."

"What about getting them a message? Ask them to disengage. Can we do that?"

"Maybe they don't want to either," said Gomez. She sighed. "Remember, this is a search program. They're looking for something. So we're in the dark until we can figure a way to contact it, or them."

"Well," Nog scratched a lobe, "I might be able to piggyback a signal. Heck, I might be able to slip in the same way Soloman did."

"A self-authorizing language?" asked Gomez.

"Worth a try."

Gold said, *"What about destroying Empok Nor's computer?"*

"That's kind of drastic. If I can get in, maybe I can shut them both down without hurting Soloman."

"If they're even willing to lis—" And that's as far as Gold got.

Suddenly, there was the squall of a red alert—and then a huge *boom* that was so loud Gomez clapped her hands against her ears. Stunned, ears ringing, Gomez fumbled with her tricorder to see where the problem was on Empok Nor.

Only the problem wasn't on Empok Nor. Not that they could see. And when they tried to reestablish contact with *da Vinci* to find out what was going on, they couldn't.

Because *da Vinci* was gone.

CHAPTER
7

"*Your Bynar's* what?" On Gold's vidscreen, Kira Nerys's image flopped back in her seat, fingered her ridges and sighed. "*Well, that's just terrific. What did Jadzia say?*"

He was alone in his ready room; Salek was on the bridge. They were on a secured channel, so he could say what he thought. Kira was good that way; hell of a woman. She was the only Bajoran Gold hadn't felt like throttling. The other religious types were so . . . pie-in-the-sky, he wanted to punch in their teeth. "Dax thinks that the Bynars were getting messages from these Prophets or something equally absurd. If you want my opinion, I think the Bynars tripped into an Androssi snare. But try getting Dax to face up to it. She's being totally unreasonable. Demands we go back to Terok Nor."

"*That could be a problem.*"

"You're telling me. You didn't get shot at. Do you think you can talk sense into her?"

"*Probably not.*" Kira took a sip from a tall mug of something piping hot; Gold saw curls of steam. Probably Reman coffee. Wretched drink; the stuff smelled like sweaty feet. "*You've got to remember that Jadzia* did *find that Orb, and she does appear to have accessed it before it went dark. But the stories go that only a select few are allowed to commune with the Prophets. So maybe Jadzia's the Emissary."*

"Do you believe that?"

"Anything's possible, David."

"Yeah," said Gold, rubbing the knuckles of his left hand with his right. "And maybe she needs her medication upped. Maybe she's lying."

"She got evaluated, remember? All the psychiatrists say otherwise. The Betazoids swear she's telling the truth. Anyway, why would she lie? She's a xenoarchaeologist; she's Trill. Why should she care about Bajor? There was nothing in her record to suggest she was looking for an Orb, and it was only dumb luck that she stumbled on that Cardassian derelict."

"Doesn't it bother you a little bit that a non-Bajoran is the only person who's talked to these Prophets? If they even exist, I mean."

"I could say that the Prophets move in mysterious ways."

"If you want to watch me get sick," said Gold, "yeah, you could."

Kira's mouth twitched into a grin. *"Might be worth seeing. Of course it bothers me, more than a little. Makes me wonder what we Bajorans are doing wrong. Maybe our faith doesn't run deeply enough, or it could be that we just like money too much. What about you?"*

"What about me? You mean faith?" Gold's eyebrows arched for his hairline. "I'm a die-hard pragmatist and card-carrying cynic. I'm just following orders. Starfleet says jump; I say how high."

"Oh, right," Kira drawled. *"That's why you volunteered for this. I think you like rooting for the underdog."*

"Excuse me, but we *are* the underdogs, remember? This is a long shot at best. It's something to which Starfleet could commit a limited number of ships—namely, the *Gettysburg*. It's a big galaxy, Kira. Easier fights than this one."

"So why aren't you off somewhere else fighting the good fight?"

It was a good question. Because he hated injustice? There was plenty of that to go around. Didn't have to go to Bajor for that, although he couldn't exactly call the Cardassians unjust. More like benevolent dictators.

For the Federation, then? No, that wasn't it either. Gold looked at Kira and saw her passion, the set of her jaw and the fire in her eyes; and he thought back to Dax, who royally pissed him off—and made him envious as all hell.

Because I want to believe in something strongly enough that I'd be willing to die for it. His gaze dropped to the gold circlet of a wedding band he still wore, and his throat balled as he thought about a girl with a mane of chestnut hair. *Because I'd like to care about something again as much as I loved you. . . .*

Kira must have read his struggle because she came to his rescue and said, *"Whatever your reasons, I'm grateful you're here, David. The Assembly won't be able to pull together a government to ratify the Cardassian treaty if we can give Bajor a reason not to. Nothing like a little miracle or two to get folks lining up on the right side in a hurry."*

"That's all you need?" Gold managed a smile. "I got a miracle lying around somewhere, right up my sleeve. Piece of cake."

They fell silent for a moment. Then Kira said, *"I've got some bad news. Word's out that the Klingons'll throw in with the Cardassians."*

"Damn."

"Yup. They do that, all bets are off. The Remans are too busy putting down the Romulans to care, and even with the Vulcans on your side, I don't think the Federation can help but watch its influence shrink. Then? Maybe we're all going to start getting used to taspar eggs."

"Maybe. What will your people do?"

"If Starfleet pulls out? I don't know. I still can't fathom that the Cardassians might get away with religious genocide. Boggles the mind that other Bajorans would stand by and let it happen just because the religious sect is a minority."

"It happens," said Gold. "Study Earth. It happens. Why not get off Bajor?"

"Bajor's our home. We have a right to worship as we please. No, we have to take the battle right to the Cardassians."

"With what? Harsh language? You have maybe ten ships?

Fifteen? You know, I hate to be the one to break this to you, but most Bajorans don't care. They're not waiting around for you to rescue them. The Cardassians aren't oppressing you. There are no Bajoran slaves. Your government's in bed with the Cardassians, and no one gives a damn because life is good. There's money, there's food; everybody's happy. So you'll get yourself killed for nothing." He rubbed his face with his hands, then scrubbed his hair. His wife used to complain about how he never really learned to use a comb. What would Rachel have said about all this Prophet nonsense?

Gold wasn't aware that Kira had spoken until there was an expectant pause. "Sorry. You said?"

"I said maybe not for nothing. We're willing to die for our right to worship as we please."

"What . . . are you . . . are you serious? You're serious. What, kill yourself to make a statement?"

"Not just me." Kira's voice was hard-edged and sharp as a knife. *"We take a couple hundred Cardassians with us, then that's a statement."*

"I'm supposed to stand by and let you?"

"I don't see how you can stop me. Look, I think we can all agree that the wormhole is our primary objective in terms of yielding maximum dividend. If the Bajoran legends are correct, once the wormhole is open, it's stable—and whoever opens the wormhole is the One, the Emissary the religious Bajorans must follow. Think about it this way, David: What would happen if your Messiah suddenly appeared? You don't think your people would notice? I don't see how Bajor is any different. Believe me, if we get the wormhole open, give something tangible to Bajorans, they'll think twice about the Cardassians. Even if all we give to my people is a martyr or two that calls attention to our cause. We win either way."

"I'm not sure dying's a win-win proposition. You'll get people's attention with a nice, big explosion and a couple dead Cardassians, yeah. But there's nothing noble in that, Nerys . . . and don't even start with that these-are-desperate-times crap. What you don't like is the suppression of your religion. That's your beef. You think you're going to get people to wake up by slaughtering Cardassians? Killing yourself in the process?"

"There are some things worth dying for."

"Precious few."

"You have a better idea?"

"Beyond living to fight another day? Not at the moment, no." Gold sighed. "Just—hold on. Let us try working with the Bynars."

Kira stared at him for a long moment. *"All right, we'll wait. As soon as I get there, I'll have my chief engineer beam over. That ought to speed up your repairs."*

"Thanks. He's a good man."

"Yes, he is. David, we have to give Bajor something to believe in other than money and science. Deep down a person wants to believe in something greater, whether those are prophets, gods, heaven, hell; angels and demons and everything else in between. Life doesn't make any sense, does it?"

"No." Gold's gaze flicked to his ring, and he felt the prick of an old pain in his heart. "But you forgot one thing that's even more important than being a martyr to a sometime god."

"And what's that?"

"Love," said Gold, looking up from his memories of a girl who blew a kiss twenty years ago as she boarded a shuttle— and then disappeared without a trace, taking everything that was best with her. "You forgot about love."

CHAPTER
8

Nog and Gomez and Hawkins looked at each other. "That didn't sound good," said Nog.

"You're telling me." Gomez wasted a few seconds trying to reestablish contact. "Hell." Then she felt something; no, correction: she *didn't* feel anything. Well, not as much anyway. "The rumblings . . . the station's not moving as much." Gomez opened a channel. "Conlon, how you doing?"

"Deflectors are up and running. I've just got to work on this manifold relay circuit and get it to settle down, but I've managed to stabilize a portion of the station around the central core and habitat ring. I wouldn't be so sure about those pylons, though. Anything we feel here is about eighty times worse out there."

"That is not what I wanted to hear," said Gomez. "We just lost contact with the *da Vinci.*"

"What?"

"Relax, it's probably nothing," Gomez lied. She frowned over her readings. Her tricorder had enough range to confirm that the temporal-spatial displacement waves were now propagating in all directions, reaching out far enough to wash over the *Kwolek*. "I don't think it's *lost*-lost. Probably just moved out of communicator range."

"*Without telling us?*" Then, after Gomez told her about their last communication with *da Vinci*, Conlon said, "*That doesn't sound good.*"

"Yeah, that's what Nog said. Look, I'm going to secure the shuttle on one of the runabout launch pads. Beam-out will be faster than walking and now that we've got the deflector going, probably safe. I'll check for the *da Vinci* with the *Kwolek*'s sensors. They have better range." She looked over at the Ferengi. "You okay here, Nog?"

"Sure," said Nog, though he didn't seem too happy about it. "I got stuff to do, and Soloman's not going anywhere."

"I can go to the shuttle," said Hawkins.

"Negative that. You're security, remember? So, you and your nice, shiny phaser rifle watch Nog's backside. I'll be right back."

Snapping her tricorder shut, Gomez slung the strap over her shoulder and tapped her combadge to contact the shuttle's computer for a beam-out. An instant later, she heard the familiar whine. Her skin tingled as the annular confinement beam caught and read her pattern while the transporter's phase transition coils simultaneously disassembled her body into a phased matter-energy stream.

But after that initial second of dematerialization, when her mind invariably froze for the span of a heartbeat, she saw something. In the stream. *With* her. Stasis or not, Gomez could still think, and her brain digested the suggestion of a face—yes, a face, because this wasn't some *thing*. The pattern was some*one*, and she registered that *one*'s eyes widen in shock—just as the realization of who that was smacked her in the face as solidly as a good, hard slap.

No. It can't . . .

Sonya Gomez was fit to be tied. The *Gettysburg*'s matter/antimatter reaction chambers were acting up, and she was still struggling with that pesky intermix. . . . She exhaled, blew

hair away from her face because she was flat on her back, futzing with the damn valve, her hands smudged with grime.

Her combadge trilled. "Gomez."

*"Commander, we've made it to the rendezvous site. The Li's
chief engineer's standing by. Thought you might need the extra
hands."*

A surge of relief flooded her veins. *Oh, thank God . . .* She
scrambled to her feet, tugged on her soiled uniform to smooth
it into place. "Well, don't just stand there, Feliciano, energize
the crap out of him."

Feliciano laughed. *"Hold your horses, lady. Energizing . . ."*

A scintillating column appeared three meters away, and
Gomez watched as the sparkles resolved into an outline, coalesced—then stuttered. Gomez's heart leapt into her mouth.
God, no, not a transporter malfunction, not now . . . But then
the pattern stabilized and the glitter resolved, coalesced, and
became a man. The sight of him thrilled her to her toes.

"Whoa, that was pretty freaky," said Kieran Duffy, looking
befuddled. "Déjà vu all over again."

"Whatever the hell that means. But, God," she said as she
flew into his arms. "God, how I've missed you."

. . . be.

The transporter beam let her go, and Gomez exhaled. Then
she stood, rigid, her heart hammering against her ribs. A distortion wave rolled past; she felt the shuttle jiggle on the docking pylon. But she couldn't move for a second, was afraid to.

It can't be.

Numb, she tapped on her tricorder. Nothing but residua normal for a standard beam-in. *But I'm not going crazy; I saw . . .*
She hadn't blacked out. This wasn't a dream. She'd been conscious the whole time; everyone was, unless you overrode the
system and programmed in a stasis loop the way Scotty had.

So. Transporter psychosis? No way. Multiplex pattern buffers virtually eliminated transporter psychosis. The distortion
waves weren't anything like interphase, so she could discount
interphase-induced delusions.

Okay. What if. They'd already seen that Soloman had made contact with a quantum twin. *So. What if the holes between universes also allowed for a phased matter transfer—as in a transporter beam?*

Then he could be alive. No, strike that. Duffy was alive in some universe somewhere, maybe even the one where Soloman was now. Then she had another thought: The Duffy she'd seen hadn't been wearing an environmental suit.

"God, I hope he didn't materialize on the wrong part of Empok Nor." She didn't know if such a thing was even possible, although she knew DS9 had experienced its share of visitors from a mirror universe. Those people appeared to have the technology to go back and forth. Maybe that Duffy had been from *that* mirror universe?

No. Her nose crinkled. *Didn't feel right. Most humans in that universe were slaves. In fact . . .*

She blinked back to attention as the deck jerked beneath her feet. The *Kwolek*'s onboard computer blatted a warning, and she hurried to the pilot's chair. *First things first: Look for the* da Vinci. *Secure the shuttle.* Then, think about how she wanted to talk to Gold about this.

When she brought up sensors, she didn't see the *da Vinci*, or anything that looked like debris.

"Oh, crap," she said. "This isn't good."

CHAPTER
9

"Give that to me again, Kane." Gold crossed his arms over his chest. "You think *what?*"

They were in sickbay: Gold, Salek, Kane, Dax, and 111. Haggard and paler than usual, the Bynar looked like a refugee from a month-long siege.

"I said that 110 looks to be in communication with another computer system," said Kane. "I can't nail it down precisely; that is, I know there's a code flowing back and forth but whenever I try to tap into it, it changes. I can't get a precise lock. Don't even know where or when it's coming from."

Gold blinked. "What do you mean, *when?*"

"Exactly what I said. There's something very . . . odd about this thing. I'm no computer whiz by any stretch. Bynar physiology is tough; half the time, you got to look at them more like sick computers than humanoids." Catching herself, Kane cringed. "Sorry," she said to 111.

"It . . . is . . . all right," said 111, and Gold almost winced. Listening to the Bynar was like revving up an old digital recording from centuries back on a machine that skipped and lurched from one section to the next.

If I think it's tough to listen to, imagine what it must be like for 111.

"You're not considering the obvious, you know. What if it's not another computer?" Jadzia gave an adamant toss of her head that set her earring flashing in the light. "What if 110's in contact with a Prophet? We've always hypothesized this possibility, that the Prophets are coherent energy. The Androssi specialize in using quantum dimensional shifts. But who's to say that their tinkering didn't open up a rift that connects us with the Prophets?"

"That is a logical hypothesis," said Salek.

"Yeah, but with only one way to prove it," said Kane. She looked at 111, who shrank back perceptibly and in a way that Gold suddenly felt, keenly, how much they were using the Bynars to their advantage: not as partners but tools. "111 has to be willing to try communing with him."

"What . . . perhaps . . ." The Bynar quailed. "This might . . . be . . . infection. Not . . . a Prophet."

Kane made an impatient sound, and Jadzia opened her mouth but Gold silenced her with a look. Hunkering down on his haunches, he brought his face level with 111's. "It might be an infection. You're right to be frightened. No one blames you for that. Hell, it shows good sense. But 110's *not* coming out of it. Kane can't help him. We humans value love. I don't know about Bynaus, and I can't know your heart. But what price are you willing to pay to help your bondmate?"

So was that a cheap shot, or what? Gold, you hypocrite. He watched 111's struggle, hating himself more with every passing second. He was very conscious of the ring squeezing his finger. *Or do I really mean that; if I had a second chance, would I—?*

He was saved from finishing the thought. 111's throat moved in a hard, convulsive swallow. "I wish . . . I will . . . I will try."

"All right." Gold nodded. He didn't think that what he felt was relief. More like . . . dread. No, more than that even: Finality.

Because one way or the other, I've just got this feeling. This will end. Soon.

*   *   *

Gomez said, "I'm not imagining things."

A pause, and then Conlon said, "I didn't say that." She didn't sound convinced, though.

Nog said, "Neither did I." He didn't sound convinced either.

"Don't look at me," said Hawkins. "I'm just a dumb jock."

Gomez ignored him. "Yeah. But? *And?*"

"*And,*" Conlon tapped her tricorder, "there's no evidence anywhere that there was another phased matter stream. All I've got is you."

Nog said, "I checked after you called from the *Kwolek,* and I've checked again, just now, when you beamed back." He held up his tricorder, screen out, so Gomez could see the readings. "See for yourself, you don't believe me."

"I believe you," said Gomez. She had no choice; her tricorder showed the same readings. "It's still a possibility. Let's just think a sec. Besides biofilters and phase transition coils, what else does a transporter have that nothing else on board the ship does?"

"A Heisenberg Compensator," Conlon said, promptly. "So?"

"So, what's the compensator for?" She answered her own question. "It's designed to make up for changes you make on a quantum level whenever you use a transporter. The Heisenberg uncertainty principle says that you can't know everything about a particle at once, not with any accuracy."

"Yeah, yeah," said Conlon. She looked faintly annoyed, too. Like Gomez was a teacher trying to catch her out for not studying. "The principle stipulates that you can measure *either* position or angular momentum but not both. The more you measure one aspect of a particle state, the less you know about another. The compensator is designed to override the inevitable informational drift. Doesn't tell you anything; just gives you information in a general sense and compares what it reads to what's stored in the buffer. Otherwise, I rematerialize with my arm hanging out of my ear."

"Wait a minute," said Nog, and Gomez heard the *ah-hah* in his voice. "Commander, you think your transporter beam snagged some information in a datastream and then compared it to what's *already there*. In the *Kwolek*. And . . ."

"And the transporter came up with Duffy," said Gomez. Hearing it again, out loud, set off this little electric jolt zipping through her heart. "Not the Kieran Duffy that we knew, obviously, but another Kieran. As the temporal distortions here increase, the temporal signatures of the universes must be momentarily synchronized, allowing for vacant time-space to be briefly occupied by reassimilated energy."

"In other words, that Commander Duffy filled a vacant space in this universe." Conlon's eyes held that faraway look she always got when she was thinking really hard about something. "And the *da Vinci*? You think that when I activated the deflectors, we pushed *da Vinci* into a time-space bubble, or into the other universe altogether?"

"I think so. We won't know until we bring down the deflectors."

Hawkins said, "Wait a sec. If you snagged hold of Duffy and we've got everyone's patterns on file, can we, I dunno, put the transporter on a continuous receptive mode? You know, catch pieces of them in a datastream and then have them rematerialize here?"

Gomez shook her head. "I thought of that. There are two problems: Causal directionality is one. If Duffy was a book, then his life has been written up to this point. Bringing that Duffy here—even if we could do it—is like bringing in another chapter by another author and plunking it right smack dab into the middle of a book. It won't make any sense to him, and he sure as heck won't make any sense *here*."

"And there's conservation of matter and energy to think about," said Conlon. "The only reason Duffy almost materialized here is because we've wrapped space-time around us. Eventually, we'll have to take down the deflectors, and the hole will collapse. But if we bring energy into this system that we can't release or get rid of, then, theoretically, there's this big ka-boom. Think of it the same way you do when matter and antimatter collide. Kind of defeats the purpose."

"But that does imply there's an energy imbalance somewhere," said Gomez. "Maybe on both sides of the equation.

It's like we're trading information to make up for gaps, and they've activated a search program that's trying to compensate. The problem is to figure out what's missing from there that they could possibly want here."

Nog held up his tricorder. "Why don't we just ask them?"

"You're a million kilometers away." Gomez frowned over at Duffy. They were recalibrating the plasma injectors. "Something on your mind?"

"Me?" Duffy grinned, shook his head. "Just . . . thinking."

"About what happened during transport?" Duffy had told her about catching a glimpse of her in an EVA suit but she figured stress, had to be. On the run all the time, people shooting at you. Bound to have an effect. So she'd dismissed it. "That still bothering you?"

"A little. It was weird, Sonnie, like a vision of the future, or something. I dunno."

"Wishful thinking, you ask my opinion. You saw me on a Cardassian station. Well, isn't that exactly what we're trying to accomplish here?" Then she scrutinized him more closely. "You're really bothered by this."

"Yeah. Ever since coming aboard I have this bad feeling. Something's going to go wrong."

Gomez put her arms about his waist. "Nothing's going to go wrong. We've been shot at a lot. We're still here."

"For now." Duffy nuzzled her hair, and inhaled the aroma of jasmine and musk. Tightened his grip. "You smell good. And, God, you feel wonderful."

Gomez sighed, burrowed. "Feeling's mutual."

A pause. Then: "Well?"

"Well, what?"

"Come on," Duffy said with mock severity. He pulled back and squinted down his nose. "You know what."

"Yeah?" Her eyes flicked down to his right trouser pocket. The fabric tented over something square. "Is that a box in your pocket, or are you just glad to see me?"

"Cretin. What, I'm supposed to get on my kne—?"

A hail shrilled, and Gomez threw her head back, closed her eyes. "I don't believe it."

"*Believe what?*" It was Gold.

She rolled her eyes at Duffy who smothered a giggle. "Nothing, sir. Commander Duffy and I are nearly done here. If you'll—"

"*Let your team finish up. I want you and Duffy in sickbay, pronto.*"

"Aye, sir. Gomez, out." She waited a split second to make sure the channel had closed then said, "Damn."

Grinning, Duffy planted a kiss on her lips. "It'll keep. Maybe I'll reconsider."

"You reconsider," Gomez said as they started off, "and I'll take out your tonsils."

All three stared at Nog. "You figured out the code?" asked Gomez.

"I will in a sec," said Nog. His fingers played over his tricorder.

"How?"

"It's what you said about Duffy." Nog gave a ferociously triumphant smile, all zigzag Ferengi teeth. "The *Kwolek*'s got patterns of Soloman when he wasn't Soloman, right? So if I access them now, compare the two and whittle down . . ."

Gomez saw it. "You get rid of the twin effect. Whatever remains will be the interaction between Soloman and that universe's 111."

"Yup. And that means I can talk to her. So," Nog gave his tricorder a final jab, "what do you want me to say?"

"How about," said Gomez, "what the hell do you want?"

For Soloman, it was like sitting at the bottom of an infinitely deep pool. He was aware of light shimmering overhead and a world beyond this hermetic seal. But that life was far away and strangely muffled, and he had no strength to reach for it, nor the desire. At a rudimentary level akin to instinct, he understood what he had done: caught 110 in a paradox, a recursive algorithm that could not be resolved.

Then the quality of the light above changed, and the surface seemed to split, and Soloman knew that they—someone—had come after him.

"Beneath the surface," said 111. The chip on her left temple winked furiously, and the buffer on her belt hummed. Her lips quivered, and her blue eyes were wide and liquid. "It's another line of code. Not thought."

"A *fourth* Bynar?" said Gold. "Are you sure? How do you know that the Androssi haven't planted a virus designed to simulate a Bynar's cerebral patterns?"

"No, no . . ." 111 shook her head in the exaggerated way of a little girl trying to make a point to an adult who just did not speak the same language. But her hesitancy was gone, and her speech had acquired the high singsong Gold associated with the Bynars. "This is no virus. This is not 110 either, and it is not 110's doppelgänger. Both are unchanged. This one says that the doppelgänger is Soloman, a Bynar existing outside in another temporal realm."

"It's a Prophet," Dax blurted. "Look, the reason we stole the device in the first place is because the ancient Hebitians built it, and the Cardassians can't access it. The pictographs on those Hebitian tombs on Cardassia strongly favor the view that the Hebitians were telepaths—"

"That's only legend," said Gomez.

Salek said, "Legends usually have a basis in fact. We know that there are no Cardassian telepaths. Yet the Hebitians leave behind a device that relies on the ability to access information on a digital level when combined with telepathy. The Bynars are the only species capable of both."

Dax looked triumphant. "What's happening now is precisely what's been prophesized: that the One will reach out and then His Temple will be reborn. Well, now we've got a window, a quantum fracture into a realm of space through which energy and information can be transferred. Think about it a second. We know that Bynars always come in pairs. Always. But now 110 has found his match, a twin. How is that possible? Singletons are incapable of meshing. They're unfit to do so. But this energy signature can, and he calls himself Solo-Man." She paused, her darkly brown eyes clicking over their faces. "Don't you understand? Solo-Man. *One Man. The One.*"

"No, no," said 111. "There is Soloman, and then there is this other. He is a," she cocked her head an instant, chittered in dataspeak and said, "Ferengi."

"What are *those*?" asked Gold.

Another pause. "He says it would take too long to explain. There are, it seems, many rules applying to acquisition. He says that we must shut down this device; that the search program has activated the computer on their side of the datastream on their . . ." 111's eyes were huge. "On Empok Nor. He says that temporal-distortion waves are destroying the fabric of space-time."

"What?" said Kane. "*Empok* Nor?"

"Are you sure it isn't *Terok* Nor?" said Jadzia. She dropped to her haunches now, laid her hands on the Bynar's shoulders. "Ask the Prophet if this Empok Nor is anywhere near—"

"It is not a Prophet," said 111. She raised her bright blue eyes to Gold. "This Soloman—the Ferengi says he lost his bondmate." Her voice quavered. Broke. "He says I died there."

Gold took the Bynar's left hand. Her fingers were cold, and they trembled. "111, does this—this Ferengi say why Soloman is there in the first place?"

"No. But I sense Soloman—waits."

"For what?"

"I do not believe he knows, but there is a void in him." She pressed a bunched fist to her chest. "But I cannot fill it. Much as I wish to help, I have my bondmate here." The look she gave Gold was full of anguish. "I want 110 back, whole, and yet I feel such sorrow for this other. I do not know how he has managed to live."

"I suppose he just went on." Gold had to pause, clear his throat. "People do that."

"Perhaps. But when love is gone," 111 said as a tear inched down either cheek, "there is always emptiness because the heart knows what has been lost."

"Yes," said Gold. His eyes burned. "Yes, it does."

"Well?" asked Gomez.

Nog shook his head. "I know I got the message through; 111's code changed to assimilate it."

"And Soloman?"

"He's there, but it's like he's . . . locked in tight somehow. And I . . ." Nog trailed off, squinted at his data.

Gomez waited an anxious few seconds. "What?"

Nog began toggling in data. "I am so stupid. I know why Soloman can't break free. You know how Betazoids have a paracortex that enhances their telepathic capabilities, and how Betazoid women have elevated levels of neurochemicals that further augment these abilities? Look at Soloman's psilosynine level. It's through the roof. That's what's happening with Soloman. The Bynars in that universe? They're telepaths."

Gomez gaped. "You're kidding."

"Nope. It's a logical extension, you ask me. What do the Bynars do? They interconnect with computer code. It all comes down to discharges along the electromagnetic spectrum. The brain works the same way. All neurons rely upon electrical potentials, whether neurochemically or electrically mediated. So it's not so unbelievable that the Bynars of that universe also possess some form of telepathy and that some machines only respond to telepaths."

"Okay," said Gomez. "So what are they looking for?"

There was astonishment on Dax's face, and Gold saw Gomez and Duffy glance at each other.

Then Gomez said, "Do we tell them?" She seemed unaware that she'd sidled closer to Duffy. "Maybe they can help."

Gold gave 111's hand a squeeze, then pushed to his feet.

"I'm not sure if I'm relieved it's not a Prophet. Another us? What makes them think they can help? We have no way of knowing if our two universes are compatible in any way."

"Well, sir," Duffy interrupted. He glanced at Sonya and then back at Gold. "Now that you mention it . . ."

"I just thought of something, a way to get Soloman out of there," said Gomez. "You just said that Betazoids and other telepaths have high levels of psilosynine in their brains, right?"

"Yeah," said Nog. "So?"

"So why not give Soloman a broad-range neural suppressant? Just . . . take him offline that way."

"But that will make him incapable of communing with Empok Nor's computer. Then we'll be stuck," said Nog.

"We're stuck either way," said Conlon. "Right now, we can talk to them but that's all. We can't control what's happening here *or* there, and Soloman either can't or won't deactivate the system. Probably it's the latter because they're the ones who are looking for something, not us. Either they find it, or they don't. Unless they shut down on their end, it won't matter."

It was her decision; Gomez knew it. "We give them a couple more minutes. Let's see what they say."

When Duffy finished, Gold looked from Duffy to Gomez, who'd gone very white. To Jadzia. Salek returned his stare then said, "That would seem to answer the question."

"Yes, it does. And it means they're probably telling the truth. That machine's ripping their universe apart." Gold tapped his combadge. "Feliciano, contact Captain Kira. Beam her directly to sickbay. Tell her I'll explain when she's aboard."

Then Gold put a gentle hand on 111's shoulder. "When Captain Kira gets here, this is what I want you to ask."

*   *   *

"The Prophets? The *wormhole?*" asked Gomez. "*That's* what this is about?"

"That's what they say," said Nog. "Seems they don't have one, and they thought this device would help them find it."

"It has, in a weird sort of way," Gomez mused. "I mean, it reached out and found *this* version of Bajoran space. Maybe we're the only universe with a wormhole."

"Well, I'm not sure we should tell them," said Conlon.

"What harm would it do?" asked Hawkins.

"You ever hear of the Prime Directive?"

Gomez raised a hand. "Wait a sec, let's think this through. This whole thing started when they activated that device—111 says that they think the Hebitians left it as a beacon of some sort. Whoever can access it supposedly can use it to find the wormhole. Well, what if they're right? First, you access micro-black holes; you establish a coherent datastream to a parallel realm, or you find the region of space most vulnerable to gravimetric inversion."

"In theory," said Conlon. "Okay. But if we give them the coordinates and then we, I dunno, disconnect Soloman, how do we know we've picked the right side?"

"You ever hear of Pandora's box?" asked Gomez. "Well, it's open. They know we're here. We know what they're looking for. From what it sounds like, they're running out of time. What incentive do they have to turn the thing off?"

"None."

"Right. If they don't stop, things don't get better here. Seems pretty cut and dried to me." Gomez looked at them all in turn. "We tell them."

"Once you tell them, you can't take it back," said Conlon.

"I know that." Gomez looked over at Nog. "Do it."

"The Denorios Belt?" Kira frowned. "No one goes there. It's a mess: high-energy plasma, neutrino storms, tachyon bursts. I've always assumed a wormhole would have to be in a stable, less kinetically energetic region of space. Best place for that is a black hole."

"Well, guess again," said Kane.

"But maybe that's the point, Captain," said Gomez. "The Denorios Belt we know about is pretty hot, right? Think about it. The Remans use a quantum singularity for their warp drive. To do that, they fuse material and create energy. In theory, you concentrate enough mass and energy you create the conditions for a wormhole by deforming space-time sufficiently to open it. Think of it as breaking down a gated door. The wormhole is there but closed off."

"You mean, input enough energy to bind all that plasma together, or maybe just a sizable chunk?" Duffy stroked the side of his chin with his thumb. "Well, theoretically, we could do it."

"How?" asked Gold and Kira at the same time.

"We generate a massive pulse of combined anti-chroniton and tetryon particles, then follow with a spread of photon torpedoes. The release of that much energy ought to be siphoned off by the denser tetryons, resulting in a collapse of matter into a highly compressed, dense mass and concomitant release of SEM gamma rays."

Kane rolled her eyes. "What the hell did that mean?"

"It means we can do it," said Gold. "Except there are only a couple problems." He ticked them off on his fingers. "One, all that plasma, we'll be lucky we don't go up with it. Second, we don't know if this isn't what the Androssi want us to do."

"Why would they allow us to steal a device that would tell us the location of a wormhole and not keep it for themselves?" asked Dax. She looked to be spoiling for another fight. "Clearly—"

"Clearly, because they don't want to get themselves blown to smithereens for no good reason," said Gold. "Ever think of that? We sure as hell know that the Cardassians aren't telepathic, and maybe the Androssi aren't either. So they needed us—specifically, they needed the Bynars—to find it for them." He looked at Kira. "I told you: Taking this thing was too easy."

Kira searched his face. "You think they're waiting to ambush us."

"They'll want all the glory. That's what this is about. They know that if the religious sect delivers the wormhole, the treaty has no chance of being ratified. But if the Cardassians find the wormhole, then the religious sect drops their objections. So how I think it goes down is like this. We find the wormhole; we open it, or we start to—or maybe the Cardassians and Androssi have their own plans for how to open it, I don't know—and then we get blown into subatomic particles. The Cardassians won't want anyone slipping away, or getting a transmission out to contradict their story."

"There's another problem, Captain," said Gomez. The color had drained from her face; her skin was white as bone china. "Even if we survive the initial explosion, the shock waves might rip the ship apart."

"And if we somehow managed to live through *that*, there's going to be a lot of gamma radiation out there, enough to penetrate shields in a matter of minutes," said Duffy. "No matter how you cut it, it's a suicide mission."

"Some things are worth dying for," said Dax.

"Yeah," said Gold, and his eyes slid to Kira in a sidelong glance. "There's a lot of that going around."

Kira returned the look. "The Denorios Belt is far enough from Bajor and Terok Nor that it would take the Cardassians or the Androssi several minutes to reach us."

"Assuming they aren't waiting for us. Assuming there aren't patrols."

"Okay, then," Kira said. "We wouldn't have much time. One of us would have to discharge the pulse while the other fends off whoever comes after us. But it can be done."

"Care to lay odds on that?"

"No."

"Me neither." Gold planted his fists on his hips. He sighed. "Man, oh, man, this just keeps getting better and better."

"In truth, we'd need another ship to have a real shot at this," said Kira. "But there's no one close enough."

"Well," said Gold. "That's not entirely accurate."

"Will they do it?" asked Conlon.

"I don't know," said Nog.

"They have the information they wanted. They'll have to

decide how to use it, but that's not our fight. My guess, though, is they're committed now," said Gomez. She palmed a small hypospray in her right hand, knelt, pressed the tip to Soloman's suit along his forearm, thumbed the hypospray to life and then settled back on her haunches to wait. "And so are we."

They'd forgotten all about the Bynar, and so it was a shock when 111 raised her voice in a keening wail.

It was Gold who reacted first. Kneeling beside the Bynar, he covered her tiny hands with one of his. The sight of her tears touched his heart with pain and an ancient grief that was somehow always fresh, like a wound that never healed. "111?" he asked, gently.

"He is gone, Captain," she said. Then she turned, buried her face in Gold's chest and wept like a small child. "He is gone."

Gold didn't have to look for 110's life-signs on the biobed monitors because he knew, instinctively, which "he" she meant. "Is he dead?"

"No, but he is . . . one again. They have chosen for him. But how will he live, Captain?" 111 said. "How can he?"

Gold swallowed against the lump in his throat, and then he motioned for Kane to deactivate the ancient device. They had what they needed—and he knew what he, and only he, must do.

They have chosen for him.

"Because he will," Gold said. "He'll just have to."

CHAPTER
10

Tugging on the tails of his lavishly embroidered tunic, Gul Garak activated his holomirror and twisted this way and that, admiring the view. The cut of the tunic was exquisite; the fabric shot through with latinum thread and encrusted with living gemstones: a little-known treasure found in ancient Hebitian tombs. As he watched, the gemstones splayed delicate, lacy fingers, bleeding color along the fabric the way a spider spins a web.

"I'm happy," Garak said, and he was exceedingly pleased when the gemstones responded and colored to amber. Then he imagined his Bajoran comfort woman slowly unfastening her sheer, gauzy tunic at its right shoulder and the look of the tunic slithering over the points of her breasts to the swell of her hips . . . and watched as the gemstones shaded to a deep blood-red so vibrant it seemed to pulsate.

So that is the color of arousal. Very nice. But I wonder what shade they will turn when that treaty is signed? He glanced at a chronometer. *Well, only a few hours left until I find out.*

His intercom clamored for his attention. "Yes, Lieutenant?"

"Zotat has reported in, Gul Garak."

"And?"

"There are two vessels headed for the Denorios Belt—and, sir, one is the Gettysburg."

"Very well. Tell Zotat to contact me the moment that he either determines the coordinates of the wormhole, or the wormhole has opened and been secured." Then Garak thought of something. "And, Lieutenant, relay this: Zotat may do as he wishes with the other vessel. It is of no consequence. But tell him that I want the *Gettysburg*." Garak looked into his mirror, and his reflection gave him a dark and malevolent grin. "Yes, tell Zotat: I want Gold."

Clicking off, Garak then stepped back to admire his reflection—and the color of victory.

"There it is," said Wong. If he was anxious, his voice didn't betray it. "Six thousand meters dead ahead. The Denorios Belt, sir."

"Slow to one-quarter impulse. McAllan, Cardassians?"

"None detected, sir."

"What about Androssi?" Privately, Gold didn't believe that Garak would let the Androssi in on the kill. The Cardassians would want all the credit. The Androssi were simply their go-tos.

McAllan took another second to double-check, then said, "Negative. It would seem the belt is unguarded, Captain."

"Like Kira said, it's a lot of space. But they're going to come running in a hurry." Gold balanced on the balls of his feet, too keyed up to sit in his command chair. "Salek, what's your status up there?"

"All nonessential personnel have moved from the outer hull, Captain. Escape pods are prepped. Shuttlecraft Templar *is standing by. We are ready to proceed at your command."*

"Good. Haznedl, raise the *Li*."

"On audio, sir."

"Kira, this is Gold. You ready?"

Her voice was steady and betrayed nothing. *"Ready as we're ever going to be. This is one risky plan, David."*

"I could say something apropos like risk is our business."

"Please, don't. What about my chief engineer?"

"We'll get him back to you."

"Then, as they say on Earth, bring it on."

"You're going to wish you hadn't said that." Gold gave a short nod then tapped his combadge. "Engineering, Gomez. How are you and Duffy doing?"

"We're just about there, Captain. We've had to reroute power from the backup phaser generators through the deflector grid. I've tied in an emergency relay from the shields just in case."

"Our shields? You're telling me that it might come down to a choice between that deflector, and shields?"

"No choice, sir. We're talking one big pulse."

"How much time to charge the deflector?"

"Once we're in position, about sixty seconds."

"A lot can happen in sixty seconds."

"Best we can do, Captain. We've got another problem, though. Our last run-in damaged our torpedo launchers. I had to reroute the launch assist generators, but it's jury-rigged. It won't hold up for long."

"They may not have to. Do what you can. Haznedl, signal the *Li*. Feliciano, when Duffy's ready, beam him back aboard the *Li*." Gold pulled in a breath. "All right, people, this is it."

"Almost there," said Duffy. His hair was mussed; he was covered in grime and there were crescents of dirt under his nails; and he was sweating so much his tunic was glued to his back. They'd been working at breakneck speed and barely had time to exchange two paragraphs that didn't contain the words *containment field, magnetic oscillation,* and *anti-chronitonic stream.*

Duffy thought back to the moments after Kane had deactivated that . . . whatever it was. Hebitian, Cardassian, Bajoran, or something else altogether: He didn't know, and wondered if now they ever would. 110 had awakened, finally; 111 had calmed, but there was a haunted look in her eyes: as if she'd been privy to a vision of a world Duffy couldn't begin to imagine.

Yet what he *hadn't* imagined was the look on Captain Kira's face after she and Salek and Jadzia Dax had emerged from Gold's ready room. Why the Trill had been included, Duffy hadn't a clue, but there was a preternatural glitter to her eyes that Duffy didn't like. Nor did he know what had transpired, but whatever it was had clearly left Kira shaken and her lips so thinned they cut a horizontal gash above her chin. True to form, Salek was a cipher. But when Gold finally emerged, he had the thunderous look of a black, brooding storm.

Yeah, and I can guess why: because we're all going to get ourselves killed chasing after some Trill's hallucinations.

Duffy hadn't spent much time around Dax, not enough to really understand everything about this religion she was so hot about. There had been rumors, of course; Kira's ship was a standard Bajoran assault vessel, with a crew complement that was barely a tenth of the *Gettysburg*. Word traveled fast. Duffy was one of four officers on loan from Starfleet. His shipmates were Bajorans, not all religious but none with any love for the Cardassians. Duffy listened to their gripes in the mess; his roommate was an agnostic, but even he saw no utility to allying themselves to a power that would, in effect, shackle them with latinum chains. They saw the Federation as more benevolent in its way.

So we leave them to manage their wealth and affairs as they see fit, but one hand washes the other. We get rid of the Cardassians and give them their gods, and the Federation gets resources it needs to push the Cardassians back.

Yet for all the unknowns, it was Dax who scared him the most. She was so . . . intense, so certain that hers was the correct path and there could be no other. Perhaps part was this Orb thing; Duffy guessed if he'd been in touch with something calling itself the Almighty, maybe he'd be a bit intense himself.

Looking down, he said, suddenly, "Do you believe in fate?"

"What?" Sprawled at his feet, Sonya Gomez was cantilevered on her side, a spanner in one hand, a warp calibration meter in the other. Her hair had frizzed from perspiration and there was a smear of something suspiciously like Heplart grease on her right cheek. She had never looked more beautiful. "What do you mean?"

"Do you believe in fate?"

"Why are you asking?"

"I'm curious."

"Well," she said, turning back to her work, "I think that some things are fated to happen no matter what you do about it. Sun going nova, that kind of thing. There are certain fundamentals to the universe I can't change because, you know, the universe doesn't care. It'll kill you a thousand ways to Sunday, you give it half a chance."

"Well, we are cheery."

"You asked. Given what we're about to do, it's kind of appropriate, don't you think?"

"Yeah. Goes almost without saying. But I meant people—do you think that our lives are scripted somehow so that no matter what, you can't change your destiny?"

She sat up now. Her dark eyes searched his face. "111 really got you spooked."

"Yeah. It's weird. Knowing there are an infinite number of Kieran Duffys just as there are a million Sonya Gomezes. But I can't imagine loving anyone but you, right here, right at this moment, in this reality."

"Then that's what you'll have to hang on to."

"But if I knew what was going to happen, would whatever I did be worth the cost? Is this?" He gestured with a hand to include the warp core, engineering, the ship. "Is a religion I don't practice, people I really don't know . . . are any of these things worth dying for?"

Gomez carefully put her spanner in a nearby tool kit and squared her warp recalibration meter alongside. Then she pushed to her feet, brushed grit from her hands and slipped her arms around his waist. "I don't think we can judge the value of an individual mission. We have no idea what will happen to Bajor or the Federation if we succeed. But we do know that the Federation's not getting any stronger, and the Cardassians are. I don't know about you, but I care about my freedom, and real freedom means you choose. I choose the Federation, and the rest will have to work itself out. I remember when I was a kid. I read Milton: not all that ruling in hell part but the idea behind it. About the freedom to choose. If you really read it carefully, Satan had a choice, and he chose to rule rather than serve. Everyone always assumes that meant he made the wrong choice. But he didn't. He made the best choice for him. The one thing Milton never confused was choice and happiness. So just because you have freedom of choice doesn't mean that you're fated to live happily ever after."

"So how do we know this is the right choice?"

"We don't. It's just the best one for now."

"Yeah, but—" Duffy was interrupted by a hail. "Duffy, here."

"Feliciano, Commander. You're needed aboard the Li.*"*

"Just a sec." Suddenly, he was filled with an overwhelming flood of panic that made his mouth go dry. There were so many things he wanted to say; he was full to bursting of things he'd never said and thought that, probably, were way too many to start now. "Okay, look, Sonnie—you got to watch that antimatter mix when you initiate the magnetic field to channel the tetryon particles."

She quirked an eyebrow at his sudden shift. "I'll watch it."

"And the anti-chronitons, you got to remember that the field's got to oscillate to contain—"

She put her fingers to his mouth. "I'm on it, Kieran. It'll be okay."

"God." Duffy took her hand in both of his and pressed it to his lips in a kiss. He thumbed grease from her face then cupped her cheek. "What I really mean is—why do I keep having this feeling that I'm never going to see you again?"

Gomez tried a smile, but it came out crooked. "Because you're a cockeyed optimist?"

"Yeah," said Duffy. He gave a breathy laugh and squeezed her in a bear hug. Amazingly, her hair still felt like silk against his face and he breathed her in, stamping her scent and the feel of her body, warm and alive, into his brain. "I'm scared for you."

He felt her nod against his chest. "I'm scared for us both," she said, her voice muffled. Then she looked up, and her dark eyes glistened. "But I love you, Kieran Duffy, and I . . ." She took his face and gave him a ferocious kiss that left him breathless. "And you want to know about fate? Well, this is ours: Yes."

"Yes. Yes . . . what?" Then, as he understood: "*Yes?* Did you say . . . ?"

"Yes," she said, with a smile that broke his heart. Then she patted his combadge and stepped out of the circle of his arms. "Feliciano, beam Commander Duffy back to the *Li*."

She saw Duffy reach for his pocket. "Wait, I have to gi—" Duffy began, but then there was a swirl of light; Duffy's form broke apart; and he was gone.

"Save it for the next time I see you," whispered Sonya Gomez. The tears she'd held back rolled down her cheeks. She didn't bother brushing them away. "Because, yes, I will see you, my love. Yes."

"*Li* reports Commander Duffy aboard," said Susan Haznedl from ops.

Gold nodded. "Very well. Salek, initiate saucer separation."

"*Acknowledged.*"

Gold felt a perceptible jolt and then a tremor shimmy through the deckplates of the battle bridge as the eighteen docking latches and umbilical blocks tethering the *Gettysburg*'s saucer to the battle section detached. On the main viewscreen, a green etched schematic showed the ellipse of the saucer lifting away and forward from the battle section. "And now, Captain Kira, there are three," Gold murmured.

"Saucer separation complete," said McAllan. "Automatic path termination seals to the turbolift shafts are locked."

"Good. Raise shields. Red alert." Klaxons shrilled. The light in the battle bridge section was always darker than in the saucer's bridge, and now, going to red alert, the shadows lengthened into rust-colored slashes. *Like drying blood.* "Weapons status."

"Phasers charged and ready. Photon torpedoes are online.

Commander Salek reports that shuttlecraft *Templar* is standing by, sir."

"Thank you, McAllan," said Gold. "Let's make sure we give the Cardassians something infinitely more interesting to look at. Wong, give me visual of where we're headed."

The schematic of the separated vessels winked out to be replaced by a swath of space that was smeary with the purple and deep fuchsia contrails of ion storms and superheated plasma. Sizzling bolts of white-hot energy arced into streamers of cobalt and cerulean blue that, somehow, miraculously stood out against the darker background of space. There were no stars visible at all in the densest region of the Belt where they were headed and it was as if a child had upended a pot of paints over a black canvas, splaying colors in a bright, pulsating, riotous Medusa's halo. The sight nearly took his breath away.

"My God, it's beautiful," said Wong, his voice barely audible. "Like something out of a dream."

"You have some pretty interesting dreams," said McAllan. "Captain, the area's lousy with radiation. If our shields so much as burp for more than a couple minutes, we're gonna fry."

"Well, you'll just have to make sure they don't. Believe me, if our shields don't hold when we detonate all that stuff out there, frying's going to be the least of your worries. Wong, course three-three-zero, mark one-five. Take us right into the heart of it; three-quarters impulse."

"Aye, sir."

"McAllan, how long before we reach minimum safe distance to discharge the deflector array?" They'd debated that one around and around, settling finally for the option that would lower their chances of a miss.

"Estimate we'll reach the specified coordinates in ten point seven minutes, sir."

"All right. Once we discharge the deflector array keep those shields steady. What about the Li and the saucer section?"

"Taking flanking positions, Captain, covering our tails and . . ."

Gold was instantly attuned to the hitch in McAllan's voice. "Lieutenant?"

In the bloody half-light, McAllan's skin had gone dead

white. "Cardassian vessels, Captain, on an intercept course. Two *Keldon*, one *Hideki*. Their shields are up; I read that they have energized their weapons and—Sir, Salek and the *Li* are moving to cover! The Cardassians are firing!"

"Hard about! Return fire!" Kira was up and out of her seat. Another disruptor slammed against the *Li* on the port side, and an inertial damper stuttered offline for an instant because Kira was thrown back and crashed to the deck against a weapons console. There was a blinding flash as a circuit shorted, and then someone was screaming to her right. Kira caught the acrid odor of burning metal, scorched hair and singed flesh. She twisted around in time to see the communications officer's uniform erupt in a ball of flame.

"Get a medic up here!" Charging, Kira flung herself at the woman. They crashed to the deck, and Kira went spread-eagled, smothering the flames as the screeching woman writhed beneath her. Starbursts of pain seared Kira's palms and chest, and flames licked the underside of her neck, but she held on, praying her own hair wouldn't ignite. "Return fire! Take out their disruptors!"

"Can't!" Her tactical officer's face was smeary with fresh blood and soot. He turned aside and spat out a gobbet of rust-colored saliva. A rivulet of blood tracked down his chin. "Our weapons are offline! Shields at fifty percent!"

"Engineering!" A medic came charging onto the bridge, and as Kira rolled away, another disruptor pulse battered their hull. Kira clawed her way back to her command chair. She banged open a channel with her fist, ignoring the scream of pain that lanced her scorched hand and forearm. "Duffy! We need weapons!"

"*Trying, Captain!*" Duffy's voice was frayed with static, and Kira heard the background gabble of voices. "*It's all I can do right now to keep your engines and shields online. I can steal power from life support.*"

"Do it!" Kira jerked her head to her helmsman "Initiate evasive maneuvers, best speed, Kira-Three!"

The stars on her viewscreen wheeled as the *Li* rocketed nearly perpendicular to an imaginary horizon in a steep, swirling, spiral climb. In an atmosphere, there would have been the howl of air screaming over a canopy, and anyone on the ground would have seen the assault vessel twirling on its long axis, presenting as little surface area as possible to the enemy. But the *Li* was sluggish; Kira felt it and saw how the stars cartwheeled in a giddy slow motion.

Not fast enough, we can't get up the speed; they'll take us out with the next couple of salvos unless . . . "Where's the saucer?"

"She managed to slip in between that lead *Keldon* and the *Gettysburg*, but she's angling off and dropping back, Captain. She's got a hull rupture somewhere. I read vented atmosphere and debris."

"What's her speed?"

"One-half impulse . . . now one-quarter. Slewing back our way . . . they must have lost control, Captain. She's a sitting duck!"

Kira's heart banged against her ribs. "Is the *Hideki* still in pursuit of the saucer?"

"Negative, breaking away. Turning now. Captain, they're coming after us."

A surge of elation roared through her veins, and her mouth filled with the metallic edge of adrenaline. *That's right, there are bigger fish to fry than that old, banged-up saucer, so come on!* "What about the *Gettysburg*?" Kira's voice was suddenly thinning to a wheeze. The air on the bridge was getting thick and tasted of oily soot, and wasn't going to get any better if Duffy had rerouted power for environmental controls to the engines. Her eyes began to burn. "Where is she? Is she in position?"

"Estimate seven minutes, fifty-seven seconds." Her tactical officer armed blood and sweat from his eyes. The air was thick enough that his eyes were streaming. "That second warship's come about, right on the *Gettysburg*'s tail, accelerating." Looking at the console, he added, "Incoming message, Captain— it's the *Gettysburg*!"

"On speaker." The bridge was suddenly awash in the electric sizzle of interference, a sound like butter sputtering on a hot grill. Kira strained to catch what Gold was shouting, then decided there wasn't time to worry about it. She hailed engineering. "Duffy?"

Duffy's voice was clogged, and he was hacking. "*Sorry, Captain, but you've got a choice. It's either speed or more shields.*"

"I need weapons."

"*No can do.*"

This is it. We knew it would come to this, now I've just got to trust that— "Then give me speed, Duffy. Give me all you've got." She clicked off. "Helm, come about. Course zero-nine-zero, mark four-five, z minus thirty." Her helmsman's back stiffened, and he half-turned. "You heard me," she snapped. "Bring us about."

Her helmsman's throat moved in a hard swallow. "Aye, Captain. Course laid in."

"Engage."

"Lower your shields!" Gold bellowed in frustration. "Kira, do you hear me, lower—"

"She's coming about, Captain," McAllan said. "The *Li*'s jumped to full impulse—ramming speed. Their shields are at twenty percent; they're dodging, taking evasive maneuvers—she's going to hit them broadside in fourteen point eight seconds."

"Can we help her?"

"Negative, sir, not unless we come about, and the other *Keldon*'s too close, they'll take us out for sure."

"Kira!" Gold whirled on his heel. "Haznedl, get me Salek."

"You've got him, sir."

"Salek, now, jettison escape pods!"

"*Acknowledged, Captain.*" Even in the heat of battle, the Vulcan's voice was a study of calm certitude. "*Pods jettisoned. The* Templar *is away.*"

"Haznedl, can you raise the *Li*?"

"Still trying, Captain and—got her, sir."

"Kira!" Gold roared. "*Now,* for the love of God, *now!*"

*   *   *

"Captain!" Kira's tactical officer whipped around in his chair. "The saucer's jettisoned escape pods, and their shields are down. Time to impact *Keldon* warship—nine seconds."

"What about the *Templar*?"

"She's away. No pursuit."

Because she's not worth worrying about, is she? Oh boy, have you bastards got another thing coming. "Give me visual." Kira saw the tiny speck that was the *Templar* accelerating out of the Denorios Belt; the *Gettysburg*'s escape pods tumbling wildly through space, like a child's building blocks knocked askew; the pods dispersing in a wide arc the way waves expand after a rock's ruptured the surface of water. And then the screen shimmered and there was the sickly brown hull of a *Keldon* warship rushing to meet them. "Drop shields!"

"Captain," her tactical officer shouted, "the *Keldon*'s firing."

Kira winced at a sudden flash; the *Li*'s bridge exploded in white-hot light; there was the flicker of a sensation more than the image of a fireball and then there was a swirl as the bridge dissolved, disintegrated before Kira's eyes. . . .

And went black.

McAllan cried, "She's going to *hit!*"

"Salek," Gold said, feeling the cords of his forearms knot and bulge as his hands fisted, "do it now."

And then time slowed and stretched like a broad elastic ribbon, and Gold saw it all, felt everything: the bite of his nails into his palms; the stutter of his heart as the *Keldon* spewed a salvo of glittering green death; and then there was the *Li* dodging, evading, weaving—and then the *Gettysburg*'s pods erupting one right after the other in rapid-fire sequence as the explosives packed inside detonated. The detonations pillowed, balled, grew, fed on themselves and the hot plasma streamers swirling around the *Keldon* and *Hideki*. Hit from behind, the *Hideki* lost control, tumbling end over end, and then Gold saw that the *Keldon* had one final choice: kill the *Li*, or blow the much-larger *Hideki* out of space. The warship chose the *Hideki* . . .

. And then time snapped back; the world sped up; and to Gold's horror, as the *Keldon* touched off its disruptors, the *Li* hit.

"Status." The skin of Zotat's face was a deep jade with rage. "Are they—?"

"Destroyed." Zotat's tactical officer was ashen. "The *Keldon* and its escort, and the Bajoran. The enemy saucer is moving off to flank its mother ship, but they must be damaged, sir. Their shields went down."

"Do they have shields now?"

"Yes, sir. But we have superior weapons and are more maneuverable. Shall we finish them?"

"No," said Zotat. His hands twitched with the urge to break something, and then, remembering his orders, he sucked in a deep breath. "They won't go far. Have you extrapolated a course for the *Gettysburg*?"

"Yes, sir—into the densest part of the Belt, a concentration of superheated plasma and tachyon eddies."

"How long?"

"Estimate they will arrive in one minute, twenty-two seconds."

"Do they have weapons?"

"Reading full weapons capabilities."

"And yet they haven't used them." Zotat's eyes slitted. "And I think I know why. Helm, close on the *Gettysburg*. Tactical, you will fire at my command."

"Yes, sir," said the tactical officer. "Disruptors at half power as per Gul Garak's instructions. You wish for me to disable the engines?"

Zotat spun on his heel. "Did I *order* disruptors at half?"

"Well, no." The tactical officer looked perplexed. "No, sir, but Gul Garak—"

"Gul Garak is not here. Gul Garak has not witnessed two of his ships being blown to bits. *I* am captain here and I will tell you *what* to do and *when* to do it. Understood?"

The bridge was very still. The tactical officer's eyes rolled left and right and then settled on a spot just above Zotat's head. "Of course, sir. Perfectly."

"I am so glad. Now," said Zotat. Turning, he pointed a finger that trembled with rage. "Run . . . him . . . *down*."

"Can you raise Salek?"

"Sorry, Captain." Haznedl shook her head. "With all that debris and radiation, I can't pierce the interference."

"What about the *Templar*?"

Haznedl said, "If she got away, sir, I can't tell. Commander Salek's off to port, standing by and—"

"Cardassian warship accelerating, Captain," McAllan broke in. "Disruptor cannon at full power. They're opening fire."

"Shields at maximum," Gold said with a snarl. "Target their engines, return fire. Wong, see if you—"

The battery of disruptor cannon bammed against the hull plating of the drive section. Gold staggered as the ship lurched, and the air filled with a loud, metallic squall. "Wong!"

"Sorry, sir." Wong had been thrown from his chair. He clawed his way back. His forehead was crimson, and he raised a shaking hand to swipe blood from his eyes. "I've lost port maneuvering thrusters. Trying to compensate now."

"Stay on course. McAllan, damage report."

"Shields down to seventy percent. Phasers still online and—oh my God."

"What?"

McAllan sagged. "The photon torpedoes, the launch assist generators, they're offline."

Gold fisted open a channel to engineering. "Gomez, I need those torpedoes."

"*I'm sorry, sir, I can't. Not without robbing power from the shields.*"

Then that's it. We've run out of options. "Forget the torpedoes. Charge up the deflector."

"Aye, sir."

"But, Captain," said McAllan, "what's the good of the deflector if we can't detonate our torpedoes?"

"You let me worry about that," Gold snapped. "Now hold those bastards off with phasers; just hold them off a few more seconds." The lights dimmed as phasers discharged, and Gold watched the blasts sting the *Keldon* warship at its nose. He didn't need McAllan to tell him the phasers had done little damage. Gold crowded in behind Wong. "How much longer?"

"One minute." Wong gulped and then Gold got a good look and saw that Wong had clapped a hand to his forehead to try and stanch the blood that leaked through his splayed fingers. "One min . . . one . . ." Wong's eyes rolled up in his head, and then he went limp.

Gold snagged the unconscious helmsman as he slid left, and lowered him to the deck. "Haznedl," said Gold, taking up Wong's position at the helm, "see if you can raise Salek. Tell hi—" He lurched forward as the next disruptor battery scored a hit aft, and his forehead cracked Wong's console. Gold blacked out for a second and then came to, his vision blurred with a shower of white lights scintillating at the margins. But he could see well enough—and all the feeling drained out of his body like water rushing through a sieve.

Because their impulse engines were gone.

"They're dead in the water," said Robin Rusconi. She staffed the helm where Wong usually sat and now she looked back at the command chair. "That last disruptor salvo took out the impulse engines. They haven't got torpedoes either."

"We have to do something," said Kira, who stood to Salek's left. She was still having trouble catching her breath and her eyebrows and eyelashes were singed off, but she'd bullied her way out of sickbay after Salek had beamed her crew aboard. "They're still too far away. If they discharge the deflector now, the concentration of particles won't be enough to open the wormhole without the torpedoes."

"I am aware of the situation and the logistics involved," said Salek, and his reply was so maddeningly calm, Kira wanted to scratch out his eyes. "Lieutenant Shabalala, can you raise the captain?"

"Negative, sir."

"But we can't just *stand* here." This from Duffy, his voice full of anguish. He stood off Kira's left shoulder. "Can't we draw that *Keldon*'s fire?"

"We must maintain this distance, Commander. Else all this will have been for naught." Salek's black gaze dropped to Kira, and she felt the sting of tears prick her eyelids. "And you know that I will do what must be done, when the time is right."

"Message coming in, sir," Shabalala said, and then he gasped. "It's the captain, it's . . ." His voice trailed off.

"Lieutenant?"

"Automatic distress, sir." Shabalala's forehead wrinkled in a deep frown. "He's activated the automatic distress beacon."

"Very well." Salek nodded. "Transporter room. Chief Feliciano, stand ready. Helm, plot a reverse course to take us out of the belt, full impulse."

"Reverse course?" Rusconi gaped. "But that's a distress signal, sir, the captain—"

"No, Ensign," said Salek. "It is only a signal. Carry out my orders."

A second passed, then another. Then Rusconi said, "Sir, the captain's lowered his shields and . . . Sir, they're activating *warp engines*."

"Lower shields," Salek said. "Mr. Feliciano, activate transporters. Helm, hard about, go to full impulse."

"Sir!" McAllan's eyes bulged. "The shields! Captain, what are you *doing*?"

Gomez, on speaker: *"No, Captain, you can't!"*

"But I can," said Gold, and he was amazed at how calm he was, now that the moment was upon him. He heard the high-pitched whine, looked toward tactical, saw McAllan's face break apart in the transporter beam. Knew without looking that the same thing was happening to Wong, to Gomez, to Haznedl, to the remainder of his skeleton crew left aboard.

"Because it's my choice," said Gold to an empty ship. "And I've chosen for *you*."

"No," someone said. Duffy didn't know who, didn't care because his gaze was riveted to the main viewscreen: to the *Keldon* warship still so intent on its prize that its captain likely wouldn't realize what was happening until it was far too late as, indeed, it already was—and to the fiery, brilliant whorls of plasma and gas so dense they obscured the stars that were, even now, dimming as the *Gettysburg*'s saucer sped away, in the opposite direction, running for and toward its life.

Then he felt someone at his elbow and knew who it was before he turned because she brought with her the scent he associated with love and all that was best in his life. He pressed Gomez to his side, unable to speak or tear his eyes away.

"Oh, God," she said, her voice watery. "Oh, God."

As if from a dream, Duffy heard Shabalala's voice, far away. "Commander Salek, sickbay reports the Bynars—they're not aboard. They didn't report when the saucer—they didn't get off, they're—" He broke off.

No one spoke. There was nothing more to say.

As much as he didn't want to look, Duffy made the choice to look because he knew this was a moment he must remember for the rest of his life.

Because memory is life, and I choose life.

The Belt truly was beautiful in all its lethal, glorious power. But what took his breath away was not the sight of the *Keldon* warship caught like a helpless, thrashing fly in the web of the *Gettysburg*'s expanding warp bubble, or the luminous deflector beam spearing through space into a whirlpool of colors brighter than the heart of a molten sun.

No. What captured Duffy and held him tight was the *Gettysburg*, hurtling toward destiny and pulling a rainbow behind: an arrow flying true for a fiery heart.

*   *   *

Time nearly stopped. As it should, the dilation effect of the warp bubble combining with all that gas, debris, and plasma. One part of Gold's objective mind knew that he had, at most, thirty seconds before the autodestruct blew the *Gettysburg* apart. But it was enough, and so he watched as the deflector poured its energy, its life into the belt. . . .

And the light at its center: white as bone and as pure as revelation.

Gold heard the lift doors sigh and before he could register what that meant 111's voice came from his left: "We are here."

"Oh, no," said Gold. He'd prepared himself for this moment, knowing it might come, believing that his life alone was forfeit because he' had chosen for Kira and her people, and for his crew. But now . . . "What are you doing?" Then he saw what wasn't there. "Where's your combadge? Why?"

"Captain," said 111. She laid her hand on his, and her fingers were cool. "We are telepaths—"

"—or had you forgotten?" 110, to his right. "It is better—"

"—that one not die alone," said 111. "We are here."

"And so is she; she is—"

"—here," said 111, and she pressed her hand to his heart. "Where she has always been."

"Because where there is memory—"

"—there is life," said 111.

The pain and joy in his heart were so intense it was as if he'd been touched by an angel. "Rachel," said Gold—and now he turned his face to the light. "*Rachel . . .*"

There was a flare of white light. A starburst of color.

But, most of all, there was light.

CHAPTER
11

"How do you feel?"

"Badly," said Soloman. They sat in Gold's ready room; the *da Vinci* had appeared as soon as Gomez powered down the deflectors—and their counterparts had deactivated their device. What they had encountered was, in Gold's words, "a whole other story." Soloman had been checked out by Dr. Tarses on DS9 and pronounced fit. "I chose very poorly."

"Yes, you did. And in the end, Commander Gomez chose *for* you."

"Yes. And because of her and Nog, DS9, and Bajor are safe."

"No, they didn't do it on their own. Nog and Gomez gave them information. Then they had a choice: trust us and shut down the device, or go it on their own even knowing they'd destroy us. They chose life for us, and for you. Let's hope they chose the same for themselves." Gold eyed him closely. "You have something else you want to say?"

"Yes." Soloman felt an uncharacteristic rush of heat up his neck and into his face. He forced himself not to look away. "I lied. I have never lied, and for that I am truly sorry. You would be within your rights to transfer me off your vessel, or insist upon my return to Bynaus."

"Yes, I would." Gold frowned. "Don't think I haven't considered it. But you're far more valuable to me, and yourself, if you stay. On one condition, however: You go to counseling either on a starbase, say for a few months, or perhaps with me, or Dr. Lense, since you seem comfortable with her. We'll have to ask her if she feels the same when she comes back. Anyway—" Gold's face softened. "—we have time."

"Yes," said Soloman. "There is that."

Kira saw Sonya Gomez well before Gomez spotted her. Gomez was standing in profile, looking out at the stars and the wormhole winking into view with its myriad rainbow colors. Then Kira noticed that Gomez had chosen to watch from just outside the chapel where they'd kept the Orb of Prophecy and Change before that Orb had been returned to take its rightful place on Bajor with all the others. *Some irony there, probably.* Kira had read Gomez's report and talked with Captain Gold. So she knew about Kieran Duffy: a hard thing to have someone about whom you cared so much be close enough to touch—and lose him again.

Like seeing that mirror universe version of Bareil after my Bareil died in my arms. Like Odo . . . I know what this is like.

"Captain," said Gomez, reflexively coming to attention, then relaxing as Kira waved her down. "I was just watching the wormhole before we ship out. We need to get back to Earth, return Caitano's and Deverick's bodies to their families. I just wanted a moment, and this—this a good place."

"Yes, it is," said Kira. "Sometimes I take it for granted. Then I think back to the time all the Orbs went dark and it went away, and then I remember to be thankful." She hesitated, then said, "I read your report. I talked to Captain Gold."

Gomez nodded. She returned her gaze to the wormhole and the stars beyond. "Weird to think about that other universe. Somewhere, out there, people I've cared about are alive."

Gomez looked at her. "Do you ever wish you could go back? Do things over?"

"You mean, do I wish I'd never let the genie out of the box, never released the Ohalu book, never joined the Resistance?" *Never fallen in love with a man I may never see again?* "No. I think it's normal to wish you could redo the past. But then it wouldn't be *my* past. I'm afraid I don't have enough imagination to consider choices I'd never have made in the first place." Kira paused, then said, "What about you? Do you have regrets?"

Gomez turned, and Kira would remember the look on her face—full of remorse and pain and regret—for a very long while to come.

"All the time," said Gomez. "All the time."

It was time. A clear sky and bright sun splashing gouts of warmth. A good day. One of his finest hours.

Gul Elim Garak stood on a podium, watching as members of the Bajor Assembly and those of his own government finished with the reading of the treaty. (These officials included Legate Rugal, a ruthless politician not above assassinating a Bajoran or two to clear his way. Garak was quite fond of the man, and they both shared a passion for *rokassa* juice— calmed the nerves.) The Assembly members were dressed in finely colored robes, each color reflecting their caste, and Garak could not help but notice that while the religious caste's members were few, their robes were so bright they looked to be of spun gold. He let his eyes roam over the upturned faces of the crowd gathered for the signing, and his satisfaction was reflected in the clear aquamarine of his tunic's living gemstones.

And yet—Garak nibbled on the inside of his right cheek— only one tiny fly in the proverbial ointment. He cast a quick glance at the sky. *No wormhole, and no Zotat, either.* Well, maybe the legends were wrong about the wormhole being visible from Bajor. *But, for there to be no word from Zotat . . .*

Garak's thoughts were interrupted by the Bajoran High

Magistrate as he stood, scroll in one hand, a rose-red lavanian crystal pen in the other. "In the tradition of our people," the Magistrate began, "I call upon any and all who believe that this treaty should not be enacted to speak and bring proof why—"

"*I* will speak." This from the back of the crowd: a woman's voice, proud and strong. "And I bring *proof*."

The High Magistrate was struck dumb as was the remainder of the Assembly. The Cardassians shot quick, questioning glances; Legate Rugal looked murderous. Startled, Garak tried to see who the woman was but could not. Yet she was coming; that much was clear because the sea of Bajorans parted, and then Garak saw a Trill he didn't recognize. She carried a glittering casket in her arms, and as if drawn by a magnet, the religious fell in behind so that as she approached, she pulled a vein of the purest gold in her wake. She ascended the dais, and when she cast her gaze about the ministers and magistrates and legates, they looked away. But when her eyes met his, Garak had a premonition that, for him, there were dark days ahead.

She turned aside and addressed the crowd. "Bajorans, I bring you hope. I bring you back your Prophets, and I bring you proof."

And then she opened the casket, and the crowd cried out because what blazed forth was so white, so strong, so perfect it hurt Garak's eyes. Gasping, he turned aside and then he saw that his tunic had gone as completely and utterly black as a starless night.

Because now . . . there was light.

IDENTITY CRISIS

John J. Ordover

CHAPTER
1

Commander Sonya Guadalupe Gomez was glad her shore leave had come to its inevitable end. It wasn't that she hadn't had a good time on Recreational Station Hidalgo, it was that she had had almost *too* good a time. Her body was sore from dancing and her head a bit achy from imbibing liquids that were definitely not made with synthehol. As she threw her belongings into a small knapsack in preparation for the *da Vinci*'s arrival that afternoon, she glanced over at the bed in her small tourist quarters. She had slept alone the entire time, but not for lack of the opportunity to do otherwise.

She had spent much of her shore leave with Tobias Shelt, a dashing, live-by-his-wits trader who had made showing her a good time his own personal mission over the last several days. Together they had taken in all that Hidalgo had to offer, which wasn't all that much compared to a modern, sophisticated pleasure center. Gomez had chosen Hidalgo over someplace like Risa for two reasons: first, her parents had met on the station a few decades back and kept nagging her to go there, and second, the station had been preserved in pretty much the same condition as it had been when her parents had been there, and it had been quaint and old-fashioned even back then.

That meant food slots rather than replicators, that meant com units on the walls rather than a combadge communications link, that meant entertainment that was live rather than holographic, and most important, it meant a break from the cutting-edge technology Gomez faced every day as an engineer assigned to an S.C.E. ship.

Gomez had met Tobias Shelt her first evening on the station when she was moping over the fact that her original plan called for her to be sharing this vacation with Wayne "Pappy" Omthon. She had intended to spend her next leave with the owner of the freighter *Vulpecula* ever since they spoke shortly before Captain Gold's granddaughter's wedding on Earth. Unfortunately, the *Vulpecula*'s last cargo damaged the ship and Wayne was currently on Lissep engaged in a massive legal and mechanical hassle to get his ship fixed and get the client who did the damage to pay for it.

Of course, she didn't find this out until she had already arrived at Hidalgo and found a harried but very apologetic recorded message from Wayne explaining the problem.

Things looked up immediately when she met Tobias. He was polite, gentlemanly, and not at all insistent on the bedroom being a part of how they spent their time together. An old-fashioned guy to go with an old-fashioned station. He was attractive, interesting, made her laugh, and was clearly waiting for some sign from her before he took the relationship further than dinner and dancing. *Why,* Sonya thought, *didn't I give him that sign, or just drag him back to my cabin? Ten years ago I would have. Even five. Even two.*

Her packing done, Gomez double-checked around the cabin to make certain she hadn't left anything behind, wondering while she did so if all the grieving and growing she had done since the death of Kieran Duffy had forced her to leave so much of herself behind that she wasn't even the same person anymore. She'd been having those thoughts ever since their odd adventure with parallel universes on Deep Space 9 and she briefly encountered an alternate Kieran.

It made it damn near impossible to know what to do with poor Tobias.

A loud chirping suddenly sounded, breaking her reverie and doing nothing to reduce the ache in her head. Gomez recognized the archaic beep as the sound of the wall-mounted communicator. She walked over to it and flipped the ON switch. The burst of static that came out turned the minor throbbing in her temples into a full-blown headache.

The static died down for a moment and a soft, officious voice confirmed her identity, then asked if she would hold on for a moment. Static filled the room again, making Gomez wonder if she had time before the *da Vinci* arrived to stop by the medical suite for a headache cure.

"Commander Gomez," a strong, feminine voice said, *"I'm Director Jerifer of Recreation Station Hidalgo."* There was no static, but a sudden silence spoke to Gomez of a communications malfunction. Then there was static again, and then Jerifer was back on, her words barely audible. *"The station has been experiencing a series of unexplained malfunctions, including in communications."*

Gomez flipped the return switch. "I hadn't noticed," she said. The communicator went dead again. She waited, and Jerifer's voice came back on. *"Could you come up to control and take a look at our communications array? You're S.C.E., right?"*

Gomez sighed. The *da Vinci* was due to pick her up in a few hours anyway, so getting back into harness a little ahead of time wasn't all that much of a problem, and she would rather work than think right now anyway. "Sure!" she said loudly, hoping Jerifer could hear her.

"What?" Jerifer said.

"Sure!" Gomez repeated loudly. "I'll bring my kit."

"Thank y. . . ." Jerifer's voice began, but was drowned out by static. Gomez turned the communicator off and headed for the door, her knapsack on her shoulder. She punched the antique door switch, and the door opened—then, as she tried to walk through it, closed again. Another push of the switch, the door opened and closed very quickly, then opened partway, then closed, then finally opened and stayed that way.

Well, isn't this lovely, Gomez thought. Her head pounded.

*   *   *

It took longer than Gomez had anticipated to reach the control room. The trip there had been more than a little stressful on a couple of levels. The lighting in the corridors had kept switching between blinding brightness and total darkness, turning the corridors into surreal strobe-lit tunnels that made it more than a little difficult to find the turbolift; and when Gomez had finally found it, the voice commands were nonfunctional, as was the wall communicator. She had been about to step out and ask someone where the control room was when Tobias Shelt stepped in.

"Hi," he said to her, and flashed her a wide happy smile. "I was just looking for you. Today's your last day, right?" Gomez saw his face fall as he picked up that she had her knapsack with her. "Sonya," he said in a sad, scolding tone, "you weren't leaving without saying good-bye?"

Gomez had hoped to do just that. Better, she had thought, to just sneak away.

"Uh, no," Gomez said, sounding unconvincing even to herself, "I'm headed to the control room; they asked me to take a look at what's causing the malfunctions."

"Place is just old," Shelt said. "Nothing a few upgrades can't take care of."

"I hope you're right." Gomez smiled up at him without meaning to. "But for now, I can't even get there. I don't know what level it's on, and the lift has gone deaf. Won't take voice commands." She kicked the side of the lift a little harder than she had intended to.

"*Please choose a destination,*" the elevator said suddenly.

"Control Center," Shelt said quickly, and the turbolift started upward, although its motion was far from smooth. "That was easy," he said. "If the rest of the problem is that simple, you'll still have time for a farewell breakfast."

"These things are rarely as simple as they seem on the surface," Gomez said, hoping that this wasn't the one time they were. With any luck a few complications would eat up the rest of the time before the *da Vinci* arrived and she'd be able to make the clean getaway she'd planned in the first place.

"Well, look," Shelt said reasonably, "if there's time, there's time. If not, we had fun, didn't we?"

"Uh, yes, we did," Gomez said. Shelt tilted his head like he was expecting a good-bye kiss, but at that moment, the turbolift stopped, the door opened, and there were five or six people in the corridor outside.

"If you have time," he said to her as she stepped out. "I'll be around. . . ."

"Right," Gomez said over her shoulder. There was an actual physical sign on the wall outside the turbolift door with an arrow that pointed the way to the control center. Some old-fashioned things were extremely practical. By the time she reached the control center, the strobing in the corridors had slacked off to a slight flickering that still pulled painfully at the corners of her eyes.

CHAPTER
2

The control center door was heavy and thick, Gomez noted as it slid open. The precautionary radiation shielding was as out of date as the rest of the station, ten times as bulky as modern photoclastic materials. The rest of the center was of the same period. Gomez hadn't seen a room like this anywhere outside of images in her history of engineering class. It was overstuffed with consoles whose lights, switches, buttons, and dials played an electronic symphony of unfamiliar clicks, buzzes, and pops. *The place doesn't lack for spit and polish,* Gomez thought. *The systems are old but I'd bet they're in great shape.*

Above the consoles were old flat-panel displays, although the status readouts they showed were in modern style. The thing Gomez found the strangest—and the most old-fashioned—was that the visual readouts were above her head rather than being in essentially the same location on a unitary touch-screen interface. The control center also contained three Hidalgo Station engineers, who were, it seemed, frantically tracking down and resolving all the malfunctions as quickly as possible.

"Hey, guys," Gomez said. "Any idea what's causing this?"

"Haven't had . . ." one of them said, as he threw switches that clicked and checked dials that whirred.

"A chance . . ." another picked up, sliding a squeaking chair back and forth between a console on one side of the room and a console on the other, spinning around as he went.

"To look into it." The third one finished as he slid down to the floor and began pulling open a creaking access panel.

"It's all we can do . . ." It was back to the first one, who was now on the other side of the room.

"To stay ahead . . ." the second, from under a control panel.

"Of the breakdowns." The third, now on his feet, reading quickly through a readout screen.

"Make sure . . ."

"No one . . ."

"Runs out of air . . ."

"Or anything else bad. . . ."

"Happens."

Gomez nodded, following the rapid interchange easily enough and pleased that it seemed the team here knew what they were doing. It was just that they were shorthanded in this crisis. *Fair enough.* "Okay, you guys keep doing what you're doing, I'll start looking for the top-level problem."

The three of them acknowledged her plan with nods as they continued to rush around the room responding to various lights and alarms.

Gomez sat down at the only free console and took a deep breath. As she familiarized herself with the system she noted that there were sections that were slightly more modern than the rest of the setup. They were still decades old, but looked recently installed. There were things Gomez had to know, so she grabbed the sliding chair before the engineer could slide away and spun him to face her. "Anything new go in before this all happened?"

"A couple of weeks ago we put in a new interswitcher, a new power gauge, and a new memory unit." The engineer rolled his eyes. "The crap was no more than twenty years old, untested, unreliable, and buggy. What could we do? They don't make the good stuff anymore. Bet that's where the problem is."

As she released him to continue his frantic tour around the room, Gomez smiled at the notion of twenty-year-old equipment being called new. She understood, though, what he was getting at. If safety and unbroken functionality was your primary goal, then a tried-and-true system was often better than a new one, because over the years, all the bugs got worked out, all the patches on the patches on the patches got integrated, and the system was finally made near one-hundred-percent reliable. Problem was that usually happened long after new, improved systems came online, and you wound up back at where you started ironing out problems. *Just as well that's how it works,* Gomez thought. *It keeps us engineers in business.*

The room suddenly got quiet, almost ominously so. The alarm beeps and squawks faded out. The lighting in the room was stable. Gomez scanned the status lights, which were carefully labeled by hand as to whether they reported on shields, life-support, or other station systems. They were all showing green.

"Looks like you got it," she said to the three.

"Won't last," One of them said.

"It's not stable," another said.

"You have any idea what's causing it yet?" the last one asked.

"Come on, guys." Gomez's eyes ran over the switches again. "Give me a minute or two." She stood up and checked the more familiar readouts on the overhead display. There were fluctuations in several major systems, too many to be accounted for by random malfunctions. Sabotage? Gomez couldn't imagine that anyone would think of Hidalgo as worth the effort. So it had to be something higher, something at a control level. . . .

"Maybe it's a synchronistic leveling problem?" one of the station engineers said.

"Or a failed N-space conformation in the hyperbridges?"

"No, more likely a bug in the negotiation buffers . . ."

"A pattern breakdown in the—"

"Stop!" Gomez heard herself say, then instantly regretted it. These weren't Starfleet engineers under her command, they were civilians who most likely knew this equipment better than she did. But with this headache she wasn't going to be able to work this problem while trapped in a hailstorm of out-of-date techspeak.

The engineers stopped talking and looked quizzically at her. They also looked a bit disappointed. *Oh, God,* Gomez thought, *they saw this as their chance to show off for an S.C.E. officer and I just slammed them. Great.* "Look," she said, "I'm sorry, it's just that I couldn't hear myself think. It's going to take all of us to solve this, and you know this stuff much better than I do."

"So," one of them began, the oldest of them, and the other two stayed silent, quietly accepting him as spokesman, "what do you want us to do?"

Gomez thought about it for a minute. There had to be something that sounded good but got them out of her hair. She pulled up the specs on the station routing conduits. "I think we need hands-on inspections of the data interfaces at these three nodes." She pointed on the display. "I think they might be futzing out on us and causing feedback throughout the system."

The oldest of the engineers—still a young man from Gomez's point of view—looked thoughtfully at the station schematic. "That . . ." he began, and Gomez held her breath, worried he'd seen through the make-work she'd just given his team, ". . . just might be it." He turned to the two younger men and nodded. "Okay, guys, let's split 'em up north, south, and east." He turned to Gomez. "We'll call in when we get there, call in again when we have status for you. That work?"

Gomez nodded, still uncertain whether he'd seen through what she was doing and was just playing along, or if she had randomly put her finger on something that might actually impact the problem. In any case, she would have a chance to work in peace. "Thank you," she called after them as they opened the large blast door, left the control center, and closed the door behind them.

That left Gomez alone in the relative quiet with only the faint buzzing of the equipment filling the room, and that gave her a chance to think. They'd said that they just put in a new—relatively new—interswitcher, a new power gauge, and a new—*what was it?*—memory unit. Newly added equipment was always the first place to look for a malfunction—that was Engineering 101 stuff. *So think this through.* An interswitcher was just a glorified dimmer switch—it couldn't cause this much trouble. Nor could a power gauge, especially one that was right in front of her and clearly working perfectly. *So first things first, check out the memory unit.*

A quick diagnostic showed the memory unit filled to capacity. *That's odd,* Gomez thought, *this station doesn't have enough data traffic to fill up any memory unit, even one this old-fashioned.* She checked the specs on the unit. It was a fourth-generation version of the ones now in general use throughout the galaxy, although those were on their fiftieth or sixtieth generation by now. Still, it should have had plenty of storage.

So, Gomez thought, *let's see what's filling it up.* A second-level diagnostic pulled up a repeated pattern, and Gomez downloaded one unit of the pattern and then uploaded it to the overhead display screen.

To her surprise it was pure text that read:

To Whomever This Reaches:

I, and my planet, are in desperate need of your help. I am the Finance Minister for Sigma V, a small world in Sector 861, on the far edge of the galaxy. The peaceful, freedom-loving, and democratic republic for which I work is under siege by a horrible military power who will bring ruin upon us and upon any other planet that falls within their reach.

As Finance Minister, I am in a position to access the wealth of our entire planet. I am contacting you in hopes of gaining your assistance in moving this gigantic sum, an amount equal to almost five billion bars of gold-pressed latinum, off our world before it falls into the control of the opposing forces, who will use it to oppress my people and to export their terror to the rest of the galaxy.

I realize the difficulty of what I am about to ask, but I am desperate. I need access to any and all latinum accounts you may have, so I can transfer my world's funds there. I recognize that there may be substantial risk to your person involved, so in recompense I am offering to pay you ten percent of the entire planetary wealth of Sigma V, which amounts to just under five-hundred-million bars of gold-pressed latinum.

Before you accept this offer, please think over the risk carefully. If you have the courage to accept, simply reply to this communication with all your latinum account information and wait for the funds to be transferred to you. I will arrange to recover the bulk of the monies that rightly belong to the people of Sigma V at a later time. Any interest that accrues over that time will belong to you as well.

Please, help me and my people.

Ardack Sprachnee, Finance Minister, Sigma V.

Gomez laughed when she read it. In form and function it was clearly a piece of tribblecom, a letter sent out with the intent of reaching the maximum number of communication links in the hope that someone somewhere would be foolish enough to fall for the obvious scam. The letter contained subprogramming that enabled it to eat up as much memory space as the target system had, reproduce itself to the extent of the "food supply," and then broadcast itself to every connected user on the system—as well as to every communications address the system contained. Uncontrolled, a tribblecom could clog up an entire computer system—which was what seemed to be happening here.

Gomez ran a few tests to confirm her theory, and was relieved to see her first thought was right—the recently installed memory unit was just advanced enough to be accessible to a modern tribblecom, but not advanced enough to have built-in safeguards against them.

A few buttons punched brought up the hidden subcode behind the letter, and it was the work of only a few moments for Gomez to decide which of a dozen glommer programs would be most effective. Named for a tribble predator the Klingons had genetically engineered way back when, a properly targeted glommer would turn the tables on the tribblecom, tracking it to wherever in the system it tried to hide, devouring it, and leaving behind clear and usable memory.

By the time the three station engineers called in with their status data, Gomez had a working glommer written—it had been a little tricky, the tribblecom was a little different from others she'd dealt with. She told the three of them she'd found the problem and to come on back. It took a few runs through a compression compiler to get the glommer to run on a memory system this old and so cramped for space, but it was working. Gomez got up and recovered her knapsack from where she'd dropped it on the floor. As the tribblecom was wiped from memory, she could see system lights going from red to amber to green as station control came fully back online.

That's that then, Gomez thought, and headed for the door and pushed the open switch. The door, she was glad to see, swung open quickly and smoothly. She was about to step through and head for the departure lounge when the communications system beeped behind her, and her headache, which had been forgotten in the heat of problem-solving concentration, came back in full force. With a sigh she stepped back into the room and answered it.

"May I ask with whom I am speaking?" a mechanical sounding voice said.

"Commander Sonya Gomez," she replied. "S.C.E. What can I do for you?"

"Could you hold a moment, please?" the voice said, and Gomez waited, patiently at first, them impatiently. When it seemed there was no one there, Gomez cut the connection and headed out again. At that moment the door to the control center slid smoothly and firmly shut, with an ominous sense of finality. Gomez hit the open switch again but nothing happened.

Gomez sighed. Maybe she hadn't cleared the system after all. She went back to the board, but found it nonresponsive. As far as the computer was concerned, she might not have been pushing the buttons at all. She tried to resolve it on her own for a few moments, then bit the bullet and flipped the communications switch back on. *I'm not above asking for help when I need it,* Gomez thought, *but it'd be embarrassing to have to ask the guys I threw out of here to come to my rescue.*

The communications switch was dead.

No reason to panic, Gomez thought. *They'll realize their control center is cut off pretty quickly, and someone will come get me out of here.* One of the overhead display screens popped into life just as she was moving toward the communications console. Gomez turned to look up at what she expected to be the face of the oldest of the three engineers, or that of Director Jerifer. Instead, the face of Captain Gold stared out at her. And he was not at all happy.

"Gomez," he said, his slightly careworn face showing a combination of anger, concern, and curiosity, *"what the hell do you think you're doing?"*

Gomez was taken aback. Yes, it seemed she hadn't fixed the computer problems on Hidalgo Station as quickly and easily as she had hoped, but the captain's reaction was way out of proportion to the situation. She wasn't even late getting back to the *da Vinci,* although she might be if it took more than a few hours to get out of the control center.

"Well, sir," Gomez started, but Gold continued.

"That's crazy talk. You're putting the lives of hundreds of people at risk." Gold's voice softened. *"Gomez, is something wrong? You've never expressed a single political thought in all the time you've been on the* da Vinci—*and now this?"*

"Sir," Gomez began again, "in my defense, and with all due respect, what in God's name are you talking about?"

Gold sighed and paused, but not as if he'd heard her. To Gomez it looked as if he was listening to someone offscreen. Then he continued.

"Gomez, it's very hard for this old man to hear you speak like that. For your sake, I hope it turns out you're under some kind of mind control, or possessed by an alien life form, or some other equally valid excuse. For now, all I can do is ask you to restore the station's life support to full strength. Please, those are real people you're dealing with, not abstract political concepts."

There was another pause. Gomez quickly checked the readouts—station life support had been cut to ninety percent.

"Agreed, then." The sadness in Gold's voice was palpable.

"I'll make sure Starfleet and the Federation take your demands seriously. We'll speak again in two hours."

"Sir!" Gomez shouted. "Don't—" But then he was gone. She tried the door switch again, tried the communications switch four or five times, and ended by slamming her fist down on the computer console. Something bad was happening, and she was obviously involved, and she was very, very interested in finding out what the hell was going on.

CHAPTER
3

On the bridge of the *da Vinci*, Captain David Gold sat with his back straight despite his exhaustion, wondering what the hell was going on. He asked Ensign Haznedl at ops to replay the conversation he'd just had with Gomez, beginning with the sector-wide onscreen announcement that Gomez had made.

"Attention Federation government," Gomez had said, reading from a padd she held up in front of her, *"this is Commander Sonya Gomez, formerly of Starfleet. I can no longer sit by and let the Federation continue to compromise its ideals and its principles by holding thousands of people in prison for no crime greater than differing with the Federation on issues of policy.*

"I have been forced to take drastic steps to secure the release of these prisoners of conscience. The computer system of Hidalgo Station is under my control, and I have just reduced the life-support settings by ten percent. I will reduce life support by another ten percent every two hours that the prisoners on the attached list remain incarcerated."

"Gomez," he had said, fighting to keep his voice steady, *"what the hell do you think you're doing?"*

There had been a pause as Gomez's image on the viewscreen looked up at him sadly. *"Captain Gold,"* she had said, *"I'm sorry that you are involved in this. I am only doing what has to be done. Someone has to take a stand."*

"That's crazy talk. You're putting the lives of hundreds of people at risk. Gomez, is something wrong? You've never expressed a single political thought in all the time you've been on the da Vinci—*and now this?"*

Gomez's image looked at him sadly. *"The Federation is drunk with power, Captain. It must be brought to its knees. This is only the first stage of a Federation-wide rebellion that will wrest the reins of power from those who oppress the masses."*

"Gomez," Gold had said, choosing his words very carefully, *"it's very hard for this old man to hear you speak like that. For your sake, I hope it turns out you're under some kind of mind control, or possessed by an alien life-form, or some other equally valid excuse. For now, all I can do is ask you to restore the station's life support to full strength. Please, those are real people you're dealing with, not abstract political concepts."*

"That's something the Federation should have thought of years ago. Two hours, Captain, or I lower the life support. I'll speak with you then. Agreed?"

"Agreed, then," Gold said wearily. *"I'll make sure Starfleet and the Federation take your demands seriously. We'll speak again in two hours."*

This is the last thing we needed, Gold thought. The crew was exhausted, stretched almost beyond endurance by the just-completed mission to Artemis IX. The mission to reverse-engineer million-year-old alien crystal technology had seemed tedious but manageable at first. Yes, the airless environment and high gravity of the planet meant working in bulky, specially modified EVA suits, but at least no one had been shooting at them—until the Androssi showed up to take the technology for themselves.

Gold was already short four people, with Lense at her medical conference, Gomez on leave, and the replacements for Caitano and Deverick not having reported yet. Still, he had had to deploy almost the entire crew, sending Corsi and her remaining security people with phaser rifles to defend the engineers as they worked under fire to evaluate and understand the long-abandoned technology, which had turned out to be pretty nasty and a serious threat to the inhabited planets of the Artemis system.

In the end the job was done, and no lives were lost among his crew—for which Gold was grateful; they had only just returned from Deverick's and Caitano's funerals—but at the moment his people were all but burned out, Gold included. Since they were headed for the Hidalgo Station anyway to pick up Commander Gomez, Gold had secretly scheduled shore leave on the station for as much of the crew as could be spared. Now not only was that out of the question, but Gomez—whose expertise had been sorely missed on Artemis IX, Tev's protestations to the contrary—was at the center of a new, improved crisis.

"Do you think that's possible, sir?"

The voice of Lieutenant Tony Shabalala from the tactical station behind Gold's command chair pulled Gold back to the present.

"What's possible, Shabalala?" Gold asked.

"That Commander Gomez is under mind control, or that she's been possessed by some kind of alien entity?"

"I certainly hope so," Gold said. "It's a strange galaxy. That kind of thing seems to happen a lot—it happened to me about fifteen years back, for that matter."

"Love to hear that story someday, sir."

"Sir," Haznedl said, "I'm getting an urgent communication from Starfleet Command."

"Well, I wonder what they could possibly want?" Gold said to the air in front of him.

The communication from Admiral Pishke had been surprisingly brief, Gold thought, considering the seriousness of the topic. Since Gomez was his officer, and all efforts at reaching anyone trapped on the station by the shields had been blocked by a static field, he was being given point on resolving the situation. In the meantime, Starfleet was reviewing the lengthy list of prisoners Gomez was demanding be released—it turned out there were thousands of them from hundreds of worlds within and without the Federation. The admiral had promised to get back to Gold with the results of the review just under the two-hour deadline.

The question was what to do now. Gold's answer was to do whatever they could with the materials at hand, just like always. It was just barely possible that Gomez had harbored these feelings for days, months, or years and that Duffy's death had pushed her over the edge. Even as Gold thought it, though, he all but dismissed it. For one thing, Duffy's death was a while ago, and she'd shown no sign of cracking. He also didn't believe this was something she would do, even if she *did* break down. As captain, though, he had to check out all options.

Another possibility was that something happened to Gomez when they dealt with that quantum foam mess in the Bajoran system. *But that doesn't track, either—we were* all *exposed to that, and we've had the added stress of Artemis IX on top of that, and none of us are demanding that political prisoners be released.*

Gold spun his chair around to face the aft stations. Soloman, the Bynar computer specialist, was working there by himself, as much of the rest of the crew was on mandatory downtime to recoup after the last week's efforts. The Bynar seemed to feel Gold's eyes on the back of his neck, or perhaps had heard the captain's chair swivel in his direction, because he turned around and looked at the captain with a quizzical expression on his face.

"Soloman," Gold said, "I hate to ask you this, but needs must. Could you break the security profiles on Commander Gomez's personal logs? We need to see just how much of an aberration this is, if there's anything in her personal writings that would have predicted her behavior."

Gold sometimes found the expressions on his Bynar officer's face hard to read, but Soloman did seem a little uncomfortable at being ordered to invade Gomez's privacy. *I'm not happy about it myself,* he thought, *but under the circumstances, I really have no choice.*

"When you pull the logs up," he said to Soloman, "wake up Abramowitz and ask her to go over them."

Carol Abramowitz's official assignment to the S.C.E. was cultural specialist, but she also had the most psychology training of anyone on board, with Lense unavailable. She was the best choice for a quick on-site analysis of whatever was in Gomez's journals—and while Gold could just have them sent to Starfleet for expert analysis, if it turned out that the journals had nothing to do with the situation, which was what Gold thought was most likely, he wanted Gomez's intimate thoughts to be kept as private as possible.

CHAPTER
4

Gomez was flat on her back, legs in the air, her body buried up to its intimate parts in the Hidalgo Station communications console. Working on archaic technology without a manual was just the kind of challenge she normally got a charge out of, but people's lives were at stake and this was no time for the joys of tinkering. Rerouting the com circuitry past the systems block had taken almost the entire two hours before Captain Gold had said he'd call back, but she'd done it—she hoped.

Gomez slid out from under the console, scraping her back painfully on a metal edge as she did so. She stood up too quickly, waited for the dizziness to pass, and then flipped on the communications switch. "Commander Gomez to Director Jerifer," she said. Nothing. The light on the unit that showed its status was green, meaning her voice should be getting out—unless, as sometimes happened, all she'd done was reroute power to the status light. "Commander Gomez to anyone who can hear me," she said again, resisting the temptation to shout into the com unit. There was no reply. She tried again, and the communicator sprang to life.

All she had managed to do was open an incoming channel from the interior communications links, so she could hear the station crew talk about breaking out emergency equipment and ways to break into the computer control center. Meanwhile, Director Jerifer and Tobias Shelt kept trying to reach her. None of that was helping her concentration, so she tried to cut it off—and failed. Instead, it got louder, which didn't help much.

From the reports and from the gauges in the control room, Gomez saw that station shields were on full, preventing anyone from leaving, that the power systems were still fluctuating like they had on her way up to the control room, and that people were starting to feel the negative effects of the truncated life support. Director Jerifer was doing an excellent job keeping the panic down and the engineers she had gotten rid of were jerry-rigging spot bypasses for the power lines and reactivating mothballed air regenerators with S.C.E.-level efficiency. Even so, conditions on the station were getting harsh, if not yet deadly. Gomez noticed she was breathing more quickly in the thinning air and that it was starting to get cold in the control room.

Just as Gomez was regretting not having even one of the station engineers inside with her to help, the overhead display popped into life all by itself. *Aha. Maybe I accidentally rerouted the audio circuits through visual?* As long as she could get a message out, she'd count that as a success. She waited while an image formed on the display. As surprised as she had been to see the image of an angry Captain Gold the last time she'd checked the screen, Gomez was far more surprised to see her own image up there—not as she was, tired, cold, and pissed off, but instead sitting calmly at the communications console.

Then the image of her on the screen began speaking in her voice, not to her, but to Starfleet in general and Captain Gold in particular. It was reminding the captain that his deadline for releasing the political prisoners had run out, and that the tyranny of the state over the common people had to be reversed, and that left her no choice but to reduce station life support another ten percent. Then the display dissolved into a split screen, and Gold's image faded in.

Gomez's blood boiled with frustration as she watched Captain Gold trying to talk "her" out of this rash action that endangered people's lives. Gold went on to ask for more time, which the Gomez simulacrum denied. *How could he really think that's me?* Gomez thought. *I'm nothing like that.* The result of the conversation was that station life support began falling another ten percent, and as the lights dimmed and Gomez felt the control center become colder and the air even thinner. Gomez took a dozen deep breaths, got down on her knees, reached into her kit for the appropriate tool, and began opening the panel under the life-support console. *If Captain Gold thinks I'm the cause of this problem,* Gomez thought, *I'd better keep trying to be part of the solution.*

Captain Gold stared at Hidalgo Station as it grew larger in the window of the observation lounge. His second conversation with Gomez had not gone well, in part because Starfleet Command had not been able to finish analyzing the list of prisoners by the time the two-hour deadline was up. Now Abramowitz had asked to meet with him and Soloman in the observation lounge to discuss what she had learned from reading Gomez's personal logs. She hadn't sounded happy, and as Gold turned to take his seat at the table perpendicular to the cultural specialist and the computer technician, he could see from their faces that they were not the bearers of good news.

"I take it," he said to Soloman, "that you were able to override the security profiles on Gomez's personal logs?"

"Yes," the Bynar answered softly. "And having done so, I stored the logs in a general access file."

"Which I scanned through," Abramowitz put in. "There was a lot of material there, Captain, too much to do more than get a cursory overview in such a short time. But I pulled out a few telling passages. This one is from about three months ago." Gold steeled himself as Abramowitz lifted up a padd and began to read from Gomez's logs. "'I must find a way to force the Federation to realize what it has become, what it is becoming: a nightmarish dystopian state that stifles dissent, imprisons those who love freedom, and builds horrible weapons like the Wildfire device to serve its need to destroy all those who oppose it.'" Abramowitz stopped reading from the padd and looked up at the Captain. "It only gets worse from there."

"The Wildfire device wasn't developed as a weapon," Gold said, "no matter how many lives it cost us in the end."

"Correct, Captain," Soloman said tonelessly, "and Commander Gomez was certainly aware of that."

"So," Carol continued, "this shows her thinking had become distorted and delusional by three months ago at least; perhaps Commander Duffy's death hit her harder than we thought."

"I requested her Starfleet psychological profile," Soloman said, "and it does not show a propensity for this kind of mental instability. I'm at a loss to explain how she came to be in this state."

"Humans are often more complex than our psych reports would indicate," Captain Gold said to the Bynar. "We like to think we know each other, but there are always things that remain buried within us that can erupt unbidden."

"Sir," Abramowitz said, "this means that it's really Commander Gomez doing this. I was hoping—"

"For mind control or alien possession? So was I." Gold took a deep breath and accepted the situation for what it seemed to be. "So we switch tactics." He tapped his combadge. "Gold to Corsi." A half second later the *da Vinci* security chief responded, even though she was under orders to sleep and heal after being wounded in the violent encounter on Artemis IX.

"Yes, Captain?"

"I need you in the observation lounge as soon as you can get here."

"Acknowledged."

Gold turned his attention back to Soloman and Abramowitz. "When Corsi gets here, we'll bring her up to speed. She's trained for negotiating in this kind of situation."

"Yes, sir," Abramowitz said. Her expression told Gold that dealing with one of their own on this level was as hard on her as it was on him.

"Carol," he said softly, "Gomez needs help. She's sick, same as if she'd broken her leg. We'll stop her, get her out, and get her through this."

Abramowitz smiled wanly back.

"Sir," Soloman asked, "I still remain uncertain that we have properly assessed the situation. There is something. . . ." The Bynar trailed off, his speech hesitating almost the way it had when he first became solitary. "I request permission to continue my investigation into Commander Gomez's records over the last three months."

"Granted," Gold said. Over the years, he'd learned never to stand in the way of a subordinate with a hunch.

The door to the lounge slid open and Corsi stepped in, still favoring her left foot. The EMH had patched her up after she was wounded on Artemis IX, but it didn't have quite the deft touch Dr. Lense had.

It hadn't been six minutes since Gold had asked Corsi to join them, and he was certain she'd been sound asleep when he called. Yet here she was, her eyes bright, her uniform pressed, her blond hair pulled back in her usual bun. "You move quickly," Gold said to her.

"Part of the job. So," Corsi said, "someone want to fill me in? Has the commander gone nuts or what?"

Commander Gomez was busy fighting with the life-support controls. The computer was still ignoring her inputs, and the brilliant idea she had come up with to bypass the blocks was taking a lot more effort than she had thought it would going in. Gomez had noted that the readout lights were still providing accurate information, and had to be maintaining a connection to the life-support and communications nodes, so she might be able to piggyback on the connection and send control signals down the same line.

It was cold enough that her hands were getting a bit numb, she was panting in the thin air, and it wasn't helping her concentration to have to listen to Domenica Corsi using what were colloquially called "nutball" negotiating strategies to try to convince the fake Gomez on the screen to give up her insane plan. That sharp-as-a-tack "Core-Breach" Corsi couldn't tell that the Gomez on the screen wasn't her hadn't made sense until the security chief had begun reading passages from what she claimed was Gomez's personal log—things she'd never written.

Whoever did this to me, Gomez thought as she worked one end of the console board out of its slot to get access to the circuit connections underneath, *put a ton of effort into it and is no slouch technically—they've had had to bypass not only Starfleet security protocols, but the extra ones I put on my personal logs.* It wasn't impossible, obviously, since Corsi was able to read out parts from her logs—even if it was nasty things about the Federation that she'd never even thought of writing. But it would take someone with expertise at least as great as Soloman's—and the Bynar knew the Starfleet security protocols going in. Gomez decided she wanted to meet whomever set this thing up, first to congratulate them, then to punch them in the eye.

Who has it in for me that bad? Gomez thought, blinking her eyes against an arc of electricity that burned out what she had hoped would be the last circuit of her brilliant improvisation. *The Androssi? This isn't their style. Those Ferengi we met a while back? No, we helped them. Luaran? She's still in custody, and besides, it'd be Corsi she'd be peeved at.* Gomez sighed. The S.C.E. so rarely dealt with anyone on a personal level that it was hard to think of anyone she had irritated so much that they would go to all this trouble to get back at her. *As far as I know,* she thought as she burned her fingers pulling out the blown circuit, *I haven't killed anyone's brother, mother, sister, father, or even their second cousin. I don't live a perfect life, but I can't think of anyone I've pissed off badly enough to single me out for something like this.*

The wiring finally replaced with ones cannibalized from other consoles, Gomez fed power into the reworked circuitry. It had been difficult, detailed, and intermittently painful work to wire up a device that would backfeed along the readout connection, send control signals back to the life-support nodes and put them under her command. It was brilliant, innovative engineering done in the midst of a high-pressure situation with lives at stake, just what the S.C.E. had built its reputation on. The only problem was that it wasn't working. Gomez sighed. Back to square one.

Soloman sat across from Carol Abramowitz in the observation lounge and reviewed everything the computer had on Gomez. The Bynar found nothing out of the ordinary. The commander, as mentally uncompiled as she had become, had nonetheless managed to stay on top of her duties right up until she left on her ill-fated shore leave. On her most recent mission, the one that took the *da Vinci* to Empok Nor, she had acted with her usual top-notch professionalism—and saved Soloman's life. There was simply nothing in her words or actions to show that her thought processes were getting buggy.

Soloman knew little of human psychology, but pattern recognition of many different kinds was part and parcel of how to deal with computers, and it seemed to him there was no pattern here. Soloman sighed. He was still tired from working desperately to reprogram an ancient defense device before it could disintegrate his crewmates, and he couldn't help but feel that if he were at his best, he would be able to pull together the sprites of insight that kept flittering just out of his reach. Perhaps Abramowitz was making headway, or perhaps she would see something he had failed to perceive.

"Carol," he said, "may I interrupt you?"

The cultural specialist looked up at him from where she had been poring over the list of prisoners that Gomez has requested be released. Her eyes took a second to refocus on him. "Please, interrupt," she said, "I'm getting nowhere with this list. It's not what it claims to be, and that's all I can tell you."

"What do you mean?" the Bynar asked. Anything that was the slightest bit off might be the clue he needed.

"It's not a list of political prisoners. With a few exceptions, it's a list of mass murderers, torturers, rapists—a who's who among the most evil sentients in the galaxy. No culture in the galaxy would call these people oppressed revolutionaries—they're criminals pure and simple, and dangerous, deadly ones at that. Like I told Corsi, there's only a handful of these people it's safe to even think about letting go."

"The list, though," Solomon said, "it was carefully compiled?"

"Clearly," Abramowitz said, "very carefully, and very completely."

The idea flittered by him like a sprite on a computer display. Mentally, he reached out for the controller, took command of the sprite, and brought it back to center screen. He had it.

CHAPTER
5

On the bridge of the *da Vinci*, Corsi was making progress. Whatever had happened to Gomez, whatever psychosis she was suffering from, she wasn't totally devoid of reason or reasonableness. She could be negotiated with, and she had to be, because the list of "political prisoners" she had provided had finally been reviewed by Starfleet and it was a worst-of-the-worst list chosen from throughout the many different intelligent species of the galaxy, all of whom Gomez was insisting were convicted in show trials on the basis of made-up charges.

Abramowitz had gone over the list in detail, though, and had found one exception to the rule. On the planet Sigma V, the list of criminals wasn't quite so bad as on the other planets, in part because, it seemed, Sigma V had far less in the way of crime overall. These were the greatest criminals on the planet, yes, but it was a remarkably law-abiding place and not one of them had been convicted of anything more serious than a drunk-and-disorderly charge. All of them were scheduled to be released within three days anyhow.

"So we have a deal?" Corsi asked the image of Gomez on

the viewscreen. "A show of good faith on both sides. We'll release prisoners from the agreed-on planet, and in return you move the station life-support up ten percent. Agreed?"

"*Agreed,*" Gomez said back. "*I really don't want to hurt anyone; I'll move the life support up five percent when I receive word from my confidential sources that the prisoners have been freed from confinement, another five percent when I have word they've been taken on a Mark 17 hauler-class ship to Bartha IX and released to go their own way.*"

"Not a problem," Corsi said. Hauler-class ships were heavy cargo vessels that also carried a few dozen passengers on each run—they were the workhorses of that area of the galaxy and available in great numbers. All that was left was to contact the government of the planet in question and arrange for the prisoners to be released, a problem for diplomats since the planet was non-Federation, but not one that struck Corsi as complex. "We'll talk again in one hour," Corsi said, "I should have all the details for you then." Gomez agreed to that, too.

In the observation lounge, Gold took Corsi's report as somewhat positive news in a bad situation. "So that's the deal, Captain. Starfleet has made the arrangements, and the prisoners on Sigma V are being prepared for immediate release. Station life support has already gone up five percent, and when we get word the hauler has arrived at Bartha IX, I fully expect the life support to go up another five."

Gold nodded. As hostage situations went, this one seemed to be working out relatively smoothly, and if it weren't for his personal involvement, he would have been much more relaxed and upbeat than he was. Even if they managed to keep everyone on the station alive, and to get Gomez out alive as well, he had lost his first officer. As all captains were, he was prepared to lose those under his command—but not like this, not to a mental collapse no one had seen coming.

"I realize this seems like only a short-term solution, Captain," Corsi said, "but the books all say that if you can get the target to give an inch, you're well on the way to getting the mile."

"Maybe," Gold said, "whatever has driven Gomez to this behavior isn't strong enough to turn her into a mass murderer." *And perhaps she can be helped back to a normal life*, Gold thought, *even if Starfleet would no longer be part of that life.*

·"Let's hope," Corsi said, "but the books also say that nothing is one hundred percent." She was interrupted by the lounge door opening. Soloman and Abramowitz stood in the doorway. The Bynar asked the captain for permission to enter.

"Granted," Gold said. The expressions on their faces spoke of a certain amount of embarrassment, but on the whole they seemed upbeat. "Tell me you two have better news this time."

"We do," Abramowitz said, as Gold motioned her and Soloman to seats near Corsi.

"Good, I could use some. What is it?"

The two of them glanced at each other, and then Soloman began. "We do not believe that the entity you have been conversing with is Commander Gomez."

Gold almost didn't process that. It took Corsi a moment to pick up on it too, which Gold used to ask the heavens above to make this true.

Corsi raised an eyebrow and turned to the Bynar engineer. "Then who have I been negotiating with for the last two hours?"

"We believe it to be a computer simulation of Commander Gomez."

"Oh, that's just great," Corsi said.

Soloman was not in the habit of making statements he couldn't back up, but this was almost too good to be true. Gold said, "That would be one heck of a simulation, and what about Gomez's personal logs?"

"On closer review," Abramowitz said, an apologetic tone to her voice, "we think they are an elaborate fabrication."

"That's hard to believe," Gold said, playing devil's advocate above the table while his fingers were crossed under it. "Personal logs have very tight security, as do Starfleet computer systems. Your revised conclusion is based on what?" Gold asked. "You found something in her records that didn't ring true?"

"No," Soloman said, "It's what we didn't find." Before Gold

could ask, the Bynar began to explain. "Carol," Soloman indicated the woman to his left, "reviewed in detail Starfleet's report on the prisoners whom 'Commander Gomez' was demanding be released, to aid Commander Corsi and give her some insight into Commander Gomez's current psychological state."

Abramowitz cut in, their back-and-forth reminding Gold of when Soloman had been part of a Bynar pair. "The choices were entirely consistent with the extremist positions that had been expressed in the commander's logs, so I thought nothing of them beyond their obvious insanity. Soloman, however, focused on the extent and complexity of the list. There are thousands of names on it, spread out throughout the galaxy, from Federation and non-Federation planets."

"I know that," Gold said, "Please continue. Soloman, no need for false modesty. We're burning time here."

"Yes, sir," Soloman said. "As you acknowledge, the list is quite extensive and detailed. Compiling it would be the work of months, at least. It took Starfleet hours just to confirm it. To dig up the information in the first place would have been a monumental task."

"And?"

"And Commander Gomez never did any such thing. To compile the list would have taken myriad contacts with myriad planetary governments and their criminal tracking systems. The *da Vinci* records show no such communications transmissions or data exchanges between the *da Vinci* and any planetary government on that topic—none at all, from anyone."

"It's out of our line." Gold then asked, "Could Gomez have gotten the information when she was off-ship? Or could she have wiped the communications files?"

Abramowitz shook her head. "Ship's records, compared with the time of the incarceration of a number of prisoners on the list, show that Commander Gomez was right here on the *da Vinci* when some of that information became available. And what my modest Bynar friend here is reluctant to say is that while it might just barely be possible for her to have wiped the communications files on the *da Vinci* beyond his ability to trace—barely possible— it's not possible for her to have wiped systems on worlds all across the galaxy to that extent. We've checked those systems, and they show no such inquiries from anyone who could possibly have been Sonya Gomez.

"The only reasonable solution is that the commander could not have collected that information. And yet the Sonya Gomez we have been dealing with clearly does have it. Therefore . . ."

Soloman picked up the thread. ". . . that is not Gomez, but a simulacrum, a very good one."

Gold leaned forward, while allowing himself to believe in this new, much-wished-for scenario. "In that case," he said, "where the hell is my first officer?"

Corsi jumped in. "Sir, sensors confirmed that she is alone in the station command center. So unless sensors have also been rendered unreliable, she's in there." Gold was impressed by how quickly Corsi had changed gears, adapted to the new situation. Not surprised, but impressed. "If she's okay . . ."

"No reason to assume she isn't unless we learn otherwise, Corsi," Gold said, his natural optimism enhanced by the sudden change in the situation. "Go ahead."

"Then despite the static field that's been placed on station communications, a tight-beam transmission focused on her specific combadge frequency should be able to establish a link with her."

Gold raised his eyebrows at that. Technical information was not the security chief's forte. Soloman and Abramowitz seemed a bit surprised themselves.

"What?" Corsi said. "You work with engineers all these years, you pick stuff up."

Gold stood up, and as he did so he allowed the edges of his mouth to turn upward for the first time since they had received the first message from the computer simulation of his first officer. "Soloman, get that signal to Gomez. Corsi, continue the negotiation with the program. It may be reporting to someone, let's keep it—or them—from suspecting we're on to it. You two," Gold said, addressing Soloman and Abramowitz, "good work."

*   *   *

Commander Gomez was taking a forced break from her struggles with the equipment. She lay on her back on the floor with her legs above her chest just as prescribed by Starfleet hypoxia training. The position diverted her poorly oxygenated blood to her brain and cleared some of the fog out of her head. She was worn out, not just by the thin air but from banging her metaphorical head against metaphorical walls and was worried that if she didn't take it easy for a minute, she might start banging her literal head against the literal walls. Besides, lying on her back on the floor and watching Corsi negotiate terms with the fictional Gomez was entertaining, in a bizarrely surrealistic way. Rooting against "herself" was particularly mind-bending.

Corsi had just finished explaining the precise details of a prisoner release from Sigma V to "Gomez" and was now confirming with "her" the particular prisoners who were included in the release. To Gomez's earthborn ears and oxygen-starved brain, the alien names sounded like a bunch of nonsense syllables strung together: Rendar Grepnackten, Yarnat Netgrel, Jertnal Echtoy, Ardack Sprachnee, Lemanr Tacketo, Sibkel T'Nuncen. In her current state Gomez found Corsi's recitation hypnotic, and she caught herself falling asleep. In low-oxygen conditions, that could be deadly. With an effort, she rolled to one side, then forced herself to stand up. She walked on shaky legs over to the control console to start trying once again to get a handle on the situation.

Something nagged at her as she pushed switches and dials almost randomly, looking for some kind of reaction that would give her a clue to a way in. Something on the list of names Corsi had read off sounded familiar, but she was certain she knew no one from that planet. But there was something, something recent, maybe something important. What was it? With some effort she was able to bring the conversation between Corsi and "Gomez" back up on the display and replay it. It took almost a dozen run-throughs before she spotted it.

Okay, she thought, *now I understand what's going on. But I can't do anything about it from in here. If only I could tell someone outside this goddamn control room. . . . .*

At that moment her combadge chirped.

Gomez almost didn't recognize the sound, then for a moment, couldn't believe she'd heard it. The combadge chirped again.. *"Corsi to Gomez, respond please,"* Gomez heard, and struggled to her feet while simultaneously tapping her combadge.

"Gomez here," she said. "Very happy to hear from you." Gomez held her breath for a tense moment—for all she knew, this communication wasn't meant for her, but for her computer-generated duplicate.

"Hate to have to ask you this," the security chief's voice came back, *"but what was the last thing I said to you before you left for shore leave?"*

Gomez could feel her combadge getting hot—whatever signal they were using to punch through the static field around the station, it packed a pretty good punch. She took a deep breath and thought back. "You said, 'Live it up.' You satisfied it's really me, now?"

"Yes. You up to speed on what's going on?"

"Actually, I may be a little ahead of you," Gomez answered. "Just wasn't able to tell anyone about it. With some help, I think I can get the station back online, and catch the bastard who did this."

"Anything you need," Corsi said.

"Great. Patch me through to Soloman right away."

"He's listening. You owe him a thank-you when this is all over. We'll explain later."

"Soloman," Gomez said, "I need you to lower the security levels on the *da Vinci* communications array and find me a particular piece of tribblecom."

"That," Soloman's soft voice came over her combadge, *"is an unusual request."*

"I know," Gomez said, "here's what I'm looking for . . ." She rattled off the key components of the tribblecom she had deleted just before all this started. "I have work to do here—flag me when you've found it." Gomez smiled for the first time since the whole nightmare had started.

CHAPTER
6

It had taken Soloman only moments to locate the particular tribblecom Gomez had requested, but it had taken her several hours of hard work to link her combadge directly into the station communication and computer systems. It was dual access—it would let her talk to the *da Vinci* via the station's communication array, and it would allow Soloman, on her command, to upload the tribblecom directly into the station computer's memory unit. In the meantime, to keep the program busy, and in case what Gomez had in mind didn't work, Corsi was continuing to "negotiate" with the false Gomez, which added the bizarre note of Gomez's own voice ranting on in the background as she worked.

At last she was ready. She hoped this would work, because if it didn't, she was entirely out of ideas. "Okay, Soloman," she said, "let it rip."

"Upload commencing," Soloman replied.

For a long moment, nothing happened. Then the Gomez on the display screen began to falter, as if searching for her next word. The Gomez image froze, then moved again but in a jerky, unrealistic fashion. It tried to speak, but its voice was first garbled, then became more of an incoherent squeak like nails on a blackboard. The screech got loud enough to make Gomez cover her ears, but then the picture on the screen broke up into a random array of tiny squares, each containing a different distorted image of Gomez.

Then the screen went black, and at the same time, the lights on the board in front of Gomez flashed green: shields were down, life support was climbing back to normal—and while the systems were running slow, due to the tribblecom, they were holding steady. A noise behind her made her turn quickly, but it was only the control center door sliding open, at long last able to obey the signal from the switch she had pressed . . . just how long ago it was Gomez wasn't certain. On the other side of the door stood Tobias Shelt and the three station engineers. All four of them started talking at once, but before Gomez could even start to answer them Captain Gold's voice came over the comlink.

"You okay in there, Gomez?" he asked.

"Just fine now," she said, waving the others to silence. That was true. Her headache had vanished the moment the control room doors slid open.

"Glad to hear it," Gold said. *"I'll let Starfleet know they can call off the prisoner release on Sigma V."*

"Sir," she said, "I think I figured out who caused all this and why. I'll want to check this with Commander Corsi, but if I'm right, Starfleet should let the release go ahead."

"Interesting," Gold said, *"then I'll tell them to let it continue. Looking forward to your explanation, Gomez. Prepare to be beamed aboard."*

"Yes, sir."

Tobias Shelt motioned to her as the transporter beam caught her—he was signaling that she should call him. She had time to signal back but didn't, and then the control center faded out.

Ardack Sprachnee, former finance minister for Sigma V, was not surprised when he was told his thirty-day sentence for drunk-and-disorderly behavior in the council chambers was being commuted. After all, he had not only arranged to be in jail in the first place, he had arranged for his and his fellow prisoners' release and for the type of transportation that would be provided.

The guards ushered him and his fellow parolees to just inside the large metal bars of the prison gate, and he listened with rapt attention as the warden explained that due to events far beyond his control, the Federation had requested their early release, and that they be transported to Bartha IX by hauler. As the protest started—his fellow prisoners objected, this close to the end of their sentences, to being released so far from home—the warden explained that the Federation had provided return transportation as well.

The warden went on to say that the whole thing sounded as foolish to him as it did to them, but orders were orders, and a free trip to Bartha IX would certainly beat another night in their cells. That, Sprachnee noted, was a point the other prisoners agreed with wholeheartedly, and so did he. So while there was puzzlement among the released prisoners, there was no resistance to the notion, especially when luxury hovercars pulled up to the gate to take them to the spaceport.

There were intoxicating drinks in the hovercars, but Sprachnee left them to his seatmates. He had to keep his wits about him, because this next part was tricky, and his timing had to be precise.

They pulled up to the cargo ship, and were led on board it by guards, but once everyone was in their seats and the door was closed, they were free—and a cheer went up from the crowd. Sprachnee ignored the noise; he was busy looking through the packet of personal effects that had been returned to him. Yes, there it was. He took a certain device in his hand and waited for the sound of engine startup. As the whirring kicked in, he pushed the button on what looked like a small writing implement. The lights on the hauler flickered for a second, but that wasn't unusual at startup.

The lighting levels returned to full power in moments, but Sprachnee stayed tense until he was certain the pilot hadn't noticed the drain on the energy levels—*and why should he,*

Sprachnee thought, *since this little gadget of mine has tweaked his readouts to ignore the massive cargo he's just taken on?*

While there were times when Sprachnee wasn't certain whether it was the lure of being fantastically wealthy or the simple intellectual challenge of the thing that motivated him, he usually tilted toward the latter. How to get five billion bars of gold-pressed latinum, the entire wealth of the planetary government, off-planet? That had been quite a problem to solve.

Sprachnee's position as finance minister was one he had worked long and hard to get because it gave him access to the codes that worked the shielding on the planetary latinum storehouse. Coming up with the rest of the scheme had taken a long time, and many false starts.

Sprachnee relaxed into his seat for the trip to Bartha IX, secure in the knowledge that, per the readout on his little device, the buffer on the cargo transporter of this very ship now contained, in supercompressed coding, all five billion bars of latinum that made up the planetary treasury of Sigma V, and in their place was a hologenerated image that wouldn't fool people forever, but would for just long enough. When they landed on Bartha, another push of the button and the latinum would be beamed to thousands of mini transporters he had hidden all over the planet on his last vacation. From there it would be a simple matter to recover the latinum piece by piece.

Sprachnee sat calmly in his seat for the entire trip, which took most of a day, not tensing up until the pilot announced their landing approach. As soon as the heat shields were dropped, Sprachnee was ready to push the button, disperse the latinum, and become one of the galaxy's richest men—under an assumed name and species, of course.

The ship landed, and Sprachnee's finger was on the button in a moment. Oddly, though, the shields weren't dropping. Probably just a malfunction. Maybe he should offer to help them resolve it?

Without his noticing their arrival, two Starfleet officers in security uniforms were suddenly flanking him. Both were very large, very strong, and were very polite as each took one of his arms and hefted him from his seat. They patted him down expertly, quickly taking his gadget and all his emergency back-ups away from him. The taller of them tapped his combadge. "It's okay, we have him, you can drop the shields."

Gomez stared at the short little balding man who had caused all the trouble. Sitting sadly in his old-fashioned metal-barred cell, he didn't look like any kind of a threat. It almost hadn't been worth the high-speed shuttle run it had taken to get Corsi and herself to Bartha IX, but Gomez just had to meet the man who had done this to her. She needed to learn what she had done to him to make him single her out.

"Are you sure that's him?" she asked. Corsi nodded. "I've never met him before. I have no idea what his beef with me might be."

"Well, let's ask him. Hey, Sprachnee," Corsi said. "Come over to the bars. Somebody here wants to see you."

The little man stood up and walked over, and it was clear to Gomez that he didn't recognize her any more than she recognized him. Gomez looked at him, looked him up and down carefully. "Why me?" she asked him.

"I'm sorry, ma'am," he said politely, "but I don't know what you're talking about."

"Why me?" Gomez asked again. "Why did you pick me for this thing out of the entire galaxy?"

"Oh," Sprachnee said, "was that you?" The little man paused, then continued. "I was in a cell, remember, I wasn't able to watch my program play itself out. I'm sorry for the inconvenience."

"Everything that happened was done automatically, by your program?"

"Yes."

"But," Gomez was losing patience, "why did the program pick me?"

"Tell me," he said, "did you get a call on a communications link just after you deleted the tribblecom?"

Gomez thought back. Yes, there had been a call, with no

one there. It had asked who she was, then disconnected—oh, no. "Yes. It asked me my name."

"Well, there you go," Sprachnee said. "Once the program realized its surroundings were apropos to the mission, it found a target subject, asked for your name, ran your records, found your image on file, located your personal logs, rewrote your journals on the basis of what your mission records said you'd been through, et cetera, et cetera." He sighed. "It could have been anyone, anyone at all, almost anywhere in the Federation. It was my bad luck, Commander, that it was someone like you. If you hadn't figured it out . . . or," he said wistfully, "if even one of the billions of sentients who have read the tribble-com by now had taken me up on the prima facie offer, I'd be a rich man instead of rotting in a cell, for good this time, I fancy."

"So my involvement in this was just—bad luck?" Gomez said.

"That's correct."

That wasn't possible. He'd known enough about her daily schedule to track her to Hidalgo Station. Enough to rewrite her journals. Enough to create a simulacrum of her that fooled her closest friends and associates for quite a while. The only way that would have been possible without detailed knowledge of her background and security codes. . . .

"You wrote a multivariant, adaptive, artificially intelligent superworm that can propagate via subspace, penetrate Starfleet security, and invade personal logs? That can, on its own, extrapolate from personal writing style and records exactly how to convince someone's closest friends and associates that they are talking to them instead of a program? That can run on equipment with as little processing power and memory as Hidalgo Station has? And that works at nanosecond speeds?"

"Well, yes," Sprachnee said modestly. "I was pretty proud of it."

Gomez was stunned. *He should be proud,* she thought. Sprachee had written one hell of a sophisticated program, so sophisticated it had taken her quite a long time, trapped in a freezing-cold control center, to figure out even part of what he'd done. What she'd realized was that Sprachnee had hidden coding in the text of the tribblecom that was set to activate when someone used a glommer to delete the message. When Gomez deleted the tribblecom, she had triggered the hidden code, resulting in the station shutdown and initiating the entire incident that followed.

If Gomez hadn't been listening to the conversation between Corsi and the simulation, she would never have known that the planet mentioned in the tribblecom and the planet where the prisoners were being released was the same planet, and that Sprachnee's name, which was on the bottom of the tribblecom, was also on the list of prisoners. She had almost missed it anyway.

Armed with that knowledge, when Soloman figured out it wasn't really her on the screen and established communication, she had had Soloman locate Sprachnee's tribblecom, the one that had started all the trouble. As the tribblecom reentered the Hidalgo computer system through the combadge link Gomez had set up, it clogged up the memory unit again—and crashed the complex program controlling the station, allowing the established station programming to reassert at least intermittent control. Gomez had figured that Sprachnee's program wouldn't be set to defend against itself, and fortunately, she had been right.

Back on the *da Vinci,* with full information in hand, Gomez had suggested, and Corsi and Abramowitz had then confirmed, that the list of prisoners to be released had been set up to manipulate Starfleet and the Federation. The only prisoners on the list who didn't seem a real threat were the batch of prisoners on Sigma V. It was therefore predictable that Starfleet would offer to release them first—especially predictable to someone who had read the Starfleet negotiation manual, as Sprachnee, Gomez thought, most likely found a way to do.

The records on Sigma showed that Sprachnee had made certain he was among those prisoners by acting out so badly in the council chambers that he would not only be fired, but would be thrown into jail. The tribblecom had also made clear what Sprachnee was trying to get away with—the biggest latinum heist in history. From there, the specification of a hauler-class ship, the only ship class in the area with both a passenger complement and transporter buffers large enough to contain that much latinum, was a dead giveaway.

Gomez looked quizzically at the little man who had caused her so much trouble. "Why'd you bother with all this?" she asked. "Don't you know how much you could have sold your program for? It would make five billion bars of gold-pressed latinum seem like lunch money."

Sprachnee waved the notion away. "Where would the fun have been in that?" he asked her. Then he stopped and looked thoughtful. "I don't suppose we could cut a deal now? I show you everything I know about the program, you get me out of here?"

"We'll see," Gomez said. She was angry at what he'd done, to her, to her reputation, the risk to the lives of those on Hidalgo Station. Gomez wrestled with conflicting emotions, but in the end she was an engineer, and the program he'd written would impress the best engineers in the galaxy. "I'll talk to someone. But don't hold your breath." To her own surprise, instead of punching Sprachnee in the eye as she'd thought of doing, Gomez stuck her hand through the bars in a gesture of respect. Sprachnee hesitated for a moment, then took her hand and shook it firmly.

As Gomez and Corsi left the holding area, Gomez wondered what would be next for the strange little genius. "What adjudication facility is he being sent to?" Gomez asked the security chief.

"I'm not sure," Corsi said. "Why?"

"Because it had better have damn good security tech, or we'll be hearing from him again really soon."

Shortly thereafter Gomez found herself back where she had been a week ago, about to beam down to Hidalgo Station. This time she wasn't going alone—most of the crew of the *da Vinci* would be visiting the station, some to help put all their systems right, others simply for much-needed shore leave. Gomez was doing a little of both—she would help the day shift with repairs on a part-time basis as well as having some time for herself.

She'd already sent word to Tobias Shelt to clear his schedule for dinner, dancing, and who knew what would happen afterward? Seeing "herself" doing things so far from her character had brought things home to her. She could accept that she wasn't entirely who she had been. What she had gone through with Duffy had forced her to leave some of herself behind, and that empty space in her would have to be filled with something new. Maybe Tobias Shelt would be part of what filled it. Maybe someday Wayne Omthon would be. Or maybe it would be somebody else entirely. She'd take it one day at a time. Smiling, she vanished from the *da Vinci* in a cone of light.

FABLES OF THE PRIME DIRECTIVE

Cory Rushton

PROLOGUE

Stardate 51623.3,

Commanding Officer's Log. We're abandoning Coroticus III. Hell, we're abandoning the entire sector. I remember previous wars, against the Cardassians or whoever. Limited engagements, minimal losses. They lasted forever. What was it? Thirty years against the Cardassians? But those wars were what used to be called cold conflicts. This one, though—I don't think we're going to get through it. We take twenty years to create someone who can pilot a starship or fire a phaser. The Dominion takes weeks to raise a Jem'Hadar soldier. I thought I would see out my commission here, studying these people on this planet, but now I frankly don't know if I'll survive the day. Even if I did, what a final day this is. Wiping the computers. Destroying the physical evidence of the observation lounge. Abandoning a primitive but wonderful humanoid race to the tender mercies of the Dominion. And for hours and hours now the repetitive wailing sound of the red-alert sirens. It's enough to—Oh, that's it. Enough!

*   *   *

"Turn that bloody noise off!" shouted Commander Tarsem Johal. "It's driving me mad."

"Red alert muted," replied the calm voice of the tactical officer. Lieutenant Saed Squire was young, barely out of the Academy where he'd taken a joint degree in security and ancient galactic civilizations. It was a rare degree, but it made him perfect for a sociological observation post on a pre-warp world orbiting Coroticus. "We've just heard from the *U.S.S. Valletta*, an *Istanbul*-class vessel. They'll enter orbit in five minutes and request that we be ready for immediate departure."

"How did we do with the transporter apparatus?"

"All outposts destroyed with minimal sign of their presence."

Johal nodded and glanced at his second-in-command. "Moseley, how's the data backup going?"

Sheila Moseley tucked a stray lock of red hair behind her ear as she read the progress reports. "We're at seventy-five percent, Commander. We need another hour."

"We don't have it," growled Squire. "Commander, I recommend we dump it now."

"We'll lose all that information." Moseley turned to Johal. "Commander, I—"

The red-alert siren started up again, triggered by some new disaster. "We have four . . . no, six! Six Jem'Hadar warships entering the system right behind the *Valletta*!"

There was a silence for a few seconds.

"The *Valletta* is four minutes away." Squire's voice remained muted.

"And the Jem'Hadar?"

"I can't be sure. Fourteen minutes if we're lucky."

"Lieutenant Moseley." Johal reached out and squeezed her shoulder.

"Aye, sir," she whispered. "Commencing total data purge."

"The Jem'Hadar are being joined by a Cardassian frigate."

"Data purge at seven percent."

"Keep an eye on the Jem'Hadar. Begin evacuation procedures. All nonessentials get out now in order of seniority." The outpost could only transport three people at a time, but with only six permanent personnel this wasn't much of a problem.

"That leaves who, exactly?" muttered Moseley.

"Well, us and the commander," Squire said with a wry grin.

"Data purge at twenty-nine percent."

"The first three personnel are away, Commander," Ensign Zophres called from the transporter station.

"The *Valletta* is two minutes, five seconds from standard orbit and have reported our personnel safe and sound."

"Except for the warships right behind them."

"Except for that. Definitely an occupying force."

"Doesn't seem big enough for a whole planet."

"The local population uses pointy wooden sticks, Sheila."

"Point taken. Data purge at fifty-four percent."

"The second group is away."

"Ensign Zophres, get yourself up to the *Valletta*. Lieutenant Squire, run the transporter."

The two men obeyed instantly.

"Two Jem'Hadar just entered orbit!" cried Squire, his composure broken at last.

"Where'd they come from?" asked Johal.

"I don't know! Commander, you need to get out of here."

The commander turned to Moseley. "You too, Sheila. Let's go."

"The data purge isn't complete, sir."

"We're being jammed. The Jem'Hadar are beginning a planet-wide scan." Squire looked at his commander. "They can't be allowed to find the post, sir."

"I'm praying you have options for me."

"I'll secure the base. There won't be much left to come back to, but a limited-spread photon grenade inside the shields should keep the base hidden and wipe out the relevant data. The shields should also mask the explosion itself. I hope."

"Get it done, Lieutenant." Johal took up his position on the transporter pad, Moseley beside him, her hair in her eyes. She didn't bother to tuck it away this time. "Follow us up."

"Aye, sir." The lieutenant engaged the transporter and the beams took Johal and Moseley away.

The *Valletta* lurched under fire, causing Johal and Moseley to stumble even as they coalesced on the ship's pad. Johal hadn't experienced ship-to-ship fire since his time on the *Grixalon*. He stumbled off the pad, trying to control his movement with a burst of forward momentum.

The young crewman at the controls nodded. "We're taking Jem'Hadar fire, sir. Are you the last ones up?"

"No," said Johal. "One of my officers is still—"

"Shields down to fifty-six percent," said the familiar voice of the ship's computer.

"Prepare for warp." The voice was female and authoritative, and coming from the transporter chief's combadge.

Johal slammed his hand against his badge. "Johal to bridge. Belay that. I have a man still down there."

"We can't wait, Commander. It's one officer or an entire ship . . . my crew and the rest of yours." A pause. *"We just read an explosion from your previous coordinates."* Another pause. *"No life-signs. I'm sorry, Commander."*

Johal felt the sudden, indescribable alteration in the vibration of the deck plates as the *Valletta* went into warp. It matched the sinking feeling in his stomach. *I'm sorry, Squire.*

CHAPTER
1

Two years later

Fabian Stevens and Tarsem Johal stood above the treeline, perched on a rocky outcrop that allowed them a vantage point over the village far below. Coroticus III was a class-M world, and Stevens allowed himself a moment to breathe in the scent of alien pine drifting up on the mild wind. *This almost makes it worthwhile*, he thought. The S.C.E. was to begin the process of rebuilding a dozen cultural observation posts on pre-warp worlds throughout the sector, with the *da Vinci* handling Coroticus III and Sachem II. Stevens was leading a small team on Coroticus, training a group of young technicians in the process before they could be left on their own, while Corsi located the Dominion headquarters for the planet and Abramowitz observed whatever cultural contamination the Dominion might have left behind. It was not a mission that promised to be much of a challenge. At the same time, escape was impossible; the *da Vinci* wasn't due to pick them up for seven days. The ship was now dropping off another team—with P8 Blue, Chief

Hawkins, and Bart Faulwell in Stevens, Corsi, and Abramo-witz's roles, respectively—then would report to Avril Station for a week to conduct upgrades on their outdated systems.

"You're not pleased to be on this assignment." Johal's smile was gentle.

Stevens dragged his attention away from the scene below. "I'm sorry if I seem distracted, Commander. The S.C.E. is happy to assist however it can. That's what we're here for."

Johal shrugged, the smile never leaving his eyes. "Rebuild-ing duck blinds is hardly a challenge worthy of the Corps of Engineers. Nevertheless, your expertise is appreciated. This sort of mission hasn't been the highest priority lately, but it is what we're out here for. Exploration. Discovery."

Stevens nodded. High above them, a dark green bird floated serenely. There was nothing Stevens could see that even hinted at this world's recent past as a Dominion conquest. Of course, that didn't mean Coroticus III wouldn't reveal some scars eventually. Rebuilding Starfleet's observation posts here wasn't simply meant to resume the original mission. It was to study the effect of alien conquest on a pre-warp civilization. "We take that duty seriously, sir. You'll be back at work in no time."

"I won't be staying on when the post is up and running again. I'm only here to patch things up, and then only because I know the place better than anyone else." His eyes lingered on the vivid forest, and beyond toward the purple mountains in the distance.

"So, what is your next assignment? Or should I say, where?"

Johal chuckled. "Picking strawberries."

"Strawberries?"

"An Earth fruit. A delicacy the galaxy over. The Mizari-ans will pay almost any price for a kilo of strawberries." He shrugged, smiling faintly. "It acts as a mild narcotic for them."

"I know the fruit, Commander. I'm guessing that Starfleet isn't assigning you to strawberry duty?"

"Good guess, Mr. Stevens. My sons own a large farm on one of Shiralea's moons. Turns out the equatorial belt is virtually perfect for strawberries. Just as good for blueberries in the right season. My whole extended clan lives there: sons, daughters, grandchildren, various in-laws." He paused to allow a faint, wistful smile. "And my wife."

"It sounds . . . idyllic. Very idyllic."

Johal laughed. "No need to be polite, Mr. Stevens. It's not for everyone."

"No, sir, it isn't. I tried it, before the war started. It didn't take, and I found myself off Rigel and on the *da Vinci* before I knew it. If you don't mind my asking, if retirement beckons, why not leave this assignment to one of your officers?"

Johal looked out at the vista before them. "My tactical officer died destroying the post so that it wouldn't fall into enemy hands. My first officer was lost when the *Ogun* was destroyed a few months later. She'd been reassigned as a yeoman. It was only supposed to be until the war's end." He smiled faintly. "It just goes to show that you can never take anything for granted."

Stevens remembered Salek and Chan Okha, who died during the war, and 111, who died shortly afterward, and Ken Caitano and Ted Deverick, who died just a couple of weeks ago, and Diego Feliciano and Stephen Drew and all the other crewmates who died at Galvan VI—including his best friend, Kieran Duffy. He whispered, "Amen."

Domenica Corsi, head of security on the *U.S.S. da Vinci*, sniffled and pinched her nose in annoyance. She growled softly, but the growl became a kind of peep before ending in a surprisingly delicate sneeze.

Carol Abramowitz glanced away from her padd, her fingers poised over the keys mid-task. "Is something wrong, Commander?"

Corsi glanced up at the cultural specialist, a look of mingled guilt and defiance on her face. "No."

Abramowitz watched for a moment as Corsi sniffed repeatedly. To her surprise, Corsi broke first, pulling a handkerchief from her pocket and wiping her nose. Above the handkerchief, her eyes glared. "Do you have a cold, Commander?"

Abramowitz tried to keep the amused disbelief from her voice. "Core-Breach" was never slowed by anything as commonplace as an illness.

"No." Corsi looked away to where her team was setting up the research post's security perimeter. Unfortunately, neither T'Mandra nor Makk Vinx was doing anything wrong with the equipment, and Corsi couldn't find any excuse to walk away. "It's . . . it's an allergy."

Abramowitz frowned. "Didn't the EMH take care of all that before we left?"

"Apparently Coroticus III has something new with which my immune system disagrees. I'll be fine." She sneezed explosively as the breeze brought some foreign pollen or microscopic feather dust to her nose's attention.

"Gesundheit," chuckled Abramowitz.

"That's a nasty word in Klingon," muttered the security chief, stalking past Abramowitz and determined to find somewhere else to be.

"I'm a cultural specialist," called Abramowitz toward her retreating back. "You know that I know that *gesundheit* isn't a Klingon curse word."

"It's bound to be a curse somewhere." She walked out of sight, down toward the proximity sensors along the hidden path leading to the nearest Corotican settlement.

Abramowitz shook her head, smiling softly despite her sympathy with the security chief. Modern medicine was full of miracles, but the universe was equal to the task of throwing the miraculous off track. Something Corsi had said caused her to pause. *The Klingon meaning of "gesundheit,"* she thought. Corsi was wrong—it wasn't a swear word. In Klingon, "gesundheit" (properly, *ghISong Heytlh*) simply meant a calendar. A particular type of lunar calendar that had gone out of favor after the destruction of Praxis, but the point remained. Yet that wasn't really what Corsi had said that made her consider. Rather, it reminded her of a conversation she'd had with the *da Vinci*'s captain, David Gold, just before they'd been beamed down to the surface of Coroticus.

*   *   *

Gold had asked her to stay for a moment after the mission briefing. The cultural specialist paused at the door as the others filed out. "Yes, sir?"

"I wish I had two of you, one for each team. I'm sure Faulwell will do fine on Sachem, but we don't know the depth of the cultural contamination in these places." Bart Faulwell was the *da Vinci*'s linguist, and although his profession demanded a certain knowledge of cultural issues, Carol was the ship's acknowledged expert. "The Federation has barely begun rebuilding itself, much less the pre-warp cultures under its care. But reports indicate the Dominion was more involved with the locals on Coroticus. Your observations will be crucial."

"Firsthand observation of a pre-warp civilization." Abramowitz whistled. "I considered becoming a proper archaeologist, once. Patient observation, good old-fashioned field work, that would be the dream life."

"Well, I wouldn't expect dreams when the place has been under Dominion rule for over a year."

Carol waved a hand dismissively. "I doubt they'd make that big a difference to the planet. Coroticus III was a strategic move. There was nothing about the natives which would have riled up the Dominion."

"Except that they were solids."

Carol paused. "Well . . . true. Still, there's no indication that the Dominion committed any kind of genocidal crimes on Coroticus. During the treaty process, Dominion negotiators claimed not to have interfered with the local populations."

"But the Dominion doesn't have a Prime Directive. Unless it's something about worshipping the Founders as gods."

The sociologist looked lost in thought for a moment. "Then we should have fought harder to keep them off the planet."

Gold shrugged. "We didn't have the resources to protect Betazed, let alone Coroticus or Sachem II. Besides, it was a Prime Directive issue."

"I've never understood this obsession with the Prime Directive anyway." Carol folded her arms. "I can never keep it straight, and I did quite well in Professor Gyffled's class. It seems to change from year to year."

Gold's eyes twinkled dangerously. Carol could feel a lecture coming, and had nobody to blame but herself. "What's not to keep straight? Don't interfere with pre-warp cultures."

"Or the Klingons. When the Klingons had a civil war, we stayed out because of the Prime Directive."

"Ah!" Gold smiled, warming to the subject. "That's because it was an internal matter."

"Of an ally, and part of the problem was that we were an ally. So we were already involved. It just looked lazy. Or cowardly. What about Bajor?"

"There are different facets and interpretations, but generally it means don't interfere if you can help it."

"So maybe the next time the Dominion attacks we should surrender, so that fighting them doesn't break their natural development?"

The captain frowned. "You're exaggerating, Abramowitz. I expect you might even be pulling my leg—playing devil's advocate?"

Carol grinned. "Color me red."

Gold chuckled. "You remind me of my old friend Gus Bradford. We used to argue about things like this—although, to be fair, I usually took your position." His smile faded. "Seriously, Abramowtiz, can I trust you with this? Nothing tests our characters like the Prime Directive. I've seen it before. Misplaced pity, inappropriate anger. It's so easy to stand on high and see what's best for other people."

Carol nodded. "I'll do my best, sir."

Gold was silent for a long moment, observing her and stroking his chin. When he finally spoke, his voice was soft. "Are you sure you're up to this?"

She suppressed the sudden, irrational spurt of anger. "With all due respect, sir, people have to stop asking me that. I'm a cultural specialist on a Starfleet vessel. This is what I *do*."

He held his hands up in mock surrender and smiled. "I know, I know. But you know me, I have to ask." He let his smile disappear. "Given what happened on Teneb."

"You mean when I was nearly stoned to death by xenophobic refugees who caught me with a magically disappearing tricorder?" She kept her face expressionless. "I'd completely forgotten about that."

Gold looked straight into her face for another long moment before shaking his head, chuckling again. "Sorry to have reminded you. If you're okay, I'm okay."

"I'm okay."

He ducked his head in a friendly dismissal. "Okay."

Now Abramowitz was on the surface of the planet itself, standing in the midst of the forest clearing where the observation post had stood, hidden from the locals. The post was currently visible, the holographic duck blind down while the *da Vinci* team surveyed the damage done by self-sabotage and time. The emitters had apparently kept working throughout the Dominion occupation, and it was an open question whether the occupiers had found it.

The main post was a series of four buildings high up in the boughs of the large *jopka*, cedarlike trees that dominated this stretch of the forest. The buildings had been connected by high-tension suspension bridges, which were to be the first things reconstructed. Visual and auditory sensors hidden throughout the region had fed information back to the post's computers, and secondary posts elsewhere on Coroticus collected similar information about the world's other civilizations. Those cameras, located in places with heavy native traffic, would have to be replaced last, given the inherent difficulties of working with advanced technology around pre-warp aliens.

The Coroticans were humanoid, and close enough to Terrans on the surface that no cosmetic surgery was deemed necessary beyond slightly tapered ears, at least for the humans of the *da Vinci* crew. The cars of the Vulcan security guard, T'Mandra, were deemed within acceptable physiological parameters for Coroticus. The locals wore rough clothing, cloaks and trousers, generally in peacock colors, with tall boots reaching to midcalf. Even the men wore some jewelry on the wrists and ears, although they were more heavily bearded than either Federation woman was used to.

In fact, it was one of Abramowitz's jobs to explore the closest Corotican settlement, Baldakor. While tiny by Federation standards, Baldakor was one of the most important political and spiritual centers on the planet. Further, Starfleet Intelligence believed that the village had been the closest spot to the Dominion presence, and thus most likely to have been affected. Granted, information was sketchy, but that was where she came in.

There was no time like the present to start out on the hour's hike to Baldakor, although she would need to locate Corsi, her bodyguard, first.

A loud sneeze from behind a nearby copse of shrubs gave her a fairly good starting point.

CHAPTER
2

The outpost was a mess.

Inside the shields, the photon grenade had destroyed the base's equipment, causing the walls to collapse on themselves. Even if a Corotican native had managed to slip past the holographic shielding, he wouldn't have known what he was looking at. A Jem'Hadar soldier, on the other hand, would have been potentially quite interested in the outpost and the information on Coroticus contained within it.

"There's nothing left," said Stevens, running his tricorder in a slow circle around the room. "I can't detect the smallest trace of information, encrypted or otherwise."

Johal nudged a fallen support beam with his foot. "That's good. It was a great source of concern at the time. We had to abandon Coroticus to the Dominion, but we certainly weren't interested in providing research that could help them control the local population."

Fabian was searching for something to say, something about the lost research and horror of war (something that wouldn't sound trite) when he was distracted by approaching footsteps, crunching in the fine debris of Starfleet sensor banks and swivel chairs. He turned and nodded to Lauoc Saon, the diminutive Bajoran security guard.

"Mr. Stevens, I've found evidence of footprints in the area."

"Normal local traffic?" asked the engineer.

"I'm not sure. They're humanoid, but they appear erratic, as if they were looking for something."

Stevens raised his eyebrow. "Something like a Federation observation outpost?"

Lauoc nodded. "The chronology is confused, but they've definitely come back more than once."

Johal cleared his throat. "It could be locals. If a hunter noticed that wildlife avoided a certain area, and the duck blind has the effect of making it appear that way, then he might have been curious. The Coroticans are just like us, in that way."

Stevens nodded before turning to Lauoc. "Have you informed Commander Corsi?"

"Yes, sir. She'll look into rumors regarding the outpost in Baldakor."

"Is there anything else you've found?" asked Johal.

Lauoc turned to the older officer. "Sir," the Bajoran said, scratching idly at the scar on his face with one hand and holding a tricorder in the other. "If I understand the situation when you evacuated the outpost, you left your tactical officer behind?"

The older officer's face colored lightly. "Saed Squire, yes. I wouldn't say we left him behind. It was an unfortunate bit of timing between the *Valletta*'s arrival and the explosion. I think . . ." Johal paused for a moment before sighing. "I think he knew he wasn't going to make it."

Lauoc nodded. "I didn't mean to imply anything. Everyone who joins security knows the risks, and we're glad to take them."

Security personnel seemed to share this sense of sacred duty, thought Stevens. *Dom sure does*. Stevens found his attention wandering back to Lauoc's scar, the result of a Breen neural whip encountered during the war. Security always seemed to pay the heaviest price. In fact, Lauoc was one of seven replacements for security personnel who died at Galvan VI.

"It's just that I can't find any sign of that, Commander." He stepped closer so that he could show the tricorder's screen to Johal. "Even given the powdering of the outpost, there should be some sign of the lieutenant's body, even if it's only at the molecular level. The shields should have kept some of the . . . material . . . localized."

Johal frowned and took the tricorder. He grunted in acknowledgment. "May I ask what you're suggesting?"

"It could be the local background radiation, Commander," suggested Stevens. "There's some low-level thoron radiation throughout the region, which is interfering with our sensors."

"From the grenade explosion?" asked Johal.

Lauoc shook his head. "Definitely not. It might be related to some sort of weapon discharge, but it would need to be on a fairly large scale to have these effects."

Johal looked out in the direction in which, Stevens knew, the nearest Corotican village lay. "Do we think the Dominion attacked the locals?"

"We couldn't tell based on the *da Vinci*'s sensor readings before we beamed down." Stevens felt like apologizing. The man was clearly affected by the possibility of the locals suffering at the hands of Jem'Hadar weaponry. For that matter, so was Stevens, and he had no firsthand knowledge of Coroticus at all. Meeting the Jem'Hadar and their level of military technology would have made the meeting between the Aztecs and the Conquistadors look almost equal.

Lauoc glanced at Stevens before continuing. "But more than that, there's a small chance that Squire survived the explosion. I don't want to get your hopes up, but if Lieutenant Squire learned anything from his Academy survival classes, this wouldn't have been a bad world to put them to practice." He shrugged. "Even with the Jem'Hadar around."

"Squire was one of the last officers to take survival from Owen Paris before he was kicked upstairs." Johal rubbed his bearded chin thoughtfully. "Can we make a search?"

"I'll ask the commander when she gets back from the village," Lauoc replied with a nod.

*   ʌ   *

Stevens's attention was drawn by one of the computer technicians. Ensign Hj'olla was a Tiburonian woman straight out of the Academy, and a year early at that. She was ostensibly in charge of the small team of young computer specialists and engineers temporarily assigned the S.C.E. for this mission, and had made her eager nervousness well known to both Stevens and Commander Gomez from the moment she boarded the *da Vinci* at Starbase 212.

Stevens wandered over. "You look like you wanted to speak with me, Ensign?"

"Yes, sir. I was wondering if we could get started clearing debris? I noticed that you were speaking about the missing officer, and that perhaps we've learned all we can?"

Stevens felt an uncustomary twinge of annoyance. "Were you eavesdropping, Ensign?"

The Tiburonian turned slightly blue under her cauliflowered ears. "No, I mean, I heard . . . I mean . . . Yes. I suppose I was, sir."

The annoyance passed and Stevens chuckled. "You don't need to call me 'sir.' You're an officer, I'm just a noncom." He smiled sweetly. "Granted, I'm a noncom in charge of this particular operation. Still 'Fabian' is fine, or 'Mr. Stevens' if you *really* want to be formal."

"Until my team is ready to take over reconstruction efforts throughout the sector on our own, yes, sir."

Fabian got the distinct impression that Ensign Hj'olla would continue to show him the respect due to him by virtue of the mission, for the duration of the mission, and not a moment longer. *No respect for the noncommissioned*, he sighed to himself, *even when we routinely save the day*.

"I suppose you're right, though," he said at last. "No reason not to start cleaning up. Your team's on a pretty tight schedule, even with our help."

Hj'olla's face lit up with a sudden transforming smile. "Thank you, sir! I'll keep one member of the team scanning for trace elements of, of whatever, while we work."

Stevens nodded and smiled back, slightly overwhelmed. *I didn't know Tiburonians could smile like that*. "That's a good idea."

Again, she said, "Thank you, sir." She put her hands behind her back and her feet together, almost unconsciously. "I'm sorry if I came on strong. Again. I really do appreciate everything you've done to help me." She smiled again, softly this time, almost shyly. "Fabian."

Stevens swallowed. "Carry on, then," he managed.

Did the ensign just . . . flirt? His first instinct was a certain self-satisfaction. His second was to look around and make certain Domenica Corsi hadn't seen. He might not be sure what his relationship with the security chief was, exactly, but he was very certain that flirting with attractive young ensigns wasn't a part of it.

Not if he wanted to keep all of his internal organs intact.

CHAPTER
3

Abramowitz breathed in deeply. The smell of livestock and inadequate sewage systems made for an unpleasant aroma, but experiencing it was part of her job. She took another deep breath and frowned.

"What's wrong?" wheezed Corsi, her own nose red and thoroughly protected from Baldakor's scent.

"It doesn't smell as bad as I'd expected." Abramowitz breathed in again, held it longer. "No, not as bad at all."

Corsi shook her head. "You make it sound as though that's a bad thing." Her stuffed-up nose made all her th's sound like d's.

Abramowitz tilted her head to the side thoughtfully. "It might be." She pointed her tricorder toward one of the larger buildings in the village, a three-story wooden structure decorated with weathered stone statues adorning the top floor. To her trained eye, the statues looked like grimacing lizards holding sticks and blades, protective spirits rather than honored ancestors. "That building has a more sophisticated plumbing system than I would have expected."

"All cultures develop in different areas at different rates," said Corsi. "Maybe these people value sanitation above weaponry or vehicular transport."

Abramowitz nodded her head appreciatively. "Well said, Commander, and certainly a possibility. You're full of surprises."

"And pollen." Corsi growled.

Abramowitz touched her left-hand little finger to her right shoulder as two Corotican women passed. They returned the gesture, but frowned at Corsi, who had neglected to do so. "Commander, we need to blend in."

Corsi glowered. "Are you saying they don't have cranky, rude people on Coroticus? Why does Starfleet always assume we all need to be friendly?" She sneezed, snarling at herself immediately afterward.

"We need to get you another hypospray. We could try another medley, maybe mix anti-sheep with anti-Omicronian orchid?"

"I'll wait for a real doctor. I'm fine."

Abramowitz refrained from pointing out that their "real doctor" was off being up for some medical prize or other and wouldn't be back until this mission was over in a week. Instead, she turned her attention back to the locals as they went about their business. "Their culture approximates that of medieval Europe on Earth, with a strongly agricultural basis." She touched Corsi's shoulder lightly, pointing to a nearby domed building, one of the few stone structures in the village. "They even have stained glass."

Corsi narrowed her eyes thoughtfully. "Isn't that Hodge's Law of Parallel Planetary Development?"

Carol chuckled softly. "Now you're just showing off. It's actually Hodgkins's Law, which describes how separate planets develop similar or even identical cultures, like the Nova Romans. Anyways, it's no longer in favor since the Palmieri Hypothesis."

"How's that work, then?"

"Well, Professor Palmieri always felt that Hodgkins's Law was . . . deeply flawed . . . and . . ." Abramowitz wandered toward the domed structure as her voice trailed off.

"Oh, very nice," muttered Corsi, following the cultural specialist.

Placing her hands against the domed building's stone, dark gray and cool to the touch, Carol stood on her toes and strained to take in the glass above. The building seemed to be a religious structure, the spire above the dome straining toward the skies, home of the gods across the galaxy. "I need to get in there."

Corsi glanced over the building's front, which was dominated by two sets of massive wooden doors, one of which was carved and the other nearly plain. The wood of the second set of doors was yellow and smelled strongly. To Corsi's eyes, it looked as though it were unfinished. "I've been watching, and I think the unfinished doors are for women, the other doors for men."

"Sounds about right."

Inside, the building was lit by a combination of braziers lit with coal and reeds, and sunlight streaming in colored beams from the ornate glass. There were no seats and no altar. Some sweet smoke, native incense perhaps, immediately overpowered the senses. A native stood in the room's center, muttering to himself and occasionally referring to the sheets of paper in his hand. Carol thought she heard the name Ushpallar, and the words for abandonment and sin, punishment and forgiveness. She moved closer to the small crowd of believers, hoping to hear more of the sermon.

". . . for the Scriptures told us, verily, that the *tuilgpaswee* would be yoked to the *jimjim*, and the *kuilka* to the *gomgom*."

The universal translater isn't even trying anymore, thought Carol with an amused inner sigh.

"And these things came to pass when Ushpallar, He Who Blesses and Condemns, son of Ashpa of the Sun and Vwainleila the Earth, moved among his people and dispensed gifts to those who fell upon their faces, and curses to those who stood tall against the wind like the *tjib*-reed."

Standard fire and brimstone, mused Carol, glancing around the domed interior. The ceiling was remarkably free of ornament where it should be brightly painted, but perhaps that had more to do with the newness of the building and not any cultural change.

"The believers cowered unto the earth when the fires came and consumed our brethren, and—"

"AH-CHOO!" Corsi waved her hands across her face, trying to dispel the smell of the incense. "It's the resin!" The man with the papers glanced up and scowled, but Abramowitz couldn't tell if it was with annoyance or concern. The gathered faithful glanced back in alarm, and many of them whispered to each other and began rushing for the doors.

"You just provided some kind of signal, Commander. The captive flock can't wait to leave." She smiled at the scowling security chief. "Maybe you should wait outside." Abramowitz held up a hand to stall Corsi's protest. "I'll be fine, and you need the fresh air." She restrained herself from physically pushing the security chief back outside, and was relieved when Corsi allowed herself the briefest of scowls before agreeing.

Carol moved toward the entrance, preparing herself for close observation, and praying the universal translator would be able to handle Corotican theology. *At least Domenica didn't ask me if I was "okay" with this.*

Outside, Corsi drank in the relatively harmless air with relief. She'd probably pay for gulping away at it due to the certain presence of trace elements of resin and whatever else was driving her sinuses to distraction, but for the moment it seemed to help more than harm.

The sudden ringing of bells caught Corsi's attention even through the allergic haze. There was no obvious bell tower on the domed building Abramowitz had entered, so Corsi looked around. Most obviously, Baldakor's people were now on the move; where moments ago they were carrying on what looked like the daily business of trading and gossiping, now they were rushing for their homes, slamming doors as they hid themselves away. A few unfortunates hid in alleys between buildings, obviously caught well away from their own homes. To Corsi's eye, the sudden activity didn't look like complete panic, but rather had the air of anxious practice. Whatever the bells meant, whatever these people were hiding from, it was something they'd encountered many times in the past.

At last she spotted the source of the bells: a small procession of five Coroticans, four of whom were carrying a bier covered with a shimmering dark red cloth; the material was the darkest Corsi had yet seen in this culture of bright blues and vibrant greens. The man at the head of the procession was wearing robes made of a similar fabric, and it was he who was ringing the handheld bells.

There was something on the bier, something lumpy. Corsi narrowed her eyes. She assumed the covered object was a Corotican; covering the dead was an almost universal tradition among humanoids, at least at some stage of the grieving process.

From the nearest alley, a Corotican male was staring openly at her. His expression was one of faint puzzlement and, perhaps, more than a touch of curiosity. The man leading the procession was slowing now, the bells ringing with less force, softly chiming to a halt as he lifted a hand. The procession stopped behind him. There was complete silence as they all stared at her.

If I wasn't so bloody slow-witted just now, she thought in annoyance, *I would have spent less time observing the local behavior and more time emulating it.*

Abramowitz turned her attention back to the lone Corotican in the building, who was now gazing after Corsi with mild interest. *And why not? The commander chased everyone else from the room.* "My sister is ill. I'm to pray for her. We apologize for the interruptions."

The Corotican, a large man who obviously had the wealth necessary to live luxuriously, held up his hands and smiled pleasantly, tucking his sermon into a flat square pouch on his belt. "Not to be troubled, daughter." He extended his arm toward a particular alcove, dominated by the glass Carol had come in to see. "Might I point to our shrine of Ushpallar? The glass is but newly installed, and the god is delighted to take offerings therein."

Carol bowed slightly, allowing her left leg to sweep forward until her foot rested on top of her right. The man smiled and bowed in return, and Carol breathed a sigh of relief that she had the gesture correct. She'd only had camera images and a written description to go on. "I would be pleased to pray to He Who Blesses and Condemns." She brought out a handful of coins, carefully constructed by the *da Vinci's* replicators based on the post's field work.

The man took them and they disappeared soundlessly into the folds of his robes. He withdrew with a bow, smiling softly. "Be never found wanting," he intoned.

"Be blessed by the clouds," she answered.

When he was gone, she turned to the shrine, stepping carefully into the alcove and letting the light wash over her for a moment. She took a stick of incense from a basket to her left and lit it from a small candle on her right, then placed it in a wooden rack projecting from the wall beneath the glass. When she wasn't attacked from behind, she assumed her mastery of local ritual was complete, and she put her hands together and looked up at the glass.

Even half-expecting it, Carol still gasped softly. *This is not good*, she thought.

The glass was made of all colors, but the blue of the god's robe dominated the scene. Three Coroticans bowed before a being on a dais, his hand raised in benediction. The god, Ushpallar, had long black hair and pointed, scalloped ears that seemed to grow straight out of his chin. Behind him stood two reptilian beings carrying black sticks, cradling them strangely in their arms.

Ushpallar, He Who Blesses and Condemns, was clearly a Vorta.

CHAPTER
4

The procession leader stepped forward, holding up his hands as if placating a madwoman. "Are you quite well, daughter?"

"Yes," Corsi said, and barely suppressed a small sneeze. "I apologize for . . . standing here."

The man smiled gently. "That is no crime. It is just that most do not wish to be so close to those who've gone on." Closer now, he stopped and glanced at her eyes and nose. "You are clearly ill." His voice was sympathetic, but the speed with which he pulled a handkerchief from his pocket and slapped it over his face startled her.

"It's nothing." Corsi was growing concerned. The man looked extremely anxious now, his body tensed as though he were fighting the urge to step back. "It's just an allergy," she said, trying to soothe him. Even Corsi realized she wasn't a soothing presence, even at the best of times. Not surprising that the man didn't seem at all calmed.

He nodded quickly, but did not remove the handkerchief from his face. He motioned to his followers, who lifted the bier with a single coordinated movement. The covered lump shifted, and a humanoid arm swung down, its blood-covered hand pointing languidly to the earth. The forearm was open from wrist to elbow, revealing mangled sinews and white bone.

Corsi glanced sharply at the man's face. "What happened to him?"

He swallowed visibly, and for a moment Corsi thought he would turn away without another word. "This man died in the woods," he said at last. "A wild animal. Pray you do not contract his condition." He turned his back on her and hurried away, his associates struggling to keep up while carrying their morbid burden.

Contract a death by mangling? thought Corsi, scowling. The phrase might have been the result of a problem with the universal translator, but that was still an odd way of putting it.

"Are you quite well, daughter?"

The soothing voice of the priest dragged Carol's attention away from the disturbing new window. She smiled at his concerned face. "Yes, I'm well. Thank you, father."

He smiled back tentatively. "It's only that you mentioned that your sister was ill, and I was worried."

Sister? Oh, right, Corsi and her allergies. The Vorta window was flustering her more than she'd like to admit. "I am well," she repeated.

The priest still hesitated. "Perhaps . . . ?" Carol was surprised to realize that the priest seemed nervous. Had she done something wrong? A newcomer in the community might alarm the locals if she acted strangely, especially if their recent alien "guests" had been cruel or oppressive. Although, she admitted sourly, the window and its implied respect probably meant that aliens and locals had worked out some arrangement. "I wondered if perhaps you had been vouchsafed a vision?" he asked hopefully. "Your eyes were wide in contemplation, your brow furrowed in deep thought."

Carol looked back at the window as if it had some answers for her. She glanced back at the priest. "No, no visions. Has someone in the community been given visions by . . . by the god?"

The priest smoothed his robes over his ample belly and stepped forward to stand beside her. "Not as such, I'll admit, although the community was blessed by the presence, the corporeal *presence*, of the god and his servants." His eyes had begun to shine with excitement, and Carol thought she saw the barest hint of a tear. "For three turns he lived near to us. He spoke to us, shared his wisdom, protected us from our enemies, made the crops grow."

And improved the plumbing, reflected Carol wryly. In the days before the war, the Dominion had always claimed a certain benevolence; perhaps, if unchallenged, the Founders really were inclined to act kindly. "Protected you from your enemies? Why would the God Who Blesses and Condemns choose sides?"

The priest glanced down at her, thoughtful. "Not for our sakes, our sinful selves. No. Our enemies and rivals blasphemed. They did not look to the god for truth. They did not obey. They called Ushpallar a false god." He waved a hand dismissively. "The people of Ajjem-kuyr were always of the heretical persuasion. They worshipped the gods on the *third* day, and not the *fourth*. Can you imagine?"

Abramowitz immediately recognized the pompous statement as a test. She wracked her brain for an appropriate answer. "Do we speak of the month of growing, or the month of sky-seeing, holy father?"

He smiled. "The month of growing."

She nodded in a manner which she hoped implied humble sagacity. "Then heretics they were."

The priest chuckled. "You are not from Baldakor, daughter. Have you traveled far?"

Carol could never resist that question. "Far enough. I am delighted to learn I have come to a place in which a god walked. Might I ask where he lived, in his time among you?"

"You may ask." The priest folded his hands into his sleeves monkishly. "But we do not know for certain. He would appear among us all suddenly, and his guards with him. It is said that they were seen in the forests to the north, but I do not know the truth of this. They were seen in many of the towns and cities, and the god even spoke with humble farmers in their hovels. Imagine! Humble farmers!" His eyes shone with delight.

"It must have been a great honor for those so fortunate."

The priest smiled softly. "I've been unforgivably rude, questioning your faith so. The Siblings should be here to assist faith, not trouble it?"

The Siblings, Carol recalled, were the holy orders, men and women who had dedicated their life to the service of the gods and their villages.

"I am honored by your attention, father." She repeated the awkward bow.

He nodded in acknowledgment. "I shall make myself available to you for as long as you stay, daughter." He began to glide across the floor, silent and graceful for a man of such size. Carol imagined he knew the building inside and out. "My name is Dyrvelkada, should you or your sister need me." He sketched a small bow, a gesture familiar from her own culture but not contained in the Corotican database; either it had never been observed by the outpost's research team, or the information had been lost in the data purge.

Or it was something new, something introduced since the Starfleet evacuation.

"May I ask," she called out spontaneously, "what happened to Ajjem-kuyr?"

Dyrvelkada stopped and glanced back at her over his shoulder. "It is not for the weak of heart, or of faith, to delve into the righteous wrath of the gods."

It seemed to Carol that this was another challenge. She nodded once, as firmly as she could. The priest's face was solemn as he nodded back, before continuing on his way through the clouds of incense.

"I appreciated his offer of spiritual guidance," mused Abramowitz. "But what troubled me wasn't anything he'd understand. Dyrvelkada's culture has been damaged by Dominion rule, to an extent that I don't know yet. I'd be asking him to question his gods. . . ." She glanced at the security chief, who had remained silent since Carol had emerged from the temple: no acerbic comments, no interested questions, not even a sneeze. "Are you all right? We could try a Benecian flour/Elaysian tear hypo next?"

Corsi's look might have stripped the duranium from a shuttlecraft hull.

Every so often I remember why they call her "Core-Breach," thought Abramowitz. "Forget I offered. You seem distracted."

"There was a procession while you were inside." Corsi told Abramowitz about the frightened priest and the mangled body. "I still can't figure out what he meant by his last comment."

Carol ducked her head to the side, chewing her lower lip as she thought. "Maybe it doesn't mean anything. Cultural specialists need to remember that sometimes an errant phrase is just a slip of the tongue, or a speech pattern unique to an individual. Still, Dyrvelkada seemed concerned about your condition, and worried that I might be ill as well. I took it for simple kindness, but I suppose it might have been more."

"I'd like to get a look at that body." Corsi grimaced. "If there's a wild animal out there that isn't afraid to attack humanoids, my team needs to know." She sneezed again, this time with an amusing degree of delicacy.

"Fair enough. Baldakorans burn their dead, though. We can try to crash the funeral, but given the priest's reaction to your sneezing . . ." Carol shrugged. "We could try that Benecian cocktail, if you like."

Staring straight ahead with a look best described as annoyed resignation, Corsi rolled up her sleeve and thrust her arm in Abramowitz's face.

The funeral grounds were outside the community, in a vast field of orange and gray flowers. Small burial mounds dotted the landscape, topped with tall wooden poles adorned with silver flags, some more ragged than others. In the growing breeze, Carol found it difficult to make out the flag's designs, sewn in black. All she could tell for certain was that each flag seemed different. A small crowd of Coroticans had gathered near a flagless mound, an access door open to the sky.

"There's the priest I met," said Corsi. He was standing before the bier, still held by the four followers. He was holding his arms to the sky and chanting.

"Long-winded, isn't he?" asked Corsi after half an hour.

"I don't think the shroud is coming off anytime soon," replied Abramowitz with a sigh. She glanced at Corsi. "You sound better."

"I feel better." Corsi's admission sounded grudging. "Not perfect, but better."

"We'll try another orchid combo later."

Corsi decided not to growl. She was beginning to suspect that Carol was baiting her deliberately. "I think that shroud isn't coming off anytime soon," she said.

"I just said that," moaned Abramowitz. "I don't think—"

"You're right," said a voice behind them. "The shroud doesn't come off until he's in the mound."

Carol's quick glance at the unconcerned Corsi confirmed that the security chief had been aware of the man's presence all along, probably the reason for her distracted contributions to their conversation.

"Thank you," said Corsi calmly. "We're not from around here."

The man chuckled softly. He was dressed less colorfully than the average Corotican, in drab browns and grays that did nothing to complement his pale skin and gray eyes. "I gathered that when you stood like a tree in the square upon the approach of the corpse."

The two humans turned to face their unexpected contact. "You're the man from the alley."

He touched his forehead in a polite gesture which, Carol recalled, meant "well-met." She repeated the gesture, and Corsi followed suit, albeit slightly awkwardly. Carol frowned when Corsi's gesture was accompanied by a sniffle. If these people were paranoid about illness, they had to find a way to suppress Corsi's symptoms as soon as possible.

"I am Jarolleka. I, too, am a stranger to Baldakor."

His smile, Carol noticed, did not extend to his eyes, but she had the impression it wasn't unfriendliness. It was wariness, perhaps even weariness. A traveler's eyes. "I am Carolabrama, and this is my sister, Domenica."

"I am pleased to meet you. You were lucky, Lady Domenica. A few turns ago, and the priests would not have let you stand before them so brazenly." He held up a dirty hand to stop her protest, a protest Corsi didn't know to make. "Forgive the word, 'brazen,' but it is one that the Siblings of Baldakor had much occasion to use but recently. When their god lived among them."

"Their god," Abramowitz repeated. "Not yours?"

Jarolleka smiled bitterly. "Not mine. Never mine." He leaned forward, his voice dropping to a whisper. "I am of Ajjem-kuyr."

"When the god began sending his lizards out to the other cities and villages, farther and farther every turn, only Ajjem-kuyr refused to bend the knee. We were the home of the Academy, a place of reason and philosophy. At the Academy, we had taught that the gods were mere stories, meant to explain natural phenomena. Why did the rains come? What were the stars? Why did people die? There was no reason to believe in the gods. When had they ever shown themselves to mortals? Only in old fables."

Jarolleka tapped the burning logs of the campfire with a stick. Beside him, Abramowitz and Corsi chewed quietly on their rations. "You didn't believe in the gods?"

He shrugged. "They might live somewhere, I suppose, but if so they don't concern themselves with us." He spat suddenly. "Until the God Who Blesses and Condemns arrived with his lizards, all scales and black armor and horns."

"And then the Academy began to believe, I imagine?"

The Corotican smiled. "No, not at all," he said with quiet pride. "At first we asked why the god would come to live among mortals, when the stories say the gods live a life of bliss in paradise? He said he came to bring things to better our lives, and certainly Baldakor prospered. Better medicine.

The stench of the city, a stench we never realized was there, disappeared. More food."

"Sounds good," offered Corsi.

"Too good, and all explainable through natural laws. There were no miracles. An Academician from a hundred years ago drew many of the same conclusions about farming, and she was no god." He shook his head. "We still refused to bend the knee, even when Ushpallar threatened to call his fellow gods. More lizards, and shape-changers. Mighty spirits." Jarolleka's tone was sarcastic, his shoulders hunched and tense. "Still we refused. Worse, I think, we began to implement many of the 'miracles' in Ajjem-kuyr, which the god had brought to Balda-kor. That was the last blasphemy, I believe. To think that we mortals could achieve the work of the gods? Unthinkable!" He laughed without humor. "Unallowable."

"What happened?" asked Carol, spellbound despite herself. A world on the cusp of a renaissance, only to be held in the grip of enforced superstition.

Jarolleka looked into her eyes, and Carol saw a barely concealed pain. "I can't tell you," he said at last. "I can only show you. It's the only way you could ever understand."

CHAPTER
5

As far as the eye could see, the ground had been turned to a rough and lumpy glass, dully reflecting the Corotican sun back into the blue sky. There was no life, no birds in the sky above, nothing skittering along the ground below. There was no smell to the place at all. "Now we know where that ambient radiation came from." Corsi's voice remained impassive and neutral, but Abramowitz knew it concealed the same deep horror she herself felt at such utter devastation. If this was Ajjem-kuyr, literally nothing had survived the Dominion's assault. It had undoubtedly taken less time to destroy the town than it had taken to deliver the threat.

"You're wondering how I survived the vengeance of Ushpallar." Jarolleka shrugged languidly. His eyes were glazed, not showing any of the bright curiosity or quick wit Abramowitz had come to expect of him in the three days it took to reach the site. "It was quite . . . fortunate, really. I was away, visiting one of the nobles on the Qrantish Coast. He wanted someone to tutor his youngest son." Another bitter laugh escaped his lips. "As it turned out, I was turned down for the post." He glanced over at the women. "Ushpallar's priests advised against my employment. I returned in time to see a bright cloud erupt over the heart of Ajjem-kuyr."

"I am sorry for your loss," said Carol, meaning every word.

He shrugged again and glanced at Vinx and Lauoc, who were examining the edge of the destruction, where the grasses and shrubs of the surrounding plain grew smaller and sicklier, until there was no growth at all and the ground itself grew glassier. If Jarolleka had been at all disturbed by the sudden appearance of Domenica's "brothers," he had never shown it.

"Did you have any family in the city?" asked Abramowitz tentatively.

"My elderly mother. I had just managed to buy her a home in the city, and only moved her from the country the year before." There were no tears; Carol wouldn't have been surprised to learn that the man was still in some form of shock, even years after the event. "I lived here for a month after my return. I don't know why. I never found another survivor. I would have been content with even a single page from one of the Academy's books, floating charred on the breeze." He smiled, his lips pale and thin, shaking his head slowly. "And still I do not believe they were worthy of my worship."

Carol nodded. "I am so sorry," she repeated.

"There was nothing you could have done in the face of their power."

She shot him a look, guilt racing coldly along her spine. *We abandoned this sector, without a fight, because of the Prime Directive*, she thought. *Our most sacred law, designed to protect the innocent on pre-warp worlds*. She stared again at the shimmering devastation, like a motionless and chill northern sea stretching out to the horizon. *Some protection*.

It was only after a moment of indeterminate length that she noticed he was watching her with faintly curious eyes. "I'm still sorry," she answered at last. "Even if it wasn't my responsibility." Did her voice break on the last word?

"I believe you," he said, and turned away to walk along the edge of the destruction. He nodded as he walked past Vinx, who was working on building a fire against the approaching night. The Iotian security guard restricted himself to a nod, rather than risk confusing the native with his peculiar manner of speech. Vinx was a native of Sigma Iotia II, a planet famously contaminated by outside influences. Their culture had obviously adjusted by now, though.

Carol sat on a fallen log, after testing its strength. It was ossified somehow, almost as strong as stone, and no creep-crawlies were disturbed by her actions. Even past the obvious signs of Ajjem-kuyr's death, there was very little alive except for the thin and colorless grass. Judging that Jarolleka wasn't coming back right away, Abramowitz surreptitiously took out her padd.

She called up the Sigma Iotia records, not certain why she was bothering. She knew the Prime Directive debate inside and out; but something had been bothering her since her conversation with Captain Gold. While the Prime Directive, Starfleet General Order Number One, seemed set in stone, in practice it led to a confusion of policies and results. The same captain could save a pre-warp planet threatened by a faulty sun, and a month later watch, with somber but grim resolve, as another planet in similar straits was destroyed. On paper, the Directive was simple; in the breach, it was anything but.

What do you do when a planet is contaminated, but nowhere near ready for further contact?

Abramowitz stole another glance at Vinx. Sigma Iotia seemed as good as place as any to start looking for answers.

Personal log, Lieutenant Michael Theivamanoharan, Stardate 7822.4

Sometimes I get the distinct feeling that Starfleet's cultural specialists have spent the last twenty years following James Kirk around. True, this particular mess isn't really his fault, but his solution left something to be desired. He's turned the Federation into a protection racket, collecting a cut of the profits gathered by the planet's mob bosses.

Granted, the profits have been steered into creating a

more democratic and open society, with free elections and a growing planetary consensus. The Iotians might even be ready for an official first contact within fifty years, and Federation membership soon after that. But that's only because the Federation Council threw so many of us at the problem after Enterprise *left; call it collective guilt over the damage wrought by the* Horizon's *unintended gift of a single book,* Chicago Mobs of the Twenties. *The Iotians were quick to emulate the culture they found in the book (why couldn't the* Horizon *have left* Pride and Prejudice, *I ask?), but once adopted, some of these cultural patterns have proven to be lasting. Speech patterns, for instance; talk to any Iotian and it's like being in a twentieth-century Mafia film.*

Much of the progress made has been from encouraging a small subculture, which has found its model in Eliot Ness and other so-called "untouchables." Iotians like Kall Porakan have worked to form honest police forces that bridge the gaps between the mob-controlled territories. These police forces have formed the basis for a rudimentary planetwide government, kept honest by their allegiance to the ideal they found reading between the lines of Chicago Mobs.

All in all, I can report that from an unpromising beginning, the Iotians are making this work. A word of caution is always necessary, however: We still don't entirely understand the mechanisms by which the Iotians filled in the sociocultural gaps in their book. How much was guesswork, how much was precontact? It might be decades before we understand everything. Despite my cautious optimism, I can't recommend expanded contact at this time.

That didn't sound so bad, thought Carol, stealing another glance at Vinx. Sigma Iotia eventually won a place for itself in the Federation. But not all such cases turned out so well.

*   *   *

Mission Report, Commodore Göller, Stardate 34675.8

It is with deep sadness that we report the loss of Lieutenant Shewer Freeman, U.S.S. Crockett, while on assignment on Zeon in star system M43 Alpha. Lieutenant Freeman showed great courage under Ekosian fire, assisting local evacuation efforts and ensuring the survival of the Federation cultural team assigned to the planet.

As you're aware, Admiral, the Zeonian culture was nearly eradicated by their neighbors, the people of Ekos, in 2268; the actions of James Kirk prevented a genocide at that time. The situation was created by John Gill, a Federation historian who defied the Prime Directive in an attempt to create the perfect planetary government, based on a combination of progressive ideals and an ancient national socialist political model. The political model proved overwhelming, and Dr. Gill died denouncing the government he'd created. Captain Kirk had, at the time, expressed optimism that peaceful relations between the planets could be restored, and Ekos returned to its own cultural roots.

It was not to be. Both Ekos and Zeon eventually became xenophobic and aggressive as a result of their experiences with Gill and the Federation; further, cultural contact with the Klingon Empire resulted in an arms race which led to full-scale conflict by 2287. The withdrawal of Klingon interest following the explosion of Praxis did nothing to alleviate tensions. Federation cultural teams, accompanied by security contingents, worked behind the scenes to broker a peace. Lieutenant Freeman died trying to fulfill those ideals.

I recommend immediate withdrawal of all Federation personnel from the system until the Ekosians and the Zeoni are able to achieve peace by themselves. You can't win them all, Admiral.

My condolences have already been sent to Lieutenant Freeman's family.

*   *   *

Two relatively contemporary contact situations, two attempts by the legendary Kirk to solve the problem, two very different outcomes. What was it Soloman had taken to joking lately? A fifty-fifty chance for everything. There will either be peace, or there won't. A culture will survive, or it won't.

Carol's next entry was a familiar one.

Mission Report, Carol Abramowitz, Stardate 47532.7

> *Damn if I didn't see this one coming. Nikolai Rozhenko went and broke the Prime Directive while observing a pre-warp civilization. Surprise, surprise.*
>
> *Assigned to observe a village on Boraal II, reports from the* Enterprise *indicate that Rozhenko fell in love with a local woman, married her, impregnated her, and then found himself with a conflict of interest upon learning of the planet's imminent destruction by atmospheric dissipation. He tricked the* Enterprise *into evacuating a village (his village, needless to say) to a similar M-class planet, Vacca VI.*
>
> *Have I said I'm not surprised yet?*
>
> *It's not that I don't have any sympathy for Nikolai or the Boraalans; of course I do. I frankly don't see why Jean-Luc Picard was so adamant about allowing the death of the Boraalan culture when, in exactly similar circumstances, he acted to save the inhabitants of Drema IV from tectonic instability. I suspect it might be the record deposit of dilithium found on Drema, but maybe I'm just cynical.*
>
> *You asked me for recommendations, Commander, and having spoken with Nikolai I have to say that he won't be budged. Further, the solution he found seems workable, barring anything unforeseen being discovered on Vacca. I further wonder what it is you expect me to counsel. Take*

*it on ourselves to fix the cultural contamination by blow-
ing up Vacca VI? What's done is done, it seems to me,
and what makes me so angry is that it's the exception that
makes a mockery of the rule. Why Boraal or Drema and
not Cholmondeley III or T'Lakana?*

*Is Starfleet enforcing General Order Number One, or are
we pleased when we're tricked into breaking it?*

I was so young, thought Carol, wincing as she read her own
angry words. She realized now what she only half knew then:
it wasn't Rozhenko she was angry at, irresponsible and arrogant though he was. It was Starfleet and the Federation,
creating a law that they barely knew how to administer, and
the meaning of which seemed to keep changing depending
on which way the winds were blowing. Lord only knew what
Commander Uxmen had really made of it, but as far as Carol
knew the Boraalans (or Vaccans or whatever) were still there,
dancing attendance on their savior Nikolai.

And so the log entries continued: planets saved, planets destroyed but witnessed, planets that made contact too soon and
either prospered or failed utterly. Of course things were always
trickier in reality than in theory; her years with the S.C.E. had
taught her that. She knew now to give Starfleet some credit
for trying to make sense of the Prime Directive, and further
she acknowledged that the Federation got it right at least as
often as they got it wrong. The fact remained, however, that
when they did make efforts at fixing cultural contamination,
it was usually because the Federation had somehow been
responsible for that contamination in the first place. It was
about cleaning up your own mess.

On Coroticus, the Federation could only be held responsible through indirect and perverse reasoning. For decades,
the Federation and Starfleet had taken their responsibilities
toward the Coroticans seriously, protecting them from the
power struggles and economic necessities of the galaxy's citizens until such a time as Coroticus would be ready to join the
family. But the day had come when Coroticus had been in the

path of a power potentially greater than the Federation itself, and although the Dominion at least hadn't handed the planet over to the Cardassians or the Breen, they had muddied the waters. By destroying the Ajjem-kuyr Academy, it looked to Carol as though the Dominion had set back the planet's cultural and scientific development by centuries. What had looked like a nascent renaissance had become a glassy, radioactive dead end.

The question now wasn't the rights and wrongs of Federation withdrawal or Dominion aggression. Captain Gold was right about one thing—the Federation hadn't been able to protect Betazed from Dominion occupation, much less Coroticus. No, the choice was now much more stark: interfere again and try to put the Coroticans back on course, or wash her hands of it?

I wish Vance was here. The deputy chief of security had been more than a lover to her the last few weeks—since the very Teneb mission that Gold had thrown in her face before departing the *da Vinci*—he had been a friend and confidant. Vance Hawkins was an excellent listener, someone she could talk a problem out to without interruption. There were few on the *da Vinci* who were adept at the noninterrupting part, and it was one of *many* aspects of her relationship with Vance that she treasured. But, because of their relationship, he was assigned to head up the security detail on Sachem II.

"You look troubled, doll."

Carol glanced up and realized that Vinx had somehow come up behind her without her hearing. The big man with the brash accent could be silent when he wanted to be. "Just thinking."

"About these Coroticans, right?"

Nodding, Carol was grateful he'd said that rather than asking if she was pining for Vance. Not that their relationship was anything like a secret, but the Iotian was hardly somebody with whom she'd talk about her personal life.

The security guard shrugged languidly. "It's a tough break but it can work out okay. Look at us Iotians, we're livin' the high life now that we're in with the Feds."

"Don't you ever feel a little lost? Don't you ever wonder what Iotia would've become without that book?"

He grinned. "The Book changed everything, and that's no lie. But it gave us the stars. Before the Book we were alone in the universe, wonderin' what the score was. Sure there was some trouble, some mooks ate lead, but then capo Kirk came along and wham! We was in business, and the stars was ours." He touched his forehead as though he expected to find a fedora on his head, and winced comically when he didn't find one. "It's all growing pains, Doc. Every species has them, ours are just different. Unique. Infinite Diversity in Infinite Combinations, ain't it?"

Before Carol could correct Vinx—she didn't mind being addressed with an honorific representing her doctorate, but "Doc" made it feel like she was horning in on Lense's territory—Corsi came up behind them.

"Lauoc found another mangled body. The mission's in danger."

CHAPTER
6

"The replicators are online," announced Ensign Hj'olla with a slight hint of satisfaction in her tone. "Would you like to test it, Fabian?"

Thank goodness for that, thought Stevens, allowing himself a small grin. No more field rations, and not a moment too soon. Only the hated roast beef and blueberry pie packs were left after four days on the surface without replicator technology, and by unspoken agreement the remaining party seemed to have decided that starvation was the preferable option. He threw his caution concerning the ensign's flirtatious behavior to the winds. "I certainly would, Ensign." He laced his hands together and stretched his arms out, cracking his fingers. "A cup of Colombian coffee, two creams, one sugar. Warm."

With a welcome hum, the cup materialized, and Stevens gingerly took it to his lips. "Smells about right." He took a tentative sip. "Tastes about perfect. Good job, Hj'olla."

The Tiburonian woman blushed, resembling the northern oceans of Rigel in a storm.

Better stop that line of thinking. He and Corsi had a good thing going—he wasn't sure what kind of a thing it was, but it was a thing nonetheless, and he didn't want to mess it up.

Hj'olla smiled and placed her fingers lightly on his arm, the one holding the coffee. He almost jumped and spilled the precious brew.

"Corsi to Stevens."

This time, Stevens did jump. Scowling at his own case of nerves, he tapped his combadge. "Stevens, Commander. What's up?"

"We've found another body, exhibiting signs of being mauled. It's been dragged a fair ways."

"An animal of some kind?" T'Mandra's searches hadn't revealed any further sign of their mysterious humanoid prowler, or any hint of dangerous animals. The area around Baldakor had been settled for a long time, and the wilderness was hardly wild at all.

"Uncertain, but I don't think so. We're staying out for a while, see if we can track it."

Fabian frowned. "It's your call, obviously, but I don't know if you should be interfering. Animal or not, local maulings aren't our business."

"Abramowitz suspects this one is our business." Silence, long enough that Fabian wondered if he was supposed to respond somehow. *I'm just enlisted personnel; I don't* have *opinions*. Stevens felt a chill as Corsi's uncharacteristically dramatic pause lengthened. When she finally spoke, her statement caused his stomach to drop. *"She thinks it's a Jem'Hadar."*

The body was Corotican, dressed in the robes of a Sibling. The woman's eyes stared upward, her final look of terror etched forever into her expressive features. Bluish blood covered her face, streaked through her hair, spattered throughout the small clearing. The amount of gore was not surprising, given the way whatever did this had pounded through the chest cavity to find and remove the organs within: heart, lungs, liver.

A trail of blood on matted grass showed where the body

had been dragged from the remains of the Ajjem-kuyr road to the north.

"Is your sister going to be all right?" asked Jarolleka, his hands folded before him, glancing back at Carol, who continued to dry-heave under a shrub.

"She'll be fine. She was just startled." Corsi looked into the Corotican's eyes. "Are there any local animals that operate like this?"

Jarolleka shrugged. "Natural history was never my specialty, but no. I don't think so. The only predator large enough to attack a Corotican is a hill *vajell*, and it hunts in packs. There'd be nothing left of the body."

"Unless we startled them when we arrived, see?" drawled Vinx.

The Corotican shook his head, his eyes never leaving Corsi as she examined the body *in situ*. "There'd be other signs of their presence. Ask your . . . sister. She can confirm that."

Corsi glanced up sharply. Was the man starting to suspect that her "family" wasn't what it appeared to be? *Control your stomach and get back here, Carol.*

Lauoc appeared at her shoulder, keeping his voice low. "This can't be a Jem'Hadar. None of them could survive this long without ketracel white. The footprints I found at the observation post were inconclusive, but probably not large enough to be a Jem'Hadar."

"The prints might be unrelated. Commander Johal thought they could be native. Besides, it's not unknown for the rare Jem'Hadar to be born without a need for white. Dr. Bashir from Deep Space 9 encountered one a few years back, and Taran'atar, that guy the Dominion sent to observe on DS9, doesn't need it, either."

Abramowitz was getting to her feet now, wiping at her lips. She glanced at the group, and Corsi immediately saw how pale she looked. It was gruesome, she thought, but Abramowitz was bravely making her way back to the bloody scene, albeit shakily.

Jarolleka stepped back as she passed, and slowly made his way to the edges of the field. Corsi wondered about his behavior, but it was fortunately timed; now the Starfleet party could talk without fear of contaminating the local culture further.

Vinx moved in to share his thoughts. "Ya think it's a Jem'Hadar mug, yeah? I think you're right, doll."

Corsi narrowed her eyes.

Vinx grinned in embarrassment and corrected himself. "What I mean is, I concur, Commander."

Lauoc shook his head and met Carol's eyes. "I'm not convinced. You said the locals felt completely abandoned by their new gods. Surely someone would have seen a Jem'Hadar and reported back to the village?"

"Maybe they did see one," said Vinx, nodding with his chin toward the decaying corpse. "Maybe seeing one was too hot for them, *capisce*?"

"Don't say '*capisce*'," muttered Lauoc.

"What other possibilities would you suggest, Lauoc?" Corsi stood to her full height between the two men, eager to sidetrack any diversionary conversation of the type that seemed to constantly infect the *da Vinci* crew.

"A local, something completely unrelated to either the Federation or the Dominion. Or a religious ceremony, meant to call back the gods through sacrifice." He ran a hand through his short hair. "Is it possible that we've got a changeling?"

Corsi thought for a moment. "I hope not."

"I doubt it," added Abramowitz. "Think about it. If there was a Founder here, I suspect we'd have seen or heard evidence of more than one god appearing to the locals, not just Ushpallar. Further, we've seen evidence that the locals are replacing artwork that depicts Ushpallar, which implies that the god appeared at least marginally different than they expected. A Founder would have just taken the most appropriate and expected form."

Corsi nodded. "Makes sense."

"There's one final possibility, but you aren't going to like it, Commander." Lauoc scuffed the ground with his boot nervously.

"Try me."

The Bajoran looked off into the distance. "Starfleet potentially has a man missing down here. Stevens couldn't find any sign, even at the molecular level, of Lieutenant Squire, last man at the observation post prior to its destruction."

Vinx whistled, low and nervous. "That'd mean he'd gone kinda wacko."

Corsi tried to fight the headache, tucking an errant strand of ash-blond hair behind her ear. "Near death, isolation, and possibly eluding Jem'Hadar soldiers every day for two years. Sounds like a recipe for wacko to me too, Vinx."

CHAPTER
7

The party had been hiking for the better part of the day, Lauoc ranging widely for hours at a time. Jarolleka had kept his distance as well, rarely speaking to anyone other than Vinx, and averting his gaze whenever one of the women spoke to him. He was never outright rude, but Carol's attempts to ascertain what was wrong went unfulfilled. Neither Corsi nor Carol was terribly happy that he had decided to accompany them, but they seemed unable to ditch him short of knocking him out; given the local situation and his obvious lack of friends, that might well have been a death sentence. Carol assumed that, after seeing his town destroyed by a Dominion weapon, seeing a Jem'Hadar base wouldn't do any further harm. It could always be explained, or his memory erased.

Now they had found a small farm in a forest clearing. *One of Dyrvelkada's humble hovels*, thought Carol, suddenly eager to visit a Corotican after days in the wilderness. Without a second thought, she began trudging toward the small wooden building with its tiny three fields carved out of the woods.

"Wait, Carol." Corsi held up her tricorder. "I'm not reading any life signs. Vinx?"

The Iotian checked his own tricorder. "She's as empty as a speakeasy after the cops've raided, sir."

Corsi sighed, turning her attention back to the cultural specialist. "There isn't even any livestock. I think it's been abandoned."

Carol suppressed a mild feeling of disappointment. "Well," she said finally. "I can still learn a great deal from firsthand observation of whatever's left."

"Could be trouble with that killer around," growled Vinx softly.

"I agree," Corsi replied, "but we both determined that the coast was clear." She raised her voice again. "Okay, Carol, go ahead. Vinx, do recon and then wait for Lauoc to return."

She jogged toward Carol, catching up without any visible loss of breath. Her professional eye took in a wealth of details related to the safety of the party, even as she knew Carol was collecting a similar amount of information related to the planet's culture.

Corsi's eyes narrowed. "The door's off its hinges." She drew her phaser with one hand while stepping forward and halting Abramowitz with her other arm. "Wait here."

She stepped forward into a single room, noticing the lack of decoration. There was a single wooden table and two chairs, a small cot, and shelves holding jugs and tableware. Some of this lay broken on the floor, signs of a struggle or an earthquake; it was impossible to say without more information. Whatever had happened, it had happened months ago at least. Everything was covered with a thick layer of dust.

"Abramowitz to Corsi."

Corsi tapped her combadge. "Carol, you've got to give me time to check the situation before you start complaining. It's hardly been two minutes."

"There's something you should see out back."

She felt her headache coming back, and closed her eyes for a moment. "If you're out back, I assume you didn't obey my orders to wait."

Carol didn't answer for a moment. *"I really think you should see this."*

The security chief kept her phaser ready while she left the

building and jogged to Carol's position behind the farmhouse, near to a large wooden structure that seemed to be a barn.

Carol was standing with her arms crossed, staring at a rough mound of dirt covered with leafy green shrubs. "How many people do you think lived here?" she asked quietly.

Corsi mulled the question briefly. "Two, three at most. If that mound is a grave, it would certainly be big enough." She ran the tricorder over it. "And if I don't miss my guess, the mound was dug out and filled back in just the once."

"Meaning everyone on the farm died at the same time."

"Why hasn't anyone taken the farm for themselves? Land seems good, building structures are sound."

The wind began to whistle past the wooden buildings. Carol hugged her cloak closer to her body. "Unless their deaths were considered ill-omened," she said. "They could be the victims of a disease, but we've discovered no signs of a plague. I'd guess they were murdered."

"Perhaps by an entity which at that time still had enough self-control to bury the remains." Corsi was about to signal for Lauoc and Vinx to join them, when Lauoc contacted her.

"I've found the Jem'Hadar base, Commander. It's about two hours from your position."

"Wait there. We'll join you." She severed the link. "I think we might be getting closer to our killer."

They moved into the forest cautiously, Vinx on point, weapons hidden from Jarolleka. The Corotican had decided to move closer to the group now, after Vinx had explained that the mysterious killer was possibly nearby. Corsi walked behind Carol and Jarolleka, keeping an eye on the Corotican as much as on the dark woods. There was no reason to assume their strange companion wasn't dangerous, perhaps even the very quarry they hunted.

"Why have you been avoiding my sister and me?" asked Carol, trying to sound as unassuming as possible. Either woman might have inadvertently broken a cultural taboo at some point, something that governed relations between the

Corotican genders. Still, she had been given very few opportunities to ask, and subtlety was not always an option. He had
seemed less bound to local traditions than the other Coroticans they'd met, and more inclined to philosophy.

He was silent for a few minutes, and Carol feared she'd lost
him altogether. "You're sick."

"What?" For a moment, Carol was confused, before she
recalled Corsi's allergies. "You mean Domenica's sneezing?
That's an . . . that's a reaction to something in the air. It's not
contagious."

Jarolleka scowled. "All disease can be spread, through the
air or by touch. I would have separated from you, if we were
not in danger of catching a bloodier death."

"I'm not ill, though," replied Carol.

"You vomited when we found the mangled body."

Carol almost chuckled. "That was because I was . . . disturbed, by the body. It was a reaction, not an illness."

"Sick is sick," he barked, and walked faster, trying to out-
pace her. Vinx turned and hissed at him, and Jarolleka reluctantly resumed his place in the formation.

*These people believe that everything can be spread like a cold
or a flu,* she realized. Even stress reactions. Carol suddenly recalled Corsi's priest, who had said something about catching
a disease from the first murdered victim. Could they actually
believe that you could "catch" murder?

"Jarolleka," she asked slowly. "Are you worried that you'll
be killed by the murderer, simply because you were so close to
the body?"

He looked away. "It was one thing Ushpallar was right
about."

After another awkward silence, she realized he wasn't going
to give her any more willingly. "About what?"

"When Ushpallar told us about 'disease' and 'germs,' some
at the Academy were thrilled. Ixardes had been arguing for
tiny atoms invading the body and causing illness for decades!
But when people angered the god, he would predict doom, or
kill every one of ten. And sure enough, soon the nine would
follow. Dead in their homes, and sometimes their families
with them. Sometimes there was no sign of violence or dis-

ease at all. The people were just *dead*." He turned back to her, and the anguish and confusion was written on his face. "This was 'germs' at work. Some force called 'bacteria.' What natural science did we have to face that? All one could do was cover one's face when death passed, or avoid being on the same street as a dead man. That's all anyone can do." This time, when he began to march forward, Vinx looked ready to let him pass.

"Look out!" shouted Corsi.

A dark shape leapt from the trees, hammering Jarolleka to the ground in a flurry of leaves and noise. A limb shot up and caught Abramowitz under the chin, throwing her back into Corsi's line of fire. Carol arched her back, arms flailing, as Corsi's shot hit her in the shoulder.

Vinx spun on his heel and lashed out with his right arm, but failed to connect with anything solid. The whirling shape, covered in filthy rags, threw itself forward. Something cracked against Vinx's forehead, and he wobbled backward against a tree. Without a pause, the shape leapt into the thicket and crashed away.

Checking that Jarolleka was still facedown on the ground, Corsi aimed her phaser toward the noise and fired three times, aiming with five degrees of difference with each shot. She knew she'd hit nothing. "Vinx, are you up?"

"We'll put 'im in cement shoes if we got to," said the Iotian unsteadily.

"Damn." Corsi knew she couldn't leave Abramowitz alone with a potentially dangerous local and an addled security guard, and it was always possible that there was more than one killer, trying to trick the party into separating. She'd have to trust that Vinx would recover his wits while the trail was still warm. She glanced at Carol, who was sitting up and groaning.

Concentrate on what you can do, she thought. "Carol, did your tricorder get any readings on what that was?"

Abramowitz shook her head. "Not sure." She quickly picked her tricorder up. "The radiation must still be interfering. This says that our attacker was a Gallamite. And it was too dark and the attack too quick to make it out visually."

Corsi rubbed the back of her neck. "It seemed too small for a Jem'Hadar."

"The mug seemed pretty big to me." Vinx was rubbing his eyes and getting slowly to his feet.

Carol got to her feet and pulled out a small flashlight. Taking Vinx's head in her left hand, she shone the light into each of his eyes while he stood still and blinking. "No concussion, I think. You'll be fine."

"Shake it off, soldier." Corsi grinned. "I want to follow that trail. Vinx, get these two to the Jem'Hadar base."

"Aye, sir." He watched as his commanding officer moved into the woods, following the attacker. After a moment, he turned to Carol and Jarolleka. "C'mon, guys and dolls. Let's motor."

CHAPTER
8

Corsi was following the trail as best she could, her tricorder all but useless in the radiation. Sometimes it would flash a warning that there was a Klingon ahead, or a Tiburonian, or on one exciting occasion, that there was an Andorian, a Tellarite, and a Vorta three kilometers to the west. *That sounds like a very bad joke*, mused Corsi.

Regardless, the tricorder's problems were the main reason why the discovery of Lauoc's prone body was such a surprise. Corsi didn't need her faulty equipment to tell her that the Bajoran wasn't moving, and with her allergic reactions still suppressed by Carol's last cocktail, her nose was enough to inform her that the area was covered in blood.

She knelt and quickly took Lauoc's pulse. It was faint, but steady. She rapidly took stock of his injuries: lacerations on the face and chest, a broken right leg where he'd fallen, and a bite mark on his arm. She frowned and shone a light on the last injury. Tooth marks, humanoid tooth marks, and it wasn't a simple bite taken in the heat of battle.

Someone had eaten a chunk of Lauoc's arm.

"That's disgusting," she muttered, even as she realized her quarry might still be close.

She pulled an emergency hypospray. "Sorry, Lauoc, this is going to sting." She pressed the device against his neck, and a groan informed her that Lauoc was waking up. A second groan told her he was feeling the bloody wound on his arm.

Corsi touched her combadge, cursing the little bleep that accompanied its activation. "Vinx, I'm heading back with Lauoc. He's injured. Whatever this thing is, it's not averse to eating us."

"We're almost at the base, Commander."

Corsi cut the contact without another word; as much silence as possible was best under the circumstances. "Let's get you up and back to the others." Letting the creature that did this go, even for the moment, gnawed at Corsi's conscience. But there was no alternative, not if it meant letting Lauoc fend for himself with his injuries. She draped his right arm around her shoulders and forced them both to their feet, and began moving back the way she came.

The small group was silent, each nursing their own thoughts. The news of Lauoc's injury confirmed their worst fears: There was something sentient out there, attacking both natives and Starfleet indiscriminately. *Madness is disturbing in every culture,* thought Carol.

"What if it's one of us?" asked Vinx quietly, Jarolleka well behind them. "What's if it's that Starfleeter who was left behind?"

Carol shook her head. "It doesn't matter. Whoever it is, they're not well, and we have to help them."

Vinx shuddered. "But . . . cannibalism, doll? Even Iotia at its worst, we never ate nobody." His gangland accent was as thick as Carol had ever heard it, the stress of the moment causing him to revert to his most basic speech patterns.

Carol placed a hand on his shoulder. "It's the madness, not the person. We'll do what we can to stop it, and then we'll do what we can to make certain it doesn't happen again."

The Iotian shook his head in horror. Carol was reminded, as she had been again and again in this mission, that Sigma Iotia had only been a member of the Federation for a decade, and had only known about the Federation for a century or so. They hadn't had the benefits of living with modern psychological practice. Madness was madness to them, a thing to be avoided, to be feared. Just as any kind of illness was a frightening mystery to the native Coroticans. The idea that this savage wandering the woods might be a representative of the Federation, possibly even a human, was bound to disturb a man from a society heavily influenced by old Earth.

Vinx was saved from having to respond to Carol's assurances by a sudden glimpse of a clearing through the trees. "That's the base ahead," he said, his voice rough. "I'll go down first, make sure the coast is clear." He moved silently into the brush, his Starfleet training taking over.

"Where's Iotia?" asked Jarolleka quietly, standing in the shadows behind Carol.

Corsi was barely making any progress at all, and with the team obeying an unspoken command to radio silence except in dire circumstances, she couldn't be certain Vinx had managed to get the team safely to the Jem'Hadar base. Worse, she wasn't certain what they'd find there if they had arrived safely.

"Looked . . . abandoned," spat Lauoc through gritted teeth. Had they served together long enough for him to anticipate her thoughts that way, or was he just a damn fine soldier?

"I'm sure it was," she replied. "No Jem'Hadar could live without the white for this long."

Lauoc chuckled, a grim sound more pained than amused. "We both know that's not necessarily true."

One step after another, she thought. Aloud, she asked if he knew what had hit him.

"Tricorder said it was human, possibly an Alpha Centaurian."

"You didn't see it?"

"Just a shape lurching up from the ground in front of me.

The thing's fast. Taking us down earlier wasn't a fluke." He paused, drew in a shuddering breath. "There was an odor, but I couldn't place it."

Corsi nodded, aware that Lauoc wouldn't see it in the dark. "Would you recognize it if you smelled it again?"

He sucked in his breath as Corsi stumbled slightly over a root in the dark. "Not . . . sure. It was like . . ." His voice trailed off.

Corsi stopped and took him by the shoulders. His eyes were closed. "Stay with me, Lauoc."

The Bajoran's eyes fluttered open. "I am with you. And so is it. I'm smelling it again."

She let him drop, knowing the fall would do less damage than an unprotected assault from the creature. She aimed her phaser steadily and rhythmically, first behind her and then to the left, and then forward.

Something shifted in the trees above her and she glanced up, the phaser following her line of sight perfectly. She could see nothing but darkness until something shone briefly.

Eyes. Bright blue eyes, blinking.

She fired into the branches, and something black against black moved quickly away. She knew instantly that she hadn't hit it, and that it had moved in exactly the direction it had wanted to move, toward the Jem'Hadar base and her team.

CHAPTER
9

"Iotia?" Carol wracked her brain, trying to summon a visual image of the Corotican continent. "It's on the eastern coast. It's very small. Lady Domenica's family is from Iotia."

Jarolleka stared at her for a moment, calmly. "That might be so."

Carol glanced toward the Jem'Hadar base, willing Vinx to summon them down. Reluctantly she turned back to the Corotican. "You sound like you're not very sure about that."

The man shrugged with a sigh, glancing up at the stars. "My whole life," he said, not looking at her, "I believed that the gods didn't care. They weren't evil. They just weren't concerned with us. They weren't our creators, weren't our masters. They were simply another order of beings, living their lives as we lived ours."

Carol felt a wave of sadness. "And then one of them showed up."

Jarolleka nodded, eyes shining with unshed tears. "And then one of them showed up. The One who Blesses and Condemns."

Carol moved closer to him, debating whether to touch his

shoulder sympathetically or not. "And he condemned Ajjem-kuyr."

"The Academy had survived zealots before. The city hadn't always appreciated our efforts. We'd been accused of corrupting the youth, or angering the gods, or whatever. In the old days, any famine or storm could be an excuse to torch the library and kill the scholars. But gradually, over time, they learned to accept us. Ajjem-kuyr became a city of enlightenment. We kept our temples and ceremonies, but we did it for *ourselves*, because of who *we* were."

He laughed bitterly. "And then it turned out the zealots were right. We had angered the gods, and they *did* care. They cared very much. So much death because of our arrogance."

Carol fought back the lump in her throat. Her own society prized knowledge and valued human achievement beyond all else. Humans respected the beliefs of their allies, the Klingons and Bajorans who still held fast to religious belief; some humans, even her own commanding officer, participated in traditional Terran spirituality. Her ship was named after a man who had achieved excellence in almost every field of endeavor available to him. But above all else, Federation life was a journey of discovery and tolerance and liberty. Before her very eyes, this world's own Leonardo da Vinci seemed to be withdrawing into a shell of ignorance and fear. If she let him, the Federation's problem would be solved: This world's traditions would be preserved, but at the expense of its diversity.

A Nikolai Rozhenko would be thrilled; another primitive culture saved so that the Federation could babysit it, learn from it, admire its own past made visible in the present.

She still hadn't decided what to say when Vinx called from the base, his voice strained as he ordered them to hurry down.

Vinx walked to the messed-up building slow-like, an itchy trigger finger on his heater. The building wasn't nothing to write home about, maybe thirty feet tall, no windows, and a big pair of double doors with what looked like a steel strip across the middle.

People told tales back home, from back before the Book, about people that ate other people. Moms and Dads told their kids about cannibals to make them sit down and shut up, but the stories hit real close to home with *every* Iotian. Rat-a-tat-tat, and things that went bump after the music stopped and streetlights went off. Maybe it was the same for everybody in this crazy galaxy, but it also meant that Makk Vinx was as jittery as a stool pigeon at a family reunion.

He sprinted as quiet as he could to the wall of the plastisteel structure, which looked as out of place in the forest clearing as a Vulcan lyre in a jazz band. There were empty wooden poles around the perimeter, which Vinx couldn't make heads or tails out of. He knew that some folks back home, people who hadn't been touched by the Book, made wooden idols like this—least until the Feds came and brought the whole damn planet together. It wasn't like those Dominion mokes to build in wood, or to use nothing but metal and force fields for their protection. Nah, the Dominion were hard as rocks, and wanted everyone on their block to know it.

He paused and waited for something, anything, to make a peep. After a few seconds, he breathed again and started sneaking along the wall to the big doors.

The doors definitely weren't Fed gadgets—or Dominion ones, neither—since they didn't open up automatically. His heater in his left hand, Vinx reached out to the big bar in the middle of the door. As he ran his fingers across it, he realized it was welded to the doors. It was a bar to make it so that everything inside the building *stayed* inside the building.

Vinx swallowed hard, but he knew he didn't have no choice. He had to know what was what inside this dump before he called down Doc Abramowitz and the local mug. He leveled his heater and fired along the soldering point, watching as the metal turned all red and bubbly. The job had been done in a hurry, and not by professionals like the guys and gals on the *da Vinci* would do.

Another moment, and the left door was mostly unlocked. The bar's bottom was still welded on, though. Vinx didn't want it dropping to the ground in case anyone inside could hear it go clang, and he sure as shooting wasn't catching the scalding-hot metal. Nah, their first warning would be when he kicked the door in like Kall Porakan bursting in on the Yakkle Gang.

He switched on his wrist light and breathed in deeply. Using a move he learned in his Starfleet security training, he spun himself around and kicked out at the door. *Lot more sophisticated than the coppers back on Iotia, I'll tell you that.*

The door went flying open, making a big racket, and the bar hit the dirt with a sizzle. Flames burst out as it hit the dry grass, which suited Vinx fine—it'd give him cover.

Without hesitating, Vinx went in.

Stevens rubbed the back of his neck, trying to ease out the kinks that had built up over the week. Part of his aches and pains was the work itself, all the intricate wires and sensitive equipment necessary to a proper observation post, which all seemed to require awkward positioning. Fabian would've thought that spending hours under a low console would be second nature to him by now, but the treetop location of the duck blind meant that much of the work had to be done while suspended from various branches and trestles.

But Fabian was bothered by more than the work. Corsi and her team had barely been in contact since they'd decided to pursue the creature killing the locals. He knew that minimal contact was necessary, not only because of the danger but because they were accompanied by a Corotican native. Not knowing how Corsi was doing still bothered him, even though he knew she was more than capable of taking care of herself.

He'd known plenty of people who'd been capable of taking care of themselves. Past tense intended.

Stevens glanced toward Ensign Hj'olla. The Tiburonian was installing a perimeter sensor into one of the native *jopka* trees, facing toward Baldakor. The engineer had to admit that the woman had a knack for the camouflage, and she'd managed to fool him once or twice when he'd tried to tell the real bark from the fake that covered each sensor. She barely left a hair fracture between the two.

As if she'd realized she was being watched, Hj'olla glanced

up toward him. She smiled tentatively and waved slightly. Stevens pulled his hand away from his aching neck just long enough to wave back quickly, and she looked away.

Their friendship had started out flirtatiously, and Fabian had to admit he'd enjoyed the slightly guilty little secret. But as Corsi remained in the Corotican wilderness for day after long day, Stevens had found that flirting had come less and less easily.

He hadn't wanted to offend or trouble the Tiburonian officer, but Fabian only had mental space for two things: his work on the duck blind, and the safe return of Domenica Corsi.

The Jem'Hadar base was darker than a tar pit, and quieter than Rosie's Bar after closing, but even without the wrist light Vinx would've known that it was a space as big as a hangar. He smelled something like rotten meat, and some twisted shapes were looming in front of him. Vinx shone his light through the smoke of the grass fire at the floor in front of him, and jumped as it fell on the eyes of a Jem'Hadar, its mouth snarling.

Shouting, Vinx dropped, aimed his heater, and fired, holding the trigger until the Jem'Hadar started to smoke.

Panic settling into his bones, Vinx shone the light from left to right. Everywhere he looked, some Jem'Hadar mug stared back at him, eyes all blank. It was only when he doped out that they were piled on top of each other that Vinx was frosty enough to look away and try to find the light switch in this dump.

He found a panel, but tapping it didn't do nothing. Vinx looked around with the wrist light until he found a Jem'Hadar hand. Bracing for the jamoke's weight, Vinx stumbled when he yanked on the arm and realized it wasn't attached to nothing.

Holding the severed limb, all red and crusty at the end where the shoulder shoulda been, Vinx muttered the most expressive of all Iotian curses: "Mamma mia." He pressed the cold dead hand against the access panel.

When the lights came on, row by row to the hangar's back wall, Vinx realized that this wasn't no tea party. *Hundreds* of these Dominion mooks were all over the place, most of them in pieces. A bunch were piled in a semicircle around the doors. Vinx saw that the inside of the doors had scratch marks and burns that were probably from Dominion heaters.

The twisty stumps at the end of some Jem'Hadar hands showed Vinx how *that* happened.

Worse, as Vinx stepped gingerly over the mangled corpses, he saw that lots of these guys had weird scars on their arms and faces. There were green scales on the floor, like someone ripped them off, and lots of the Jem'Hadar had blood around their mouths.

But Jem'Hadar don't eat flesh, 'cause they just like to chow down on that white stuff, thought Vinx, trying to keep from vomiting all over the bodies. *Unless they ran outta white, and someone gets the bright idea of getting it straight from another mug's veins . . .*

Corsi's voice on his squawk box caused Vinx to nearly drop his heater, and he truly hoped his boss lady hadn't heard him squeaking like a little girl.

He cleared his throat. "Vinx here."

"The creature's nearly killed Lauoc and it's heading back to base. I'm pursuing as fast as I can, but it's likely going to be up to you."

"Me?" stuttered Vinx. He felt queasy. It was all too much. What the hell was a dumb kid from the slums of Grak Street doing in Starfleet, anyhow? "It's a massacre here, sir. All the Jem'Hadar, they were trapped in the building. They killed each other." He paused again, the pieces falling into place. "I think their Vorta did it."

There was a silent pause. *"Vinx, can I depend on you?"*

Vinx worked his throat, but he couldn't make the words come.

"Vinx," came Corsi's voice, with more steel in it than Vinx had ever heard. *"I need you to stop this jamoke, Vorta or not. Capisce?"*

The Iotian took a deep breath and tried to calm his nerves, his own dialect from an unexpected source working like a salve. "I got it, doll." He checked his heater, and knocked up to a higher setting than stun. "I got it."

*   *   *

Outside, Carol and Jarolleka skittered down the slope toward the Jem'Hadar clearing in a hail of small stones and twigs. Vinx's warning had been perfectly clear: The creature was coming, it was likely a Vorta, and it wouldn't hesitate to kill. Carol resisted the urge to glance over her shoulder, afraid of what she might see screaming out of the alien forest.

The doors to the base were open, and Vinx had told her that he was inside and that she be prepared for the worst. She called on the almost-forgotten sprinting she'd done in college, willing her legs to move faster.

Behind her, Jarolleka fell with a startled scream.

Carol whirled, aiming her phaser, unsure of what she'd be able to do face-to-face with an insane killing machine but unwilling to leave the Corotican philosopher to his fate.

Jarolleka's face and elbow were bleeding as he forced himself up from where he'd fallen. He kicked his right leg free from the root that had tripped him up, and Carol's anxious glance quickly told her that no murderous creature had pushed him. "Come on," she said, relief washing over her. "Let's get inside!"

Without waiting, she turned back to the doors just as a figure shimmered into view directly in front of her, its wild blue eyes filled with a mad hunger.

Corsi ran faster than she'd run in years, legs pumping and lungs burning, crashing through the scrubby brush and past the thick local pine trees.

She was just as worried about the wounded Lauoc, left on his own behind her, as she was for the team members ahead of her. If the creature wasn't as mad as she thought, if it decided to double back for the easy mark, Lauoc would pay for her gamble with his life. Everyone knew that security often had to make the ultimate sacrifice. Galvan VI had brought that reality home to Corsi rather brutally—seventy percent of her security force died there. But sometimes you had to decide who to save instead of just risking your own life. Lauoc knew that, but Corsi prayed she wouldn't have to live with the consequences of her decision. She'd only just buried Ken Caitano. . . .

All she could do was to keep running, committing fully to the decision she had made. Nothing killed faster than indecisiveness.

"Hello, meat," said the Vorta, its teeth black and rusty-red with grime and blood, barely recognizable from his image in the stained glass.

Carol tried to pull her phaser up, aware that she couldn't miss but also curiously certain that she would. The Vorta was faster, grabbing her wrist and squeezing hard enough to break it. The phaser fell to the ground. His other hand darted for her throat, his sharp nails scratching the skin. His breath was fetid, and between the stench and his iron grip Carol had to fight to retain consciousness.

Behind her, Jarolleka's knees buckled. To him, Carol knew, Ushpallar had returned, returned to kill the last son of Ajjem-kuyr and his strange allies. Tears began to stream down his paralyzed face.

"We've . . . come to help," gasped Carol. "The war's . . . over."

"The war?" wheezed the Vorta. "The war against heresy never ends. Never. I came to bless this place, and now I must condemn it. I condemn thee, disbeliever!"

Carol managed to make her arms work, but her blows were weak and getting weaker as the air left her lungs and her vision began to fade. "You're not a god!" she gasped.

"Aren't I?" His mouth opened, and the grimy teeth began to move toward Carol's cheek.

Carol shut her eyes, nearly unconscious, the blood roaring in her brain. This was how she was going to die? She survived combat, Galvan VI, and Teneb, only to be the last victim of the Dominion War, at the hands of a cannibal Vorta with delusions of godhood?

Just as his thin scabby lips brushed her skin, a shadow fell across the Vorta and his victim, and his grip loosened. Carol dropped to the ground like a stone as the Vorta lurched forward, hit from behind by a thick branch.

"If you are a god," snarled Jarolleka, breathing heavily with the effort to force his limbs into motion, both hands gripped tightly on his impromptu weapon, "you're a pretty pathetic one. We don't need your condemnation any more than we need your help."

The Vorta glanced back at him, shoulders hunched, a terrible smile playing across its pale features. Jarolleka paled and took an involuntary step backward.

"It doesn't matter what you need," said the Vorta. "You are to serve us." Shimmering, the Vorta disappeared. Dimly, through the pain that wracked her body, Carol noted that the disappearing effect didn't look like a Jem'Hadar shrouding—which was a biological ability of that species, one the Vorta didn't share—but looked similar to what happened when a Federation observer post's duck blind was activated.

Jarolleka looked around wildly, whimpering.

Carol rose to her knees, rubbing her bruised neck. "It's a shroud," she hissed, every word painful. "It's . . . it's just a kind of natural law."

The Corotican looked into her eyes, and it seemed to Carol that he calmed visibly just before something hit him hard from behind. He buckled forward, his arms barely resisting his fall. Carol tried to scream, but no sound came from her damaged throat.

A shape hurtled out from the entrance to the base, leaping up and over Carol before she had time to duck. She fell backward, looking up to see Vinx putting his shoulder into a shimmering figure.

Both combatants fell to the ground, but Vinx leapt to his feet first, catching the now-visible Vorta on the chin. Blood spewed from the Vorta's mouth, but Vinx showed no mercy, following up with another solid blow to his stomach. The Vorta collapsed to the ground, and Vinx slowly pulled his phaser and carefully set the weapon to stun.

"Good night, buddy." Vinx fired a short burst into the Vorta's chest.

Carol forced herself to stand. "How did you know where to throw yourself?" she whispered.

Vinx smiled, wiping his brow with a dirty uniform sleeve. "The bad guy always goes for the dame first."

"That's so . . . old-fashioned."

"I'm an old-fashioned kind of guy, toots," he said with a shrug that involved his entire upper body. "And I did it . . . my way."

CHAPTER
10

Tarsem Johal slowly turned his combadge over in his right hand, letting the light from the Corotican sun catch it as he repeated the gesture. The sacrifices his crew had undergone since the Dominion War began—Moseley on the *Ogun*, for example—had largely been unrelated to their work here on Coroticus. They were scientists, archaeologists, and historians, and like everyone in the Federation they'd become accustomed to pursuing their research in peace, undeterred by an angry universe. Well, barring the occasional discovery of a primitive supercomputer or the sudden appearance of an angry and omnipotent godling.

Where had he heard that before? Johal smiled softly and glanced down at the shining combadge again. Saed Squire, imparting his wisdom to the unwary scientists under his protection. He seemed to know every obscure story of Federation archaeology gone awry, and have at least three plans prepared to deal with each and every eventuality. Just as he'd had a plan for protecting Coroticus as best he could while ensuring his crew escaped safely.

Johal hadn't realized, until Corsi and her team caught the

renegade Vorta, just how much he'd been dreading the possibility that the madman was Squire. To know that the man's last actions were uncomplicated by a subsequent period of murder and insanity meant that this small story had a decent ending; it was part of a much larger story of sacrifice and despair, and eventual triumph, but Squire had gone out as he'd have wanted.

The commander had briefly considered returning to active duty, delaying his retirement to finish the job here on Coroticus and replace the memories of those last frantic, tragic moments with something better. He looked back at the S.C.E. crew, shaking hands with the personnel who'd be left behind to finish the rebuilding of the observation post.

Seeing a Starfleet crew giving their all in the service of science rather than war, knowing that every effort had been made to correct the damage done to Coroticus not because they had to or because it was their fault, but because it was a sacred duty . . . Tarsem Johal knew that those better memories had already been made.

He was looking forward to fresh strawberries.

Dyrvelkada rubbed his chin thoughtfully, glancing up at the sky with both wonder and fear. "A war in heaven?"

Walking beside him in the funeral grounds, Carol nodded. Jarolleka, recovering from his injuries, walked at a discreet distance behind the Sibling and his female companion. "Heaven has been torn by the strife of gods. Ushpallar came to you to protect you, to protect all who walk and think upon the green world, but now he has returned to defend his own kind."

The priest looked back over his shoulder at Jarolleka. "He Who Blesses and Condemns told us that he had destroyed Ajjem-kuyr for its disbelief. Now you are telling me that this was not true. Can a god lie?"

"You heard the rumors of shape-shifters?" The Sibling nodded. "These are the enemies of the gods, as you well know. They have been active among you. Sometimes, Ushpallar was your friend. Sometimes, he was your foe." *Well, it had a certain kind of truth to it*, thought Carol with a grimace.

"Our legends knew the shape-shifters of old, the Henjiqi who hunted our kind before we knew language or of tools." Again, he glanced at Jarolleka. "Please, my son, walk with us. If you believe what Carolabrama says is true, we have no reason to be enemies."

"I'm not your son," said Jarolleka with the faintest of snarls, but at a warning glance from Carol, he consented to walk beside the priest.

"Far from enmity," Carol ventured, "your causes are more alike than you know. You both seek truth, each in your own way. The Henjiqi shape-shifters knew that Ajjem-kuyr could discover the truth through observation of the stars. And so they decided that Ajjem-kuyr would be destroyed."

Jarolleka did not meet her gaze. Although they had not spoken of the Vorta or the events at the Jem'Hadar base, Carol knew that the Corotican was deeply troubled by what he had seen and felt. He seemed even more uncomfortable with Carol's explanation of their recent history, but with no greater explanation of his own, he seemed willing to nurse his doubts privately.

Dyrvelkada was less willing to gloss over the inconsistencies. His demeanor was troubled, and he paused to glance again at the blue Corotican skies. "A war in heaven." He looked back at Carol. "And how is it that your people know this?"

When Carol had come up with her plan for the containment of the cultural contamination, she had desperately tried to find a satisfactory answer to that question, which she knew would be asked. Now that the question had come, Carol surprised herself by having a sudden answer to hand, as though it had been lurking in her mind for months. She looked directly into Dyrvelkada's eyes. "We know because the dark gods came to us, and tried to rule us as Ushpallar ruled you."

The Sibling gazed at her thoughtfully for a long moment, before nodding once, and turning away to return to the safety of Baldakor's temple. Carol knew, somehow, that her story was about to enter the region's spiritual lore.

"That was the first thing you said to him that I believed," said Jarolleka softly.

"Why that?"

He smiled faintly. "Because you said it with a sadness that cannot be false." He came forward to embrace her, and she returned the hug. "I have much to do. I think that Dyrvelkada will support my application to rebuild the Academy, and help to raise the necessary funds. Your tale has seen to that. It is as though a balance needs to be restored."

Carol nodded. "It seems that way to me, yes."

Jarolleka shook his head ruefully and gave a hesitant grin. "It will be like starting over from the beginning, making the people see what we have to offer. We'll have to go through the same persecutions, the same censorships. But it will be worth it."

"Where will you seek to rebuild?"

This time, his smile was real. "In the field where I saw Ushpallar brought down by a mortal with a strange manner of speaking. It is time I began." With a nod, he turned and followed Dyrvelkada's path back to Baldakor.

She heard faint footsteps approaching from behind her. Was everyone on this planet addicted to sneaking up on her? She turned to see T'Mandra, who paused long enough to tell her that the *da Vinci* was to arrive within twenty minutes.

"Thank you, T'Mandra." The Vulcan woman nodded curtly and marched off to find other errant personnel.

Carol smiled. She had indeed restored the balance between tradition and innovation on Coroticus, but she didn't think anyone could blame her if she was pleased that innovation might have received just a little extra help on the way.

SECURITY

Keith R.A. DeCandido

CHAPTER
1

U.S.S. da Vinci
in transit between Recreation Station
Hidalgo and Coroticus III
one week ago

The crystalline walls sparkled with reflected light as the brown ball shot out arcs of electricity at the nine Starfleet personnel in EVA suits.

A bizarre structure had entered the Artemis system, and the *U.S.S. da Vinci* had been sent to investigate this unknown technology. While doing so, they found a known one: the brown ball, an Androssi security device.

One of the Starfleet people, a Tellarite officer, broke cover and headed for one of the faceted wall sections that looked like a series of sparkling icicles. Another bellowed, "Tev, what the hell are you doing?"

Two seconds after Lieutenant Commander Tev broke cover,

another followed him, this an enlisted security guard, armed with a phaser rifle, which he shot at the brown ball.

"Computer, freeze program."

At the command from Lieutenant Commander Domenica Corsi, the tableau stopped moving. Andrew Angelopoulos sighed. *Here it comes.*

"All right," the security chief said to the people under her command, gathered in the *da Vinci*'s hololab for a debrief, "who can tell me what Angelopoulos did wrong there?"

Around him, six other enlisted guards raised their hands. Angelopoulos put his head in his.

Standing before them, Corsi, flanked by her deputy, Chief Vance Hawkins, smiled. "Angelopoulos, do *you* know what you did wrong?"

Venturing a smile, he said, "Yes, ma'am—I shouldn't have bothered wasting my breath and energy defending a stupid officer who doesn't know not to break cover?"

Several chuckles started to form, then died when Corsi's facial expression managed—somehow—to get darker.

"*Most* officers—particularly engineers, a type of officer we are overburdened with on this ship—are too stupid to know not to break cover. That's why *we're* here. Now, when Hawkins beamed down with you, Robins, Lauoc, Krotine, and T'Mandra to support Tev, Stevens, and Conlon, you each had a task. Hawkins was in charge, Lauoc and T'Mandra were to secure the perimeter, and what were the rest of you supposed to do, Robins?"

Angelopoulos had opened his mouth to answer, but Corsi had instead posed the question to Madeleine Robins. She had been in security on the *da Vinci* since the ship was first given over to the S.C.E. six years ago; she even predated "Core-Breach."

The older woman said, "We were to protect the engineers, ma'am. I had Stevens, Krotine had Conlon, and Angelopoulos had Tev."

"Right. Krotine, what does protecting the engineers *mean*, exactly?"

The wiry Boslic woman gave Angelopoulos an apologetic

look before saying, "Stick by the engineers at all times—no matter what."

"No matter what, yes."

Corsi paced back and forth in the hololab. Angelopoulos wished they would get past this part and move on to their assignments for the upcoming mission—from what Angelopoulos heard from Bennett and Phelps in engineering, they were splitting into three groups. Before that, though, Corsi was taking the opportunity to pick apart their mission to Artemis IX, undertaken before their unexpected rescue of Commander Gomez from Rec Station Hidalgo.

Finally Corsi turned her pitiless blue eyes on Angelopoulos, who, for his part, was trying desperately to sink into the bench. Next to him, Makk Vinx was doing a terrible job of holding in one of his trademark guffaws.

"Angelopoulos," she said in a slow voice, "does 'no matter what' include following officers when they break cover to start playing with their crystals?"

"Yes, ma'am."

"Yet you didn't do that."

"No, ma'am. Honestly, I wasn't expecting it."

"Congratulations, that's the second wrong answer you've given in five minutes. People, we're security. Our job is to expect the unexpected and to keep the people on this ship safe. You, Angelopoulos, failed in that regard pretty spectacularly on Artemis. Most of you came on after Galvan VI, and that's because seven good people *died* protecting this ship. If you can't handle that, then you can follow Powers out the door. Understood?"

As one, all nine security personnel, even Hawkins, said, "Yes, ma'am."

Angelopoulos bit his lip in annoyance. Back on Risa, Hawkins had asked Angelopoulos what he thought of Corsi, and he described her then as "brusque." *After that dressing-down, brusque would be a relief.*

He also thought that her shot at Frank Powers was unjustified. True, Powers had complained that he signed on to the *da Vinci* because he figured protecting engineers would be comparatively easy duty, only to find the ship diving into a black hole within a few weeks of his signing on. Then he was badly injured on Phantas 61, and when Powers recovered from that, he requested a transfer. *But that doesn't make him bad security, it just makes him . . .*

Angelopoulos didn't finish the thought. He also noticed that, while Corsi mentioned Powers and the people who died at Galvan VI, she didn't mention Ken Caitano. He died, not protecting the ship or doing his duty, but from some secret weapon created by a crazy Vorta, one that also claimed his roommate, Ted Deverick, one of the engineers. Corsi had taken those two murders particularly hard for some reason, and Angelopoulos wondered if that meant she was going to be even harder on them.

Like it could get worse.

"All right, we're en route to Coroticus III—we should be there in three hours. It's one of two pre-warp planets that the Dominion occupied during the war, the other being Sachem II. We're going to help to set the observation posts back up, and also to examine cultural contamination the Dominion might have engaged in, on both worlds. Prime Directive's in full force on this one, and there'll be lots of engineers, including a bunch we picked up at Hidalgo, so the away teams will include four security per. Chief Hawkins will have Angelopoulos, Krotine, and Konya on Sachem. I'll be taking T'Mandra, Vinx, and Lauoc to Coroticus."

Thank God. Angelopoulos let out a long breath. *I thought for sure she'd stick me on her team. At least Hawk doesn't want to kill me. Probably.*

"After that, the *da Vinci*'ll be headed to Avril Station for an upgrade. Robins, you'll be it for security, but Commander Ling told me that six of her people will be detached to you to handle security for Commander Gomez and her team."

Robins simply nodded.

"Powers's replacement will be reporting to the ship at Avril, also, as will Deverick's, and the *U.S.S. Musashi* is supposed to be dropping Lense off—apparently their CMO was up for the same prize. Robins, I expect you to break the new guy in."

"Yes, ma'am."

Even though he knew full well that the best thing for him

would be to keep his mouth shut, Angelopoulos found himself saying: "Uh, ma'am, don't you mean Caitano's replacement?"

Now Corsi glared at him, and Angelopoulos was trying to bury himself *under* the bench. "Of all the people in this room who should be keeping their mouth shut, Angelopoulos, you're pretty much at the top of the list."

"Yes, ma'am. Sorry, ma'am."

"And I said Caitano's replacement."

Angelopoulos wisely said nothing. Hawkins was giving Corsi a strange look—she really *did* say Powers, and that meant something was wrong. But no way was Angelopoulos going to pursue it just at the moment.

"All right." Corsi looked out at everyone. "Dismissed."

Stepping over Vinx and T'Mandra, Angelopoulos set a land speed record getting out of the hololab. He wanted to be away from Corsi as fast as possible. He'd been in security for a little more than three years, going back to just before the war, and one truth he'd learned was that, if you were in your CO's doghouse, avoid said CO like the plague.

On his way down the corridor, he almost literally bumped into Lieutenant Commander Tev. "Sorry, sir."

"Guard," the Tellarite said dismissively, and started to walk past him.

"Uh, sir?"

Tev turned around and asked impatiently, "Yes?"

"I just wanted to apologize to you, sir."

"I was unaware of any offense you'd committed. If you had, I'm quite sure I would have reported you for it."

This is a bad idea, Angelopoulos told himself, but, as with his pointing out Corsi's misstatement, he found the words coming out of his mouth before his brain could stop them. "Back on Artemis, sir, you broke cover, and I was slow to watch your flank. I didn't anticipate your move and lagged behind. So—"

"Of course you didn't anticipate my move." Tev snorted, which sounded like a pipe bursting. "You couldn't *possibly* have worked out how to use the crystalline power systems to overload the Androssi security device as I did—you are simply a security guard. Few on this ship could have anticipated what I would do, and none of them is in security. Therefore, Guard, you have nothing for which to apologize." Tev continued down the corridor. "Now if you will excuse me, I have a most onerous duty to perform."

Well, that didn't make me feel any better.

As Tev continued toward the hololab, Vinx walked up beside Angelopoulos. "When you gonna learn to keep your yap shut, Andy?"

"At this rate? Five minutes after I'm dead."

"Which'll be five minutes from now if you get too close to the boss." The Iotian shook his head. "C'mon, I'll buy you a beer. We got three hours, and we ain't on shift till then. See if we can rustle up some grub, too."

Angelopoulos nodded. "Sounds good. Hey, Makk—what do you think's up with Core-Breach?"

"Nothin's 'up,' Andy. Just 'cause she raked you over the coals don't mean nothin'."

He waved his hand in front of his face. "No, not that. I deserved to get my aft shields blown off for that one. No, I mean the way she called the new guy Powers's replacement instead of Caitano's. What do you think that is?"

Vinx shrugged as they appraoched the turbolift that would take them to the mess hall. "I heard tell that she was buds with Caitano's old man, so maybe that has somethin' to do with it. I dunno, I ain't no head-shrinker. 'Sides, the dame's tired—after *Artemis*, we all are. I'm lookin' forward to a nice easy mission on Coroticus, lemme tell you."

"Yeah." They entered the turbolift. "Hey, why's Tev talking about the hololab being an 'onerous duty'? Thought those engineers loved it in there, playing with their techie toys and stuff."

Vinx leaned in close. "Well, between you, me, and the lamppost, I heard tell that Gomez got Tev takin' some kinda sensitivity trainin'."

Angelopoulos blinked. "You're kidding."

"That's what I heard, anyhow. Hey, if any mook needs it, it's him."

"You said it, brother." Angelopoulos winced. He liked Vinx,

he really did, but there were times where his odd way of talking—common to the natives of Sigma Iotia, who had apparently patterned their entire society after a four-hundred-year-old Earth book about contemporary criminals—rubbed off on him. *If I find myself calling Corsi "sweetheart," I swear, I'm gonna kill him.*

CHAPTER
2

U.S.S. da Vinci
in orbit around Avril Station
two days ago

David Gold exited the turbolift. He had been on his way to his quarters to reread the letter from his granddaughter Ruth. Little Rinic David was adjusting to having a baby sister, the baby was doing fine, and they had finally decided to name her Kiri, after Ruth's husband Rinic's grandmother.

However, before Gold could even make it to his cabin to peruse the letter yet again, he was summoned back to the bridge by a call from the *Musashi*, which he hoped was bringing his chief medical officer back to him. He wasn't sure, as the *Musashi* had to fly through a massive ion storm in order to get here from Station Kel-Artis, where the Bentman Prize had been awarded. Lense had been one of the finalists for the prestigious medical award. So had Dr. Julian Bashir of Deep Space 9, and they had traveled together in one of DS9's runabouts. The *Musashi*, however, had a finalist to pick up in their own chief medical officer, and was then going to Cor Coroli IX. Avril Station was on the way between Kel-Artis and Cor Coroli, so it worked out nicely for everyone.

The replacements for Caitano and Deverick—a young man named Tomozuka Kim and an older woman named Lise Irastorza, respectively—had reported aboard, and the upgrades to Avril were proceeding apace, despite occasional shouting matches between Gomez and Tev.

As he entered the bridge, Gold thought again with sadness about the senseless deaths of Caitano and Deverick. He'd been a captain for a lot of years on a lot of ships, the *da Vinci* for more than six of them, and it never stopped hurting when he lost people under his command.

Gamma shift was on duty: Martina Barre at conn, Alexandre Lambdin at ops, and Winn Mara at tactical. The latter, a tall Bajoran woman, spoke as he sat in his chair. "I have Captain Terapane, sir."

"Good. On screen."

A very concerned-looking face appeared on the viewer, along with a fortyish, balding man with a blue collar on his uniform. *"I'm afraid I have some bad news, Captain. Your doctors weren't at the conference."*

Gold blinked. "Say again?"

The man in the blue collar spoke up. *"Captain, I'm Dr. Dennis Chimelis—I'm the chief medical officer of the* Musashi. *I'm afraid that neither Elizabeth nor Julian made it to the conference. As it happens, they didn't win . . . er, I did, in fact, but the point is—"*

Having no interest in the doctor's point, Gold waved his right hand in front of his face. "What happened to my CMO, Doctor?"

"I honestly have no idea."

Gold whirled around to the tactical station behind him. "Put a call through to DS9, pronto."

Winn nodded. "Aye, sir."

"I'm sorry, if it wasn't for the ion storm—" Terapane started.

"Understandable, Captain. Don't worry, we'll get right on it."

"We need to make time to Cor Coroli IX. Again, sorry about this."

"It's all right. *Da Vinci* out."

As soon as the screen reverted to the view of Avril Station, Winn said, "I've got Deep Space 9, sir."

Gold nodded, and the screen switched, this time to a very familiar Bajoran woman in a Starfleet uniform with a red collar and four pips.

With a wry smile, she said, *"David, this is getting to be a habit."*

"Not a good one, I'm afraid, Nerys," Gold said to Captain Kira in as serious a voice as he could muster. "It seems we've both got us a problem."

CHAPTER
3

U.S.S. da Vinci
in orbit of Coroticus III
now

Vance Hawkins waited impatiently for Laura Poynter to hurry up and finish operating the transporter. *I need to see my woman. Not to mention my CO.*

Their mission to Sachem II had been uneventful. The Dominion had done little to change the lives of the natives, mostly because the natives were fairly easygoing people. P8 Blue had supervised the team of engineers who'd be running the "duck blind," Vance and his people had found no remnants of a Dominion base that might prove problematic—whatever one might say about the Jem'Hadar, they were good at cleaning up after themselves—and Bart Faulwell had found no evidence of cultural contamination. (The linguist also complained that the natives, who called themselves the O-Mor, had the most boring language he'd ever encountered. Vance gamely tried to be sympathetic.)

Now they had to pick up Commander Corsi and her team from Coroticus, which included Carol Abramowitz.

Vance and Carol had been serving on the *da Vinci* together since the war, but it wasn't until their mission to Teneb—during which the entire away team, including the two of them, Fabian Stevens, and Commander Gomez, was almost killed—that they really *noticed* each other. He enjoyed listening to her talk, her sense of humor, her interest in the nuances of how other people lived their lives—and he could even stand to listen to her music for more than five minutes at a time, which put him one up on their two score crewmates.

As Poynter energized the transporter, Vance felt his stomach drop. There had been no vocal communication with the away team to avoid possible Prime Directive issues. They simply sent a signal to Corsi's combadge indicating that the *da Vinci* was approaching. So Vance had no idea how the mission went—though the lack of any kind of distress signal from the duck blind on the planet was, he had hoped, a good sign.

When he saw one of the six members of the team beaming up in a horizontal position, he feared the worst. *Dammit, we just buried Ken and that Deverick kid, and Lense has gone missing—we're not losing another one!*

I'm not losing Carol.

To Vance's relief, the injured team member wasn't Carol, but Lauoc Soan, and Vance soon saw that he was breathing. That tough little Bajoran had been through hell and back during the war, and Vance was fairly sure that, if he was breathing, he'd be fine.

Corsi—like all of them, dressed in the brightly colored clothing and cloak that the Coroticans favored—barked at Poynter, "Get Lauoc to sickbay." She tapped her combadge. "Corsi to Lense—Doctor, you've got a patient."

"Lense isn't back yet," Vance said quickly. Before he could answer the question that Corsi's responding look posed, he tapped his own combadge. "Hawkins to Wetzel. Incoming wounded." Even as he spoke, he felt the subtle change in vibration indicating that they were going to warp speed. Lauoc's body disappeared in a shimmer of light.

"*Acknowledged,*" came Nurse Sandy Wetzel's voice. "*He's just materialized. I'll get the EMH on it.*"

"What happened to Soan?" Vance asked.

"What happened to Lense?" Corsi asked right back. "And why'd we go to warp so fast?"

Since he was the chief petty officer and she was the lieutenant commander, her questions got answered first. "The *Missouri* apparently never made it to Kel-Artis. Nobody's heard from Lense or Bashir since they left DS9 right before that Empok Nor disaster. The *Defiant*'s already searching, and we're heading out to do the same now that we've got you guys."

Shaking her head, Corsi said, "Dammit."

"Captain wants you and Stevens in a staff meeting as soon as you get changed and, uh, bob your ears."

Coroticans had tapered ears, so all of the away team—save for T'Mandra, whose Vulcan physiology gave her adequate natural cover—had their ears surgically altered to pass muster. "Screw the ears." She turned to the others. "Fabe, you're with me. The rest of you, report to sickbay—the EMH can deal with you guys after he fixes up Lauoc. Then report to the security office. The minute my senior staff meeting's over, I'll be briefing you all."

"You'll want to meet the new guy, too," Vance said. "Tomozuka Kim. Robins has been showing him the ropes."

Corsi nodded. "Good."

With that, she and Stevens left. Vinx and T'Mandra followed behind her.

After he gave Poynter a significant look, she said, "Uh, I think I need to go recalibrate something. Back in a bit."

The second the door closed behind Poynter's retreating form, Vance leaned down and kissed Carol passionately. It had been a week, after all. . . .

When he came up for air several subjective centuries later, he smiled down at her, their arms still clasped around each other. "You taste kind of peaty."

She smiled. "That would be when the crazy Vorta dropped me to the ground."

Vance's eyes widened. "*Another* crazy Vorta?"

Nodding, Carol proceeded to tell him about the Vorta who

had set himself up as one of the local deities. Deciding he liked the taste of godhood, he had stayed behind when the order to retreat came in, massacring his Jem'Hadar, and living on his own as a lunatic in the woods of Coroticus for a year, occasionally mutilating a native.

Shaking his head, Vance said, "First Luaran, now this. Did we install a wacky-Vorta magnet on the ship or something?"

"I wouldn't put it past the engineers to build one." Putting her hand to Vance's cheek, she said, "I really missed you down there. I could've used someone to talk to."

"Yeah, well, I don't see us going on a lot of away teams together from here on in, after—" He cut himself off.

She nodded, understanding. It had been a brutal year for all of them, and the most brutal part was Galvan VI, when Commander Duffy died, shortly after proposing to Commander Gomez.

I bet that's why Stevens and Corsi have been dancing around each other for months. Well, that and Corsi's an emotional coward, but try saying that to her face.

Not wanting to gossip about his CO—not even to his girlfriend—he instead said, "Look, I gotta go prep the troops for the meeting."

"And I need to have EMH get rid of these ears." Her hand went to the left one. "They itch like hell."

"Why don't we try to catch up when I'm off-shift—say, the mess hall at 1615 hours?"

She smiled. It was a beautiful smile, and Vance was one of the few who was privileged enough to see it. "It's a date."

They both departed the transporter room. Poynter was standing outside the door.

"What happened to the calibration?" Vance asked pseudo-innocently.

Poynter rolled her eyes. "Yeah, like I need to calibrate things on *this* ship. Why do you think I requested the transfer here? S.C.E. ships are fine-tuned within an inch of their lives—easiest duty a transporter chief ever had."

Chuckling, Vance gave Carol a quick kiss good-bye, then headed toward the turbolift, while she made a beeline for sickbay.

CHAPTER
4

U.S.S. da Vinci
in transit between Coroticus III
and Station Kel-Artis
now

Rennan Konya walked into the security office alongside Makk Vinx. An unfamiliar mind was inside, and when he looked around he pegged it as the very young human male sitting alone on the port side of the room. He recognized the minds sitting on the starboard side: T'Mandra's orderly thought patterns and Andrew Angelopoulos's somewhat more chaotic ones. Rennan wasn't a strong enough telepath to detect a non-Betazoid's actual thoughts, but he was able to get general impressions, and he certainly knew when he was around the people he worked with without ever having to see their faces.

"Looks like we're early," he said to the Iotian.

"That must be the new mug. C'mon, let's roll out the welcome mat."

The "new mug" was sitting ramrod straight, and he seemed eager to please in the way that only recent recruits could be.

Makk walked over to him and put a hand on his shoulder. "You nervous, kid?"

Smiling, he said, "A little, yeah."

"Nothin' here to be scared of. You signed yourself up for the best security detail in the quadrant."

"Oh, I already know that, sir."

Rennan chuckled; Makk winced. "Can the 'sir' hogwash, kid. Ain't no officers in this room—exceptin' the commander, of course, but she's a good broad for an officer, so she don't really count."

Unable to resist, Rennan asked, "Why do I get the feeling you'd never say that to her face?"

Grinning, Makk said, "'Cause I ain't got a death wish is why." He offered his hand to the new recruit. "They call me—"

"Makk Vinx," he said, returning the handshake. "And you're Rennan Konya. I'm Tomozuka Kim."

Rennan frowned. "Funny, you don't *look* telepathic."

Grinning, Kim said, "I'm not, I just know the crew roster. I've followed Commander Corsi's career pretty thoroughly, and I've kept track of the security personnel on the *da Vinci* since she reported."

"Why, you got the hots for the commander?" Makk asked with a wink.

"Got the—" Kim seemed confused at first. That was hardly surprising. Since reporting to the *da Vinci* on Earth months ago, Rennan had wondered how a nontelepath could possibly understand a single word Makk said, since without his ability to read the Iotian's perspectives, Rennan himself would have found his colleague to be incomprehensible.

When Kim finally did get it, his cheeks flushed with embarrassment. "Oh, nothing like *that*. God, no, the whole idea's crazy."

"Good thing—she got the hots for Stevens."

Rennan gave a half-smile. "Well, he has the hots for her, anyhow."

"Yeah, jury's still out on that one. So what's the story, kid, why you go around memorizin' Corsi's duty rosters?"

"I'm from Izar. My mother's a peace officer there. A while back, Commander Corsi helped one of our people stop a killer. I was just a kid when it happened—it was ten years ago—"

"You're *still* a kid, kid," Makk said with a wink.

"—but I'll never forget it. She's a big hero on Izar. One of my mother's coworkers, Christine Vale, she quit the force and joined Starfleet."

Makk frowned. "I know that moniker."

"Security chief on the *Enterprise*," Rennan said. "Remember, Phantas 61?"

Realization spread over Makk's face. "Oh, yeah. Not a bad-lookin' broad."

That, Rennan thought, *is a perfect example. How does the word "broad" come to mean a female?*

"Anyhow," Kim said, "when I was old enough, I signed up to join security, too, just like Commander Corsi and Officer—or, uh, Lieutenant Vale. I was hoping for the *da Vinci* or the *Enterprise*, but I'd have taken anything. It was just luck that this opening came when it did."

While he appreciated Kim's enthusiasm, that last line hit a bit too close to home. In a quiet voice, Rennan said, "I think Ken Caitano might disagree with the notion that luck had anything to do with it."

Kim's cheeks flushed again, and Rennan couldn't help but feel the young man's embarrassment this time. "I'm sorry, I didn't mean—"

"Caitano did his job, kid." Makk's voice had hardened, all the friendliness drained from his demeanor, making his eccentric style of speech sound downright scary—though Rennan supposed that he was feeling it more strongly, both telepathically in Makk and within himself, too. Ken was good security, and he deserved better than the senseless death he got.

Makk continued: "He hadn't been on board for more'n a couple days when he put his keister on the line to save the ship. Turned on one of the engineers' doohickeys. He hadn't done that, we'd all be worm food. And then a couple days later, he died from some weapon made by a Vorta who belonged in a rubber room."

"Our job's to protect the people on this ship," Rennan added. "That's a duty we all take very seriously."

Makk stood up. "It'd be real swell if you got your head outta the clouds and remembered that every once in a while. Otherwise, we'll be buryin' you next to Caitano—or worse, we'll be buryin' the guy you let die 'cause you were too busy droolin' over Corsi to do your job right."

With that, the Iotian went over to sit on the starboard side of the security office, with T'Mandra and Andrew.

Kim's regret was washing over Rennan in waves. "I didn't mean anything by that, honest, I just—"

"I know you didn't," Rennan said in as soothing a voice as he could muster, "but you'd better get used to it. Every new assignment in security usually means you're taking over from someone who died in the line and serving alongside that person's comrades. This ship's had it particularly rough this past year, and with only about forty people on board, people tend to get close. And the work is *very* intense. My first couple of weeks here, we explored a city inside a small ball bearing, helped terraform Venus, stopped a Ferengi time traveler, salvaged an alien ship, and went into a black hole. And that was a slow month. Not everyone can handle it. The person Caitano replaced was named Frank Powers, and he transferred off because he couldn't deal with it. Now—"

The door to the security office opened, and Corsi came in—still, Rennan noted after a moment, with the pointed ears from the Coroticus mission. Ellec Krotine, Madeleine Robins, and Vance Hawkins walked in behind her.

Indicating Kim, Vance said, "Commander Corsi, this is Tomozuka Kim, our newest recruit."

Kim stood up at attention. "It's an honor, ma'am!"

Corsi let out a breath. "At ease, Kim. Why?"

Relaxing hardly at all, Kim asked, "Why what, ma'am?"

"Why is it an honor?"

That seemed to surprise Kim. "The commander probably doesn't remember me, but we've met before—ten years ago on Izar. My mother is Officer Soon-Li Kim."

If Kim's earlier embarrassment came in waves, Corsi's anger and hostility came like a slap to Rennan's face. It happened as soon as Kim mentioned that he was from Izar. *What the hell—?*

"Sit down, Kim."

If only Rennan noticed Corsi's fury before she spoke, everyone caught it in her voice now.

Baffled, Kim took his seat. "Uh, yes—yes, ma'am."

Corsi then looked out at the rest of them. "Here's the drill. The Runabout *Missouri*, carrying Doctors Elizabeth Lense and Julian Bashir, has gone missing. It hasn't been seen since departing DS9 two weeks ago. Since the conference they were to attend was to go on for twelve days, no one was the wiser. The *Defiant* has been dispatched to begin the search, and we'll be joining them. They're tracking the runabout's path from DS9—we'll be backtracking from Kel-Artis, the station where the conference was held. Everybody's on alert status until we determine what happened to the *Missouri* and its passengers. Lauoc's out of commission for at least a few days, so we're on beta formation, with Kim in Powers's—or, rather, Caitano's spot."

Rennan blinked. That was the second time since Ken's death that Corsi had done that. Andrew rather stupidly called her on it then. Nobody seemed willing to brave that particular lion in its den now.

"Kim, since you're new, the beta form—" the commander started, but Kim interrupted her, proving he had less of a fear of lions.

"I know the formation, ma'am." Rennan could feel Kim's pride as he spoke. "It's the same as the alpha, only with you substituting for the injured crew member. In this case, you'll be joining Angelopoulos and Krotine on gamma shift, with Chief Hawkins, T'Mandra, and Konya on alpha, and Robins, Vinx, and I on beta."

Rennan was once again impressed with Kim's knowledge of the ship's duty roster. That was a level of preparation most people didn't bother with. *Then again, most people don't worship the water their new CO walks on . . .*

Corsi's anger had come back full bore, though Rennan was more prepared for it this time. "Two things you need to know, Kim. One is that the duty roster shifts every few weeks, and the one you just recited was changed a week ago, after our mission to Artemis IX. And as of right now, the duty roster is changing yet again."

That was a surprise, but only a mild one. Changes didn't happen that fast regularly, but that didn't mean they never did.

"Angelopoulos, Kim, and I will take alpha, with Lauoc slotting back in when he's recovered. Beta is T'Mandra, Vinx, and Robins, with Hawkins, Konya, and Krotine on gamma."

That threw Rennan for a loop—mostly because he felt the loop that it threw Vance into. Rennan knew that Vance had requested alpha shift the next time the duty roster shifted, so he and Carol Abramowitz would be on duty at the same time. When Vance had mentioned it to Rennan, Andrew, and Makk over dinner one night, he had seemed pretty confident that Corsi would grant it. Since Vance had served with the commander longer than anyone on board save Madeleine, Rennan assumed it to be a sure thing. *So why did she stick him on gamma?*

"The second thing you need to know," and now Corsi's anger was starting to make Rennan's head hurt, "is that I do *not* like to be interrupted. Is that understood?"

In a small voice, Kim said, "Yes, ma'am."

"Say again, Mr. Kim, I didn't hear you," Corsi barked.

More loudly, Kim said, "Yes, ma'am!"

"Good." She looked out at the rest of them. "Alpha shift will report to the security office. Kim, you'll be trained on the systems there. Beta and gamma, report to the hololab and run battle drills nine and ten. When beta shift starts, alpha and gamma will continue to do the same, this time integrating Kim into our maneuvers." She let out a breath. "Bear in mind that we could find Lense and Bashir at any minute, and that may require an extraction. Dismissed."

Rennan got up. He felt Kim's disappointment in his first meeting with Corsi, which matched Rennan's surprise. She hadn't been like this when Rennan came on board—which was alongside Makk, Andrew, T'Mandra, Soan, Ellec, and the since-departed Frank Powers.

And it all happened when Kim said he was from Izar. Rennan was glad that he'd been put on the same shift as Vance—this was a concern about the security chief that he needed to bring to the deputy chief's attention posthaste.

CHAPTER
5

U.S.S. da Vinci
in search operations between
Stations Kel-Artis and Deep Space 9
now

Vance Hawkins entered the mess hall in desperate need of a cup of coffee.

He also needed a short break. Konya and Krotine had things under control in the security office, the *da Vinci* hadn't actually found the *Missouri* yet, and Corsi had, miraculously, allowed alpha and beta shift to get some sleep, after running them all through the ringer.

The only other occupant of the mess hall was Fabian Stevens, who had a variety of tiny parts on the table in front of him, along with a cup of coffee that looked like it had long since gone cold.

"What're you doing up?" Hawkins asked as he walked to the replicator. "Coffee, black."

As the steaming drink materialized with a hum in the slot, Stevens looked up and said, "Hm? Oh, uh—couldn't sleep. Commander Gomez, Pattie, Nancy Conlon, and I were up half the night recalibrating the sensors. Nog was kind enough to send over the specs of the *Missouri*, and we've been fine-tuning so that the sensors will find the runabout's seat cushion, if we have to."

"Nice." Hawkins took a seat perpendicular to Stevens and noticed that several of the small pieces on the table were charred and/or broken. "Hope that's not the sensor array."

Grinning, Stevens said, "Nah, these are the tattered remains of my pet project."

Hawkins nodded. "The mobile emitter that Luaran blew all to hell?"

"Yeah, but at least it *worked*. Haven't had the time to save it from Humpty Dumpty status." Stevens took a sip of his coffee. "Gah, this tastes almost as bad as you look."

"Thanks a lot," Hawkins said dryly.

"I ain't kiddin', Hawk, you look like the seventh level of hell. What's Dom been doing to you guys?"

"That answer'd be shorter if you asked what she *wasn't* doing." Hawkins hesitated. He had no more desire to gossip about his boss to Stevens than he had to Carol, but Corsi and Stevens had *something* going on, and maybe the engineer could provide some insights. So he told Stevens about the meeting, and what Konya had told him afterward, and then discussed the training that went on during beta shift. "Angelopoulos has been in her doghouse since Artemis."

Stevens frowned. "Why?"

"He didn't break cover with Tev right off."

Snorting, Stevens said, "You can't expect a 'mere' guard to keep up with the Great One's thought processes. You know, I think he's gotten worse since the *Hyperion*. In retrospect, inviting him along to that wasn't one of my brighter moves—after bossing those cadets around for days, he's expecting the rest of us to act like they did. Commander Gomez didn't come out and say it, but I think she's actually making that jackass take—"

Hawkins held up a hand. "Uh, Fabe? I'm on a break here

and I honestly could give a damn about your problems. I'm
here to bitch to you about my boss, not listen to you bitch
about yours."

Laughing, Stevens got up and headed to the replicator.
"Fine, fine, so what's the problem?"

"Well, Andy talked out of turn a bit during the Artemis debrief, so I can see why the commander's crawling up his butt.
But all Kim did was show initiative and enthusiasm. I mean,
yeah, he was wrong, but it was only because the latest duty
rosters haven't made their way to Command's database yet."

Stevens took a fresh cup of coffee out of the replicator. "And
she's kicking his ass as much as Andy's?"

"More, actually. Give the kid credit, he's taking everything
she's dishing out, but all she does is ride him harder."

Sitting back down, Stevens said, "Well, isn't that what she
does?"

"Not like this." Hawkins drank some of his own coffee, the
hot beverage clearing the cobwebs from his brain. "She had
the off-shift personnel running scenarios in the hololab. When
alpha came in, she whipped out battle drill number twenty."

His eyes widening, Stevens asked, "Galorndon Core?"

Hawkins nodded.

"Ouch."

"And she included the random sensor-blind traps that you
and Duffy put in last year."

"Why do you think I said 'ouch'?" Stevens shook his head.
"When we showed her the gussied-up version of that, she said
she was gonna save it for the next war. Seriously, that's intended for ten-year veterans in security, not newbies."

"I know. Hell, *Robins* was having trouble with it, and it's
actually designed for someone like her."

"And you think it's because of something with Kim being
from Izar?"

"I don't think that, Rennan does, but I trust his judgment."

Chuckling, Stevens said, "Wasn't he the one you thought
wasn't worthy to be on your hallowed security team?"

Hawkins fixed Stevens with a glare. "I expressed a concern
when Rennan signed on. I later retracted it."

"Was that before or after he knocked you down?"

"You do realize that I can just kill you and make up a reason why, right?"

Stevens frowned. "Hang on a sec—you said you're on a break? You're on gamma now?"

Unable to help himself, Hawkins chuckled. "Nice of you to catch up to where the conversation was half an hour ago. Yeah, she put me on gamma, after I specifically requested to be put on alpha next go-round."

"Right, because then you and Carol would have two shifts to go all smoochy-face."

Hawkins raised an eyebrow. "We do *not* 'go all smoochy-face.' I'm not even sure what that means. Anyhow, something's gotten the boss's back up, and I don't know what it is. I don't think it was Coroticus."

Shaking his head, Stevens said, "Not that I noticed, but I wasn't with her as much."

"Not that T'Mandra or Vinx noticed, either—their after-action reports are pretty straight-up."

"On the other hand," Stevens said while rubbing his chin, "she hasn't been entirely right with things since Ken died. You know about them, right?"

Hawkins shook his head, unaware that there was any history between Corsi and Caitano.

"Dom tried to keep it under wraps, but—well, Caitano's dad was her mentor back at the Academy. So when he died—especially like *that*—she took it pretty hard."

Leaning back in the mess hall chair, Hawkins said, "Damn. I didn't know that. That explains a lot, actually." Finishing off his coffee in one gulp, Hawkins then rose. "Listen, I need to get back. Do me a favor—I don't know what exactly you and the commander have going, and I honestly could live a happy life without ever knowing any specifics—"

"This from the man who can't shut up about how wonderful Carol is."

Hawkins shot Stevens another look. "That isn't the point."

"Easy for you to say—I need to wear polarized goggles just to keep from being blinded by your glow."

"Are you gonna listen to me, or are you gonna run your mouth off?"

Grinning, Stevens said, "Evidence to date indicates I can do both."

Hawkins rubbed the bridge of his nose with his right forefinger and thumb. The coffee was doing nothing to alleviate the headache that he'd had since Corsi announced he was on gamma shift. "Can you just talk to her? See if anything's bothering her? And if it is—I don't know, *do* something about it?"

"What do you suggest I do?"

"Didn't I just get finished telling you I don't want specifics?"

"That you did, yes." Stevens sipped from his coffee. "Fine, I'll do what I can, but I can't promise it'll do any good. Believe me, if I had any real impact on the way Dom behaves—well, let's just say that you wouldn't be so unclear as to what we have going."

That brought Hawkins up short. There was a depth of feeling to Stevens's words that he'd rarely heard from the usually freewheeling engineer. "You really care about her, don't you?"

For a second, Stevens's face remained serious, then broke into his trademark grin, though the jocularity didn't quite extend to his entire face. "To a degree that scares the hell out of me sometimes."

Hawkins was about to turn and leave the mess hall, then hesitated. "Carol told me something after we became a couple. She said the thing she got most from both Galvan VI and Teneb was that this is the only life we got, and we don't know when it's gonna be taken away, so it's stupid not to make the most of it."

"Smart lady, is our Dr. Abramowitz." Stevens tried to make the comment sound facetious, but failed.

"I'll talk to you later, okay, Fabe?"

"Definitely."

Hawkins left, still unsure as to what was wrong with his CO, but also a lot more confident about at least one person's ability to take a shot at getting it out of her.

CHAPTER
6

U.S.S. da Vinci
in search operations between
Stations Kel-Artis and Deep Space 9
now

Tev sat at an aft station of the bridge of the *da Vinci*, looking over the recalibrations that Commander Gomez, Chief Engineer Conlon, and Specialists Blue and Stevens had done. The work was excellent, almost as good as Tev himself would have done.

From the tactical station that faced Tev's console, Ensign Winn said, "We've reached the coordinates, sir."

Standing up, Tev looked toward the conn at the fore of the bridge. "Full stop and commence search pattern."

"Answering all stop, sir," Ensign Barre said from conn as she ceased the *da Vinci*'s forward thrust, and applied the reverse thrusters in the configuration necessary to bring the ship to as close to sitting still as was possible in the depths of space.

From next to Barre at the operations console, Ensign Lambdin said, "Beginning search pattern."

Gamma shift was almost at a close, and soon Captain Gold would be arriving to relieve Tev of command of the bridge. The captain and Gomez had, he noticed, taken to walking to the bridge together in the mornings. According to Bartholomew Faulwell, it was a habit they'd developed early on in the commander's tenure as first officer, but one that took some time to redevelop after Tev's predecessor's death. Tev thought that was an odd reason for discontinuing a practice that gave the two top-ranking officers on the ship an opportunity to compare notes and discuss command strategies. However, he said nothing, since he apparently could not communicate with Commander Gomez in any way that would not result in an awkward confrontation.

Awkward primarily from her perspective, of course. The woman was obviously smitten with Tev—not that he could blame her, given his expertise in her chosen field, she would naturally be drawn to like, just as she was to Tev's predecessor—but could not properly express her passion. Tev sympathized with the poor woman, but it sometimes got in the way of the work. Witness the tiresome arguments at Avril Station. If the commander would have just admitted that Tev's diagnostic program was more efficient than hers, he would have been spared the distasteful task of going directly to the station administrator.

The worst were those absurd sensitivity lectures he had to endure in the hololab. The program was apparently designed by Vulcans who were supposedly trying to educate people in how to deal with the more emotional species. Tev failed to see how this advice could possibly have been of use to a Tellarite.

Still, he endured them. As Bartholomew had so succinctly put it, it got the commander off his back.

At 0800 hours, the start of alpha shift, the turbolift doors parted to reveal Lieutenants Wong and Shabalala and Ensign Haznedl. They relieved Ensigns Barre, Winn, and Lambdin, respectively. At 0809, the captain and Commander Gomez entered. Tev had long since come to grudgingly accept that engineers who weren't him had no concept of punctuality, and so did not let his irritation at the fact that his relief was nine minutes late show in his face.

Gomez looked right at him upon entering the bridge. "Tev! Just the Tellarite I want to see." The commander's voice sounded a bit tighter than usual. Tev wondered if she was feeling ill. "We need to have a conversation. With your permission, Captain, we'll be in observation."

Gold said, "Sure."

Tev, however, was not particularly in the mood for one of the commander's flirtations. "I am now off-shift, Commander, could it possibly—"

"You seem to have a certain difficulty with following direct orders, *Lieutenant* Commander, so let me spell it out for you. Go to the observation lounge or go to the brig." She smiled. "Your choice."

If she is going to hide her lust behind rank, then so be it. Snuffling with minor irritation, Tev exited the bridge and entered observation, Gomez right on his heels.

Bartholomew was in the lounge, working on a padd, with several other padds laid out in front of him. Tev didn't recognize the writing that was scanned into one of the padds, but he assumed it was some arcane tongue that the linguist was working with.

At their entrance, he stood. "Oh, sorry, Commanders. I just needed to spread out a bit for my article."

Gomez peered at the table. "That's the Syclarian language, isn't it?"

Nodding, Bartholomew said, "The Sato Linguistics Institute asked me to do an article for their journal."

Tev snuffled. "Would they not ask a Syclarian to write one?"

"They did, and got a big no for their troubles. So, since I translated a Syclarian scientist's journal a while back, they tapped me. Been working on it in what I laughingly refer to as my spare time."

With a smile that was much more friendly than the one she had given Tev on the bridge, Gomez asked, "Bart, can we have the room, please?"

Something changed in Bartholomew's face, but Tev wasn't sure what it was. "Uh, yeah, sure. I could use some coffee anyhow, so I'll do this in the mess hall." He gathered up his padds and left via the opposite door, which would take him to the turbolift.

Turning to face Gomez, Tev said, "By the way, Commander, I have been studying the upgrades that you supervised to the sensors. Excellent work." To show that he was sincere, he added, "Almost as fine as I would have done."

Gomez said nothing in response to that, but simply walked over to the window that showed the darkness of the interstellar void in which they searched for the elusive runabout. Her back was now to Tev as she spoke. "I just got contacted by Commander Ling. It was a pretty weak signal, because their comm amplifiers were down—along with most of Avril Station's other systems. They managed to get a signal through to the nearest relay station, but it was tough."

This surprised Tev. The upgrades they had performed were of the finest quality. "I do not understand."

"It seems that the diagnostic program that we provided for them crashed the entire system. That really surprised me, since I designed the diagnostic program we provided, and it should've been compatible with the station's hardware." Now, she turned to face him. "Except, it turns out, they *didn't* use the diagnostic program I designed, did they?"

Tev chose his words carefully. "I felt that the best way to—"

Holding up a hand, Gomez said, "Stop *right* there, Tev. I told you that your diagnostic program would not suit the needs of Avril, yes?"

"I found that conclusion to be faulty, Commander. I should think that with my—"

Gomez walked around the table so that she stood face-to-face with Tev. "The reason *why* I came to that conclusion is because the computers on Avril were never given the Sitok upgrade because it crashed their system. The upgrade really wasn't going to do them enough good for it to be worth overhauling all their hardware."

That surprised Tev. He wasn't aware of any major Federation computer system that was not given the security and diagnostic upgrade pioneered by the Vulcan computer scientist Sitok two decades ago. Soloman had been handling the computer elements, so Tev had not bothered to familiarize himself with the specifics of their network. "Why did you not tell me that?" he asked, genuinely confused.

"Why didn't you just trust my judgment?"

"I have always found my own judgment to be—"

Waving her hands in front of her face, Gomez said, "Forget *your* judgment for a second, Tev. Forget *you* for a second. Yes, we all know you're brilliant, and if we're ever in any danger of forgetting, you'll be sure to remind us. But the thing that you have continued to not get in all the time you've been on this ship is that the rest of us know a few things, too."

"You're all quite competent in your fields, it's true," Tev said, "but—"

Using a tone that Gomez had never used, not even when she reprimanded him while trying to decipher the pyramid the Koas had placed their planet into, she barked, "I did *not* give you permission to speak, Lieutenant Commander Tev! I hear one more word out of you without leave, and I *will* toss you into the brig."

Tev, wisely, stayed silent.

Gomez waited for several seconds.

Then for several seconds more.

At last, she broke into a grin. "See? That wasn't so hard. You should try it more often."

Unable to resist such obvious prompting, Tev asked, "Try what?"

"Following orders. It's way past time you got comfortable with something, Tev: There are going to be occasions when other people know more than you. And it won't necessarily be because they're smarter than you or cleverer than you, but because they *have* to. I'm a commander, you're a lieutenant commander; I'm first officer, you're second officer. Not only does that mean I outrank you, but it also means that sometimes I'm going to be given information that you're not allowed to have because of your lower rank and position. That is one of about a thousand reasons why it is critical that you trust *my* judgment—more than I trust yours, because I'm the boss."

Snuffling with disgust, Tev said, "You mean that you didn't tell me about Avril as some sort of test?"

Gomez put her head in her hands. "You really don't get it, do you? I didn't tell you because I had no *reason* to tell you. And because you didn't trust my judgment, you went behind my back to Commander Ling, and caused Avril Station to fall to pieces. Now they're purging your program and installing mine, and it should work out all right." She looked straight at him. "That was the last straw, Tev. That was the last time you disobey my orders or flaunt my authority. I've gone easy on you up until now, partly because I prefer a more casual command style, but that obviously isn't going to work with you. A formal and lengthy reprimand is going into your record, and I can promise you that any hopes you may have had of making commander next promotion go-round are pretty much in the waste extractor."

Tev could not believe what he was hearing. "A reprimand? I have done nothing to deserve this!"

"You've done *everything* to deserve this, Tev. And the fact that you can't even see it makes it all the more clear that it's the right decision."

"This is outrageous." Tev shook his head. He was willing to concede a certain amount to the commander's infatuation, but—

"Tev—we're not going to steal credit for your work."

That brought Tev up short. He looked over at Gomez, and saw that the anger had left her face, replaced with a kind of sadness—no, that wasn't right. The expression he saw was pity.

"That is . . . ridiculous, Commander. I thought we went over this."

"Yes, after our mission to Kharzh'ulla, you insisted that you didn't hate Eevraith for stealing your work twenty years ago, and you didn't have any regrets about the life you were leading in Starfleet. But I have to wonder if that didn't engender a certain fear in you—a worry that someone else might do what Eevraith did. A worry that became so strong that you refuse to work well with anyone else."

How dare she accuse me of that? So livid was Tev, he was unable to say the words aloud. Plus, while her accusations of his fears were wholly baseless, he did have a legitimate fear that she might take disciplinary action against him. It would be out of character—he learned early on that she had no taste for true leadership—but so was her earlier outburst. She had threatened his career enough for one conversation.

Instead, he simply said, "Is that all, Commander?"

"Think about what I said, Tev. Dismissed."

He turned on his heel and left the room, intending to do no such thing.

Domenica Corsi stared at the axe.

She lay on her bunk, feet flat on the bed, knees bent and pointing to the ceiling. The box the axe was in leaned against her raised thighs. After the last session in the hololab—after the fourth straight time that Tomozuka Kim fought hard and got back up off the metaphorical mat no matter how much harder she made it—she realized that she could no longer stand the sight of the young Izarian, and told everyone to get some sleep.

Luckily, nobody gave her that order, as she would have had to disobey it. She had no interest in sleeping, because she knew exactly what would happen: She'd dream about Dar. Bad enough he still invaded her dreams on the anniversary of that miserable day on Izar. Last time, she'd banished it by seducing Fabian Stevens. *That's not happening again*, she vowed. *That's gotten way too messy for my tastes.*

She knew she was conveniently ignoring that her relationship with Fabian had been what kept her going these past months, that she really enjoyed his company, and that she desperately wanted to take it to the next level. But Caitano's death and Kim's Izarian face served as regular reminders as to why that was a tragically bad idea.

The axe stared back at her. It had been a family heirloom for three hundred and seventy-five years, and was remarkably well preserved, though the wood of the handle was cracked in spots. She'd taken the axe with her to Starfleet Academy, and it had survived through dozens of missions, from the other-dimensional trip the *U.S.S. Soval* took when she was assigned there as an ensign to that living ship that almost literally ate the *U.S.S. Roosevelt* to the Galvan VI disaster here on the *da Vinci*. It had even provided a useful mental *nudzh* in solving Caitano's murder.

But it provided no answers now. It was just an old tool in an old box.

The door chime rang. Corsi ignored it, not having any great desire for company. Her combadge was on the nightstand, placed there after she tossed her sweaty uniform into the recycler. She had showered and then put on the flannel robe her mother had gotten her when she graduated the Academy and which was still in fairly decent shape.

Again, the door chime rang, this time accompanied by a voice. "Dom, it's Fabian. I know you're in there. And I know you're alone, since we haven't found Lense yet."

Fabian. Perfect. She sighed. She couldn't really use the excuse that she wasn't properly dressed, considering that Stevens had seen her in much less on more than one occasion.

"Come," she muttered just loud enough for the computer to hear and allow the door to slide open.

Stevens entered, a look of concern on his pleasant features. His dark hair was mussed, like it usually was after he'd been working all day, as he tended to run his hand through it. That meant he had been up all night, since alpha shift was just starting.

"I hear you've been riding the newbie pretty hard."

Hawkins has a big mouth, Corsi thought. Her deputy chief and Stevens had become close since their shared trauma on Teneb, so it had to be him. Either that or Hawkins talked to Abramowitz and she talked to Stevens. *Hell, it could be anyone—Fabe's always making friends with people.* Regardless, it was completely inappropriate. "Are you part of security now?" she asked in a tight voice.

"Of course not, but—"

"Then keep the hell out of security affairs, Mr. Stevens."

Rolling his eyes, Stevens said, "Oh, come *on*, Dom, this isn't a chat between officer and enlisted, this is you and me in your quarters. Forget the ranks for a second—what's wrong?"

Placing the axe on the deck, Corsi swung her legs around

and sat up, facing Stevens. "Nothing's wrong. Tell Hawkins or Abramowitz or whichever other gossipmonger told you to come talk to me to stay the hell out of my business."

"Nobody told me to come talk to you, Dom, I came on my own."

Corsi regarded him angrily.

He relented. "Yeah, okay, Hawk and I had a talk, but that was it. Besides, he's worried about you, and he figured I had a better chance of finding out what was wrong than he did."

"Well, he's wrong. Get out of here." She stood up and pointed at the door.

Stevens shook his head. "You know, you really should start wearing a sign around your neck."

"I beg your pardon?"

"So I know which Domenica Corsi I'm talking to. It's hard to keep track."

Corsi moved closer, looking Stevens right in the eye. "I am two steps away from ordering you out of my quarters, Mr. Stevens, now—"

"'I just worry that she's going to completely close herself off.'"

Blinking, Corsi stared dumfoundedly at Stevens. He was obviously quoting something. "What the—?"

"You know who said that? You—right after you broke several regulations trying to set Commander Gomez up with Captain Omthon."

Turning around, Corsi went back to the bed. She needed to sit down. "Yeah, well, that was stupid."

"No, Dom, it wasn't." Stevens sat down on the bed next to her. She wanted more than anything to reprimand him, to remind him that she kicked him out of here, but one look at that goddamned earnest expression on his face, and she couldn't do it. "You've been prickly ever since Ken and Ted died, and it's gone into overdrive since we got back from Coroticus. Did something happen down there that I missed? Or is it because of Kim and where he's from?"

That brought Corsi up short again. "What?"

"He's from Izar. Hawk isn't the only one concerned—Rennan noticed that you went a little crazy when the new guy said he was from Izar. So I did a little digging, and you've been there, when you were deputy security chief on the *Roosevelt*. Solved a big homicide and everything. Kim was the son of one of the peace officers you worked with. What's-her-name from the *Enterprise*, Vale, she was there, too." He shook his head. "You know, I remember when Vale and Commander La Forge came on board to help us out with the *Beast*, Vale said you were the reason why she joined Starfleet. La Forge said he asked you what that was about, but you wouldn't tell him." He put one of his hands on Corsi's. "What happened on Izar, Dom?"

Corsi wanted to tell him to get his hand off hers. She wanted to tell him to get the hell out of her quarters and mind his own damn business. She wanted to tell him to stay out of her life.

But then she remembered the conversation from which Stevens had quoted. It was right before they went to the Lokra system, and she had said something else then: "Life is too short to waste it."

So instead, she told him about Izar.

CHAPTER
7

U.S.S. Roosevelt
in orbit of Izar
ten years ago

Lieutenant (j.g.) Domenica Corsi shivered as she entered the
security office. The *Roosevelt*'s security chief, Lieutenant Heinrich Waldheim, always kept the office at arctic temperatures.
He said it was to keep people sharp, but Corsi was convinced
he just did it to annoy everyone.

When Waldheim summoned her, she had been doing her bridge
rotation at tactical, keeping an eye on both the planet below them
and the massive telescope nearby. Izar's orbit took it in proximity to the Heyer Array, the largest telescope in this sector, for the
next two months. The *Roosevelt* was providing some maintenance
on the array, which meant shore leave for those members of the
Roosevelt's complement not involved in the Heyer mission.

That shore leave was especially welcome to Corsi. She'd
been waiting for this mission for *months*.

Waldheim was sitting in the security office behind the big desk covered in padds, his massive frame barely fitting into the standard-issue Starfleet chair. His thick arms were folded over his equally thick chest. Corsi had been serving under Waldheim since she graduated the Academy, first as a grunt on the *Soval* where he was deputy chief, then here, taking her along to be his deputy chief when he was promoted to chief of the *Roosevelt*. As a result, she knew what his arms being folded meant: he was about to give her a duty she wouldn't want, but for which he—and she—had no choice.

If this means I don't see Dar, Heinrich, I promise, I'll take that outsized head of yours right off with the family axe. Don't think I won't. It had been hell maintaining her long-distance romance with Academy-mate Dar Ableen—everyone told them they were insane to try to keep it going after graduation, that Academy relationships had a shelf life of about six seconds after you got your commission—but they'd done it, through her two shipboard assignments and his four planetary or starbase ones. But this was also their first chance to be together since that trip to Pemberton's Point more than a year earlier, and she was not going to let anyone blow it.

The other person in the office probably had something to do with what was going on. A pale, petite woman with long auburn hair, she wore the drab blue one-piece uniform with the flag of Izar emblazoned over the heart that indicated an Izarian peace officer. Charged with maintaining law and order on this human colony-turned-Federation-member world, the flag had a rendering of the red-green planet with fireworks behind it over a white background.

"Lieutenant Domenica Corsi, this is Officer Christine Vale."

The younger woman offered her hand, and Corsi took it, noticing the stylized *D* on the cuffs of her uniform. "You're a detective?"

Vale nodded. "Yes, ma'am. We've had a couple of homicides."

That caught Corsi off guard. Homicides were rare beasts in the Federation, much less multiple ones on the same world—though she had a vague recollection of Dar mentioning something about some murders on Berengaria when he was assigned there. "Really?"

Breaking the handshake, Vale said, "Really. Two women have been killed by a phaser set on burn, one a week ago, the second last night. I think it might be connected to some other cases in the Federation. However, for something that crosses jurisdictions like this, procedure is for the nearest Starfleet ship to coordinate."

"Okay." Corsi was familiar with the regulation, but anyone in security could handle this.

Waldheim spoke up then. "You will serve as liaison between Officer Vale and Starfleet for the duration of the investigation, Lieutenant, starting first thing in the morning."

Corsi opened her mouth to complain, then stopped. She didn't want to air her dirty laundry in front of a stranger.

"Thank you *very* much, Lieutenant Corsi," Vale said. "I'm looking forward to working with you." Turning to Waldheim, she said, "If you'll excuse me, sir, I need to get back to the surface. I'm expecting the full lab report on last night's victim."

Waldheim unfolded his arms and nodded his head. "Of course, Officer Vale. Please, if you could forward that report to us, it would help us to get started."

"Sure." Vale gave Corsi a quick nod and then left.

As soon as the doors closed behind her, Waldheim held up one of his large hands. "I know what you're going to say, Domenica, and I'm sorry, I didn't set out to ruin your leave, but—"

"It's okay." Corsi had thought about it and her anger had already burned to ashes. "I take it the Izarian authorities are in a tizzy?"

"You bet—and can you blame them? Every time I think we've finally achieved paradise, something like this bites us on the ass. It's like an asymptotic curve—keeps getting closer, but never quite makes it." He shook his head. "Starfleet Command's in as big a tizzy, believe me. Captain Van Olden got a fifteen-minute lecture from Admiral Toddman."

"Right, so obviously this liaison work can't be handled by anyone less than the deputy chief of security." She smiled wryly. "So why isn't it being handled by anyone *greater* than the deputy chief of security?"

Corsi was, she knew, the only person on the ship besides Captain Van Olden and Commander Znirka-Tul who could get away with snarking Waldheim like that, as proven by his chuckle in response. "Because, Lieutenant, if I handled it, I'd have to put you in charge of the security detail on the Heyer away team in my place. That team is transporting over in forty-five minutes. By giving you liaison duty, it means you don't have to start until 0830 tomorrow morning—which gives you the entire evening to do whatever your little heart desires."

Realization dawned on Corsi. It obviously showed on her face, because Waldheim folded his hands on the table in front of him, which he always did when he was about to impart good news. "So as of now, you're off duty. I've already ordered DiGennaro to take the rest of your shift at tactical. Go on, shoo! Have fun with Lieutenant Ableen."

Backing toward the door—which parted, letting in the blessedly warmer air from the corridor—Corsi said, "Heinrich, thank you. You are a prince. I take back most of the things I've said about you."

He grinned. "Do I get to pick which ones?"

Chuckling, she double-timed it to her quarters, and immediately put a personal call through to the supply office on the Starfleet base outside of Garthtown.

A few minutes later, the beautiful face of Lieutenant Dar Ableen appeared on the small viewer on the desk in her quarters. Dar had sea-blue eyes that matched Corsi's own, perfect cheekbones, and a hook nose that on anyone else would have looked awful, but worked with his face for some reason. He had no chin to speak of, but he covered that by wearing a Vandyke beard that was as dark as his semi-curly hair. They had first met in a martial arts class; he joked that it was there that he fell for her—over and over again. In fact, he had always had a superb grasp of the martial arts of many different worlds, so much so that many of his instructors—and Corsi, for that matter—encouraged him to focus on security. But Dar had preferred a career in supply, citing it as "less stressful."

On those occasions when she saw him, she was always drawn first to his eyes. She could just get lost in them.

"Hey, you."

"Hey. Well, I've got good news and bad news. . . ."

CHAPTER
8

Officer Christine Vale stared at her reflection and decided she hated her hair.

Oh, this is good. You're facing the first double homicide in the planet's history, you're about to spend the day with the most intimidating woman you've ever met, the bosses, the government, and Starfleet Command are all going to be taking up residence in your posterior, and you're thinking about your hair? Get with it, Christine!

The voice in her head sounded distressingly like her mother, especially since her Mom hated when frivolity got in the way of the work.

That, of course, didn't change the fact that Vale hated her hair. She hated the color and hated the length.

As she exited the cramped one-person bathroom that was

apparently the best the government could provide for the main Peace Officer Headquarters in Pibroch City, she wondered what color she could try next. *And maybe I'll cut it shorter.*

That thought got pushed to the back of her head when she bumped into Soon-Li Kim. Her fellow detective was practically rolling her eyes. "That Starfleeter's here."

Vale blinked and double-checked the chronometer on the wall. "She's early."

"You know how they are about promptness." This time Soon-Li really *did* roll her eyes. "That one's pretty typical— probably spits and polishes her socks."

Snorting, Vale tried to picture the uptight blonde she met yesterday performing that rather absurd action. To her lack of surprise, the image took.

Soon-Li wasn't finished. "We really should be able to do this on our own—I mean, you start bringing Starfleet into this, and everything becomes a major to-do."

That prompted another snort. "It already *is* a major to-do. We've got two dead bodies, and not a shred of useful evidence. Besides, this is *Starfleet*. They deal with crazy stuff that doesn't make sense on a weekly basis."

"I guess." Soon-Li turned and looked back at the detective office where she, Vale, Johannsen, and Malvolia did their work, and where Vale assumed Corsi was waiting. "Still, I don't like it, I don't like Starfleet, and I don't like her."

"Nobody's asking you to." Vale didn't add that she didn't like the situation or Corsi much either. She did like Starfleet, had always admired the work they did. There were times when she had thought about going to the Academy instead of following in her mother's footsteps.

Right, and then have the whole family disown me. That'll happen. Vale knew that her becoming anything other than an Izarian peace officer would devastate her mother. Never mind the fact that Starfleet security looked a lot more challenging . . .

She went on to the office, while Soon-Li continued to wherever she was going. *Probably checking into that missing person's case. Can't have the rest of law enforcement grind to a halt just because two people died.*

Expecting the same stick-up-her-ass officer she'd met on the *Roosevelt* the previous day, Vale was surprised to see a much more pleasant-looking person standing in the stuffy office that she shared with the other three detectives. Where yesterday, Corsi looked like she'd rather be cleaning the waste extractor with her tongue than take on this duty, today she looked— well, happy.

"Lieutenant, good to see you."

Corsi turned and faced Vale. The lieutenant was a lot taller than the young officer; Vale was used to that, as most people were taller than her. However, this one, she noted, used her height to her advantage. She didn't just stand, she loomed.

"Is it always this hot in here?" Corsi asked.

Vale couldn't help but smile. "Little different from the arctic tundra in your CO's office?"

Corsi smiled right back. "Actually, it's a nice change."

"Let me show you what we've got." Vale walked over to her desk and took a seat, indicating the guest seat for Corsi. She called up the records on the two homicides.

Or, rather, tried to. After banging the side of the comm unit, the records actually came up. "Sorry," she said sheepishly. "This thing hasn't been upgraded since Praxis exploded."

"Really?" Corsi's eyes widened.

"Well, no," Vale said quickly. That Klingon moon blew up more than seventy years earlier, after all. "This is actually better than what they had in my mother's day, a fact she never tires of reminding me when she wants me to know how good I have it."

"Your mother was a peace officer, too?"

Vale nodded. "Until she retired last year, yeah. Her father before her was also, as were both his parents before him. Kind of the family business."

"I know what you mean. My family's got a long line of service of some kind in it. In any case," Corsi said quickly—Vale assumed she didn't feel comfortable talking about her personal life—"you should have access to the records of all homicides in the last ten years in Federation space, as well as any allied powers that share those types of records with us."

"Good." Vale turned to the computer station and started entering in commands. When she banged the side again, the commands took. *If I joined Starfleet, I'd get to use up-to-date equipment, probably.* "What I'm doing right now is a basic search to see if there are any commonalities to our case."

"Like what?"

Vale realized that Corsi didn't really know the specifics of her own case, and if she was to be the liaison, she should know. *Of course, she could just read the reports,* she thought, once again in her mother's voice, but Vale didn't mind repeating the facts again. Sometimes you caught something in the retelling you didn't before.

Once she got the search running, she called up the images of the two dead bodies to her screen and turned it toward Corsi. The images were stacked one over the other, both human women—ninety percent of Izar's population was human—both looking to be in their thirties or forties, both with long darkish hair of about the same length as Vale's own, and both lying on a sidewalk. The one on top was facedown; the one on the bottom was on her back, so on her you could see the circular chest wound.

"The victim on top is Marianne Getreu, a librarian working at the Garthtown Public Library, in the special collections section. She lived alone, and was walking back from a late night working at the library to her house. The murder occurred on a side street about half a kilometer from her home."

"She walked?" Corsi asked.

Nodding, Vale said, "The weather's pretty nice in Garthtown this time of year. But it was late at night, so there were no witnesses. Cause of death was a phaser shot to the chest that vaporized skin, several ribs, and twenty percent of her heart. Death was probably painful but quick. It was a type-two phaser set on level four."

"The burn setting," Corsi said unnecessarily.

"Yeah, hence the 'painful but quick' part." She pointed to the other victim. "That's Kelly Fleet, an actor with a troupe called Mermaid's Revenge. They've been specializing in neo-classical Betazoid theatre."

"Why is a Betazoid theatrical troupe called *that*?"

Vale smirked. "Some mysteries even a detective of my skill can't solve. Anyhow, same COD."

"Same phaser?"

She nodded. "That's the one thing these two do have in common besides being female and having long hair. The resonance pattern is the same for both phasers."

"Have you scanned for the phaser with that pattern?"

"The scan's been running constantly, both in Garthtown and elsewhere, but Garthtown is a city of six hundred million, plus the rest of the populace of Izar. It's a big planet, and picking out one phaser from all that isn't easy."

"Starfleet has top-of-the-line sensors. I'll have the *Roosevelt* scan for the phaser also."

Vale hadn't thought of that. "Couldn't hurt. I'll send the resonance pattern up there." She called up the autopsy reports. "Fleet lived with three other members of the troupe in a house in the suburbs of Garthtown. She liked to take walks in a park near their house. She was on her way to the park when she was killed." She leaned back in her chair. "The thing is—there are no witnesses and *no* trace evidence in either case. No DNA residua, nothing left behind at the scene, not a goddamn thing."

"No commonality between the two women?"

"Nothing we could find." Vale let out a breath through her teeth. "We've checked everything, tried everything. Unless that phaser turns up, we're stuck. And even if it does, given how clean the scene is, I'm willing to bet there's nothing on the weapon, either."

Corsi looked dubious. "C'mon."

Throwing up her hands, Vale said, "I just call 'em like I see 'em."

"I can't believe there isn't *anything*."

Vale couldn't blame her. She didn't believe it, either. Before she could say anything, however, the computer beeped. The search came back to the front of her screen. "*This* is interesting."

Corsi leaned forward to look at the screen. "What?"

Vale read off the results of her search. "Tarsas III four years ago. Three Vulcan women, all of whom had short brown hair, none of whom had anything else in common, all killed with type-one phasers set on burn. No trace evidence, never solved.

"Berengaria two years ago. Three Bolian women, all of whom had medium-length white hair, also nothing in common besides that and being killed by laser drills. No trace evidence, never solved.

"And Alpha Centauri six months ago. Three Trill women, all of whom had red hair of varying lengths."

Corsi was also reading. "Killed by type-three phasers set on burn. I'm amazed there was anything left of their chests."

Vale checked the autopsy reports. "There wasn't much. And the same lack of evidence." She leaned back and blew out a breath, running a hand through her hated auburn hair. "This is bad. We've got a major serial killer on our hands, one who's good enough to leave *no* trace behind at eleven murders."

Standing up, Corsi said, "I need to call the ship. Starfleet Command needs to be aware of this, and we need to get *full* information from Berengaria, Tarsas, and Centauri."

Vale peered at the screen. "I think we've got it all, but sure, go ahead." She looked up and pointed to the doorway out into the large squad room where the regular officers had their desks. "If you go out to the squad room, find Officer Giacoia. He can set you up with a comm link."

"Thanks." Corsi moved to the door, then stopped. "Listen, Officer Vale—we're gonna get this guy. Starfleet's got your back, and we don't lose."

Vale said, "Thank you, Lieutenant." In her heart, though, she didn't believe it. *Eleven murders. This is insane. How the hell can anyone get away with this?*

Corsi contacted Commander Znirka-Tul and filled her in on the situation. While they were talking, the commander reported that Vale had sent the resonance frequency along, and they'd start scanning.

Then, since she had a comm unit to herself anyhow—Officer Giacoia had taken her to a small room that had a comm unit and a large viewer—she decided to contact Dar.

"Hey there, gorgeous. Can't get enough of me, huh?"

Corsi smiled. After last night, she never wanted to leave

Dar's side. Duty managed to get her away—his and hers, as he was in the midst of a major inventory—but she numbered their time together last night, from the glorious dinner at the Bolian restaurant to dessert at the Italian café to the entire night in his bed to falling asleep in his arms, as one of the best nights of her entire life.

"Maybe not, but I'm afraid I'm gonna have to beg off a repeat performance tonight." She filled him in on what Vale told her, and what they found on the other three worlds.

Dar looked devastated. *"God, I remember what happened on Berengaria—this is connected?"*

"Looks like."

"I thought this kind of thing didn't—" He visibly shuddered.

"Anyhow, I need to stay on here until this guy's caught. Vale's *way* out of her depth here."

"I would think anybody would be. This isn't exactly run-of-the-mill."

Corsi smiled. "I'm security. Not run-of-the-mill is our specialty. We'll catch this bastard, don't you worry. And then—I promise the biggest celebration of your life."

Dar's beautiful face broke into an incredibly goofy grin. *"Sounds like something to look forward to. Hurry up and catch this guy."*

"I'll do my best." Then she hesitated, and said, "I love you, Dar."

"Right back at you, Domenica."

She signed off and leaned back in her chair. For the moment, she didn't think about eleven dead bodies and a killer who'd gone from planet to planet without getting caught.

That prompted a thought. She tried to call up a record, but the comm unit was *only* a comm unit, not multipurpose like any decent Starfleet station would be. Going back out into the squad room, she sought out Officer Giacoia.

The diminutive officer was nowhere to be found, but she did see the woman who'd greeted her—Kim?—standing with a little kid who bore an obvious resemblance.

These people are taking their children to their work in law enforcement, and we're supposed to trust them to solve this?

"Can I help you, Lieutenant?" the officer asked.

"I need a computer terminal. I just thought of something from Starfleet records that might help."

"Are you with Starfleet?" the kid asked.

Smiling down at the boy, Corsi said, "Yes, I am."

"You're an engineer, right?"

God, what a revolting concept. Corsi hated engineers. "No, I'm with security. We wear the same colors as them."

"So you're like my mom?"

No, I'm more professional. But Corsi wasn't impolitic enough to say that out loud.

The mom in question said, "That's enough, Tomo." The boy clammed up, and Kim looked at Corsi. "I apologize for my son, Lieutenant. I'm heading home anyhow, so why don't you use my terminal? It's the one across from Christine's."

Nodding, Corsi said, "Thanks."

Leaving mother and son behind, Corsi went back into the detectives' room. Vale was right where Corsi left her.

"I just thought of something, and I want to check it out. About a hundred years ago, there was this thing called Redjac—"

"I know what you mean," Vale said without looking up from her reading. Corsi walked over to the younger woman's desk to see that Vale was reading the reports from Berengaria Enforcement on the second set of murders. "I read up on that right after we found Getreu's body. The thing is, even if it *is* that Redjac thing, we still need to find the person Redjac's possessing to do these killings," she looked up, "and did I just casually talk about people being possessed?"

Corsi shrugged. It wasn't even close to the weirdest thing she'd seen in Starfleet. "We should contact the *Roosevelt*, see if—"

"I did that as soon as you guys made orbit. I heard back from your operations officer after I left the meeting with you and Lieutenant Waldheim yesterday. She told me that, accounting for a hundred years of drift, Redjac wouldn't be anywhere near any inhabited planets, and the chances of it encountering a ship in interstellar space are infinitesimal."

"But it's still possible that we're dealing with Redjac."

It was Vale's turn to shrug. "Maybe. But it doesn't really fit the MO—Redjac always used blades. And even if it is him, like I said, it doesn't really change anything useful, like what we do to find him."

Corsi had to grudgingly admit that the officer had a point. Still and all, she requested access to the *Roosevelt*'s computer. She wanted to refamiliarize herself with the Starfleet mission that discovered Redjac on Argelius a century ago.

CHAPTER
9

U.S.S. da Vinci

in search operations between

Stations Kel-Artis and Deep Space 9

now

Tev awoke from his nap, feeling very refreshed. The fact that his bunk was located in a Kharzh'ullan passenger shuttle didn't seem to matter all that much.

"Mr. Tev is expressing a valid concern. Giving me something to think about. A little bluntness is a good way to do that."

A Kharzh'ullan was sitting in the seat opposite Tev's bunk. "How long until we reach the base station?" Tev asked.

The Kharzh'ullan checked the chronometer on his wrist. "I never was good at math. Should be soon. Half an hour, perhaps."

"Good."

"What I'm trying to say, in the nicest possible manner, Tev, is that I'd like to work on this solo.*"*

Something went wrong. Tev realized that the shuttle wasn't decelerating, even though at half an hour from their destination, the slowdown should have commenced. The shuttle was bringing them down the elevator that took one from the massive orbital ring around Kharzh'ulla to the planet's surface. Realizing that his engineering acumen could be of use, he clambered out of his bunk and started down the ladder to the conductor's level.

"You're wasting your time," the Kharzh'ullan said, and only then did Tev realize that his fellow passenger was Eevraith, the one who took credit for Tev's own study of the orbital ring.

Ignoring Eevraith, Tev continued down the ladder.

"Why allow everyone to believe the paper was his and not yours?"

By the time he got to the conductor's level, alarms were blaring. "What's happening?"

The Kharzh'ullan conductor turned around—this was also Eevraith. "Who are you?"

"You know who I am," he said impatiently. "Tell me what's happening, Eevraith."

"The brakes appear to have failed. We're in free fall."

Tev asked, "What of the emergency brakes?"

Eevraith shook his head.

"There must be something we can do," said Tev.

"There is nothing *you* can do, Mor glasch Tev. You know nothing about the Ring."

"I'd say you were right about everything except about its being unoccupied. There, you're dead wrong."

Ignoring Eevraith's words, Tev said, "I think if we restart the computer system, we might be able to restore the electromagnetic polarity." He went to the nearest console and began the shutdown sequence.

Then the station went dark. As it did, the shuttle rocked as it bounced off the guide rails, out of control. "Can you restart that console?" he asked Eevraith, who looked ridiculous in the conductor's uniform.

"Of course I can. I know everything about the Ring, thanks to my stealing your work."

"The next time you step out of line with me, I'll have your ass in front of a court-martial at warp ten."

"Tev? Tev, I don't want to die."

At first, the voice was Eevraith's. Then Tev realized it was a woman's voice.

"Mother?"

"That was the last straw, Tev. That was the last time you disobey my orders or flaunt my authority."

"Tev?" she repeated, but it wasn't his mother this time.

It was Commander Gomez.

"We're not going to stop, are we? And that's because you screwed up. Just like you did on Kharzh'ulla. Just like you did at Avril."

"She's right," Eevraith said. "And now we're all going to die because of you."

The shuttle crashed into the surface of the planet.

And Tev awoke with a start, sweat matting down the hair on his body and soaking through the sheets of his bunk.

That dream had been a gift from an ancient species known as the Furies, whom Tev encountered while serving on the *Madison*. It was years before the dream stopped recurring every night, and he hadn't had it for months—until the *da Vinci's* mission to Kharzh'ulla and his reunion with Eevraith.

This time, though, was different. Neither Eevraith nor Commander Gomez had ever been part of the dream before.

"Computer, time."

"The time is 0950 hours."

Tev snuffled. Not even two hours' sleep. "Computer, locate Specialist Faulwell."

"Crewperson Faulwell is in the mess hall."

Tev got up from his bunk and changed into uniform. *Bartholomew is probably still working on his Syclarian article.* Tev needed someone to talk to, and Bartholomew was the only person on the ship he'd even consider a personal conversation with.

A scattering of crew members were in the mess hall when Tev arrived. Several engineers—Hammett, Lankford, Bennett, and Phelps—were drinking coffee along with a woman Tev did not recognize, but whom he presumed to be Lise Irastorza, the replacement for the late Theodore Deverick. The gamma-shift bridge crew were also just getting up to leave after what appeared to be a large post-shift meal.

Tev went straight for Bartholomew, who had a table to himself, his padds spread out as they had been in the observation lounge. "Excuse me, Bartholomew, may I join you?"

The thin linguist looked up and smiled when he saw Tev. "Sure, have a seat." The smile grew and he added, "I'm afraid I don't have any apple rancher candies."

"It is a bit early for those." Tev found himself returning the smile. He wasn't sure why he felt so much at ease around Bartholomew. Perhaps it was because he did not seem intimidated by Tev's brilliance.

"What can I do for you, Tev?"

"I am in need of counsel, and you are the only person on this ship I trust to provide it. I am having—difficulties with Commander Gomez." He filled Bartholomew in on their recent conversation. "The poor woman is obsessed with me, and now, because I refuse to return her affections, she is sabotaging my career. I cannot go to Captain Gold—he would likely take her side."

Bartholomew was frowning now, and scratching his chin. "Uh, Tev? I don't know how to tell you this, but—" He sighed. "You're wrong. Dead wrong."

Tev found that impossible to believe. "About what?"

Shaking his head, "I honestly don't know where to start. But the biggie is Commander Gomez's alleged affection for you. Trust me—that is all in your head."

"Don't be ridiculous. She has gone from indecisive and hesitant to aggressive and hostile. Of course, she—"

"Tev, you're thinking like a Tellarite."

Confused, Tev asked, "How else would I think?"

"Well, if you're gonna psychoanalyze a human, then you should think like one. Humans don't court each other that way. Hostility isn't a sign of respect—especially from her."

"What is it a sign of then?"

"That she's really really really pissed off, and if you don't do something about it—and not what you think you should do about it—it'll be more than your promotion prospects that you'll have to worry about." Bartholomew took a quick sip of his coffee. "Tev, you are an incredibly brilliant engineer, but you're not perfect. And you're not among Tellarites."

"You have not said anything of which I wasn't already aware." Tev snuffled. This conversation was starting to annoy him. He supposed that Bartholomew's insights were useful, since he, like the commander, was human, but still . . .

"Then you should probably start acting appropriately. You're third in command, Tev, not first, and not second."

"I am also aware of *that*. I suppose you will also tell me that I fear that others will steal my work."

"Do you fear that?"

Tev snuffled angrily. "Of course not. I can't imagine why anyone would believe that I would think the crew of this ship to be on a level with Eevraith."

Bartholomew raised an eyebrow. "This is the same Eevraith who took your definitive work on that orbital ring around Kharzh'ulla and claimed it as his own, a brilliantly written monograph—I read it, remember—that made Eevraith's entire career. *That* Eevraith?"

"I do not appreciate your sarcasm, Bartholomew." Tev snuffled again, and made to get up from his chair. "The life Eevraith now has would not have been for me. I'm better off."

"Sure, you know that now and feel that way now. But twenty years ago? When Eevraith first stole your work, Romulan puns and all?"

Tev stopped rising and remained seated, remembering that Bartholomew had been the one—at Commander Gomez's instigation—to read the monograph Eevraith claimed as his own, and recognized the Romulan curses he'd worked in as puns to an audience that knew nothing of the language.

Bartholomew continued. "You were just a young student. The betrayal had to hurt, and I can imagine that you would've sworn to yourself—even subconsciously—that you wouldn't let that happen to you again."

Tev almost smiled. "You're thinking like a human."

"Maybe." Bartholomew did smile. "That doesn't necessarily mean I'm wrong." He dropped the smile. "Look, whether you like it or not, this is a team, and a small one at that. I know you can work with people. You've come close more than once. But you've got to set aside your ego."

"And my arrogance, too?"

"No, you need that." Bartholomew chuckled. "I know Tellarite, remember? I know that the word for *arrogance* and the word for *self* are one and the same."

Tev nodded. He remembered his surprise that the primary human tongue didn't consider the concepts synonymous.

"But you can't just barrel through on your own brilliance and hope everyone will catch up. Before you know it, you're going to fall behind."

"*Senior staff and S.C.E. team, report to the bridge.*"

Lieutenant Shabalala's voice snapped Tev to attention. He stood up, as did Bartholomew.

"Looks like we're needed," Bartholomew said.

"Indeed." Tev turned to the linguist. "Thank you, Bartholomew, you have given me . . . a great deal to think about."

Nodding, Bartholomew said, "I just hope that they're calling us to the bridge because they found Elizabeth and Dr. Bashir."

"That is my hope as well." And with that, they departed the mess hall together.

CHAPTER
10

Peace Officer Headquarters

Pibroch City, Izar

ten years ago

Lieutenant Corsi was still wiping sleep out of her eyes when she entered Officer Vale's office. "You called me?"

"Yes, I did." Vale sounded stiffer and more formal than she had over the past three days of their investigation. She was standing behind her desk, leaning forward, her hands flat on the desk's surface.

It had been a tiring few days, as Corsi and Vale had spent every waking hour—which outnumbered their sleeping hours by a ratio of twenty-one to three—going over the records of the previous homicides and talking over subspace to everyone involved that they could track down. They also determined that the killer was likely to be humanoid—the wound patterns all indicated that the angle of the killing blast was likely to be from someone of average human height standing about a meter away. Since the majority population on all the planets where the homicides took place was humanoid, this was hardly conclusive of anything, and the lack of any kind of trace evidence made it even less so. It was frustrating that, with sensors that could detect a particular grain of sand on a desert planet, they couldn't figure out who'd killed eleven people.

Izar itself had been all but locked down, with temporary curfews put in place and regular sensor sweeps looking for the phaser in question. All the previous murders had come in threes, so everyone was waiting for the third in this sequence to be completed. In particular, human women with long dark hair were encouraged to stay in their homes until the person was caught.

Corsi couldn't help but notice that both Vale and Kim fit the bill.

She had managed to steal a few hours' sleep with Dar—which meant she had gotten very little sleep at all—until the summons came on her combadge. Dar had barely noticed the call, and she told him that she had to go to work and she'd see him later.

Vale stared at her now with a rather intense expression. Corsi wondered if that meant they'd found something.

"Lieutenant Corsi, after I first briefed you three days ago, did Officer Giacoia give you access to one of our comm terminals so you could contact the *Roosevelt*?"

Not liking the tone in the officer's voice at all, Corsi asked, "You know I did. You're treating this like an interrogation—why?"

Vale did not answer the question, instead posing another: "After doing so, did you then make an unauthorized call to a Lieutenant Dar Ableen?"

"It wasn't unauthorized," Corsi said tightly. "And if it was—well, I'm sorry, it wasn't my intention to break any regulations. What is this about, Officer?"

"When I summoned you here this morning, did you come from Lieutenant Ableen's quarters at the Starfleet base in Garthtown?"

Putting her hands on her hips, Corsi said, "I'm not answering any more questions until you answer some of mine, Officer."

Finally standing upright, Vale ran her hands through her auburn tresses. "I did a search on equipment that could hide all traces of evidence in a manner that would allow these crimes to take place. I found something in the Starfleet database, something that was only just declassified a month ago, so any of the locals investigating the previous homicides wouldn't even have been allowed to know about it. It's a stealth suit, one that is to be used for anthropological observation of pre-warp civilizations."

"Okay." Corsi had a vague recollection of reading an update about the declassification of that technology. "What does that have to do with this?"

"Only one of the murders had a witness—the second one on Centauri."

Corsi nodded. "Elra Gren." The Trill was a computer programmer who was engaged to be married.

"Right." Vale sighed. "That witness claimed that the phaser blast seemed to come out of nowhere. Since it was dark, the detective in charge assumed that the witness just didn't see the murderer, but what if he *couldn't*?" Vale turned her screen around so Corsi could see it. "Starfleet has a presence at all four locations—Starbase 74 is in orbit of Tarsas III, there's a base on Berengaria, a supply depot on Alpha Centauri that Starfleet leases, and the base here in Garthtown."

Now Corsi was getting irritated. She didn't even bother to look at the screen. "What of it? I doubt that there's a planet in the Federation that doesn't have *some* kind of Starfleet presence *somewhere*. And you can't possibly believe that a Starfleet officer could do this."

Vale snapped. "I can't possibly believe that a *sentient being* did this, Lieutenant! But the evidence sure as hell indicates that one did."

"You will modify your tone when speaking to me, Officer," Corsi said in a low, dangerous voice. She had had just about enough of this amateur civilian as she was likely to take.

"No, Lieutenant, I don't think I will. You see, I found something interesting when I did a search of Starfleet personnel who were either assigned to or in the vicinity of the four facilities in question, and then cross-checked it with people who'd have access to classified technology. We only got three hits. One of them was Lieutenant Dar Ableen."

Corsi felt her mouth go dry. "What?"

"Lieutenant Ableen was on or near the site of all eleven murders, including working in the supply office of Starbase 74. The stealth suit was developed by a research team on that starbase, and Lieutenant Ableen was assigned to them as their supply officer. Lieutenant Ableen's height and build also match with the likely height and build of the murderer."

Corsi could not believe what she was hearing. "This is absurd. Dar would never do anything like this. He can't possibly—" She shook her head, as if coming out of a daze. "You said there were three hits."

"I've already been in contact with Captain Van Olden, and the other two are also being tracked down. Meantime, I intend to question Lieutenant Ableen."

Now Corsi was furious. "You went over my head? I ought to—" And then she cut herself off. *Of course she went over my head. The evidence makes Dar at least to be a suspect, and she had to eliminate him. Naturally, she's going to treat me suspiciously. Stop being an idiot.* "I apologize, Officer, you're right. I have a relationship with a suspect in a homicide investigation. It would be—inappropriate for me to remain as the liaison between the Izar Peace Officers and Starfleet."

Vale let out a long breath, sounding relieved. "Thank you, Lieutenant. Honestly, I don't believe you have anything to do with this—you've been too thorough in digging through the evidence. But I had to be sure."

"Don't worry about it. Look, let me call Dar in here. He'll come in on his own, answer your questions, and everything will be fine. I've known Dar since we were first-year cadets. I can't believe he'd do something like this."

"Like I said, Lieutenant, I can't believe *anyone* would do this—which means that *anyone* could be responsible. I'm not feeling very trusting right now."

Corsi smiled at that. "I'm in security—we're *never* trusting. It gets in the way of the work."

Vale returned the smile. "That sounds like something my mother would say."

Sure enough, Dar was more than happy to beam over from Garthtown. A few minutes later, his lean form beamed directly into Vale's office.

"Lieutenant Ableen, I'm Officer Christine Vale." She stepped around her desk and offered her hand—but not, Corsi noted, in a handshake. "I'm afraid I'm going to have to ask you for your weapon."

Corsi hadn't even noticed that Dar had his sidearm. *Damn, Dar, how dumb can you get?* Corsi had her phaser, of course, but she was security—she needed to be armed at all times. There were times when Corsi wondered why they even bothered to issue weapons to supply officers like Dar. Besides, this building had a scattering field that prevented unauthorized weapons from firing—even with that, though, regulations stated that only peace officers could carry any kind of weapon in here. Corsi's status as a Starfleet liaison let her off the hook—though that was murkier now—but Dar wasn't allowed to have his, even though it didn't work at the moment.

Dar gave Vale the melting smile that he had perfected on Domenica by their third year at the Academy. "Be happy to, Officer." He unholstered the phaser, held it out to Vale—

—then grabbed her wrist with the other hand and yanked Vale toward him in a modified *sok-pal* grab from the Vulcan *V'Shan* martial art, at which Dar was at the level of *ahn-was*, which was as high as any human had achieved. Before Corsi had had a chance to register what had happened, he had Vale in a *rol-shaya* grip. Corsi had been in Dar's *rol-shaya* before—the officer wasn't moving until Dar let her.

"You know the grip, Domenica," Dar said. "I make one slight muscle movement with my right forearm, and her neck snaps like a twig. Pity, really." He smiled again, but this wasn't the melting smile, it was one she'd never seen on his face before. "I'd rather the third kill was like the first two. The rush is *so* much better that way."

Corsi shook her head. "So it *was* you."

"Of course it was me! How could you even doubt it? Now

put your phaser down, Domenica. Let me go with the officer here, so I can kill her *properly*, like the other two."

Glancing down, Corsi saw that she had, in fact, drawn her phaser as soon as Dar grabbed Vale. The action hadn't been conscious, but drilled into her after all her years of security training.

The next action she took was completely conscious. Pausing only for a second to aim, she blew Dar Ableen's head off.

CHAPTER
11

U.S.S. da Vinci
in search operations between
Stations Kel-Artis and Deep Space 9
now

Fabian Stevens stared at Domenica Corsi in shock. "My God, Dom, you—" He shook his head, barely able to parse what she'd just told him. "What happened next?"

She shrugged. "It was over. Izar went back to normal. Vale and I both got commendations. I tried to point out that she was the one who did all the legwork, but she insisted that I was the one who saved the day. She told me—" Domenica hesitated. "She told me that she could never have done what I did—just shoot him like that, especially given our . . . our relationship." Chuckling bitterly, she added, "She applied to Starfleet Academy the next week. Said she'd always wanted to, but didn't want to let her family down. But after seeing me in action, she knew that it was the right thing to do. I told her then that she was nuts."

"Yeah," Fabian said dryly, "I can see how you'd think that. I mean, she's just security chief on the *Enterprise*, after all—not like that's a major assignment or anything . . ."

Harshly, Domenica said, "I didn't mean that she would be bad security, Fabe, I meant that she was nuts to use me as an example. All I did was shoot the man I loved."

His thoughts still whirling, Fabian asked, "Why did he do it? How—"

"I don't have answers to any of that." Domenica's voice was a rough whisper now. "He was dead as soon as I shot him. I didn't have a choice—he'd already killed eleven people, and Vale would've been number twelve if I didn't do something. I couldn't afford to hesitate, or try to talk him down. This was someone who'd *gotten away* with eleven murders, I couldn't—" Her voice broke. She was staring down at the deck. Fabian's hand was still on hers.

Fabian had known Domenica since he signed on to the *da Vinci* during the Dominion War. In those two years, he'd never heard her voice break—not even when they went to visit her family at Fahleena III, when they both fell apart in front of each other.

Then he did some mental calculations recalling the dates on the reports he'd looked up before coming here. "I just realized something. The night you came to me, right before we helped Nog drive the Androssi off Empok Nor—" *The first time we made love*, he didn't say aloud. "—that was the anniversary, wasn't it?"

Domenica nodded.

He cupped her chin with his hand and guided her head up so he could look at her. Tears marred her beautiful blue eyes. In a soft voice, he asked, "Is that what that night was all about?"

Again, she nodded. "Wasn't the first time—usually I tried to spend the anniversary with someone, just to remind myself that I was capable of *feeling* something. And also . . . also to distract myself. Most of the time, I don't think about Izar or Dar or Vale at all. It was a little hard when she came on with La Forge that time, but I managed. On the anniversary, though . . ."

Shaking his head, Fabian said, "God, no wonder that new kid set you off. And Ken and Ted's death—must've been *déjà vu* to have another crazy homicide like that."

Domenica wiped her eyes with the back of the hand that Fabian wasn't holding. "Actually, no, it wasn't. Honestly, it didn't occur to me to consider it similar. Like I said, I don't think about it." She let out a snort. "And when I *do* think about it, I don't consider it a homicide investigation, I think of it as the day I had to kill the man I loved."

Fabian couldn't help but hear bitterness and guilt in her tone. Life in Starfleet had given him plenty of firsthand experience with both, and he quickly said, "Dom, this wasn't your fault."

"Right." Domenica yanked her hand out from under Fabian's and stood up. Her flannel robe swished about her legs in a manner Fabian might have found erotic under better circumstances. "Eight years, Fabe. Dar and I were lovers for *eight years*. In all that time, I had *no clue* that he was psychotic. You mind telling me whose fault it is?"

"His."

That brought Domenica up short. She turned around and faced him with a confused look on her face. "What?"

"It's Ableen's fault, Dom. You say you had no clue—how were you supposed to? There've been, what, two documented cases of this kind of homicidal insanity in the Federation in the last hundred years?"

"Something like that," she said quietly.

Getting up from the bed, Fabian put his hands on her broad shoulders. They were about the same height, with Domenica a few centimeters shorter—which had always struck Fabian as odd, since he *felt* shorter than her—so he could look her right in her tear-streaked eyes when he said, "There was no way you could've known, Dom. The only thing you could have done was what you did."

She looked away. "I wish I could believe that."

"Well, since it's actually true, there's no good reason why you shouldn't."

Blinking away more tears, Domenica looked back at him. "Fabe, I—"

"Senior staff and S.C.E. team, report to the bridge."

Fabian closed his eyes and sighed. "Timing is everything."

Wiping the tears, Domenica was suddenly "Core-Breach" again. "They must have found Lense and Bashir." Without any hesitation, she removed her robe and went over to the closet to grab a uniform.

Fabian found himself admiring the view—and was encouraged by her lack of self-consciousness around him. "You want me to meet you there?"

As she started to get dressed, she said, "No, we can go up together."

That prompted a smile. After that first night, she had formally requested that they never speak of it again, and when they were summoned to the observation lounge, she had gone ahead, not wanting to be seen walking in with him.

After she got her uniform jacket on, she walked up to him and kissed him. Fabian was a bit taken aback, and so it took him a moment to return the kiss. There was a bit of a salty taste from the tears that had streaked down to her mouth, but Fabian found he didn't mind.

"Thank you," she whispered after the kiss broke.

"For what?" he whispered back.

"A lot of things. For being there when I needed you on the anniversary. For—" She chuckled. "—for ignoring me when I said that it wasn't the start of something. And for getting me to talk tonight. Honestly, I think it's the first time I've really *talked* about Dar and Izar since—well, ever, really."

They started to walk toward the door. It parted on their approach. "You feel any better about it?" he asked.

"Not sure. But I'm glad I did, and I'm glad you're the one I told."

They held hands as they walked to the turbolift. Fabian was stunned—a public display of affection was unheard of in the Domenica Corsi Code of Proper Behavior—but he wasn't about to say anything. And, in fact, when they passed by Rai Lankford and Rizz walking the other way down the corridor, the human and the Bolian gaped openly.

Domenica didn't even pay attention as they entered the

turbolift doors. However, after the doors closed on Rai and Rizz's astonished faces, she burst into a giggle.

"Dom, did you just giggle?"

"You know, I think I did. I also think I kinda liked it."

He grinned. "Me, too."

However, the new, improved Domenica Corsi was only going to last so long. As soon as they arrived at the bridge, she let go of his hand and "Core-Breach" was back.

Captain Gold was in his usual seat, of course, with Commander Gomez and Tev standing on either side of him. Soloman, P8 Blue, Carol Abramowitz, and Bart Faulwell were standing or sitting at the aft consoles behind Tony Shabalala at tactical. Domenica went to stand next to Tony; Fabian took a seat next to Bart.

Bart whispered, "Coming in together? Isn't *that* interesting."

"Very interesting, yes," Fabian said completely seriously, which brought Bart—who had only been teasing—up short.

"I assume we'll talk later." It wasn't a question. Bart, Fabian's roommate, was the only person who had known about Fabian and Domenica's one-night-stand back when it was just a one-night-stand, and he'd been a good sounding board on more than one occasion.

But that was for later. Gomez had turned around and was now addressing the S.C.E. team. "About ten minutes ago, we detected a duranium fragment that matches the information we got from Nog—it's from the *Missouri*. We slowed to impulse, and that's when we found this." She turned around. "Put it up, Tony."

The forward viewer flickered to show an area of space the center of which was—well, Fabian couldn't say what it was. He found his eye wandering from it, unable to focus directly there.

Immediately, he turned around and activated the sensors from the console at which he was sitting.

"You're wasting your time, Specialist," Tev said disdainfully. Fabian turned to see the Tellarite's disapproving glare. "Because the sensors were retuned to detect the *Missouri*, they are unable to extrapolate what this anomaly is."

Gold spoke for the first time, turning around his center seat to face them, a grave look in his blue eyes. "Whatever that thing is out there, it's right on the *Missouri*'s flight plan, and there's a piece of the *Missouri* near it."

"So we need to retune the sensors back?" Pattie asked.

Gomez shook her head. "Nancy's on that—she'll have them back to normal in the next five minutes. When that's done, I want to know everything there is to know about that— whatever it is—and what it did to our people, and I want to find out yesterday."

Fabian heard a determination in the commander's voice that led him to think that, if they didn't do what she wanted, her response would make Domenica's recent treatment of To- mozuka Kim be a walk in the park by comparison.

CHAPTER
12

U.S.S. da Vinci
in search operations between
Stations Kel-Artis and Deep Space 9
now

Sonya Gomez sat in the science lab on deck five of the *da Vinci*, staring at the unknown.

This was why she joined Starfleet in the first place: seeking out the new, the unknown, the unexpected. That was why a lot of people joined Starfleet, of course, but because she was an engineer, she also tended to add, and learn what makes it tick.

What kind of year has it been? she thought as she stared at the sensor readings of the bizarre anomaly they found near the distressingly small fragment of the *Missouri. Has it really been less than a year?* She shook her head. Admiral Ross had come to her after the war and her promotion to full commander with the offer of becoming first officer of the *da Vinci*, a duty that included supervising that ship's contingent of

S.C.E. personnel. It was a fantastic opportunity, and one she never regretted accepting.

Well, maybe once or twice, she thought with a small smile, grateful that she could smile about the doubts she'd had after Kieran Duffy died.

Thoughts of her dead lover prompted thoughts of his re-placement—*God, what a terrible association*—and she looked over at Tev, hunched over another sensor station, wondering what she would do with him. The S.C.E. team she ran was as good a group of people as she'd ever worked with. And Tev was as good as any of them, truly, but his attitude . . .

"Commander."

Sonya looked away from Tev to Soloman, who was at one of the consoles with Fabian Stevens. When she saw the look on his face, she flinched a bit. *I didn't know Bynars could look like someone had walked over their grave.* "What is it, Soloman?"

"We got a doozy here, Commander," Fabian said. "The en-ergy readings we're getting keep fluctuating."

"So does the structure," Pattie Blue added. "Every time I think I have an idea of this thing's shape, it completely alters."

"However," Soloman said, "I recognized one of the energy signatures. It matches the data patterns we found emanating from Empok Nor."

Now Sonya understood Soloman's apprehension. Only a couple of weeks ago, they'd encountered another universe that was seeking out information in this one, a request that almost destroyed the Bajoran system. Both Soloman's dead bondmate 111 and Kieran Duffy were alive in that universe; it had been a bit of an emotional roller coaster, but especially for Soloman, who had, for the first time, lied to Sonya and the captain in order to get a chance to see 111 again, even an alternate one.

"The pattern's changed again," Fabian said, "but I'm start-ing to think that this may be another gateway between uni-verses."

"Not another one," Sonya said with a sigh.

Tev suddenly stood up. "Commander, I need to go to engi-neering."

Sonya frowned. "Why?"

"I must modif—" Tev cut himself off, took a breath, and

then spoke in a much calmer voice. "Request permission to modify one of our class-1 probes to investigate the anomaly. When I was assigned to the *Madison*, I devised a program—"

Well, that's a little progress. Aloud, Sonya said, "I'm familiar with the program, Tev—that's why Nancy's people are already modifying one of them with a variation on your program. Should be ready in another two minutes or so."

"Ah." At first Tev looked deflated, then perked up. "A variation? Of what sort?"

"It's something we came up with here right after I signed on—a form of sensor compression that triples the amount of information the probe can take in. Soloman and Stevens rewrote your program about six months ago to utilize that angle as well."

"Why was I not—" Again, Tev stopped himself. "Six months?"

"Yup—we pay attention to what engineers on other ships are doing, too."

Fabian chuckled. "For example, Lieutenant Rao on the *Musgrave* makes a mean set of *asna* dumplings."

"Conlon to Gomez. It's done and loaded, Commander."

Tapping her combadge, Sonya said, "Good work, Nancy. Gomez to bridge—Tony, there's a modified class-1 in the probe launcher."

"I'm reading it, Commander."

"Launch it, please, and have the telemetry sent down here."

"Yes, ma'am."

Seconds later, the probe's telemetry started showing up on her screen, fed from Tony Shabalala's tactical station.

"That's what I thought," Pattie said.

Walking over to the specially modified chair the Nasat was sitting in, Sonya asked, "What did you think?"

"I finally figured out this thing's structure—it's perfectly spherical."

"That's ridiculous." Tev got up and walked over to Pattie's station. "The structure has been inconsistent. It is obviously of variable construction, that—"

Pointing at the sensor results with two of her pincers, Pattie said, "No it isn't, unless that program of yours doesn't work right. And anyhow, I figured this out five mintues ago—the probe just verified it. What that thing does is change the structure of *space* around it, at the subquark level, making it look like there's a structure there, but there isn't. What *is* variable is the way and amount of space it changes."

Tev was now staring at Pattie's screen. "I believe you are right, Specialist. Congratulations."

Fabian shot a look at Sonya. Sonya just smiled and said, "Okay, now we have a better idea of what it does—the question is, can we find out what happened to the runabout?"

"My best hypothesis is that the runabout did not detect the anomaly," Tev said.

"Yeah," Fabian said, "we only saw it at all because we slowed down after finding the fragment. If they weren't looking, the *Missouri* could've barreled right into it."

Suddenly the lights in the ship dimmed. Half a second later, the red alert Klaxon blared.

"I've lost probe telemetry," Pattie said.

"We're moving," Sonya said as she felt the vibration of the deckplates through her boots. "Backing off at one-quarter impulse."

"A wise precuation," Tev said.

"Gold to science lab. Reassure an old man, Gomez, that my ship, it won't get blown to bits."

Sonya walked back to the console she'd been using to verify her readings. "Probe's been destroyed, sir. As far as we've been able to determine, the anomaly is caused by a small spherical object that's altering space around it."

Tapping his combadge while hunched over his own console, Fabian said, "Sir, I've just verified that every time it changes the fabric of space, not only does the size of the area it alters vary, but each time it does, the space has a different quantum signature."

"In English, Stevens."

Sonya and Tev both verified what Fabian just said. "Confirmed," Tev said. "This device is a gateway to parallel universes, akin to the one we communed with on Empok Nor."

"The current configuration," Fabian said, "is a diameter of about two hundred meters." He looked up. "If it was this big, there'd be no way the *Missouri* could miss it."

"What are you saying, Stevens?" Gold asked.

Sonya gritted her teeth. "It means that the effect of this device is expanding."

A tinkling noise was followed by: "I found something!"

Dashing back over to where Pattie sat, Sonya asked, "What is it?"

"I was going over what we got from the probe. Take a look." With three of her pincers, she pointed at the screen.

Sonya saw what she did—they had detected another fragment of duranium, one that matched that of the material that made up the *Missouri*.

As David Gold sat down in the observation lounge, he said without preamble, "Tell me we have some way of getting Lense and Bashir out of that mess."

"Working on it, sir," Gomez said as she took her seat to Gold's right. Tev sat on his left, with Soloman next to him. Stevens took his seat next to Gomez, Corsi next to him. Gold noted that Corsi and Stevens came in together and sat together naturally, moving almost as one. Blue was at her specially modified seat at the other end.

"Talk to me. We've lost too many people off this ship already, I'm *not* standing for it happening again."

"Sir," Tev said, "I feel constrained to point out that we have no empirical proof that either of the passengers aboard the runabout are still alive, nor that the runabout is still intact."

Quickly, Gomez added, "Having said that, at least we now have a working theory about what happened."

Gold nodded. Over the past year, he'd learned to trust Sonya Gomez's working theories a lot better than most people's facts.

Touching a control in front of her caused the viewer on the wall to light up with a sensor scan. In red was a spherical object. Random shapes appeared around it, one yellow, then replaced with a differently shaped blue, with a third shape in green, and so on.

"The sphere in the middle is the device that's causing all this. It's opening up a gateway between quantum realities."

"Before it was destroyed by the device's expanding field," Tev said, "the probe was able to scan the surface of the device, but not penetrate its interior workings. The technology is unfamiliar."

Stevens put in, "But it probably opens up quantum fissures somehow. Back when he was in Starfleet, Ambassador Worf encountered a natural fissure that sent him on a joyride through about a dozen quantum realities. This thing probably does artificially what that fissure did naturally."

Although he was listening, Gold was also watching the colors change. "There's a pattern to it."

Smiling in the way a professor smiled at a student who got a right answer, Gomez said, "That's it exactly, sir. The device is currently cycling through six different quantum realities. In addition, the field keeps expanding, which is why we got shook up—the *da Vinci* was right at the event horizon of the fissure. If we'd been even ten meters closer, we'd have been dragged into the fissure and into another quantum reality."

"Which," Tev said, "is what we hypothesize happened to the *Missouri*."

Blue added, "We were able to detect debris from the runabout in one of the quantum realities."

"Sir, there's something else." Gomez hesitated.

"I can take it, Gomez—spill."

"Based on the rate of expansion, we think that the device was activated a little more than two weeks ago—about when Empok Nor started endangering the Bajoran system. We think that whatever the Bynars did in that other quantum reality, it also set this thing off."

"*Gevalt*," Gold muttered. Unable to help himself, he glanced at Soloman, who looked a bit guilty.

"I am sorry for what happened, Captain Gold," the Bynar said.

"Stop *shvitzing*, Soloman," Gold said, although Bynars did not, as far as he could determine, sweat, "it wasn't your fault, it's the fault of whoever it was in that universe who thought probing ours was such a hot idea." He leaned back in his chair. "All right, looks like we have two things to accomplish: get our two doctors back, and shut this thing down."

"Something else this device does," Gomez said, "is alter the quantum signature of whatever passes through it. The debris that Pattie detected is a molecular match for the *Missouri*, but its quantum signature matches that of the universe it's in. Which means," she added quickly, probably noting the expression on Gold's face, "we can go in after the *Missouri*. But when we do, we'll only have seven minutes and twenty-two seconds to find the runabout, rescue Elizabeth and Dr. Bashir, and come back."

Gold sighed. "I know you can't answer this, but I'm gonna ask anyhow. What happens if we take longer than seven minutes and twenty-two seconds?"

"We wait for the thirty-six minutes and fifty seconds it'll take to cycle through the other five quantum realities and hope for the best."

Blue said, "The good news, sir, is that we continue to detect the *Missouri* in the quantum reality in question. That means we'll have that thirty-seven minutes."

Testily, Tev said, "Thirty-*six* minutes, Specialist, and fifty seconds."

Making a tinkling noise of annoyance, Blue said, "I was rounding up."

Before his engineers could devolve into an argument, Gold said, "What about the other part?"

"That part's pretty straightforward," Stevens said. "According to Worf's report, the fissure was closed by using a broad-spectrum warp field to collapse it."

"Creating that will not be a problem." Tev spoke with his usual confidence/arrogance. "It will require only twenty minutes—less, if I am not forced to make tiresome explanations."

And here I was about to compliment Tev on how well he seemed to be getting along with others. Gold sighed. "Good."

"Sir, there's only one problem," Corsi said. Everyone turned and looked expectantly at her. She didn't usually contribute to an engineering discussion, but Gold figured she had a security concern. "That solution worked on a *natural* quantum whozits. But this is an artificial one."

"I fail to see what difference that makes," Tev said.

Staring daggers at the second officer, Corsi said, "If I was building something like that, the first thing I'd program into it is a failsafe against something that could stop it prematurely."

Stevens was nodding. "You're saying they may have built in a countermeasure to the warp field."

"Like I said, it's what I'd do."

Gomez folded her arms in front of her. "All right, Pattie, Fabian, start working on a Plan B in case the warp field doesn't work. Soloman, your job is to get the sensors and transporters and engines to talk to one another. We'll only have a few minutes, and we need to set it all on automatic: find either Elizabeth's or Dr. Bashir's combadges, or their lifesigns, beam them up, and get us back through the fissure before it cycles."

"Yes, Commander." Soloman bobbed his bald head.

"Tev, you and I will recalibrate the warp field."

The Tellarite started to say something, then stopped. "Of course, Commander."

Maybe he is getting better, Gold thought with a smile. *It's just a work in progress.*

"Sir," Corsi said, "if we don't find them in the seven minutes we have, then we have to come back." She didn't phrase it as a question.

"Yes," Gomez said, "but then we can take another shot half an hour later. We'll find them, one way or another."

"That's what I want to hear," Gold said before Corsi could do her wet-blanket impersonation again. "Let's find our people. Dismissed." As everyone rose from their chairs, Gold said, "Corsi, stay a minute, would you please?"

"Of course." Corsi gave Stevens a look, followed by a smile. It was a pleasant smile, and one Gold had never seen on his security chief's face while on duty before—and damn rarely off duty, either.

Once they had the room to themselves, Gold said, "I hear tell you ran the new recruit through the Galorndon Core scenario."

Corsi's face clouded over. "Sir, I was under the impression that security was my responsibility."

"It is—and the *da Vinci*'s my responsibility. I just want to make sure that you aren't pushing your people too hard."

Stiffly, Corsi said, "I'm not pushing them any harder than reality will push them, sir."

"I only signed off on that scenario even being installed because it came with a notation that it would only be used for ten-year veterans. Kim's service record indicates that he hasn't been in the service for ten years."

"No, sir." Corsi shook her head, and smiled once again. "I actually met him ten years ago, on Izar, and he was just a kid. Sir, I had some—some concerns about Kim when he signed on. That's why I ran him a bit rough. Those concerns have been addressed, however, and it won't be happening again."

"Good." Gold looked at the door through which Stevens had walked a few minutes before. "So, is there anything else going on I need to know about? Say between you and Stevens?"

She stiffened up again. "Nothing that will affect my duty, sir."

"That wasn't what I asked, Corsi. Humor an old man, will you?"

Again, she relaxed; again, she smiled. "You asked if there was anything you *need* to know about, sir."

Gold laughed. "Fair enough. I trust both your judgments. Just be careful, Corsi. I don't think anybody on this ship needs to be reminded—"

"No, sir, I don't—in fact, I need that reminder less than anyone else, quite frankly." She stiffened yet again. Gold thought she was going to strip her treads, switching gears so often like that. Then she relaxed yet again. "But I'll be careful, sir—we both will."

"Good. Dismissed."

Nodding, Corsi departed the observation lounge. Smiling, Gold headed for the bridge. His people were on the case, and he had every confidence in their ability to do their jobs.

Corsi stood in the transporter room, Angelopoulos and Kim by her side, with Poynter, Gomez, and Tev all standing at the transporter station. Corsi thought that was overkill, especially since the transporter was on automatic—all they could do was monitor what was happening, and Poynter could do that just as easily—but she understood why Gomez and Tev would want to be present when the doctors were rescued.

If they were rescued.

It was, of course, as likely as not that the *Missouri* didn't survive the encounter with the alien device, that the debris that Pattie found was all that was left of it, and of the two doctors.

Corsi had insisted on a team's being present, and since it was alpha shift, that meant her, Kim, and Angelopoulos. She regarded the two younger men; they both were in full at-attention mode, hands hovering close to their sidearms.

Taking a breath, she made a decision.

"While I've got a minute," she said quietly to the two of them, "I just wanted to say something. Kim, I know I've been a little hard on you. I'm not going to apologize for it—I don't apologize for anything. This isn't a pleasure cruise, and this isn't an opportunity for you to relive the glory of your youth, or indulge in hero-worship, or whatever reason you had for joining."

"Sir, I—" Kim started, but then Angelopoulos spoke.

"Hey, don't interrupt the commander. Apologies, sir—please continue."

Inwardly, Corsi smiled. Angelopoulos had been a model guard since he made an ass of himself during the Artemis debrief. That didn't mean he was out of her doghouse yet, just that she knew his being there was doing some good. "Thanks, Angelopoulos. My point is, Kim, that—as hard as I'm driving you—reality will drive you harder. This isn't an easy road you've chosen, and it's one that can get you killed if you're not careful. Sometimes, it'll get you killed if you *are* careful. I need people I can count on to protect this ship. Period."

"You can count on me, Commander," Kim said. "I didn't join so I could serve with you—or with Lieutenant Vale. I mean, I'm glad that I am serving with you, but that doesn't change my desire to serve." He hesitated. "I'll do my best to live up to Caitano's example, sir."

Tev had moved off to an auxiliary station that was tied into the bridge. "Approaching event horizon."

Corsi turned back to face the transporter. "That's a tall order, Kim."

Although she wasn't facing him, Corsi could hear the cheeky grin in Kim's voice. "If the orders weren't tall, ma'am, they wouldn't need security."

She could also hear the wince in Angelopoulos's. "God, you got trained by Pelecanos, too?"

"Best teacher I ever had," Kim said.

Agosto Caitano was the best I ever had. And I let his son die. Corsi shook her head. *No, that's wrong. His death, and Deverick's, led us to a weapon that would've killed millions. Maybe it wasn't the standard way, but he died doing what security's supposed to do.*

And when I shot Dar, I was doing what security's supposed to do. For the first time in ten years, she realized that *that* was what Christine Vale—and Tomozuka Kim—saw on that day on Izar ten years ago. *Maybe it's time I gave both of them credit for it.*

"Now entering new quantum reality. Sensors indicate our quantum signatures have been altered."

For some reason, Corsi had expected some kind of fanfare. But if there was any transition that the *da Vinci* experienced by going from one universe to another, it wasn't felt in the transporter room. She found that vaguely disappointing.

Poynter said, "Soloman's program's running—sensors have found a planet. Checking for combadge and human lifesigns. They—got it!"

"That was fast," Gomez muttered. "Oh, no."

Corsi didn't like the sound of that. "What is it?"

"We've got Elizabeth's combadge and two human lifesigns— plenty of other lifesigns, but these are the only two human ones. But one of them's in bad shape—near death. And we're reading projectile weapons fire!"

Shooting Gomez a glance, Corsi saw the look of horror on her face. She, along with Hawkins, Abramowitz, and Stevens, had been on the receiving end of more than their share of projectile weapons fire on Teneb, and all four of them were nearly killed.

Tev said, "We are about to achieve a standard orbit of the planet."

"Transporter's activating," Poynter said.

Gomez tapped her combadge. "Medical team to transporter room, incoming wounded."

The transporter hummed to life, and two figures appeared. Corsi barely recognized the one who was crouching as Elizabeth Lense, who was shouting something that sounded like "finish" as she materialized. The naked, scarred, prone figure was hardly at all recognizable as Julian Bashir.

"Leaving orbit," Tev said, "two minutes remaining."

Lense jumped up. "No, dammit, you've got to send me back!"

"Elizabeth, we detected gunfire," Gomez said quietly. "Besides, if we don't leave now, we risk never getting back home again. I'm sorry."

Wetzel and Falcão came in with two gurneys. Lense refused to get on one, but helped Bashir onto the other one. "I could've saved her, dammit."

Corsi wasn't sure what that meant. Did she have a Dar of her own on that planet? Or had her Dar succeeded in harming her Vale?

Tev's voice snapped her out of it. "Crossing the event horizon back into our quantum reality. Quantum signatures reverting to normal."

Lense led the team out into the corridor without another word.

"Well," Gomez said after a moment. "I'm betting there's a story there."

"Mhm," Corsi said with a nod.

CHAPTER
13

"So then we hit the thing with a broad-spectrum warp field, and it worked the first time. The fissure collapsed, the alien device shut down, and we're no longer poking into other universes. I was stunned."

Corsi smiled at Stevens's words. "Why?"

"Because that was Plan A. Plan A *never* works."

"First time for everything, I guess." She smiled as she sipped her *raktajino*. She had just come off-shift, but was letting Lense have their quarters to herself for the time being. Whatever she and Bashir went through in that other quantum reality—an ordeal that apparently, on that side, took a lot longer than the two weeks she was gone on this side of it—had a huge impact on her. Corsi assumed that Lense would talk about it when she was good and ready—*which, if past history is any guide, will be approximately never.* So she and Stevens were sitting in the mess hall, sharing a couple of *raktajino*s. She added, "I guess whoever built that device wasn't as smart as me."

Stevens deadpanned, "Or it was just one of those engineers who always have their heads in the clouds so they don't think about the real world."

"Gee, do we know anybody like that?" she asked with a cheeky grin.

"One or two—but we're working on 'em." He winked. Then he checked his chronometer. "Crap, I need to get to the holo-lab. Tev called a staff meeting. Apparently, his royal highness has some 'ideas' about how to streamline our procedures." He gulped down the rest of his *raktajino* and stood up. "On the other hand, he actually was playing well with others when we were searching for the runabout, so maybe he's improving. God knows, he couldn't get any worse. I'll see you later?"

She also rose. "Count on it."

Then she grabbed him and kissed him.

To her amazement, part of what she enjoyed about the kiss was that she was doing it right there in front of everyone in the mess hall—including Hawkins, Krotine, and Lauoc, who had just entered. Lauoc was just released from sickbay that morning—Lense's second official act upon reporting back for duty, following saving Bashir's life—and was already back in uniform, even though he wouldn't be back on duty until alpha shift the next day.

Grinning ear to ear, Stevens departed the mess hall. He and Hawkins exchanged some quick words, accompanied by laughter, then he departed.

The trio then went to the replicator—Hawkins got a synth-ale, Lauoc a tarkalian tea, and Krotine a *frimlike*—and then approached Corsi's table. "Mind if we join you, boss?" Hawkins asked.

Indicating the other chairs at the table, Corsi said, "Have a seat. Lauoc, good to see you up and around."

"Ready for duty, Commander," Lauoc said, sounding no worse for the wear despite the horrid beating he took from the mad Vorta on Coroticus.

"You're not on duty until 0800 tomorrow."

"That's just a technicality. With the commander's permission, I'd like to run some scenarios—maybe with the new guy."

And Kim thought I was rough—wait'll Lauoc gets through with him. "Knock yourself out, Lauoc. But you'll either have to do it in the next hour or wait until 2100. Tev has the hololab until then."

Krotine asked, "Is Commander Gomez *really* making him take sensitivity training?"

"I wouldn't presume to know why Commander Tev is using the hololab," Corsi said seriously. Then she chuckled. "But, as it happens, there may have been something about that in a conversation with Commander Gomez a while back."

"Couldn't happen to a nicer guy," Hawkins said emphatically, holding up his ale in a mock toast.

"I'll drink to that," Krotine said, then gulped down some of her *frimlike*. After placing the mug down on the table, she turned to Corsi. "Uh, Commander—what was that with you and Mr. Stevens?"

"I was wondering that, myself," Hawkins said with a wide grin.

Corsi let out a long breath. "I guess I should tell you all that Mr. Stevens and I are a couple."

Still grinning, Hawkins asked, "With all due respect, boss, was that supposed to be a secret?"

Corsi laughed, and the others did the same—except Lauoc, who didn't really laugh so much as smile enigmatically. "Yeah," she said, "it was a secret—from me."

A little while later, Corsi went back to her cabin, having determined that Lense was in sickbay. She had spent the better part of an hour just talking with her people, and she found it to be quite pleasant. Hawkins was a good deputy, and she had herself a security team that was as good as any she'd served with.

Eventually, though, she excused herself. There was something she needed to do.

She entered her cabin, went to the replicator, and asked for a glass of water, then sat at her desk. With a shiver, she recalled that Caitano had asked the replicator for a glass of water before he dropped dead in his cabin. *Stop being an idiot*, she admonished herself.

Entering several commands into the comm station, she opened a channel to the *Enterprise*.

A few minutes later, the deceptively innocent-looking face of Christine Vale appeared. She had cut her hair and changed its color since that day on Izar—it was currently brown and in a pixie cut, as opposed to the long auburn it was then—but she still looked very much like the detective Corsi had naïvely assumed to be incompetent ten years ago.

"Commander Corsi!" Vale seemed stunned. *"Is something wrong?"*

"No, Lieutenant, nothing's wrong at all, I just—" She hesitated. "I just wanted to tell you something, Christine, something I should've told you a long time ago. You should be proud of what you've accomplished. I know I am—proud, that is, to be in the service with you."

Now Vale looked even more stunned. *"Uh, thanks, Co—ah, Domenica. Thank you very much. I—I can't begin to tell you—"* She took a breath. *"I owe it all to you, you know."*

"Like hell. You don't owe anything to me, Christine—*you* were the one who figured out that it was Dar. It took you three days to see something that I managed to miss for eight years. All I did—" Her voice caught. Until yesterday, she hadn't talked, hadn't *thought*, about this, and it still was like rubbing an open wound. "All I did was shoot him. Anybody could've done that."

"That's good of you to say, Domenica, but—I don't think I could've done what you did."

"Sure you could've—because you're good security. We deal with the unexpected and keep people safe. And that doesn't come from outside." She smiled. "I just hope that Picard and the rest of those guys know what they have there."

Returning the smile, Vale said, *"Well, if they ever forget, I'll be sure to send them to you."*

"You do that. Take care of yourself, Christine—and take care of your ship."

"You do the same, Domenica. And thanks."

Corsi closed the connection, then got up and headed to the door, thence to the security office. True, she wasn't on duty, but like Lauoc said, that was just a technicality. She had a ship to protect.

WOUNDS

Ilsa J. Bick

CHAPTER
1

So, contestants, today's puzzler. Given the choice between a very long trip with Julian Bashir in a cramped little runabout, with nothing to do except stare at the same paragraph over and over until her eyes merged to the center of her forehead, would Elizabeth Lense rather:

- *a)* *have Tev torture her with Klingon painstiks for seven hours;*
- *b)* *be reincarnated as Tev's personal Orion sex slave;*
- *c)* *play footsie with Tev in the mudbaths on Shiralea VI;*
- *d)* *just forget Tev, and stick pins in her eyes;*
- *e)* *What, are you insane? Stop wasting my time. Just phaser Bashir, then pilot her own shuttle, thanks, and she'd be as happy as a Ferengi in—*

"Elizabeth, have I done something to offend you?"

Let's go with e. "No, why do you ask?" Lying her head off.

Bashir's brows tented in a frown. "Because ever since we got the news about the Bentman Prize, you've been, well, positively frosty."

"Frosty? Honestly, I wasn't aware." *Just shut up and leave me alone, because you really, really don't want to go there.*

"That's not true," he said, like he'd read her mind, and then she started to get mad. Bashir cocked his head a little as if she were a species of fascinating bacteria. "Is there something you want to talk about?"

The way he said it, those words . . . She felt like she was sixteen again. She felt as if they were back at Sherman's Planet and it was Gold sitting there and not Bashir. Lense felt as if she'd been having this conversation in one form or another for most of her life. All kinds of people—her parents, her captain, not to mention several doctors—asking if there was something she wanted to talk about. Like talking ever made a damn whit of difference. "No."

He gave a quizzical half-smile. "I don't think that's true."

"I'd . . . I don't want to get into it."

"Why not?"

"Because it doesn't matter," she said, knowing that no, really, it did.

"Anything that's upset you matters, especially if it's something I've done."

That clinched it. He asked, right? "Okay. Honestly?" She reeled in a deep breath and said, "I don't think someone like you should be eligible for the Bentman Prize."

It was weird watching the way his smile deflated bit by bit, like his face was painted on some big balloon with a slow leak. "Someone like me." He said it slowly, as if each word was a land mine he had to mince around. "What do you mean?"

"Oh, come on." Squaring her padd on her console, she swiveled her seat until she faced him head-on. "You want me to spell it out? Someone who's been *enhanced.* Someone who's had his DNA rearranged so he's some kind of mental superman. That's what I mean."

Color flooded his cheeks. "I don't know that I understand. What's my . . . enhancement got to do with anything?"

"Oh, don't play dumb. Nobody's keeping score; nobody's watching. Don't play dumb."

He gaped. "Dumb? What are you *talking* about?"

"You. You're such a fake. You were a fake back in medical school, and you're a fake now. Take that final exam thing . . . you threw it, didn't you? I mean, come on; the question was a gimme. But you missed it."

"*Medical* school?" Bashir looked genuinely astonished. "Elizabeth, you're still thinking about *that*?"

She clenched her jaw hard enough to make her teeth hurt. "Yes, I'm still thinking about *that*. I've always wondered why . . . no, *how* you could miss something a blind first-year medical student would've seen with a cane. The difference between a preganglionic fiber and postganglionic nerve . . . who're you kidding? It's a snap. But knowing what I know now? My guess is someone was looking at you maybe a little too closely. So, you figured, do something dumb, they wouldn't wonder anymore. Worked, too. You played people just right and it seemed like it kept on working until Zimmerman showed up and started asking questions. Thing is, I felt *sorry* for you when I heard about that. Thought, God, just leave the poor guy alone. Not his fault his parents broke the law. But then Commander Selden came after *me*, and now? I don't feel sorry for you anymore."

Then everything came boiling out, stuff she'd stoppered up a good long time: about how she had lost a month of her life staring at the four walls of a dingy little room on Starbase 314 where she got to twiddle her thumbs while they poked and prodded and questioned and sampled her stem to stern. Came up with a big fat zero, too, because—gee, look at that—she *was* a pretty sharp cookie, and she hadn't had a single base pair on any DNA strand tweaked anywhere, thanks. And, oh, by the way, while she was sitting around most emphatically *not* doing her job? A whole bunch of people, including the *Lexington*'s Captain Eberling, got killed, and for what? Because Commander Selden was a righteous pain in the ass. Because Selden made hunting down people like Bashir something of a mission, and no worries if people died because Lense wasn't there to put on the save. Gosh, what's a few dozen Starfleet so long as Selden got rid of Bashir and anyone else who—

"All right, all right." Bashir held up both hands, palms out. "Enough. I get the picture. I don't suppose it matters that I didn't know about any of this; that it happened in the context of a greater paranoia about the shape-shifters; and that I'm not responsible for Selden *or* that paranoia. But I hear you, Elizabeth, I—"

"Don't call me that," she snapped. "'Elizabeth.' Like we're friends. We're not friends. You don't even know me, Bashir."

"My God." He looked as if she'd slapped him in the face. "So now I'm your *enemy*? Elizabeth, that's irrational, that's—"

"What, *crazy*?" Oh, that just burned her. Gold, Bashir, people, her whole *life* . . . everyone treating her like someone who needed *care*, so much *understanding*. *Poor Elizabeth; she's so fragile*. Like she was some crazy woman ready to crack an airlock without a helmet. "I came by my degree honestly. I came by my *brain* honestly."

"God, I can't believe we're having this conversation. First Trill, now this; I can't fathom this run of bad . . ." Sighing, Bashir pinched the bridge of his nose between his right thumb and index finger as if he were very weary. Like she was just one more thing in a series of spectacularly *bad* things heaped on at once. "Look, I was six bloody years old. Everything that happened when I was a child was utterly out of my control, and, enhanced or not, I still have to work hard. And I fail, I make mistakes, I bollix things up more than you can imagine, and a good deal more often than just in medicine. We both must. We *have* to because we're only human. I'm just a person, Elizabeth. Whether I'm theoretically better, what's the difference? What counts is what we do with what we've got."

"Yeah, right. Except we're going for the same prize. I'd like to see a level playing field myself. Gee, what's it like to succeed all the time? Must be kind of nice."

"Oh, completely. But, you know, people are so very uncooperative; they're so *fallible*. They insist on dying before you can do a damned thing, or their feelings for you *change* and then—" He broke off and stared at his fingers knotted in his lap. When he looked up, his eyes were bright. "Would you like me to withdraw? Oh, wait, no, I can't now, of course, can I? What was I thinking? Because then you'll blame me for making it all too easy. I'm really in one of those no-win scenarios, aren't I? I do nothing, you hate me. I do something, same result. Or you blame me, and that comes out to the same thing. I don't suppose it's occurred to you that there's absolutely no guarantee that things on the *Lexington* would have worked out differently even if you'd been there. Maybe you'd have been killed."

"Unlikely. Sickbay's a pretty secure area." A lie. That first shot blasted a chunk out of the *Lexington*'s sickbay and took out virtually her entire staff, and she was wondering just what the hell was wrong with Starfleet engineering specs, that they couldn't reinforce sickbay better than *that*.

"But not impossible." He paused. "Since we're being so very honest, then I'd point out that you're making me out as some sort of monster: your personal scapegoat for all the failures you've had, real or imagined."

She wasn't expecting that. "What? I haven't failed. I've *never* failed," she said, knowing she was lying again. (What, after all, was her paper about? Not one of her more shining moments, that was for sure. And why *had* she written about Dobrah? Was it because Dobrah was unfinished business? Because thinking about him was like a claw ripping her heart, making it bleed?) "This isn't about me. Let's just stay on point, okay?"

"No, let's not. What, did you think I'm your personal punching bag? Not on your life. You give me far too much psychological importance."

"So you're my counselor now?"

"Stop that," Bashir said. "You may be narcissistic and more than a little grandiose—"

"And you're not? Fancy that, the great Julian Bashir, Frontier Doctor—"

"But you're not a stupid woman," he said as if she hadn't spoken. "So don't act like one. You want to hang something on me, go right ahead. But this isn't about my competency, or even my enhancements. This is about you. This is about *your* competency."

"My competency's not the issue here."

"The hell it isn't. Now maybe without my enhancements, I'd have been a big zero. Just a nit. But it takes more than intelligence to make a person. No amount of enhancement can change fate, Elizabeth. You can't control everything. The universe will do what the universe will do."

She knew it was cruel and wrong, but she said it anyway. "Gee, I wouldn't know about the universe, not being perfect and all."

His face seemed to crumple. He looked away. She stared at him, every muscle quivering, her brain screaming that she was being unfair, that she *was* narcissistic, and Bashir was right.

No, that's wrong. You're a doctor; you can't have doubts. In an emergency, you act first, have second thoughts later. You have to believe in the rightness of your constructions, or else everything falls apart.

Bashir let go of a long sigh. "You're wrong, Elizabeth. Perfection, real or imaginary, has nothing to do with fate, and I'm not perfect. Never have been, and never will be. I'm not a freak, not a monster. I make mistakes all the time. I'm human, and I have feelings to hurt."

She never had a chance to reply. Later on, she wondered what she'd have said and thought. It would probably have been something just as cruel because she didn't want to cut him a break. Couldn't afford to because being kind meant taking a good, hard look at herself and she sure as heck wasn't going to do that. But, right then, she never got the chance.

Because in the next instant, the computer screamed, and everything went to hell.

CHAPTER

2

It was like being whacked in the face with a club. Something broke over the runabout. Or the *Missouri* simply plowed through something, shattering space the way an icebreaker smashes through a thick shelf of solid ice. Her neck whipped back and forth, like a heavy flower on a slender stem. Her console rushed for her face, and she shouted, twisting to one side, throwing her arms out. But she wasn't fast enough, and her left temple cracked against plasticine hard enough that her vision blurred with pain.

Dazed, she heard Bashir hit: a solid *smack* as his face connected with the forward viewing port. Crying out, he fell back into his seat, and a fount of bright red blood gushed from his nose. More spurted from a rip in his scalp.

"Oh, my God." She half-stood, and then the *Missouri* spun in a drunken, counterclockwise whirl. There was a sputter of circuitry followed by the ozone stink of fried relays. The runabout porpoised and bucked and then their gravitational unit must have stuttered because the impact caught Lense like a punch to the midsection. Her feet left the deckplates and she smashed against a science console aft. The duranium hull groaned and the deckplates shuddered so much the vibrations rattled into her teeth.

The waves kept coming. They were so fast, the runabout's inertial dampeners couldn't keep up. Lense gasped for breath as centrifugal force palmed her back, pinning her to the deck like a bug to cardboard. Her muscles quivered as she pushed up. She made it to all fours but another hit sent her pitching forward. The point of her chin banged off the deckplates the way a billiard ball ricochets against a bumper. Gagging, she coughed a spray of bright red blood.

"What is it?" Choking, she backhanded blood from her mouth. "What the *hell* is it?"

"Some kind of distortion waves!" Bashir was at the helm, battling for control. "All around! Like rips in space! Can't pinpoint the origin! Are you all right?" He spared her a quick glance over his shoulder, and her gut iced. An oily slick of blood coated his face like a mask, staining his teeth orange. The ooze was turning his uniform from blue to purple.

Then his eyes widened: black rimmed with white outlined in blood. "Oh, dear God. Elizabeth, *fire*, there's a fire; the *transporter*—!"

She smelled it then: the astringent odor of molten plasticine. Balls of black smoke boiled from the ceiling-mounted transporter assembly, and her throat seized against the smoke's acrid sting. Then there was a brilliant yellow flash that left her dazzled as a shower of sparks arced to the deck, and tongues of red-orange flame licked along a bulkhead.

Get up get up get up! Rolling, Lense snagged the edge of a seat, hauled herself to her feet, then staggered to an emergency locker. Dragging out an extinguisher, she clicked it to life. White fire suppressant spewed in a white cloud, and she aimed up, but then the ship yawed to port and flipped so violently she lost her balance, her boots skidding like she'd slipped on sheer ice. She lost the extinguisher; the back of her head cracked against the deck, and then she saw the extinguisher spinning high as a baton before arcing down, straight for her face.

"No!" Tucking her head to her knees, she rolled. But she was too slow. The extinguisher glanced off her spine with a solid, brutal *thwack*, and she screamed.

"Elizabeth!" Bashir, frantic. *"Elizabeth!"*

"I'm all right!" Through a haze of pain, she saw Bashir's back; the drizzle of his blood; the way his shoulders hunched as he fought with the ship.

Got to get to him . . . he's losing too much blood . . . got to put out the fire . . .

Somehow she made it to her knees and then she was crawling on all fours, grappling for a handhold on the science console just aft of Bashir's seat. Only everything was blurry and she was breathing hard, and sour bile burned the back of her throat.

Head hurts . . . can't breathe . . . where's the control for . . . can't black out, not now . . .

She was shaking and it took all her focus and concentration to get her fingers to obey. But they did, and in the next moment, there was the faint electric blue shimmer aft. She huffed out in relief as black smoke and flames flattened against the force field. Then she did the only thing she could think of: shut off life support from the field aft and evacuated all the air.

No air; fire will suffocate. Her head was fuzzy and she shook it clear, hard to do when the ship was still jittering so badly it was a wonder they hadn't already broken apart at the seams. *Bashir's bleeding; have to get to him; we've got to call for help . . .*

"Bashir," she began—and then her voice died in her throat.

Because all of space gathered, knitted into a tight ball, a single point, and the stars winked out.

CHAPTER
3

The rainbow blur of stars and black space peeled back, and they shot into a vast stretch of absolutely nothing the way a toboggan hurtles into a long, dark tunnel. There was a pause, a sensation of jumping from one place to another. And then, faster than thought, the *Missouri* rocketed through, and then there was space and there were stars. The turbulence was gone, and things should have been better.

But they weren't. They were speeding up, not slowing down; she could tell by the heavy drag of gravity's fingers pulling at her skin. Then she looked forward and saw why: a murky, soot-stained ball of a planet, dead ahead, filling the viewing port and looming closer by the second.

"Bashir! Bashir, we're in a gravity well; you've got to pull up, *pull up!*"

"I can't!" Bashir armed blood from his eyes. "The plasma injectors shut down. All I've got are maneuvering thrusters, and our shields . . ."

"I see them," she said, her voice grim. Shields were at thirty percent, plus the runabout had taken major structural damage along the starboard hull. If Bashir couldn't correct their approach angle or get into a stable orbit somehow, the runabout would simply split open and spit them out in a rush of sudden depressurization. Or they might just burn up. Or, more likely, both. "Can you ditch us?"

"I can try. What about the planet?"

She brought up sensors, thanking whatever deity was watching over them that they still worked. "M-class, high levels of atmospheric contaminants, pollution, silicates and copper arsenicals, lots of radioactive decay. Partial pressure of carbon dioxide's higher than Earth."

"Can we breathe it?"

"Not very well, but we don't have a lot of alternatives. Sensors reading three continents: two north, and an island continent, about the size of Australia, to the south with a big inland sea or lake. Low salinity, no aquatic life there; mountains north, stretches of desert, and some kind of big industrial complex south."

"All right, I'll try for the water. Jettison a distress buoy. Then break out the suits just in case, a medical kit, whatever supplies you can."

"I'm on it." She was already moving but with aching slowness, the gravity sucking at her legs like thick mud. A wash of harsh yellow light fanned in, bright enough to throw shadows. Startled, she glanced over her shoulder and saw fire sheeting over the front viewing port, the friction of their passage through the atmosphere igniting a ball of flame like a meteor. The *Missouri* was burning up.

No time! We'll never make it down in the ship! Got to evacuate now, now! The runabout was jittering again, and there was a guttural roar so loud that she gritted her teeth as the sound pummeled her brain. *Just focus, get the suits; get Bashir into his suit; then we blow the hatch, use the suits' thrusters to get us down and pray like hell our force fields don't cut out before we hit or . . .*

The equipment locker was aft of the force field she had thrown up against the smoke, but the transporter fire was out. She stabbed the controls, bleeding in air to equalize pressure before bringing the field down. Then she dragged two suits and helmets from the equipment locker. Even as she tugged one on, her mind was already skipping ahead.

Job one's to get him into his suit. She jammed her right leg into her own, and then her left before cinching it up around her waist. She shrugged into the arms, toggled the clasps. *Need to slap on a fast-clot pressure bandage then bring up his suit's force field, program his thrusters to correct for speed and distance, tether us together so I can control his descent if he passes out; he'll pass out; he's got to, he's losing way too much blood; patch him up as soon as we get down. Got to hope to hell the impact doesn't kill us.*

"Bashir, come on!" She fumbled out a medical kit, clicked it open, pawed through for a pressure bandage. *Got to be quick, quick . . .* "Come on, it's no use! *Leave* it! Let's go!"

"Just a few more seconds!" The runabout was thrashing like a roped steer, and he was straight-arming his console, working fast while his blood puddled on the deck. "We're still too high! If I blow the hatch now, the depressurization will suck us out; we won't have any control!"

He was right. She knew he was right. But what made her furious was that she was getting suited up, and he wasn't.

This is nuts; he has to get back here now! Jamming her helmet down over her ears, she thumbed the catch, heard the click and hiss as the helmet sealed and the suit pressurized. She banged open her external mike. "Bashir, *now!*"

"*Almost there!*" His voice was a little tinny and sounded small and very far away through her internal speakers. But he did turn, and she tossed his suit forward, then his helmet. He fumbled for the suit, nearly lost it because his hands were slick. But then he had it, shook it open, shoved in one foot, then the other. Tugging the suit past his waist, he wriggled in one arm, then the other. But then, to her dismay, he turned back to his controls.

"*I'll try to level us!*" he shouted over the staccato sputter of maneuvering thrusters. "*That way when I blow the hatch—!*"

"Forget that! We can blow it from here! Now you've got exactly three seconds to get your ass back here, or I'm going to drag you out by your thumbs!"

"*No, Elizabeth, stay where you are!*" And then Bashir stiffened and he turned. Their eyes met and for one brief instant, it was as if time stopped. Everything fell away, and she would remember the look on Bashir's face for the rest of her life: his horror and his regret, and all that blood.

Then time began again. The runabout streaked toward its death; the alarm shrilled its ululating cry; then there was a weird, wrenching metallic scream and Bashir was shouting, wildly, *"Elizabeth, she's breaking up, she's breaking up, she's breaking—!"*

"Julian!" she shrieked. She lunged for him, one gloved hand hooked to a bulkhead, the other outstretched and they were so close she could nearly touch him, she was almost there, she could save him, she *had* to! "Julian, for God's sake, give me your hand, *give me your hand!"*

Maybe he started for her. Maybe not. But she'd never know because the next thing she heard was an enormous *ka-bang*. Flames sheeted through the runabout, and the air roared. Her right hand closed reflexively but her fingers clutched air, and then she was screaming because suddenly there was no deck, no bulkhead. No Julian.

The entire starboard hull erupted like someone had touched off a bomb.

Lense was swept away in a hail of debris. She smashed through murky clouds, tumbling head over heels so she saw dun-colored land and then an orange sun and then a vast gray-green smudge that undulated like oil. And then she was on her back, looking straight up, and she saw a bright fiery ball: the runabout, or rather what was left of it, arcing south and away from the water, shedding bits and pieces in its passage, streaming a jet of superheated plasma behind and breaking apart like some sort of angel fallen from grace.

Then clouds swallowed her up and she couldn't see the runabout anymore. There was only the sound of her guttural sobs, the wet of tears upon her skin, a swirl of vertigo. Her vision dimmed as she accelerated, and she went by feel, the *g* force hammering her body, squeezing her until she could barely take a breath. Her fingers crawled over her suit's controls as she activated a force field to cushion her impact and programmed reverse thrusters.

Her last coherent thought was that she would never survive. The impact would kill her. She was going to die, and only a fool would think otherwise.

The very last thing she heard was the full-throated bellow of the wind.

Then there was silence, and her mind slid into darkness. But that was a mercy.

CHAPTER
4

Another primate had died during the night, the third in six weeks. Dr. Idit Kahayn knew because of the smell. The primate lay in a pool of vomit and feces: black eyes glassy as a doll's, purple tongue lolling from a mouth stretched in a rictus of death.

Death and more death. That was her life now. Death for breakfast, death for dinner. Death in her dreams: the image of soldiers and rifles and Janel's face exploding into a mist of blood spray and bone, and her screaming a warning, too late. That same dream every night, like her mind was stuck in an endless, recursive loop. No way off; no way out.

The remaining primates tracked her as she passed through the animal room to fetch gloves, a gown, her safety glasses. But she paused, staring them down. "It's not my fault. I didn't mean for this to happen. But I don't have a choice."

The primates didn't answer. They just looked at her with their grave, liquid brown eyes, and she could sense the room getting thick and electric and icy.

"It's not my fault," she said again. Then she went to the isolation room, pulled the body from its cage, bagged it, and lugged it to the lab, leaving the animals to throw their thoughts back and forth in the air above her head.

The lab was chilly and smelled of antiseptic and old death. The counters were metal, the walls were white ceramic tile, and the floor was scuffed gray linoleum. A metal autopsy table stood on rolling casters in the center of the lab. The table was fitted with gutters all around to funnel away blood and other fluids. She unbagged the body and placed the primate on the table where she hosed it down, sluicing away vomit and filth, grateful that the water was triple-filtered at least so its color wasn't black but a shade of watery ash. Then she braced the primate's neck on a block so the head hung back and those blind eyes fixed on a point somewhere far away.

She used a scalpel for the skin along the crown and from ear to ear, incising through tough, calloused scalp and stringy muscle all the way to bone. Then she pulled the front flap down over the primate's face and tugged the back flap to the base of its skull just above the spine. She took up a rotary bone saw, thumbed it to life. The saw whined, then dropped in pitch as the blade bit bone. As she cut, watery wine-colored blood dribbled into the gutters. She buzzed the circumference of the skull, notching the bone at the occiput. If the skull slid off when she bagged a dead animal for cremation, it made a mess.

When she'd cut through, she lifted the calvarium from the brain. The skull and tissues made a hollow sucking sound, like picking up an overturned bowl of thick gelatin. The primate's brain was so edematous that once the cap of bone was removed, gray matter (though it was never really gray but a dirty pinkish purple like thin jelly) lipped the edges of the cranium like an underdone soufflé. The dura mater clung to the underside of the skull cap, so she got a good look at the brain in situ. The gyri were plump and choked with fluid, and she saw the bruise at once: a purplish-black splotch fanning around the implant like a squashed bug. She nudged away brain until she spied a clear bulb that was the proximal end of the implant: a thin, nearly filamentous metal cylinder bristling with synthetic dendrites.

Inflammation and swelling; probably a reaction to the separation. But how to beat that? After an easy dozen primate deaths in the past twelve months, she still wasn't sure. Either way, the animal's brain had swelled with fluid. Intracranial pressure had built up and the brain—really nothing more than a gelatinous mass of tissue and fluid held together by the thin bag of the meninges—had nowhere to go except the spinal canal. There would have been pain. The animal would've lost the use of its arms and legs, then bowel and bladder control. It would have been frightened. A horrible way to die but, then again, Kahayn didn't know too many ways that were terrific either.

After separating the brain from the spinal cord and the tentorium, the dural connections between cerebrum and cerebellum, she scooped out the brain with both gloved hands. The cooling brain was tepid against her right hand but cold in her left.

She suspended the brain with a string in a formalin solution. She'd leave the brain in the preservative for the next ten days or so while the tissue firmed enough for her to section and see where she'd gone wrong—again.

By six-thirty in the morning, she was done, and then it was time for a stim and the OR. She wasn't hungry. As she passed through the primate room, she didn't look at the animals but she could feel their eyes on her back and their thoughts chasing her down the hall and out of the research wing.

Late afternoon now, and on her fourth procedure of the day: a rail-thin man with lung rot. Her pager shrilled as she was wrist-deep in a small, plum-colored lake of blood that smelled like an old clot. She had a fistful of rotted left lung and the tip of her left pinky plugged an arterial rip. There was so much blood, she'd gone by feel, tweezing through stiff, filamentous lung until she felt the rhythmic pulse of a tiny gusher a third of the way down the aorta. The blood was warm, but the tip of her pinky was cold and she needed her right hand free to do the fine work.

Her pager nagged again. "Someone get that, please? I'm a little tied up here."

A surgery tech patted at Kahayn's left hip, found the pager, killed it, glanced at the display, then hip-butted his way out of the suite. Kahayn jerked her head at the lieutenant standing opposite: a new girl who was all round blue eyes set in pale blue skin above a white-edged blue mask. "C'mon, c'mon," said Kahayn, "get some suction going so I can see what I'm doing here."

The lieutenant jumped to, stabbing the patient's pleural cavity with the suction tip.

"Easy, go easy," said Kahayn, grabbing the lieutenant's gloved wrist with her free hand. Grape-colored beads of blood pattered onto green surgical drape. "Not so hard; you're going to give him another bleeder you keep that up."

"Sorry." But the lieutenant slowed down, working with exaggerated care. Blood gurgled through tube, and the blood lake receded until Kahayn saw first the knuckles of her gloved left hand and then the spot where she'd plugged the artery. The rip was, thankfully, small, and the artery not yet so brittle that she couldn't simply suture it shut. But rot had eaten into the left lung, and the normally spongy blue tissue had morphed into tough, stringy, prune-colored filaments that had insinuated through pleura and into the patient's rib the way ivy suckers clung to old brick.

"Okay," she said to the chief OR nurse, who stood with anesthesia behind a green drape at the head of the surgical table. "We're going to need a left lung here."

"I think we only have nine lefties on hand," said the nurse. She was a major, and a perennial hard-ass. "Besides, this casualty hasn't built up enough credits for a lung and if people get wind that he got one without . . ."

Kahayn drilled the nurse with a look. "Maybe you didn't hear me. I said, get the lung, *Major*."

"Colonel, I am just following protocol—"

"I don't care. Now either get the lung, or get out."

"Colonel, there are established procedures for—"

"That's it." Kahayn cut her off with a jerk of her head. "You're out. Breynar," she called over to the circulating nurse, "I need a left lung."

The nurse, a first lieutenant, shot a hesitant glance at the major, then nodded and scurried out, his booties whispering against linoleum. The major's eyes narrowed over her mask before she did a quick pivot with the precision of a drill instructor. She hipped the door. "I'll be reporting this," she said and pushed out through the scrub room. The doors had hinged flaps and *fwap-banged*.

No one said anything, so the suction gurgle was very loud in the silence. Then the anesthesiologist said, "You got to go easy, Colonel. She has a point."

"Don't start," said Kahayn.

"I'm not. But you think we're busy now, all they got to do is riot out there and then you'll be getting up before you go to sleep."

"Yeah, yeah, and eating gravel for breakfast. Look, this guy needs a lung. So you have a better idea? Like I'm supposed to go to all this trouble to stitch up an artery but let him suffocate?"

"I'm just saying. She's doing her job."

"Yeah, yeah," Kahayn said again, exasperated. She blew out. Her blue surgical mask puffed then crinkled back in a papery rustle of accordion folds across her nose and mouth. He was right, of course, not that it mattered much because the patients just kept on coming. The medical complex was short-staffed, nothing new about that either because they were *always* short-staffed, the casualties streaming in for replacements, and there was never enough to go around. Kahayn felt like one of those rats on a little wire wheel, running and running and running nowhere really fast.

Nothing was getting better either. The air was bad and getting worse, and there were a lot of people with lungs so sooty they looked more like bloody bags of pulverized charcoal. Cancers in the bone, the liver, the gut, eating people alive a piece at a time. The whole thing was so damned futile.

Don't think. Kahayn stared down at that ruin of a chest, what was left of a man's lung. *Nothing you can do. Just work and keep on working but don't think.*

So she worked steadily like an automaton and was a suture away from finishing with the artery when the surgical tech banged back in, door *whap*-flapping in his wake. "That was the ER. They want you down there."

"Uh-huh, well, I'm kind of busy now. Major Arin's on; he can handle it."

"It was the major who called."

"Did he say what it was about?" Kahayn held her hand out again, palm up, and the nurse slapped a needle holder into her gloved palm. Kahayn poked the wire-thin tip of the curved needle into arterial wall, rotated her right wrist counterclockwise until the needle appeared, and then tied off a friction knot in a double-wrap throw followed by a single. She nodded. "Okay, that'll do it for the artery. Now all we got to do is wait for that lung. We're just damned lucky he didn't need a new hose. Arguing with the major about that would've been fun." She looked over at the tech. "Well? What did Arin say?"

"Major Arin didn't say, exactly."

"Meaning?"

"Just . . . he said it was some sort of casualty brought in under heavy guard."

"So it's a Jabari? Or some other freak? Whatever it is, Arin's going to have to harvest this one on his own. But let me know if there's a good lung. I could use it up here."

"No, this one's still alive. Major Arin said he wants you to break scrub; he needs another opinion. He sent Captain Storn up to scrub in for you." A pause. "Major Arin also wanted you to know that Colonel Blate's on his way."

"Okay," said Kahayn, though it wasn't. If Security Director Blate was involved, things never worked out well. She'd had a lot of experience with that. With Janel . . .

Can't think about that now. Just go do the job.

She peeled off her smeary gloves, then said to the lieutenant, "Wait for Storn, and don't touch anything."

On her way down to the ER, she passed Breynar hustling back with a lumpy polystyrene sac full of the lung she'd wanted. He looked a question, but she hooked a thumb over her shoulder and he skedaddled. As she turned right to take the stairs, she happened to glance left down the long hall. She spotted the major marching hard-ass-style and double-quick at the head of a phalanx of administrative types, and as they did a hard left for the OR and disappeared, Kahayn figured she'd just done a whole bunch of really good work for nothing.

Death for breakfast. Death for dinner. She banged open the door to the stairwell. Yeah. Typical day.

CHAPTER
5

Bashir was screaming; there was blood everywhere, and there were flames. But no matter how hard she tried, she couldn't get to him; he wouldn't take her hand, damn him, and then it was too late because she was swept away by black water that was infinitely deep. So she hung there now, alone, just like a diver so far down the world above was a memory, or maybe a nightmare, a very bad dream . . .

Lense's eyes jammed open in panic. Her head hurt; there was blood in her mouth; her face was wet. And she couldn't see. There was nothing. No light. No stars. No clouds. Nothing.

Oh, God! God, no! I can't be blind, I can't!

She thrashed and the blackness gave, and that's when she realized that she was floating facedown and that this was water, or maybe oil because the stuff was dense and viscous and sucked at her limbs. Something was still screaming. But it wasn't Bashir. It was her suit nagging that she'd better get a move on because her air was nearly gone.

I made it. She remembered Bashir's bloody face. She remembered churning clouds and a flash as the runabout blew apart and then her stabbing at controls, programming in a descent. *Reverse thrusters must have engaged before I passed out. Must have landed in that water.* She rolled, and then she was on her back and staring through gooey rivulets more like molten tar than water.

Somehow she made it to shore. The sea was rimmed with brown sand hemmed by gray bluffs of bare rock. She was gasping by the time she pulled herself from the muck, every breath feeling as if she were sipping air through a straw. Then she cracked her helmet, twisted it, dragged it off and hoped like hell her sensors hadn't been completely whacky. (But, really, she didn't have much of a choice and there was no way she was suffocating in that suit, no damn way.) She sprawled, gasping like a hooked fish on a dock.

Eventually, she pushed up to a sit. She didn't exactly feel better, just less horrible. The air stank like rotten eggs, and tasted worse, like something had crawled into her mouth, defecated, and died. She worked her mouth, spat out a gob of rust-brown saliva. The air was loaded with sulfur dioxide; she remembered that from her sensor readings. What else? She tried to think past the roar in her head. Nuclear waste but not lethal in the short term. (Give it a year, two, then she was in trouble. But she sure as heck wasn't going to be here by then.) Methane, copper arsenicals, crystalline silica, and ozone: all bad. Sensors had said there were mountains north of the sea, so she must've beached there. A lot of land around but mottled, almost moth-eaten. A patchwork of parched, dusty brown tracts alternating with barren stands of twisted, shriveled trunks. What looked like a broad, red-brown desert valley, brown and yellow-banded mesa west and east sprouting from the desert like flat-topped mushrooms.

But there was a city to the south. She remembered that, too. An image flashed in her brain: crashing through clouds, rolling away from the fireball of the *Missouri* and looking south. Spying a dense carpet of metal, glass, and odd jumbles of remnants that had to be buildings. But they were haphazard and set at weird angles, like the blocks of a toy city kicked over by a kid sick of playing games. She remembered that there was one, very big structure, a central hub with four spokes that fed to a large outer ring. Maybe she could get there, blend in, figure what she was dealing with . . .

Because I'm marooned here. The thought hit like a phaser blast in the chest: an explosion of pain and heat, and her innards scooped out all rolled into one. Her stomach lurched, and her forehead filmed with clammy sweat.

They're never going to find me. They won't even know where to look. It could be days before they figure out we're missing and now I'm never getting out of here, I'm stuck, and I'm never getting out, I've got to get out, get out, get me out, let me out . . . !

"Shut up." She squeezed her eyes tight. "Shut up, *shut up!* Don't panic. Nothing's for sure. They might find you; they're probably looking right now, so just shut up, nothing's certain, absolutely nothing." But she knew she was lying because there was, of course, one thing of which she was very certain.

Julian Bashir was dead.

CHAPTER
6

Kahayn smelled the ER before she saw it: a sick, gassy odor of wet gangrene mingling with the full, ripe stink of feces, old blood, and fresh vomit. Stronger than usual today, and when she turned the corner down the last hall, she saw a double line of gurneys wedged head to toe along the left and right walls; a patient cocooned under a sheet, a ream of paperwork on a clipboard, triaging each casualty by diagnosis and urgency. (They were all sick, and they were all urgent. Again, typical.)

A lanky man with pewter-gray hair stepped into the corridor. Arin wore blue scrubs that blood had dyed black and a dingy white coat that never seemed to come clean no matter what. Spotting her, he stumped down the hall, favoring that gimp knee of his.

"You took long enough," he said, jabbing a finger at the bridge of a pair of owlish, steel-rimmed specs that had slid to the tip of his nose.

"Bleeder," she said as they headed for the triage suite. "Lung rot. The usual. So, what's all the fuss about?"

Arin blew out, stabbed his glasses back into place again. "All kinds of craziness." Older by almost two decades, Arin wore glasses because he was a tad old-fashioned. Said he'd keep the eyes, until they fell out on their own; no marbles for him just yet, thanks. She envied him the eyes. They were so . . . natural. Pupils worked very smoothly; you could see the iris muscles contract or lengthen like some sort of miracle, and the tracking from side to side was phenomenal. So efficient. No glitches at all. "Some casualty that slipped past the guards at the perimeter," he said.

"Hunh." She was impressed. "That takes some doing. Guards found him?"

"On patrol, yeah."

"How'd he get in?"

Arin shrugged. His limp was worse today, and his knee squealed. "They don't know. One look, though, and they brought it here. Figured they sure weren't going to get stuck without getting some kind of clearance."

"So clear him. Shouldn't be that difficult."

"It's really not that simple," said Arin. "Trust me on this."

"Why do I feel like the worst is yet to come?"

He eyed her over his glasses and didn't smile. "Because it is."

They pushed into the ER, past a knot of nurses and one physician working frenetically over one patient who Kahayn could tell by the blood spatter wasn't going to make it. The ER was arranged in a long rectangle, with curtained bays lining each wall and a triage station centered at the head. Behind the triage station were two critical-care bays. (A joke: You made it to the ER; you were critical. The staff was so overwhelmed that, anything less, and they just laughed in your face.) Kahayn spotted a quartet of uniforms, three with their rifles at the ready. That was bad. She didn't like rifles anywhere near the ER.

But it was the man who wore the fourth uniform that told her, instantly, whoever this patient was, he wasn't run of the mill. The uniform was a bullish man with a neck so thick and short his head seemed glued to his shoulders, and a pair of goggle, walleyes that always unsettled her.

"Oh, hell," she muttered. "How'd he get here so fast?"

Arin grunted. "Like I said, it's not that simple. Blate's people told him about the intruder, and then he showed up just as I was getting started. Since then, they haven't let me near it.

Been making all kinds of noise about taking the patient over to detention. I wouldn't let them, not unless you ordered me to. Even threatened to call Nerrit over at High Command, and then they kind of backed down. Barely, but enough to buy me enough time to get you down here."

"This must be some patient."

"You have this really annoying habit of reiterating the obvious." An exasperated sigh. Arin flexed his left knee, and his prosthetic clicked and whirred. "Sorry. Dragging you in was the only way I could think of to keep them from taking it out of here."

"No, you did right," she said, only belatedly registering that Arin kept saying *it*. But then she was within earshot of the security director and attempted what she hoped was something bordering on a neutral expression. "Director Blate."

"Colonel." Blate's left eye was especially bad and wandered, giving him a walleyed stare that Kahayn always found disturbing because she was never sure which artificial eye to focus on. She suspected that this was precisely what the security director wanted. Blate said, "I hope Major Arin didn't pull you from anything important."

No, no, just a little chest bleed, lung replacement, nothing big. "As I understand it, you've kept Dr. Arin from examining his patient."

"Indeed." Blate's right eye zeroed in. "This is not your ordinary casualty."

"Gee, you can tell all that without an exam?" She nodded beyond the guards at a back bay curtained from view by a gauzy yellow, nearly full-length drape. There was a gap between the floor and the bottom of the curtain, and Kahayn saw the gurney's black rubber-wheeled castors and the disembodied off-white flats of a nurse crossing left to right. "And I thought that's what you needed doctors for. If you're so good, Blate, why the hell do you need us then?"

"Idit," Arin murmured.

"I didn't require your assistance," said Blate. "I still don't. I ordered Major Arin to stand down. He became belligerent and threatened to call High Command, and then he insisted that you had to authorize release of the casualty to our custody."

"Damn straight," said Kahayn. "Now, as I get it, your people brought the patient here. I hate to point this out, but we're doctors. Yeah, sure, we're all military, but this is a hospital. We see casualties, only we call them patients. We even treat them. So since this is a patient and we're on *my* turf, I have command authority, not you. The only person who can override my authority is the base commander, or Nerrit. You're welcome to call the CO, but I suspect he'll side with me. So the faster you let me clear this guy, the sooner your people can get at him. What say you get out of my way?"

Blate raised a hand, his right, the one that clicked when the fingers moved. "It's not that simple. We need to—"

"Anyone says something's not simple one more time, I'll gonna rip out his tonsils." Kahayn pushed past and yanked at the curtain. There was a rasp of metal; the curtain scrolled to one side. "Now, what . . ." she began—and stopped dead in her tracks.

Two nurses and a tech hovered uncertainly around a gurney. On the gurney was a biped, lying prone. The fact that the patient *was* bipedal and had two arms to boot was a relief because, with all that radioactive sludge out there, she didn't take anything for granted. But she couldn't tell about the head because the patient wore some sort of soot-stained, off-white suit with a bulbous helmet of a design she'd never seen in her life. There were patches of something rust-red and black smeared on the suit. Red and yellow lights winked on some sort of control panel mounted like a bracelet on the left wrist. There were more red than yellow lights, and that was usually a bad sign. But she didn't have a clue about what the lights meant, nor could she figure the power source. The helmet probably had some kind of polymer faceplate but whether it was clear or not, she didn't know because the helmet was seared and sooty as an old filter of an air repurifier that hadn't been changed in three weeks.

But one thing she did understand. The patient was writhing, restless, pumping his legs in slow motion and getting nowhere fast. She knew pain when she saw it. She knew trouble.

"As I said, Colonel," said Blate. He stumped between her and the gurney; his right eye tracked in with a tiny whirr. "Things are really not that simple."

CHAPTER

7

There was this big joke about S.C.E. Those engineer guys show up, and everything goes terribly wrong. Some kind of cosmic curse thing going. Lense figured she had the S.C.E. curse but good because everything that could go wrong had, and in a really big way. Like now, for instance: stranded God-knew-where with nothing but the clothes on her back, and a bulky EVA suit whose only useful item included an emergency locator beacon. Otherwise, no emergency rations, no tools, no water. No Julian. No nothing.

Tacky with sweat, Lense battled through a thicket of prickles, her arms full of spiky boughs sticky with sap and stinking of resin. She'd stripped to her black tee, and her arms were crisscrossed with scratches. The branches were from some sort of stunted, indigenous conifer with a gnarly black trunk. Only thing growing besides these damn prickles and a heck of a lot of scrub grass and chaparral. She was headed down-hill toward a natural depression she'd discovered near a slow creek slicked with scum northwest of the inland sea.

She was huffing like she was making an ascent. Her dark curls were plastered to her scalp, and sweat trickled down the back of her neck. Maybe it would get cooler when that weird orange sun went down. Then she eyed that sky and figured no way. Maybe four degrees C cooler, and that'd be it. Too many clouds trapping way too much heat, leaving the air hot and turgid as sludge. Her chest was tight, as if a metal band were twisted around it. Her head roared with a headache so bad, she thought her brain was going to dribble right out of her ears. Her gut was doing flips, pushing bile into the back of her throat.

The air was death by slow poison. She had symptoms like making altitude too fast the way pikers did with Everest on Earth, or Vulcan's Mount Seleya, not acclimating first to make up for the lower partial pressure of oxygen at altitude. Probably she'd get better in a couple of days. But she didn't want to be anywhere on this rock in a couple of days and so hoped she wasn't going to find out.

And she was thirsty. Grit crunched between her teeth and her tongue felt glued to the roof of her mouth. Dying of thirst was really unpleasant, but she didn't dare drink water she hadn't boiled. For one thing, the water didn't look that inviting and there was nothing living in it so far as she could tell, except for some scummy kind of sea grass. But she wasn't ready to die *because* of desperation either. Not that she thought boiling would do a whole hell of a lot. That water was loaded with contaminants: residual radioactive ash, polychlorinated phenols, industrial waste. Probably she could boil away the more volatile phenols and other organic carcinogens. Still no guarantee, though, and there was nothing to do about the ash. Maybe filter it through her uniform top? No, that'd take a long time and the uniform was a tight weave, not very porous. Probably more would evaporate away than drip through. So that was a nonstarter.

She'd thought about scrounging for water from some of the native plants, but she hadn't spotted any water-trapping plants like bamboo, or *adun* cacti like they had on Vulcan. Maybe she could rig a solar still, but she didn't have anything clear to drape over the pit upon which water could condense. But she had to get water. More than food, water's what would keep her alive and . . .

Whoa, slow down; panic over one thing at a time.

The tricky thing had been what to do with her suit. That old Prime Directive thing cropping up—and wouldn't Gold have a field day with that one. But the real issue was her suit had an emergency transponder-locator beacon, sort of important if she wanted off this rock. Once she'd beached, there was no way she could lug it along. So she'd stayed in the suit, hiking northwest and away from the inland sea.

Eventually, she'd found the stream and a good place to construct a shelter. There were tumbles of boulders humped and jumbled here and there, and she found a wide ridge with a sixty-degree incline and a cave of sorts that led back for about fifty meters. Thumbing on her emergency transponder, she wedged her helmet and suit into a fissure but pocketed her combadge. The opening to the cave was wide enough for her to squirm into, if needed. Of course, this might also mean that an animal could do the same thing, but she hadn't seen any animals so far. There were birds here and there, black specks silhouetted like cinders against smoke-yellow clouds. A heck of a lot of bugs, though, especially those nearly-invisible no-see-ums swarming in an undulating ball around her head.

The bugs made sense. In the aftermath of a nuclear catastrophe, insects would likely adapt and survive. That was bad because she wasn't exactly sure what there was for food, and she wasn't eager to go grubbing for, well, *grubs*. If she had a chance to spy out a few of the local inhabitants, that would help because if they were similar physiologically (and she'd just have to take a guess since she was pretty near blind without a tricorder), she'd likely be able to tolerate the food.

Thinking about getting food and water, she wasn't watching where she was going. Her toe hooked on an exposed root, and she stumbled, went down, wood spilling out of her arms. Her right ankle complained. She cursed. Starfleet regulation uniform boots were made for civilized life on a civilized ship, not hiking.

She picked herself up, dusted off, and retrieved her wood. Food and water, they were just two problems out of a gazillion. She hadn't exactly aced survival training but remembered that Starfleet's version was predicated upon a few givens. For example, Starfleet pretty much figured you had access to tools or some kind of gear: phaser, a tricorder. Something. Another was that if you ditched, well, you had the shuttle for shelter and you could stay pretty cozy, break into your survival stores, and wait to get rescued.

Rescue. That was the key. Starfleet kind of drummed that into you. Your people were going to be looking for you even if you were just a plasma smear or a slew of subatomic particles. You were important; your absence was felt, and someone somewhere would worry. So she figured they were worrying: Gold, Gomez, even Tev. Not to mention the folks on DS9 who probably missed Bashir. She counted on that much.

But the problem was surviving until they found her. If they found her. She didn't have tools. She didn't have the runabout. She'd debated about trying to find what was left of the *Missouri*, maybe scavenging bits and pieces but mostly sticking close because that's where her people would look first. But the shuttle had gone far south toward that city and was too far away for her to get there in anything like a reasonable amount of time. From what she'd seen, there wasn't much left of the *Missouri* anyway—and, to be honest, she wasn't really sure she was ready to face what might be left. Of the runabout. Of Julian, mainly, if he was still in there. Maybe she should be stronger. Right now, she wasn't.

Worse than having nothing (if there was such a thing as something worse in a situation verging on the totally catastrophic), she didn't really think they'd ended up anywhere close to where they'd been going. In the few seconds she'd had at the sensors, she'd drawn a blank: no Starfleet buoys to ping, no recognizable stars. No nothing. Of course, the sensors could've been damaged. On the other hand, they'd been good enough to read this planet. So a whole lot of nothing meant they'd ended up far, far away. That was pretty bad.

So make a plan, you idiot. You'll feel better if you're doing something, if you've got a plan.

It was a psychological game. She knew that. Helplessness made people panic. You panicked, you were as good as dead. So, okay, in the morning, she'd head toward that city, keep the sea on her right and the mountains behind her and go south until she found someone.

"And what you got to think about now is what you're going to eat and drink." Her voice sounded weird and a little small because everything was so still. But talking to herself made her feel better. She dodged a tumble of boulders and angled in left toward the hollow she'd opted on for the night. "Because face it, sweetheart. You are going to be here for a nice, long time. You're on your own and . . ." She looked up and froze.

There were three of them: a woman and two men. They each had a rifle and their rifles were pointed straight at Lense.

No one spoke for a very long moment. Then the woman—with dusky, plum-colored skin, no nose, only the right half of her jaw that made her face look dented, and a zigzag scar slicing along her collarbone from left to right—said, "You were saying? About being on your own."

"That's your story?" Their leader, a lanky and well-muscled man with a square chin and brown hair that spilled in ringlets around massive shoulders, eyed her skeptically. He wore a coarse, beige linen shirt that was open to his throat, a pair of olive-drab trousers, and cracked black leather combat boots streaked with deep seams of red-ocher grit. A pistol was holstered high on his right hip. But, unlike the woman and the other man, *this* man was unmarked. No scars, no missing limbs. His only similarity to the other two was the color of his skin: a dusky purple like an underripe Damson plum but with more blue.

Not Bolian, and Andorians are more sky-blue. This is something old; on the tip of my tongue, something about hemoglobin . . .

"Why don't I believe you?" he said.

Lense gave a halfhearted shrug. "That's not my problem."

"Oh, but I'm afraid it is."

"I told you," said Lense. "I was with friends. We were on a hike. We got separated."

The man's brown-black eyes slitted. Lense forced herself not to look away. Her stomach was turning somersaults, though. If she couldn't convince these people that she was just some stupid hiker, there was no way out of this, and there sure as heck wasn't going to be any cavalry charging over the hill to come to her rescue.

She was in some sort of rebel camp: a warren of caves several hours north of where she'd been. The caves were a good ten degrees C cooler than outside, a welcome relief. The air smelled wet and there must be some sort of underground river or stream because Lense heard a faint but steady drip, like moisture pattering on rock. The place was well ventilated, too. Every now and again, a finger of cool air brushed along the nape of her neck and gave her goose bumps. Torches flared along the walls, releasing curling tendrils of sooty smoke that streaked the rocky walls charcoal black. Couldn't keep the torches going if there was no way to replenish air.

"So why didn't they go looking for you?" the man asked.

"I'm sure they did. If your people hadn't interfered, they'd probably have found me by now."

The man grunted. "My people wouldn't have come anywhere near if there'd been the slightest hint of a search party. But there wasn't one, and I have to wonder about that. They're your friends, so why didn't they raise an alarm? Those woods ought to have been crawling with Kornaks. But you were alone. So these . . . *friends* of yours, they can't be that fond of you now, can they? After all, what type of friend leaves someone with no supplies to wander around on her own? In fact, Mara here," he nodded at the blonde with the scarred jaw and no nose who stood on his left, "she says you were foraging for wood and very noisy about it. So, with friends like that—"

"With friends like that, I don't need enemies. Right, right." Lense feigned impatience. "That just goes to prove my point. If I were some sort of spy, I'd be, well, kind of stealthy, wouldn't I? Spies usually sneak around."

He arched an eyebrow, the left. "Maybe you're a very poor spy."

"Or maybe I'm not a spy. That's what I'm telling you. Look, I don't know what it is about *no* that you don't understand, but for the record: My name is Elizabeth Lense. I'm not a spy. I was out with friends. We were separated. I was trying to make myself comfortable before it got dark. I am confident my friends will be looking for me, *are* looking right now. They'll be worried sick. Period, end of story."

"Then why are you dressed like that, hmm? That looks like a uniform. And what's this?" He flipped her combadge like a coin, caught it one-handed, thrust it under her nose. "What is this, some sort of insignia?"

Her fingers itched, and it was all she could do not to snatch the combadge from his hand. "It's jewelry. I told you."

"I don't believe you. How stupid do you think the Jabari are, eh? Hiking; that's absurd. You don't have a pack. You don't even have a canteen."

Lense was silent. Mara, the blonde, had asked the same things. They'd shepherded her along a corkscrew trail that doglegged and cut along switchbacks through the mountains north of the sea. The terrain had turned progressively worse, the vegetation sparser, and Lense's boots were not up to the task of hoofing it up trails filmed with crumbly scree. She'd fallen a lot, ripped her uniform pants at the knees and gotten banged up pretty good. But it was when she started coughing that they stopped to rest. Mara and the men swigged water from canteens while Lense leaned back against a boulder, dripped sweat and wheezed. Her chest was killing her and when she could work up a mouthful of spit, it came out rust-colored, and her mouth tasted like metal. That scared her.

That's when Mara scowled. "Where's your canteen?"

Lense worked at getting air. "I . . . I lost it."

"Lost it. How could you . . . ?" Then Mara gave a horsey snort, scrubbed the spout of her canteen with the flat of her hand and thrust the canteen under Lense's nose. "Here. But don't get any ideas. You're worth a lot more alive than you are dead."

Lense hadn't argued. The water smelled of a combination of tin and petrochemicals. Probably the stuff was going to make her as sick as a Klingon on fish juice, but it was wet and she gulped it back.

Now, the man—the obvious leader—said, "I see two options: believe you, or kill you. Either way, though, you can't expect that I'll just let you walk away."

"And why not?" Lense thrust out her chin. "Did I come looking for you? No. Your people came after me."

Mara cut in. "Saad, this is a waste of time. Her family's got money; they've got to be rich. She's just too well-fed to be from one of the other Outlier tribes." Mara tossed Lense a narrow-eyed, suspicious look. "All you have to do is look at her to know that she's got connections. There's not a scratch on her, no visible prosthetics. I'll bet that if we strip her down, she won't have any scars either. No organ transplants, nothing."

"So you're talking ransom," Saad said slowly. His eyes were that shade of brown that's almost black, and now they clicked over Lense, clearly taking inventory. "Maybe. But look at her skin, Mara. See how pale she is? And that blood." He pointed at the scratches on Lense's arms and her crusted knees. "It's too red. Maybe she's a mutant that got cast out of the city."

"Or maybe they're side effects from new medicines."

"But maybe not. Mara, if she's a mutant, no one's going to pay to get her back, and we can't trade her for anyone. Then she's useless."

Lense didn't like where this was going. "Excuse me, but I'm not a piece of furniture. How about including me in the decision, all right?"

Mara opened her mouth to say something but Saad silenced her with a look. "You're right," he said to Lense. "You're not a chair. But you could be a deserter, or a spy. Yes." He stroked his chin between a thumb and forefinger. "The more I think about that one, the better I like it."

"How is that better?" Mara's lips twisted into a scowl, and this made her scar jump and wriggle like a fat, purple-blue worm. "If she's a spy, we can't let her go back, no matter what's offered."

"But if she's a deserter, she can't go back either. We win either way. I think this puts her in a rather interesting position and I suspect—" He broke off, and now Lense heard the commotion, too: a gabble of angry voices, shouts, the sounds of footsteps clapping against rock. A moment later, a wiry man with the half-moon of a scar arcing in a scimitar over his neck hurried in and sketched a hasty salute. "What is it?" asked Saad.

"Kornaks." The wiry man had chocolate-brown spatters on his shirt that looked like dried mud. "Got two of our squads."

"Squads?" Saad shot Mara a look.

"I don't think there's a connection," said Mara. "No one around where we found her."

"Unless they've come out looking for her," said Saad. The corners of his mouth tightened. "How many Kornaks?"

"At least fifteen that we saw," said the wiry man. "We killed nine, but the others kept up a suppressing fire and we had to retreat."

"No possibility you were followed?"

"None."

"What about our losses?"

"Five dead. The rest of us made it back, but we've got two wounded, both badly. I don't think we can save either one. Do you want them executed now, or—?"

"*Executed*?" The word was out of Lense's mouth before she could bite it back. "What are you talking about? Where's your medic?"

"Shut up." Mara nudged her with the point of her rifle. "Really."

"You object," Saad said, his tone more curious than hostile. "Why?"

Lense weighed the value of keeping her mouth shut, then decided she'd already put her boot in it and if Gold ever saw her again, he'd string her up by her thumbs for that Prime Directive stuff. Only these people would probably kill her anyway and deprive Gold of the pleasure.

So you might as well go down for something useful, not some dumb runabout accident, right?

"Yes," she said. "I object. Your people get hurt, you fix them up. You don't automatically decide that someone's life is worthless just because he's been wounded. You don't have that right."

"Don't talk to us about right," said Mara. "You, a Kornak, of all people . . ."

Lense kept her eyes on Saad. "You don't have the right."

"Convince me there's a better way," he said.

"What do you mean, better? Why should I have to convince

you that it's better to be humane and better to treat someone even if he ends up dying? Otherwise, you'll never know whether you might have saved him." It occurred to her that in triage situations, sorting through who was worse off and who she might save, she *did* let people die. But she couldn't think about that now.

"Interesting point," said Saad. "You talk as if you have some sort of training. What type?"

She paused. "I'm a physician."

"Really?" Both of Saad's eyebrows went up this time. "Do you have trauma experience? Combat?"

Her thoughts jerked back to the *Lexington*, and the air electric with screams and Klaxons and smelling of singed hair and clotted blood, and she thought that, yeah, she had plenty of experience and some to spare. "Yes," she said, wondering for a second if that meant she'd cinched her own execution as a Kornak spy or soldier or terrorist, or whatever and whoever the hell a Kornak really was. "But even if I didn't, even if I had only a passing acquaintance with using antiseptic and old-fashioned bandages, you don't execute people who get hurt doing their job. You don't throw people away like garbage. You people, you're out here, running around with those,"— she gestured toward Mara's rifle, an antique with a long barrel and a gas suppressor—"you get shot at and you don't have a medic, anyone with training?"

"Our medic is dead," said Mara. Her face was twisted with rage and nearly the color of a fresh bruise. "I have some training but not enough, and it wouldn't matter anyway. We barely have supplies to treat minor injuries, much less major ones. Anyway, why should a Kornak worry her head about one more dead Jabari? The only thing you'd care about was that you couldn't harvest him—"

"You shouldn't do this," Lense said to Saad. "I don't care what your customs are. You're their leader, not their judge and executioner." When he said nothing, she said, "For crying out loud, let me look at him! What can it cost you? You've already said you're not going to let me go. If I'm a spy, what more can I learn to compromise you than I have already? Maybe I can *help* this man! At least let me try."

He stared down for a very long time, though it was probably only a few seconds. Then he turned to Mara, and there must have been something in the set of his face because she huffed out an exasperated snort and said, "Wonderful. I'll get whatever supplies we've got."

"Good," said Saad mildly, but Mara had already stalked out, ducking into an adjacent tunnel. Saad turned back to Lense. "All right. I will let you examine these men." He wrapped a hand around her left bicep, and his grip was firm. "And let us see whether or not you can buy back your life."

CHAPTER

8

"Oh, this is just perfect." Enraged, Kahayn dodged around the security director and made for the gurney. The suited figure was still writhing, but she couldn't see who or what was inside. The faceplate, which she assumed was clear, was shiny with a thick layer of soot that had an astringent smell and smeared like oil when she touched her finger to it.

Cursing, Kahayn snatched up a large square of gauze. "Give me a hand here," she said to the tech as she leaned down hard on the patient's right arm and started scrubbing at the faceplate, "grab that other arm, get it out of my way. The rest of you, I need a crash cart, stat, and get me an ET tube. As soon as I get this clear, I want this guy wired for sound. Call anesthesia, get them down here, we're probably going to intubate."

"Stand down, Colonel!" said Blate. His bullish face was a mottled purple. "That's an order!"

"You don't outrank me, Blate." Kahayn threw the nurses a look. "Go."

This seemed to be all the nurses were waiting for; they moved fast, one nurse racing off for the crash cart, and the other whirling toward a wall-mounted comm.

"Arin." Kahayn craned her head over her shoulder. "Did you check for explosives?"

"Colonel Kahayn!" Blate, again. "You are ordered—!"

"Shut up, Blate." Kahayn tossed aside one stained gauze and wadded up another. *Residue's sticky like tar, like he's been in a chemical fire, maybe a fuel depot that went up—but this suit, I've never seen anything like it.* "Arin, what about it, is he packed? What about contamination?"

"No." Arin came alive. Taking the distance in three loping strides, he relieved the tech, leaning down hard on the patient's arm. "Get me restraints," he ordered, and then to Kahayn: "No explosives, and the suit's not radioactive as far as we can tell."

"What about scanners?"

"Colonel," said Blate.

"Scanners are a nonstarter," said Arin. The tech returned with brown leather restraints and Arin got busy belting down the patient's left arm. "The suit's impervious, maybe lead-lined. We can't see anything." Arin threw a restraint around the patient's left leg as the tech took the right. Then Arin crowded next to Kahayn, threaded leather through a buckle and cinched down the right arm, tight, midway up the patient's forearm. "Can't call up anything on tomography, either."

"We've got to get this suit off."

"Yeah, but those lights, the ones going to red on his wrist, they bug me."

"You're thinking countdown?"

"Maybe." Arin peered at Kahayn over his glasses. "No way to be sure, right? Except we crack it and hope we don't go boom?"

"That is precisely why you must release this intruder to me," said Blate.

"Forget it, Blate. Write me up." She grabbed another gauze. The patient's faceplate was smeary, but she caught a glimpse of a face. *Almost there.* "Better yet, arrest me. I haven't had a decent night's sleep in a week."

"This isn't funny, Colonel."

"Blate, you idiot! You think the Jabari or an Outlier have the technical know-how for a suit like this? And this junk, this crud on his suit and faceplate, this is for *real*! This isn't just charcoal smeared on for effect to trick a couple of your sentries. This guy's been toasted; he's been in some kind of fire, and . . ." She gasped, peered more closely at the faceplate then, cursing, fumbled up a pair of gloves and snapped them on. "Forget this, forget this, I need hands here!"

"Idit!" Arin said. "What about a bomb?"

"No, it's the *suit*! Don't you get it, Arin?" Frantic now, she was running her gloved fingers along the lip of the helmet searching for a catch, a way to get this thing off! "He's been in a fire! This is a protective suit, and that means he's had air, but look at the lights! He's got no air! That's what they mean! He's out of *air*! Let's go, let's go, let's get him out of this thing now now *now*!"

. She'd found two nibs, felt them give when she pressed down, and gave the helmet a twist. Then she heard a hiss, barely a sigh of escaping air and a suck of suction, a wet sound eerily like the sound of a primate's cranial cap being pulled away. And then she heard the man's tortured, agonized wheezes; saw the open mouth and flare of bloodied nostrils as he worked hard trying to pull in air; and then the smell hit her, metallic and very strong.

"My God, there's blood everywhere. Arin, get a tube down him and bring up the tomos," she said, and then she and the tech were tugging at the neck of the suit, fumbling with catches, peeling the suit away, jerking them free of the restraints. She registered the clothes underneath, a uniform of some kind and an odd piece of gold jewelry on his left chest, but then she couldn't think anymore about it because the nurse rumbled in with the crash cart. Whipping around, Kahayn tossed the tech a set of scissors. "Cut his shirt and trousers away, I want these clothes off; I'm going to throw in a CVP line; we need some access, let's go, let's *go*!"

"No!" It was Blate, just behind, and then she heard the unmistakable metallic snick of metal on metal. "Stand down, Colonel! *Now*!"

The room went so quiet that Kahayn could hear the slow drip-drip of blood from the helmet and the man in his death throes—and he was dying, he would die, there was no question because there was all that impossibly bright red blood, and the bulge of his jugulars and pink foam that frothed his lips. She saw the tech, who stood with his scissors caught in mid-snip; her gaze clicked to Arin, who'd gloved and stood, frozen, with an endotracheal tube in one hand, and in the other, a shiny metal laryngoscope with its curved blade out and locked into position. And then Kahayn turned, knowing already what she'd see.

She was right, but that was no consolation. Because there was Blate, of course, and there were his soldiers.

And there were three rifles centered on her chest, aiming right for her heart.

CHAPTER
9

Saad's men lay on rough pallets of torn linen. One had multiple abdominal wounds; his green shirt was soaked through to a dull rust; and he moaned in deep guttural groans that were as regular as a basso foghorn. He was clammy to the touch, and his skin was very cold.

Losing blood fast; probably a lake in there; what have I done, what was I thinking? Lense knew in an instant that she couldn't help him, and she'd been a fool to think she could. *Operate here? In a cave? No anesthesia, no way to keep a sterile field, no tricorder to help with diagnosis, and his anatomy's probably so different; I can't do it, I can't help, and if I can't help, they're going to kill me. . . .*

She concentrated on the other casualty. This one was sucking air in great gasps that sounded almost agonal, except he was conscious; his eyes bulged and his hands were clapped over a glistening splotch on his right chest. His fingers were streaked with dark chocolate-brown blood.

"Well?" Saad, just behind her left shoulder.

Lense felt sick. "There's nothing I can do. The one with the gut wound. It's too involved, and he's lost so much blood, I don't know . . ."

"Yes," said Saad, his voice neutral as if he'd just been told nothing more interesting than the weather. Then he drew his pistol from his right hip holster in one smooth motion, and Lense froze. The pistol grip was stippled and blocky and fit easily in his huge palm; the metal was matte black and the barrel was square with a round bore. He bent, pressed the muzzle against the wounded man's temple and pulled the trigger.

There was a tremendous *bang* that echoed off the walls, an orange spurt of muzzle flash, and the man's head erupted in a fine brown mist of blood, brain and bone. The air was instantly saturated with the brackish odor of fresh blood, scorched hair, and burnt skin.

"What are you *doing*?" Lense cried, horrified. She scrambled to her feet. "What have you done?"

Reholstering his weapon, Saad looked at her with a bland, matter-of-fact expression. "You said you couldn't help. I stopped his suffering."

"But you don't just . . . you can't just kill a man! You've got to try!"

"And how do you suggest we do that? Look around you." Saad spread his arms in an all-inclusive gesture. "This is only a forward camp, but this is very much like our home. This is who we are. This,"—he indicated an orange medical kit Mara had retrieved—"is all we have. You say that you're a physician. Then surely you can appreciate the cold calculus of life and death. We don't have the luxury of pretending that it's otherwise."

"Death is never preferable." She was trembling with rage. "It's never just another option."

Mara spoke, her tone dripping with contempt. "It is if life is a death sentence. Oh, but I forgot. You're a Kornak, and a privileged one at that. No need for prosthetics, no scars . . ."

Saad hacked the air with his hand. "Enough. We're wasting time. You, Elizabeth Lense, can you help this other man, or not?"

She was going to say that she would try when one look at Mara let her know that she'd better do more than that. So she said nothing. She squatted before the kit and stared into a jumble of medical supplies, most of which she didn't understand and had never seen. Her eyes roved over packets of gauze and bandaging materials, and thank heavens, she knew what they were, and there were brown vials of liquids—antiseptics and alcohol, she imagined, and other drugs, antibiotics, painkillers . . . she didn't know. Gloves, of course, hard to mistake those. Intravenous needles in sterile plastic packets, plastic and glass syringes: stuff from a history of medicine class to which she'd paid almost no attention.

Twentieth century equivalents, maybe twenty-first. Or nineteenth, they had rubber by then but not plastic, I think. I just don't know; what have I done?

A voice over her left shoulder. "Well?"

"It's fine," Lense lied. *Yeah, right, so get going.* Swallowing her panic, Lense knelt by the man with the chest wound. "I need some hands here," she said, grabbing the man's shirt. "Someone get over here and take his hands out of the way."

Two of Saad's men dropped to either side of the man's head and took an arm. Lense ripped open the shirt and hissed in a quick breath through her teeth. "Oh, God . . ."

A projectile wound, about as big around her thumb and forefinger, punched through the right chest just beyond the nipple and over the sixth rib. Some blood dribbling but not a lot. Skin retracting between his ribs with every breath, so he was working very hard, pulling in air past an obstruction or through resistance. Her eyes clicked to his throat; his Adam's apple was pushed left of center, and the large veins of his neck, his jugulars, were fat around as purple-brown worms. The man's nail beds were even bluer than Mara's, and his lips had shaded to a muddy plum. She brought her ear level with the wound, listened hard, didn't hear air escaping. That's when she noticed tiny blebs beneath the skin of his chest and when she pressed them with her fingers, they made tiny crinkly sounds, like bubbles in a plastic polymer.

Crepitus, deviated trachea, right lung, probably a pneumothorax . . .

"Turn him onto his left side a second," she said and then she quickly scanned his back. No exit wound, so the bullet was still in there.

That's bad; how am I going to get that out? She thought a moment. *First things first; he builds up much more pressure in there, he's not going to last long enough for me to worry about that.*

Turning aside, she riffled in the kit with only a vague sense of what she was looking for. Her fingers walked over packets of suture materials and gauze packs, tape and vials. Then she fished out an instrument: two flexible tubes connected to curved metal prongs surmounted by perforated plastic nibs at one end and a heavy dual-function metal contraption at the other end—something with a drum on one side and a bell on the other.

Earpieces, diaphragm, bell . . . they called it a . . . a stethoscope, used for magnifying sounds . . .

She'd never listened to a heartbeat in her life. She'd never heard breath sounds. Although she knew on general principle that tympanic meant hollow and something that sounded dull was either fluid or something solid, she had no idea, really, what meant what. Everything she'd ever done as a physician had been through a filter of gadgets that did the thinking for her: screens that spat out data; algorithms that ticked through possibilities and whittled down the available options; a tricorder that told her what was invisible beneath the skin. Sure, there was clinical judgment. There was guesswork. But it was really hard to argue with a computer that thought a thousand times faster than she could, whizzing through data on thousands of species, humanoid and otherwise.

She screwed the earpieces of the stethoscope into her ears, didn't hear a thing for a moment, then realized that ear canals canted forward. Forcing her fingers to steady, she removed the earpieces, twisted the prongs until the earpieces aimed forward and away, then popped them into her ears. This time she heard plenty, and it was so startling that she froze for an instant, then fingered the instrument's diaphragm. There was a loud rasping sound like fingernails running over paper or cloth, and she heard a faint background roar that she realized was the sound of air filtering through the cave but magnified tenfold.

She put the diaphragm over the man's chest, and she heard the rapid thudding of his heart—*going a kilometer a minute, sounds like . . like three sounds, not two, and they're so loud—*

but she heard virtually nothing over the right chest, only a hollow pull of air. Just to be sure, she checked the left side and was confused for a second when the heart sounds faded—and then she realized that the man's heart was in the very center of his chest just beneath the sternum. Right then, she didn't know if that was good or bad.

Doesn't matter; look at how much bluer he is; he's only got a few more minutes, I've got to move, move!

Quickly, she pulled the earpieces out, started pawing through the kit. "He's got a tension pneumothorax. It's a one-way air leak," she said, riffling through packets, chattering, thinking out loud as much to them as herself, talking herself through the problem. *Mechanics, it's simple physics, you can do this.* "Either he's got a collapsed lung and air's escaping into the chest that way, or there's only this puncture wound so that every time he breathes in, the negative pressure created in the chest is pulling air into his thoracic cavity. Either way, there's air in there that can't get out."

Negative pressure, air going in one way not coming out, need a tube. "I have to vent the thoracic cavity, let the air out, then make sure it can't get back in." *Tube, I need a tube and then something flexible to make a valve . . .*

Then she found them: packets of needles, some covered with plastic tubes and some not. Different gauges, and she knew that the lower the gauge, the bigger the bore of the needle. *Needle, I can use the needle and now all I need is something for a flutter valve; yes, a glove!* She pulled out a paper pack of unopened latex gloves, ripped open the packet, pulled out a glove and snipped off the middle forefinger.

"What are you doing?" asked Mara. She sounded more curious now than angry, almost intrigued. "What is that?"

"A flutter valve," she said, poking the needle through the snippet of pale beige latex. "It'll relieve the pressure but keep the air from getting back in." She pulled the glove finger all the way to the flange, then rooted around for a syringe, opened the packet, and fitted the needle onto the syringe. Moving fast now, she ripped open another packet of gloves, then packets of antiseptic swabs. Gloving, she splashed rust-colored antiseptic onto the man's ribs, thinking furiously: *Which rib is it, second or third; third's in line with the nipple, but does it matter which one?* She couldn't remember; the computer usually did all this for her. Hell, she'd never had to manually evacuate air from a tension pneumo in her life. Walking her gloved fingers over his ribs, starting at the armpit, working her way down. *Heart's in the center, what does that mean? And what about the intercostal artery? Is it running above or in the groove along the bottom of the rib, same as humans?* She was sweating now; her lips tasted like salt. She stared for a long moment at the space between the man's second and third rib.

Do it, just do it; either they'll kill him, or he'll suffocate, just do it!

"Hold him still," she said then jabbed the needle through his skin. The man flinched, but she was pushing now, guiding the needle over the top of the third rib. She felt the needle pushing through muscle, scraping over bone, and she winced, clenched her teeth, kept pushing, pushing . . .

She felt it go through at the same moment there was the sensation of a tiny pop—and then there was air gushing, hissing out of the end of the needle. She breathed out a sigh of relief as the snippet of glove fluttered. "Got it." She looked up at Saad and Mara and then said, with fierce satisfaction, "I got it."

Saad cocked his head to one side. "That will help?"

She nodded. "It should. I just have to cover over this wound . . . the bullet hole here, so I can stop him sucking air in that way."

There was no way to probe for the bullet, and there was no exit wound either. So there was a nice dirty bullet floating around in this man's chest and unless she could do exploratory surgery in a cave, it was going to stay there. *Later, later, one disaster at a time . . .* Quickly, she snipped up the rest of that one glove, removing the fingers and then filleting it open until it lay flat. Then she cleaned up the wound as best she could, let it air-dry and then taped the latex flap over the wound on three sides, leaving the fourth free as another relief valve.

It was only when she'd finished that she realized the man's gasps had diminished. She put the stethoscope to his right chest, heard air going in, saw that both the flutter and relief valves she'd made were limp. The air pressing against his lung was gone. His face was less blue, and his trachea had returned to center.

I did it. She felt limp. *My God. I really did it.* She sat back on her heels. Stripped off her gloves and pushed to her feet. Her hands were streaked with white talc and felt sticky.

She looked up at Saad. "I got it," she said again.

His brown-black eyes searched her face, then narrowed slightly. "Yes," he said. "You did. He looks better."

"He is. A little. He's still got a bullet in there. I don't dare try to get it out."

"Will he survive?"

"I . . ." Her gaze flicked to the corpse lying on its tumble of bloody linens. She straightened her shoulders, pulled out of her slouch. "I don't know. Maybe. A dozen things can go wrong: infection, more bleeding, the bullet wandering around and shredding something else. I don't know."

"If you had more or better equipment, could you do more?"

Yeah, right, I do just great with antiques. "I don't know. Depends."

"On what?"

Lense gave what she hoped was a negligent shrug. "On how badly someone's hurt. I wouldn't expect miracles."

"I'm not asking for any." A hint of a smile touched Saad's lips and he seemed to reach a decision. "Very well. We have to talk."

"We? Meaning you and Mara and—"

"And a few others, yes. In the meantime, you will go with this one,"—he gestured at the wiry soldier who'd brought in the news of their ambush—"and he will show you a place where you can wash, change out of those clothes. Rest. Have something to eat and drink."

Remembering the lake and its awful smell, the way it looked and felt, Lense wasn't sure she trusted or wanted either one but then figured she didn't have much choice about that. "What is this, some kind of last meal?"

"Perhaps." Saad's eyes were sober. "When we are through discussing the matter . . . maybe so."

CHAPTER
10

For a moment, no one moved, no one spoke: not Blate; not the soldiers who stood poised with their rifles aimed at Kahayn's heart. Not the nurse who'd brought the crash cart on a dead run; not Arin who'd paled to a shade of light aqua; and not Kahayn. The only person who did move was the dying, blood-soaked man on the gurney. His clothes were in tatters; his knees flexed and extended, and his legs strained against their restraints like he was trying to run in an awkward, slow-motion shuffle. His breathing had dropped off to irregular, deep gasps that scored Kahayn's heart like jagged glass.

Agonal breaths, brain's starving for air; we're running out of time!

"Blate," Kahayn said, urgently, "Blate, please, you have to let us finish!"

"It could be a trick."

"Damn you, Blate, I don't have time for this!" Kahayn shouted so fiercely that even Blate took a step back. "*He* doesn't have time! This man is *drowning* in his own fluids, and he's going to *die* if we don't help him! So either shoot me, or get the hell out!" Then she looked over at Arin, the nurses, the tech. "Let's go, people, let's do it!"

She saw the soldiers glance at one another; Blate's eyes narrowed. Arin hesitated, looked at the soldiers, then at Kahayn, and snapped to. "You heard her! Move!"

That was all her people needed. Personnel swarmed around Blate and the soldiers; the nurse rattled up with the crash cart; Arin slid a tube down the man's throat, attached a bag, and then the anesthetist pushed his way in and took over as Arin moved to bring up his scanners. Kahayn pulled on fresh gloves as fast as she could, then slapped the man's skin beneath his right clavicle with antiseptic solution. She bent over him, feeling for the notch of his clavicle with her right index finger and judging the distance before stabbing a large-bore needle threaded through a central venous catheter. There was a flash of blood in her syringe as the needle pierced the subclavian vein.

"I'm in!" She threaded the catheter into the vein and then nodded to a nurse who flicked on the IV while Kahayn threw in two quick sutures to hold the catheter in place. She snapped off her soiled gloves as the nurse moved to bandage the site. The corporal had started a line in the left arm and was taping down the tube. "Careful not to open that up wide; we don't want to overload him." She glanced behind her shoulder and saw that Blate and his men had taken up position along the far wall. *Best I can hope for.* She turned back to the corporal. "Get the rest of his clothes off! Move!"

"I want the clothes," Blate said, "and that suit!"

"Yeah, yeah, when we're done," Kahayn said, not turning around. "Arin, what you got?"

"In a second!" Arin's fingers flew over his control panels. "Bringing tomography and 3-D online now!"

"Corporal, check for wounds. Then clean off his face, I want to get a good look at that gash, and get the portable X-ray up here; I want pictures of that skull, make sure—"

"Idit, pressure's dropping!" Arin sang out. "Heart rate one-thirty-five; we've got significant pulmonary hypertension, and I'm getting atrial fibrillations here, sporadic PVCs! No periatrial waves at all!"

"What's his potassium?" Kahayn shot back.

"Calculating . . . normal."

"Dial down the IVs, then hit him with a diuretic, ten of pentalatix! Let's get some of that fluid out of him. Someone get me a catheter in there; let's make sure his kidneys are still working." She spun left toward the anesthetist. "Give me positive pressure ventilation, short bursts, pure oxygen, keep those alveoli open, don't rupture—"

"Idit," Arin said, "I'm getting couplets!"

Kahayn swore. "Pull up 3-D of that heart, I want to see what I'm dealing with here." She snatched up a stethoscope and slapped the drum to the middle of the man's chest. She frowned. "Where's . . . what the . . . what the hell . . . I don't hear . . . ?"

"Idit! V-fib! No pulse!"

Kahayn hopped off the gurney. "Corporal, start compressions! Charge up that defibrillator! Two hundred!" The defibrillator gave a crescendo whine as the machine charged, and she grabbed the gelled defibrillator paddles, rubbed them together. "Everyone off!"

The corporal jumped back, and Kahayn slapped the paddles onto the man's chest, one at the apex of his right chest and the other at the tip of the sternum. But then what she'd *heard* flashed through her brain. *Nothing in the center or to the right; heart's shifted left; what's it doing there, maybe pushed over because the right lung's boggy, but that doesn't make sense and the sound's all wrong; what am I missing?* She closed her eyes, imagined how that heart must look beneath the chest, how the electrical impulse *must* flow, and then she repositioned the paddles, the sternal paddle directly over the sternum just beneath the notch and the apical paddle on the left chest just below and left of the nipple.

"What are you *doing*?" cried the anesthetist. "Doctor, no, that's *wrong*."

"No, leave her!" Arin shouted. "Idit, *go*!"

"Clear!" Kahayn thumbed the push button of the apical paddle. There was a faint *puh* as the paddles discharged, but not the melodramatic flopping around that holodramas were so fond of. "Arin?"

He shook his head. "Still in V-fib. No pulse."

"Charging again, two hundred . . ." Listening to that crescendo whine, thinking about that weird heart: *Arin said no periatrial waves at all.* Her eyes raked over the man's body, over smooth skin and taut muscle. *I'm missing something, what's missing; what if he doesn't have a periatrium to jump-start . . . ?* The defibrillator trilled. "Clear!" She discharged the paddles, heard the *puh*, waited. "Arin, anything?"

"Nothing."

"Okay; charging up; nurse, get me an amp of xentracaine ready after this next—" She broke off as the charger whined. "Arin, you said *no* periatrial waves, right?"

Arin gave her a look. "That's what I said."

"That can't be right," said the anesthetist. To Arin: "It's not reading right."

"It's right," said Arin, giving her that look again. "I'm reading it right."

No periatrium, no way to jump-start— Kahayn gasped, then jerked around to the nurse. "Charge it to three hundred."

The nurse went as goggle-eyed as Blate. "Doctor?"

"Just *do* it!"

"Wait a second," said the anesthetist. "That's not—"

"Three hundred," Kahayn said to the nurse.

"But, Doctor—"

"Are you deaf? Three hundred!"

The nurse swallowed hard, looked at the anesthetist, who shrugged, and then to Arin, who did nothing. Then she toggled up the charge. "Three hundred."

"Clear," Kahayn said, hoping like hell that she was right. She thumbed the discharge. There was that dull *puh*. "Arin?"

"That did something." Arin looked at her over his glasses. "I got about five, six beats before the rhythm degenerated."

"I got a little flutter up here," said the anesthetist, almost grudgingly. "Though heaven knows why."

Kahayn let out a breath. "Okay; Corporal, resume compressions; nurse, push in that amp of xentracaine, see if that'll tamp down that cardiac irritability. Charge up the defibrillator again." She and Arin exchanged a wordless stare; then he gave a minute nod, easily missed if she hadn't been looking for it, and Kahayn said, "Three . . . *fifty*."

She saw the nurses glance at one another before the nurse dialed up the voltage. Without a word, she took up the paddles. "Tell me when the minute's up."

That minute crawled by in an eternity of seconds, and it was long enough for Kahayn to wonder what she would do if this man—whoever and *whatever* he was—pulled through. The corporal had managed to clear away most of the blood and she now stared at his face: black, close-cropped curls slicked with blood capping a high forehead; delicate cheekbones; a chin that was more oval than square. That forehead wound was ugly and oozing, and he looked as if his nose was broken. They would probably have to give him some blood, and that forehead would need stitches. She would make him a nice scar . . .

And then, with a jolt, she realized what was missing.

No scars. Her eyes traveled over the man's chest, his abdomen, his hips and legs. *There are no scars anywhere, nothing, as if he's never had a wound or prosthetic in his life.*

"One minute, Doctor."

"Right." But she didn't move. She stared into that face, and for a brief, disorienting instant, that wasn't a stranger lying there—*and whatever else you are because you are not like us, not like us at all*—but her Janel, because they did look a bit alike and she missed the man he'd been.

And then he was not Janel but a stranger who needed her: a man without scars inflicted by time and an unkind planet. And the difference between the two, between the man who had been Janel and the one here now, was the wound in her heart that had never properly healed.

Oh, my beloved, how I wish I could have saved you, really saved you.

"Clear," she said, and then as the corporal jumped down, she placed the paddles on the man's chest, took a deep breath and pushed the button.

CHAPTER

11

Saad came to find her after several hours though she'd lost track of time. Lense sat on a rock just outside the entrance to this system of caverns. The guard was with her, of course, but she'd wanted to go out. Maybe just to convince herself that there was an outside world, something that was not a warren of dank, glistening gray caves. That orange ball of a sun was setting to her right, its light refracted to a dark red that glowed on the undersides of a pillow of yellow clouds and turned them a peachy blush. It was a little cooler now, too, and she was more comfortable in the clothes they'd given her: a rough cotton khaki tee and matching trousers, with sturdy, worn black boots and thick socks. They'd taken her uniform, though they'd given her combadge back. Why, she didn't know. It rested in the right pocket of her trousers. Felt good there. She slipped her hand in now and again just to feel it. Knowing she still had it made her feel better.

Then she smiled a little. Probably make Gold feel better, too, her being so by the book, keeping "advanced technology" from the natives when all she wanted was to remind herself of a little bit of home. She tried hard, though, not to

think about whether she'd ever get back. No point to it. Not
yet anyway.

She was breathing better. They'd given her some kind of
mask: an adaptation of a re-breather, she figured, similar to
what divers used but with a carbon scrubber. At least, that's
what the guard told her. As long as she kept the prongs fitted
into her nostrils, her lungs didn't burn, and she was comfortable enough. Her mouth still tasted like ash, though.

There was a crunch of gravel, and then she turned and stood
as Saad slipped out. His pistol was still in its black leather holster. Saad gave the guard a look then hooked a thumb over his
shoulder. Obediently ducking his head, the guard slid into the
caves and out of sight. Saad edged closer. His leather holster
creaked on his hip. "I see that you've washed and changed.
You've eaten?" When she shook her head, he asked, "Why
not?"

She decided honesty—and a little humor—might lighten
things a bit. "I just wasn't hungry. Figured that if you were
going to kill me, somebody else could use the food more than
me. That's the way things work here, right?"

That faint smile again. "You catch on quickly. Where did
you say you were from again?"

"I didn't. Say, that is." She quickly thought back over what
she'd gleaned from the runabout's sensors during those few
chaotic moments that had happened only six hours ago and
felt more like a century. "I come from very far north, another
continent." *And please don't ask me the name.*

"Ah," was all Saad said. "Odd that you and your friends
should wander this way. I know,"—he held up a hand when
she opened her mouth—"I know. You were hiking. And they'll
be looking for you."

She clasped her hands behind her back, felt the straps of
the re-breather pack dig into her shoulders. "So have you decided, or not?"

"First, since you don't seem to know anything about us, I
need to explain a few things." He waved her over to a hump
of rock a meter long and flat on top. He sat, and indicated
that she should sit as well. "I need you to understand why I'm
going to do what I'm going to do."

Her heart fluttered against her caging ribs, like a trapped bird. "Okay," she said, though it wasn't at all.

"You were surprised when I shot Apariam, the one with the belly wounds. You were more than surprised. You were outraged. And I thought to myself that, Saad, this is a woman who truly does not understand the Jabari, or any of the Outlier tribes. Or the Kornak." His dark eyes slid to hers in a sidelong glance. They were only a half meter apart, and he was so close she caught his scent, a mixture of musk and sweat. "Truly amazing that she doesn't know."

"Know what?" she said. Her voice quavered, and she swallowed. "What do you mean?"

"I mean, Elizabeth Lense, that you are lying, and I do not believe your story." His voice was mild, not accusatory—more . . . intrigued. "I have eyes—my own, fortunately—and your skin, the color in your cheeks and lips . . . you're lying."

She wasn't as shocked as she thought she'd be. After all, it was one of those things a person would have to be braindead to miss. Standard Starfleet-speak, though, Prime Directive junk: lie your head off and hope no one catches on that you aren't just a teensy bit different than, say, oh, that guy over there with five tentacles and seven eyes. "Okay," she said. "And?"

"*And*, if that's so, then you don't understand this. You don't understand me or my people, or what we're up against. So I will explain. We Jabari fight the Kornaks because they are machines."

"What do you mean, machines?"

"Living machines. They add prosthetics when their limbs wither, or replace their organs with those they've harvested in transplant or with a mechanical equivalent. Our planet hasn't been very good to us, or maybe it's the other way around. Our air's bad; the water's polluted; there's residual radioactivity in some areas." He shrugged. "It's our life here. Mara and I, the rest of us, we don't want to be machines. We don't think the Kornaks should force their will on the planet or its people, especially not when a prosthetic is a reward for how loyal you've been, or what you haven't consumed."

The scars on Mara's neck, those people missing hands, legs . . .

*they've either removed their prostheses or declined them out-
right.* "Why not?" Lense asked, genuinely mystified. "If you'll
live better and longer lives, isn't that worth the trade-off?"

"No. Because if I accept that more and more of me isn't
flesh and blood, then I give up what it is to be a man." Saad's
eyes lingered on hers. "And, above all, I'm a man, Elizabeth
Lense. I have lived and I will die as one."

She stared back, and the insight was like the quick flash of
a shooting star: *A little like the Borg, but without the collective.*
Her eyes searched Saad's face, its clean lines and strong bones.
No scars at all, and that struck her as odd, though perhaps
his scars were hidden by clothing. But she liked what she saw,
and it had been a long time since she'd seen a man she hadn't
dismissed out of hand.

And then, on the heels of that thought, she remembered
what Julian had said: *I am a person, and I have feelings to
hurt . . .*

"And me?" she asked. She looked away and hoped that
Saad hadn't noticed that shame, not embarrassment, burned
her cheeks. "What about me?"

"You are a free woman, Elizabeth Lense. You may live and
die as one."

"But only if I stay here." She glanced at him askance.
"Right? Otherwise, I'll die free, only a lot sooner." When he
nodded, she said, "So I can be your medic, or you'll kill me.
Not much of a choice."

"No, but it is a choice. Whichever you take, however, one
thing is certain."

"And what's that?"

"Either way," he said, "there is no going back."

CHAPTER
12

Two hours later, after the patient had been stabilized and a corporal had wheeled the gurney out of the ER to an isolation unit in the ICU, Blate came and stood over Kahayn and Arin, who were seated at a workstation, busily entering their notes and data into the official computer record. Arin saw him coming first, casually stabbed a control that blanked the 3-D VR, and gave Kahayn a gentle nudge with his elbow.

"Yes, Blate?" Kahayn sighed, pushed wisps of brown hair from her eyes, and looked up. "What now?"

"Don't think that your heroics here will preclude a full account of your conduct. I intend to make my report, and I will most specifically make note of your carelessness." The security director's right eye skidded left, then tacked out to fix a glare. "You may be cavalier with your own life, Colonel, but I have a complex to think of and a command to which I owe my loyalty."

"As do I, Blate."

"Don't be stupid, Colonel. You had no way of knowing if that man was infected. For that matter, you still don't know. He could be incubating some disease."

"Well, then if I die, I won't have to worry much about what you report, will I?" Then Kahayn snorted. "You know something, Blate? I can't figure out if you're mad because *he* didn't die, or because *I* didn't keel right over and kick off from some phantom virus."

"Perhaps you will."

She was tempted to point out that then he'd likely dance a jig but quashed that as unhelpful and downright dumb. "Blate, there's nothing there. I sent off blood for culture. We'll see if anything grows. But I doubt it. As for the patient, I'll tell you what. I'll keep him in isolation. In a couple of days, I'll move him to the research wing. How about that? The wing's got no systems that feed back to this complex, and I'll be the only doctor, okay? Me and a couple of nurses, and that's it. Arin to take over in a pinch. We'll take full precautions."

Blate's eyes clicked from her to Arin and then back again. "I'm still making my report. And I expect updates and *all* your data, Colonel. All of it."

"Of course," Kahayn said and managed to sound like she'd expected that. "It's standard procedure for a potential security risk, right?"

"Yes," said Blate, and then his lips thinned to a smile. It didn't improve his looks. "Because I have eyes, Colonel, I have eyes."

"Of course you do." She paused. "And I should know; I put them in myself, and just like you wanted them, too. But you really ought to come in and let me adjust the tracking on that leftie, Blate. It's downright scary."

"No, thank you. I like my eyes the way they are. But I have eyes, Colonel. I can see as well as the next man, and I saw that patient." Blate waited a beat. "No scars, Colonel. He doesn't have any *scars*."

Her pulse ramped up. She swallowed back a flutter in her throat. "Except the one on his forehead."

"Which he got today. Which you gave him. But nowhere else." Blate breathed in, pulled himself up. "Not one. That's interesting for a . . . native, don't you think?"

She said nothing.

Blate nodded as if she had. "This isn't over, Colonel. This is far from over."

Arin waited until Blate was gone. Then he sighed, stabbed at his glasses, and looked over them at Kahayn. "That's not good."

"Don't start." Weary to the bone, Kahayn slumped, washed her face with her hands. "One disaster at a time."

"Mmmm." Arin hesitated and then said, "How did you know? Without my having to say anything?"

"I didn't." Her eyes were still closed and she cocked her head to one side. "I . . . *heard* it. Or I didn't hear it. That's what it was." She opened her eyes and gave Arin a tired smile. "No click. So, no periatrium. It seemed the only explanation."

"And the defibrillator? That was one-fifty above the recommended charge."

She hunched her left shoulder and let it fall. "Without the periatrium to kick in at the PA node, I figured there'd be more resistance. So I jacked it up. Lucky guess."

"Yah," said Arin. "Lucky." Then he brought up the 3-D VR they'd been studying just before Blate approached. The heart was outlined in green; the lungs were gray and air-filled spaces were black. Arin pointed. "A heart with four chambers instead of five. That's amazing. And look at that left lung. Two lobes."

"And not three, yah. You'd expect that, the heart shifted over to the left. No room for another lobe. How the hell does he get enough oxygen without the extra surface area?"

"That's a damn good question. And that organ on the left wedged under the diaphragm, what is that? Too small for a spleen, and his thymus is a third the normal size."

"Beats me. For that matter, why is the blood ferrous? Like it's much more deoxygenated and he requires way more oxygen, a higher partial pressure than we do."

"I don't know. But he's different, that's for sure." Arin massaged the bridge of his nose between his thumb and right index finger, then blinked and resettled his glasses. "Weird, but I'm not getting that creepy-crawly feeling you get when you *know* some guy's a mutant. Know what I mean?"

"Yah. I know. I'll bet when he's tuned up, his system's going to work just fine. That kind of throws out mutant right there."

"So, if he's not a mutant . . ."

They were silent. Kahayn thought of that weird suit. Then she said, "Don't go there. Not yet. Give it some time."

Arin nodded. "Okay. I can do that. I'd do anything for you, you know that?"

"Yah." She squeezed the back of his hand with her good one, her right. "I know. Would have fallen apart a long time ago without you."

Arin's eyes roamed her face, and his lips parted as if he were going to say something. But then he seemed to change his mind and, instead, said something else. "Idit, you won't be able to hold off Blate forever. Sooner or later, he'll be back and he's going to ask for this stuff, and we're going to have to turn this stuff over."

"I know that." Then she gave her friend a narrow, sidelong glance. "But that guy's pretty sick. I mean, *really* sick . . ."

"*Very* sick."

"And we wouldn't want a relapse."

"No. We wouldn't."

"Because he's very sick, and I think we both know what will happen if we act too soon."

"He'll relapse."

"Right. So how about we make sure that we turn these over much later?"

"How much later?"

"Say . . . a month. Six weeks?"

"That's a long time," said Arin. "I think it's too long. Remember, Blate's got the suit and that helmet. That piece of jewelry, or that pin, or whatever it was. And that uniform . . . I have to tell you, I agree with Blate on that one. That patient? He's military in someone's army, and it's sure not ours. So Blate's going to be back long before that month's up. I give him a week. Then he's going to want some answers."

"We'll give him answers."

Arin shook his head. "It's one thing not to volunteer information; but it's another to lie. We got away with it today because we didn't lie, not technically. We simply—"

"Didn't mention a few pertinent details. Like that heart, his left lung, and the iron in his blood."

"Right. And you're going to be seeing this guy every day. You'll have more data, right? So when Blate asks, how are you going to hide things? There are records, you know. Lab values in the computer any person with two neurons on a T-connector could pull up."

She thought. "I can keep two records. One here. The other on the computer in the lockout room of the research wing. That's an isolated system, doesn't tie in here at all by design. So it'll just be a sin by omission. Things that I was just kind of storing. For study, you know?"

"Might work for a little while." Arin laced his fingers in his lap in thought. "Either way you look at it: We do this, there's no going back. This is like being a policeman or a detective and not handing over evidence. You know?"

"I know that. In a way, we are the detectives, aren't we? The police? We're all part of the same military, and the military runs things."

"Runs everything."

"Yah." She paused. "You like that?"

"I don't know any different."

"But I can *imagine* different. I can imagine a time when the military serves the people, not the other way around."

Arin poked at his glasses. "Careful. Now you're talking like a Jabari. An Outlier."

Like Janel. A talon of grief snagged her heart. "I can't . . . cooperate with that kind of thing. Not now."

Arin was silent. Kahayn said, "I think a lot of the work we do is important. Otherwise people die. I'm a doctor; I don't like that. But what I also don't like is using what I do to take away a person's freedom. That's not right."

"But you're doing it anyway, Idit," said Arin. "With the primates. That neural implant." He didn't have to add: *and those test subjects*. She knew that was there, by implication.

"That's," she searched for the word, "different. You know it is. I don't have a choice about that."

"No," said Arin. "You do. You could choose to give it up. I really don't know why you haven't. But you don't like the consequences of giving that thing up, whatever you think they are. There are no test subjects anymore. Just the primates. So I don't get that. Anyway, let's just say that you aren't wild about the choices you *do* have."

She wanted to argue, but he was right and she told him so.

Then she said, "So, this guy . . . They don't ask, we don't tell. Okay?"

They stared at each other without speaking. Then Arin nodded, and sighed. "Okay. Let me ask you something, though. *Why* are we doing this?"

In reply, Kahayn tapped a command into the computer, and the image of that strange heart vanished. Not forever. Nothing, Kahayn knew, was forever except, maybe, love. Or its ghost. And Arin was right because Blate would be back, and then, maybe, there'd be more hell to pay. But she did it anyway.

She looked up at Arin. "Because it's the right thing to do."

"Right or wrong, there's no going back," Arin said again.

"Yeah," she said. "You got that. No going back."

CHAPTER
13

He came to himself in bits and pieces, and in tremendous pain. Everything hurt. Pain knifed his brain; his throat was raw and felt bloody. His lungs burned. There was something hard in his mouth and down his throat and when he tried to swallow, he couldn't.

Then he heard a weird gasping groan like the wheeze of an old bellows. There was a gabble of voices, all overlapping, like the conversation of too many people in too small a space—or maybe that was a memory. He couldn't tell. But there was someone, a woman, telling him not to fight the tube: *Don't fight, try not to fight, try to relax, let us help you* . . .

His eyelids peeled apart, slowly. Light, too bright, out of the corner of his right eye. The light hurt. Felt like a red-hot poker jammed into his eyes. Bed. Pillow under his head. Bars to either side. Linens and something scratchy on his right arm. Blanket, maybe. Something in his mouth. That queer grunt of air, pulling in, pushing out. His chest rising. Falling . . .

Falling. He remembered falling. And he remembered blood in his eyes, the iron taste of it in his mouth. The crawl of blood on his neck, dripping from his fingers. He also remembered the moment the runabout shattered in an agonized squall of metal shear that spiked his brain at the same time that a steely vice of panic squeezed his chest. He remembered the way his lungs exploded with pain as superheated air and gases scorched his throat and boiled away his voice so there was no sound when he screamed.

Runabout . . . gone . . . Elizabeth . . .

He must've moved because something stirred in the darkness. Movement to his left. He tracked it with his eyes, and then he saw the opaque white of a tube attached to a machine.

Ventilator. Tube down my throat; what's wrong with my lungs? He realized now that he was hooked to a machine that breathed for him. He didn't like it; he wanted that tube out; except when he tried to raise his arms, he couldn't move.

And then he panicked. Maybe he didn't have arms anymore; he couldn't feel them, and he was so cold, and there was the machine breathing for him. Fear clutched his chest, and suddenly he couldn't breathe at all, despite the machine. He was back in the runabout, superheated air scorching his throat and he couldn't even scream . . .

"Easy, easy. Relax." A woman's voice, and then she materialized out of the shadows: a shoulder-length fall of dark-brown hair framing a square chin, full lips, and brown eyes, but her skin was dark, an odd shade of blue, and there was something about her eyes, something not right . . .

"Listen to me." She put a hand on his shoulder, and that slight touch made him feel better. "My name is Dr. Kahayn. You're in a hospital. You were very badly hurt. We had to put in a tube to help you breathe. I kept you sedated because you kept trying to pull the tube out. You're in restraints. That's why you can't move, but I didn't want you to panic and pull out the tube before I could explain. Your lungs are better now, and that's why I let the sedative wear off so you'd wake up and I could take out the tube. Do you understand? Nod if you understand."

He nodded.

"Good." She gently tugged tape free from his mouth. "This is going to be unpleasant. You're going to feel like you can't

breathe for a second. But I'm right here. I won't let anything happen to you, so just relax and then it will be better,
I promise."

It was more than unpleasant. It was awful. A sensation of
plastic slithering at the back of his throat, like a long, rigid
snake and he gagged, tried to pull away, but then the tube was
gone.

"Take it easy," she said. Turning aside, she flicked a switch
and the ventilator wheezed to a halt. "Deep, regular breaths.
That's better. But your throat probably hurts. Would you like
some ice chips? You'll feel better."

She fed him ice chips on a spoon, one at a time; told him
to take it slow and suck the chips not chew them. The melting ice eased the pain in his throat, and he thought he'd never
tasted anything more wonderful. When he nodded that he'd
had enough, she put aside the cup of chips and then unbuck-
led the leather restraints tethering his wrists to the bed.

Then she said, "What's your name?"

It took him a few seconds to get the words out, his throat
was that raw; it felt like knives cutting him to pieces in there,
and it hurt to talk. "Bashir," he managed, finally, and he was
shocked at how weak he sounded. "Julian . . . Bashir." He
swallowed to wet his throat. "How . . . how long . . . have . . ."

"Three weeks," she said, and then as his shock must've
spread to his face, she added, "You would've regained consciousness much sooner, but I had to keep you under sedation
because of the tube."

"Tube . . . how bad?"

She explained his injuries: parenchymal damage and pulmonary congestion from breathing in smoke and superheated
gases; a concussion; a broken nose. "And that cut on your
forehead was pretty bad. Went way up into your scalp, like
you'd smashed into something."

"My . . ." He raised his fingers to his scalp, felt a ridge of
stippled flesh jutting from bristles because they'd shaved part
of his head to cut at the gash. Then he saw that a tube snaked
along his left forearm and was attached to a bag of clear
fluid hanging from a metal pole next to his bed. "What . . .
what's . . . ?"

"An intravenous line. You have another one running in under your collarbone on the right, under all those bandages. You keep down fluids today, and I'll pull the central line tonight. If you're still doing well tomorrow and can keep down soft foods, I'll pull the other IV." She paused. "You lost a lot of blood. You've been very sick. You're lucky you're not dead. But you're bound to feel pretty weak and awful for a while, and you'll be short of breath for a bit because of the damage to your lungs, even though they're much better. So take it easy and go slow." She paused. "Your scalp wound was very bad. You're lucky you didn't bleed to death."

His head was whirling. *Intubation . . . ventilator and intravenous lines . . . like being in a museum . . .* Then, another thought, this one much worse, and he felt a sudden clench of dread: *She's a doctor. I'm in a hospital and she's a doctor. She saved my life, but that mean's she examined me; she's given me replacement fluids and drugs, so she must know . . .*

She cut into his thoughts. "What happened? Do you remember?"

"I . . ." He paused, as much to gather his thoughts as form the words. "Accident. My vehicle . . . crashed. A fire. I don't remember much." Then he thought of something. "Did you . . . I was with . . . a woman. A friend. Did you . . . ?"

"No. You were the only one brought in."

Elizabeth. He wasn't prepared for how he felt: an emptiness in his chest, a feeling of grief. Guilt, too. *My fault; I should've listened to her. My fault we were separated . . .*

"Do you know where you are? That is, do you know the name of this hospital?" When Bashir shook his head, she said, "You're in Rangdron Medical Complex of the Kornak Armed Forces." She paused as if that should mean something, but he didn't know what. So he didn't say anything.

Instead, he studied her face again. That blue skin. Very familiar. Not Andorian, though, or Bolian. But familiar. And there was something wrong with her left eye . . .

"This is a secured facility," she said. "There are guards on the perimeter, and you need to have built up enough credits to be let in at the main gate. The underground trams are monitored."

"Yes," he wheezed. He didn't know what else to say. *That left eye. Not tracking as well with the right. No blood vessels. That eye's artificial, some kind of prosthetic . . .*

"You're quite different," she said. "For a Kornak, I mean. You don't have any prosthetics."

"Been . . . been lucky." It was the only thing he could think to say.

She shook her head. "I don't think so. You're not from around here."

Even whispering hurt. "No, you're right. I'm from . . . from very far away. North." He tried to remember what Elizabeth had said about the planet. Was there one northern continent, or two? He risked it. "From the northern continent. This is the first time I've . . . I've been here."

But she gave a regretful shake of her head. "That's not true and that's not what I meant. You know that. Now, *I* know that you're not Kornak, or Jabari, or any of the Outlier tribes. You're . . . *different*. Then there's the matter of your suit. And that uniform you were wearing."

"My . . . ?" he began, then stopped. She meant his environmental suit. He tried thinking of something that would explain the suit away and his uniform but couldn't. So he said nothing.

She waited for a moment, maybe to give him time to think of some new lie. Then she nodded as if confirming something for herself. "Right. Thanks for not insulting my intelligence." She paused. "You're not . . . *from* here."

He was silent.

"At first, I thought maybe you were a mutant. But I discarded that. See, by definition, most mutants don't work well. Like a machine where the blueprints get all mixed up, so that what you finally build doesn't work very well. But you work. You're injured, and it's pretty serious. But your body's healing. Everything in your body, from your organs to your chemistries . . . they all work efficiently, neatly. And your brain's even better than that. So *you* work."

He said nothing.

"Right," she said. "And then there's the not-so-little matter of your anatomy. Your skin color, your heart, that left lung of yours. Your blood, like you're used to and require a lot more oxygen." She touched the ventilator by his bed, and there was a tiny click and a whirr because, he saw now, her left hand was artificial, too. "More carbon dioxide as a respiratory trigger, too. That threw me. You were having trouble one day and I hyperventilated you, blew down your carbon dioxide level and you flat-out quit breathing. That gave me another big scare."

"Another?" he whispered.

"Yah. You tried dying in my emergency room, and very actively I might add. Then I realized that your central respiratory system needs a higher set point of carbon dioxide to initiate breathing. Anytime I tried going for what's normal—what's normal for me and everyone else here—your body tried to die. So you're different, Julian Bashir. You are very different."

He said nothing.

"That's right." She inhaled, let the breath go. "Like I said. Different. Not one of us. So, I think we need to talk about this, Julian Bashir." She cocked her head to one side. "Don't you?"

CHAPTER

14

So, contestants, today's puzzler. Given the opportunity to whack off some poor guy's leg without anesthesia, would Elizabeth Lense rather:

a) chow down on a bowl of wriggly gagh chased with shots of piping hot bahgol while simultaneously squatting naked as a jaybird with Tev in a mudbath and being tortured with Klingon painstiks;

b) have Captain Gold as her therapist forever because there's no way in hell she's going to be anywhere near normal if she ever gets off this dustball of a planet;

c) gladly go anywhere in the known universe with Julian Bashir while he gabs on about being a Remarkable Frontier Doctor;

d) all of the above;

e) What, haven't you been listening? Julian Bashir is dead; Lense is stuck somewhere hell and gone; people are trying really hard to die right and left; and you're worried about some dumb stupid game? Get out of my way.

Blood drizzled in a sludgy brown stream, soaking thin linen thrown over a makeshift surgical table, a wood pallet balanced on twin stacks of flat rocks. The wound site was a mess: a gory crater of pulverized bone and blasted flesh midway below the right knee. There was no way in hell Lense could save that leg.

You know, d is pretty damned attractive.

"Okay, okay, hold him still," Lense said. They were nine in all: Lense and the patient as well as the seven others she needed to hold her patient thanks to that lack of anesthetic. To Lense's left, Mara controlled the leg from the knee down, and Saad stood to Lense's right. The leg was flexed at a right angle and Saad pulled down on the knee until it canted fifteen degrees from horizontal.

Reeling in a deep breath, Lense spread the fingers of her left hand over the man's inner thigh. His skin jumped and his head snapped up, and his knee wobbled as he strained to kick free. "Please," he said. His teeth were bared in a grimace of fear and pain, and he was sweating so much his gray-blue skin shone as if oiled. "Please, please, please, don't take off my leg, please don't take my leg, please, don't —"

"No, I'm sorry, got to do this, just hold on," Lense said, and then simply whipped her scalpel over his skin. The knife bit through skin, slashing open his thigh and cutting fat, fascia, and muscle in the first pass.

The man let go of a high, keening shriek. Chocolate-brown blood spurted from severed veins and arterioles, and he bellowed with pain. The pallet shifted, and she heard the squawk of wood grating on stone.

"For God's sake, hold him!" she shouted. Last thing she needed was to cut herself, or send the blade through the artery before she was ready. "All I need is a couple more minutes!" This was a lie; she needed a lot more than two or three minutes. There were muscles and tendons to cut; nerves to suture to muscle; an artery to find, clamp, and then tie off so he wouldn't bleed to death—to say nothing of sawing through bone. And that was just to get the leg off.

"Hurry." Saad, at her right elbow. He was a big man, easily two meters tall and muscular, but even he was struggling. "You must work faster, Elizabeth."

She slashed through muscle and fascia. Talked herself through it: *Okay, coming across the top now; there goes the semimembranosus, and then I got to be careful because of the sciatic nerve; got to cut that fast and then tag it so I can suture it to the short head of the biceps femoris; yeah, that'd be best. . . .*

She tagged the sciatic nerve, then clamped and tied off the saphenous vein. (Were these the right names for here? Probably not. But with some significant exceptions—the heart, the left lung, a thick sternum, their very large spleen and thymus, and their queer blood—this species' anatomy was virtually identical to humans'. Lucky her, she'd had plenty of casualties to practice on, do a couple half-dozen autopsies to get the anatomy down.) She was drenched in sweat; the back of her khaki tee was plastered to her shoulder blades and the front spattered with blood that came fast and brown. But no pumpers, thank Christ, though the femoral artery wasn't too far away now.

Trickiest part; got to clamp it off and make sure you got plenty of artery there or else it'll retract. . . .

She made her next cut and saw the femoral artery now: a fat, bluish-brown, pulsating tube wedged close to the bone medial to the knee and between two large thigh muscles. The tube throbbed a rapid staccato, her patient's heart rate ramping up with fear and pain. He was still screaming and trying to kick, and she kept praying that, please God, he'd pass out because this was insanity, she was out of her goddamn mind. . . .

First proximal, then distal, because if the artery tears, at least you've got control of the business end of things. Clicking open two arterial clamps, she gently eased the teeth of one around the artery at a point closest to the hip and then snicked a second clamp shut two centimeters distant. She was already thinking three steps ahead: *Tie off the artery, then get rid of the rest of the tissue, cut the bone.*

So what happened next probably occurred because she wasn't focused, wasn't reading how his few intact muscles kept jerking and twitching, wasn't listening to how much he screamed because *everyone* screamed. So Lense slit the artery in two—at exactly the wrong moment.

"*Stopstopstopstopstopstop!*" he shrieked. The thigh above

the cut bobbled, and Lense flinched, her scalpel snagging in the handle of the proximal arterial clamp.

"Hell." *Can't lose the artery, can't lose it.* Then she heard a warning yelp from Mara and looked up just in time to see her patient's left foot angling for her face.

"Jesus!" Lense ducked but not fast enough, and the blow caught her left temple, slamming her back. She went down hard; her scalpel skittered over rock, and she lost her grip on the clamp.

"Elizabeth!" It was Saad. He'd caught hold of the patient's left leg and was forcing it back, passing it off to the men opposite. "Elizabeth, the *artery!*"

Cursing, Lense grabbed his proffered hand, clawed her way back to her feet. Her head throbbed, and tears stung her eyes. Her vision was blurry with pain, but she could see well enough and then wished she couldn't. A geyser of blood jetted over raw muscle and bare bone, but the elastic artery itself had snapped back into muscle and was nowhere in sight.

"Oh, no no no no!" She tried fishing for the artery with her clamps, jamming the curve of her instrument into bloody meat. But there was nothing to snag and so much gore Lense couldn't see worth a damn. "Hold him, *hold* him!" Quick as lightning, she slashed away at the remaining tissue right down to the bone. She was sloppy about it; her scalpel scraped against nerve-rich bone and the patient flopped and wailed in agony. Then, mercifully, finally, he fainted.

The sudden quiet rang as a high whine in her ears. The only sounds were ragged breaths and the drip-drip of blood pouring into and overflowing from a thick lake on the pallet to patter in rivulets onto rock with a sound like rain on tin.

"Okay, okay, just a few more seconds," she said, lying through her teeth. She abandoned the clamp, squirming her naked fingers into warm muscle until she felt blood spewing with every beat of her patient's heart. Grunting with effort, she tried tweezing the artery between her thumb and forefinger, pushing and tearing through thick muscle.

If I don't get it this time, either I cut away more muscle or that leg comes off right now. She concentrated, closing her eyes; then, her breath snagged in her throat. "Got it, got it," she said, her teeth clenched hard enough to hurt. "Just another sec, just another—" But then she felt her blood-slicked fingers slip and the artery pulled back like a taut elastic band snipped in two.

"Damn!" She huffed out a breath, then dug out a thin coiled wire strung between two metal handles. "Got to cut the bone, get more maneuvering room," she said, whipping one end of the wire beneath the nearly-severed leg. "Otherwise, I'll have to cut away more meat."

Or he'll just bleed and die; supply will peter out and his pressure will hit the basement; and there's no way in hell that's happening on my watch, not on my watch!

She palmed the metal handles of her saw: a very fine, very tough wire. (Admiral McCoy, guest-lecturing a history of medicine course, talking about how the principle behind this kind of primitive saw, a Gigli, proved what Thugee assassins had known for centuries—that garroting with razor-thin wire almost always resulted in decapitation.) The saw made a buzzing sound like sandpaper over stone; but she had no lubricant for the saw, and friction and thickening blood made the wire heat, then snag and hesitate. She struggled, the saw giving in grudging fits and starts.

"Let me," said Saad, and then he simply jerked the handles from her and bent to the task with a will. His shoulders strained, but he moved fast; the saw zipped through the bone in less than sixty seconds.

"Thanks, okay." She was already crowding in just as the leg came free. She pushed the disarticulated limb aside; it dropped to the rock with a sodden plop but she ignored it because that was dying meat and in the way. She grabbed up a linen and swabbed, but the linen was saturated in seconds and blood still jetted from the severed artery. However, she now had a marginally better view, looking at the stump on end, like a rump roast sliced in two: bone and its circle of bronzed marrow a little off-center, slabs of glistening raw muscle, and the spurting tube that was the artery, wide and fat, held open by the pressure of blood being forced through.

One more time. She watched the geyser pump, the blood chugging like oil. A quick nod to Mara, who sponged the area clear and then Lense was plunging the clamp deep into the muscle, forcing the tough tissue back, spreading the clamps as wide as they would go—knowing she was going to grab meat, too, but not caring—then jammed them together, hard.

For a second, she didn't know if she'd hit the artery or not because there was still so much blood—on the stump, splattered on her and Mara and Saad, pooled on the pallet—she couldn't see, and her boots squelched in coagulating muck. But the pumping had stopped. She held her breath for five seconds, then ten. Her eyes clicked over raw muscle; she registered ooze from small vessels. But no spurts, no more geysers.

"Okay," she said, releasing a long breath. She felt queasy. Because she was out of her league, and knew it. "Okay."

"Okay? This is all right with you? You call this *mercy?*" Saad's tunic was sheeted with blood. He was panting; gore slicked his hands, and he held them up for Lense to see. *"This* is your mercy?"

Her cheeks burned with shame. She opened her mouth then closed it.

Saad stared at her a second longer. He was so enraged, he trembled. "Elizabeth, whatever you think of our customs, *this* is blood on my hands, this is—" Then, whirling on his heel, he hooked his thumb over his shoulder, and one of his men stepped up to take his place.

Lense found her voice. "Blood on your hands . . . and it wasn't before?"

"Not this way." Saad's lips had compressed to a thin dark line, like a crack in stone. "Because I never made my people *beg.*" He stalked out, and Lense heard the echoes of his footfalls several seconds after he was gone.

Mara plucked up a length of teal-colored suture threaded through a needle between the jaws of a clamp. "He's right."

"Thanks," Lense said tersely. She took the needle but she couldn't look Mara in the eye. Her face flamed with anger, embarrassment. "I know that."

"Something has to give. We can't keep on like this."

I know that, too. Lense squeezed her eyes tight. She tried counting to ten and made it to three. "So what do you want

me to do, huh? Give up? Stop trying to help? We have virtually no *equipment!* But if there's even a *chance . . . !*"

"For what? We still lose men, or they stay alive long enough
to die of *complications,* as you call them. So, is this for them,
or you?"

Lense had no answer for that. "Fine, whatever. Let's just
give this guy a nice scar."

"A scar," said Mara. "And here you were so worried about
fitting in."

CHAPTER
15

"You are out of your element, Colonel." Blate's face looked more squashed than usual on Kahayn's vidcom, those walleyes so magnified she thought of some ancient, bottom-dwelling flatfish. "You've had almost six weeks. Your tactics are completely transparent. Stalling my inquiry does not change the fact that your patient is my prisoner."

"Oh, come on, Blate. I haven't stalled anything." From his seat across her desk, Arin's eyebrows reached for his hairline, but Kahayn ignored him because she had to concentrate on phrasing her lies just so. "Three weeks ago, he got short of breath just walking to the bathroom."

"He doesn't have to run a marathon, Colonel. All he has to do is answer questions."

"He's answered questions."

"But I am not satisfied. That accent, for one . . . have you ever heard anything like it?"

"No."

"Are you at all satisfied with his story?"

She hedged. "Care to be more specific? Bashir's told us

what he remembers. I can't help it that the poor man's got retrograde amnesia. People with head injuries can have huge gaps—"

"I've consulted with other physicians, Colonel. So let me ask you. What are the chances of complete and total retrograde amnesia?"

He had her there. "Small."

"Try slim to none. How many reported cases in the records since the Cataclysm?" He held up his good hand, the left. *"Three. Now your records clearly document that this . . . Bashir,"* he made a vague conjuring gesture, *"if that's even his name . . . suffered minimal traumatic damage, correct?"*

She said nothing.

"In fact, didn't your own brain imaging studies reveal several anomalies? Neural functions that have no correlate in our database?"

"Anomalies happen, Blate. We call them mutations. We call them syndromes. For all I know this is something that's already been described but the data was lost after the Cataclysm."

"Perhaps," he said, like he'd sucked on something very sour. *"But no damage other than the usual EEG slowing seen after a concussion, isn't that so?"*

"Yah. And, Blate, well, I'm impressed. Soon you'll have my job."

"No, Colonel. Soon, I will have your patient."

"Care to make a little wager?"

"Bashir is lying. You know he is. And I have eyes and ears, Colonel."

"As do I, Blate. Torturing Bashir won't get you anywhere. Keeping him alive and cooperative is much more in our interests. His physiology alone merits further study—"

"You've had time to study. But you and Major Arin withheld information—"

"Hold on. Dr. Arin was following my orders, Blate. You have any quarrels, you have them with me."

"No, I don't think so, and do you know why?" Blate laced his fingers, like a professor. *"Because loyalty is key. Loyalty is the glue that binds us Kornaks together and makes us strong.*

Loyalty allows us to function as one, with one goal, one mind, one purpose."

"But there's the individual, Blate. You can't control hope, or fantasies, or dreams."

"But we're well on the way, aren't we, Colonel? You've had your failures, of course." He paused. *"But your primates, they're an example, yes?"*

"I still can't separate them for long."

"A problem you'll solve, I'm sure. Besides, perhaps autonomy is not desirable."

"People have to be able to choose, Blate."

"You didn't always think so."

"But I think so now. Besides, we only know of one donor, and now he's gone. I can't replicate someone so unique. We need a single voice to direct the others. If not, then what's the point? The others might function as a unit, yes, but they can only go so far. Anyway, Bashir is so different, I can't see how he could be the one to—"

"We both know that your patient is no random mutation. His story is shot through with lies. I can prove it."

She had a sinking feeling in her gut. This was precisely what she'd been afraid would happen. "The fMRI? In your dreams. His brain's so different, it won't work." A lie. The fMRI would prove Bashir a liar, and that was only the first step down a road that could only end in a place she didn't want to be again.

Blate said, *"I disagree. You will run the scans in a week's time. Only I will ask the questions, not you."*

"And why a week?"

"Because General Nerrit's quite interested."

Arin muttered a curse. She felt dizzy. A week didn't give her much time . . . and to do what, exactly?

Because you believed in this once. Else why keep on with the work? Why keep separating the primates to see if maybe you've cracked it? Because we're dying, that's why; if I can't take this further, do something . . .

"Well, we'll certainly look forward to seeing the general again," she said with as much enthusiasm as she could muster. "You said there was something else?"

"*Yes,*" said Blate. "*I thought you might like to know what we determined about Bashir's very interesting suit. An amazing bit of technology. It's designed to provide air, pressure, and temperature control. It's got a battery pack that we don't understand and a novel form of computer integration my people can't crack. We know that the Jabari and the other Outliers don't possess this technology. We certainly don't.*" He paused. "*Tell me, Colonel, have you ever seen a machine that flies?*"

She was confused. "You mean, other than a propellant grenade? No. No one has. We can't . . . it's not possible."

"*Mmmm. What if I told you that Bashir's suit flies?*"

She was so stunned she couldn't speak for a moment. "Fly? You mean, off the ground, through the *air?*"

"*Yes. The suit is designed for flight. We think only for a limited period, you understand, and it seems that the suit would function better with less friction. But this thing could fly.*"

"But . . . *no one* flies," Kahayn said, stupidly. "No one knows how."

"*Not precisely, Colonel. We did know once, didn't we?*"

"But that's all ancient history, Blate. After the Cataclysm, the *ban* . . ."

"*Prohibits development and so on and so forth; I know, Colonel. But that would explain much, wouldn't it? How, after all, did Bashir get inside the perimeter? There is no other way except by underground tram, and he'd have needed a pass, which, I think we can agree, he didn't possess. But this suit flies, Colonel. That's troubling, don't you think? What are the chances that a people this advanced live in some idyllic country we've never heard of?*"

She said nothing.

"*Yes, I'd thought you'd agree. So,*" Blate said, ticking the items off on his fingers, "*Bashir's suit provides for pressure, air, heat, propulsion, and also, we think, communications. Everything you would need.*"

Her heart was hammering so hard she felt the rhythmic pounding, like a timpani drum, in her temples. "For what?"

"*Why, for traveling in* space*, Colonel.*" Blate folded his hands upon his desk and gave Kahayn a beatific smile uglier than a snarl. "*It has everything you would need for space.*"

*   *   *

After Blate rang off, Kahayn and Arin stared at each other. Neither spoke for a long time. Then Arin stirred. "You don't have to do this. You have a choice."

Kahayn pulled in a deep breath. "No."

Arin frowned over his glasses. "No, what? No, you won't do it, or . . . ?"

"I mean, no, I don't have a choice. We have to do something, Arin."

"Yeah, yeah, yeah, or we're all gonna die." Arin chewed on the inside of his cheek. Then he jammed his glasses back into place. "Explain something to me. We go through all this trouble to save this guy, protect him, keep him isolated so no one messes with him, all so you can cave? So you can kill him?"

"I was doing my job," she said, but distractedly. Her mind was going around in circles: *The suit proves it; but if I convince him to give up the information willingly . . . Or maybe I shouldn't; maybe our only destiny can be what we've already made for ourselves. . . .* "I'm still doing my job. You wouldn't understand."

"Yeah? Well, I understand this." Arin pushed to his feet. "When did we become the monsters?"

"We're not monsters," Kahayn said. She pinched the bridge of her nose between her thumb and forefinger and sighed. "We're just trying to survive, Arin. This is a war, if not with the Jabari or other Outliers then with our bodies and this dustbin of a planet." She made a helpless gesture with her hands. "We're just trying to survive," she said again.

"Until when? The military's swallowed us up and locked us down tight. When was the last time you even heard about cleaning the air or water, or doing something about the soil so radioactivity doesn't stunt crops or saturate our systems, or even helping people have a normal baby?"

"*Damn* you, Arin!" Kahayn brought her artificial fist down on her desk with a sharp bang. "Don't you understand? Blate said it. The suit can *fly!* Put it together! We figure out the principle—"

"From one dinky suit?"

"Better than a propellant grenade. It's a start. Besides, every particle of anything this guy's ever *seen* could be ours. There's an excellent chance that he knows much more that he thinks."

"That's not ours to take, Idit."

"Says who? You want to stay here? Because this is about getting us the hell off this rock! Maybe not in your lifetime or mine—"

"Oh, I don't know about that. Keep switching out parts, and we might last a good long time."

"You know we won't. Eventually, our bodies will outlive our brains. But he could be the key. Just because we can't see the stars anymore doesn't mean we shouldn't try for them."

"Nothing justifies murder."

"I won't kill him." A pause. "He won't die; I promise."

"Why should he be any different than the others?"

"Because he is, Arin. Have you ever seen a brain like his? Ever? I'm not talking simply structure. I mean, function. His brain is working better, faster, and more efficiently than yours or mine or the smartest person's on this planet could ever hope. He picks things up that would take us triple the time. He's not just intelligent, Arin. He's brilliant. And to top it all, he's antigenically neutral. So maybe he's the one who could facilitate repair and—"

"So that justifies a bargain with the devil? With Blate? What, the hell we're living in right now isn't good enough for you?"

"Don't you lecture me, Arin. Not when I spend my days ripping out organs that don't work, or hacking out cancers, or reeling out rotten gut."

"Idit," said Arin, but it was a hopeless sound. Like someone who'd used up all of his strength. "Don't you see? Blate has his reasons for wanting whatever information Bashir's got, and you have yours, except they really don't come close to overlapping. Do you really, really think Blate or Nerrit want what's best for us?"

"I don't know about what's best. All I know is war, Arin. Fighting the rot, or the planet, or Blate . . . all I know is how to fight. If you stop fighting, you might as well just walk out of here and into the desert, and keep on until you drop. Or put a bullet in your brain." She was silent for a moment and then said, a little dreamily, "In the beginning, it all seemed like such a good idea, a way we could stop fighting among ourselves. A way to keep going in these bodies for a near eternity. It can still be a good thing."

"Are you trying to convince yourself? Even you must surely see that whatever your dream was, Blate will pervert it to a nightmare."

"I still have to try."

He searched her face. "Maybe you do. But what, exactly, are you going to call this now? An experiment? Or exploitation?" Without waiting for a reply, Arin limped for the door, favoring that left knee. He yanked the door open, then paused. "You talk about reaching for stars. But maybe this is all we deserve. Maybe people like us shouldn't be allowed out there," he gestured toward the ceiling, "messing up stuff for everybody else. And maybe *he* knows that our place is here."

"Arin, if the situations were reversed, would you help his people?"

"Of course."

"As would I. So who is he to judge us?"

"He's a person, Idit. However different from us, he's still a person. *If* he's lying, maybe it's for a good reason. Perhaps that's where his honor lies. An ethical line he cannot or will not cross. There are some universals, Idit. Dignity, respect. And honor. Heaven knows, I've lost mine."

They were silent. Then Kahayn said, miserably, "I'm doing the best I can. I'm doing what I *have* to do."

"Oh, shut up." Arin's face twisted. "Lie to yourself, but don't expect me to bless you for it. You think this is a war? Do you know what they say about war?"

"What's that?"

"The first casualty in war is the truth." Arin gave Kahayn a hard stare. "That's what they say."

She was quiet for a moment. Fidgeted with a stylus. "When the time comes . . ."

"I'll be there." He sounded resigned. "I always have been."

"No, Arin. I don't want you to assist."

Arin stared. "What?"

"You heard me."

"Yeah, I just don't believe it. Why not?"

"I don't want you involved. Whatever happens, I'm responsible. Someone has to be responsible. That's me. You understand?"

"But I'm *already* involved!"

"And I've appreciated everything you've done." She was still playing with the stylus, then tossed it aside with a sigh. "But this far, and no further, Arin. You're out of the loop as of now."

"You don't trust me?"

"No, I don't." She read his sudden pain, and waited for an explosion of anger. Maybe she wanted it. But it never came.

Instead, Arin blew out a breathy laugh that had no humor in it. "Well, this is a hell of a thing." He paused, almost seemed to think better of what he was going to say and then changed his mind. "I've known you a very long time. I've been your friend. I used to think I was a little in love with you, even when Janel—"

"Arin—"

"No, let me finish. Janel was my friend, Idit, before he ever was your lover. But I . . . I respected both of you, and when he died, I stayed away."

"No, you didn't. You were always there for me, Arin."

"But only as a friend, and I knew that. I still hoped that maybe, someday . . . Anyway, now I wonder what that's like."

"Love?"

"Hope," he said. "Because here's the hell of it: I'm your friend, Idit. I always have been. You need me more than you think, because you've the devil on one shoulder, and an angel on the other, and sometimes you need reminding of which is which. Janel's gone, Idit. But I'm here, and I always will be, even when this is over. Because if you go through with this, you'll hate yourself, and you'll need me to remind you that, once, you were on the side of the angels."

He turned away. The door snicked shut.

Kahayn sagged back in her chair and exhaled a long sigh, suddenly very weary. "I know, Arin. That's just the problem."

CHAPTER
16

Almost two months. She'd been here two months. And still counting.

Lense was filthy, and her clothes—blood-stiffened khaki pants, a khaki tee ringed with a necklace of sweat edged with dried salt—could probably stand on their own. Her mouth was gummy and dry, like she'd been marooned in Vulcan's Forge for a month. But at least she'd acclimated to the low oxygen. No headaches or nausea in two weeks. Her sleep was still off, though. Dreams of fire, and Julian, always there, forever just out of reach.

She slumped on a rock slab outside a honeycomb of mountain caves about three days' travel from that inland sea. That hazy orange ball of a sun was setting now, throwing rust-red bolts across a sky filmed with a yellow-brown smear. But better here than back in her ad-hoc recovery ward, a gray dank cavern reeking of old blood, stale urine, and fresh pus.

I just want to go home. She slipped her hand into her right trouser pocket and fingered her combadge, tracing the familiar contours. *Please, I just want to go home.*

She couldn't get that near disaster this morning out of her

mind. All right, maybe that was melodrama. Worst-case scenario, she would have revised the amputation up, kept cutting until she had enough artery to tie off. But she wasn't doing anyone any good, hacking and tearing and cutting them up bit by bit. Who was she to think that she could?

She stared south. The terrain reminded her of Vulcan's Forge, too, only flatter. Long stretches of pancake-flat, sun-blasted red desert shimmering with heat waves. But where the valley opened up, there were boulders edged with stunted trees and irregular swaths of scrub. The horizon wavered with heat, and the air wobbled like something alive. This high up, she could just make up the edge of the sea, black as the blood crescents beneath her nails.

Three, four days' walk to that compound, probably. Even if she went there—if she didn't cook on the way—what then? Would things be any different, better there? Probably not.

Besides, there was Saad. Good-looking. Okay, more than that; very . . . well, drop-dead gorgeous. Very nice eyes. Beautiful hair, all that brown spilling over his shoulders. Odd thing, though. No scars, at least none that were visible. Maybe, beneath his clothes, probably had a nice back . . .

Whoa, kiddo. You start thinking about some guy, you know what you're really saying? That you're stuck. That they've stopped looking for you . . .

"Elizabeth?"

"Saad." She swallowed, quickly knuckled away her tears, blinked the others back. "Just taking a break, but I've got to get back. My clothes, I'm a mess, I need—"

"You need rest." Saad slid next to her. He'd changed out of his bloody tunic, and he smelled clean and, faintly, of musk. Beads of condensation dewed a tall gray mug he held in one hand. "I came to apologize."

"For what?"

"Getting angry. I know you're doing the best you can."

"Hunh." She gave a wan smile. "Best isn't good enough. I thought I could pull this off. Back in my . . . country, there are stories about wars from very long ago. People getting all blasted to hell, and doctors operating with cleavers. I used to think that was heroic. Frontier medicine, you know?" That reminded her of Julian—how cruel she'd been and how much she wished she could take back everything she'd said—and she had to push past a sudden lump in her throat. "Winning against all odds, that kind of stuff."

"And now?"

"Now, I think it's vanity. Arrogance. Oh, a doctor has to be pretty narcissistic to begin with. Otherwise, you'd never pick up a, uh," she'd been about to say *protoplaser,* "scalpel. A doctor's got to believe in her hands and her head. On quick thinking and no room for doubt or error."

"And what about this?" Saad flattened his palm over his sternum. "Is there no room for heart?"

"Not much. Compassion, sure. But the heart has doubts. The heart gets in the way."

"Of everything?" He said it mildly enough but she was suddenly very conscious of how close he was, his scent. The way he was looking at her now, with a degree of intimacy she didn't think she was imagining. She wasn't entirely sure she disliked it.

"Most things." She changed the subject. "Anyway, I'd do better with the proper equipment, more supplies." Thinking: *I'd do better with tools I recognize in a world you can't imagine.*

"Such as those in this . . . country to the north?"

"Yes," she said. She wasn't prepared for what she thought next: how much she wished he could have seen her in *her* world. *A world that's gone.* "But I wouldn't leave now anyway. You don't just walk away from responsibility."

"So you've *never* walked away, Elizabeth?"

"Never," she lied, thinking that, of course, she couldn't tell Saad the truth: *Well, see, there was this kid, only he was really old and he harbored this incredibly deadly virus and . . .* The point was she *had* walked away; knew there was no choice. No use telling herself that Dobrah would outlive her by centuries; that time would heal him in ways she couldn't. "I wouldn't mind leaving *here,* though."

"Is *here* so very bad?"

"You know it is." Again, she felt this tug of danger and steered the conversation somewhere safer. "Why is it that the Kornaks don't just wipe you out?"

WOUNDS 453

Saad blinked as if perplexed by her sudden jump. "Beyond the obvious? That there are stretches of desert and rough terrain and water so mucked with pollution you could practically walk over it? That we'd simply fade into the mountains and our caves?" He shrugged. "It's a good question. Actually, I think the answer's deeply psychological. Every power needs an enemy, even if it's just a vague theory that there's someone out there who wants to do away with your way of life."

"You do want the Kornaks gone, though."

"No, I want them *different*. I want them to see how perverse their reality is."

"Yeah?" Her gaze skipped to the blasted desert, then to Saad. "That looks pretty bad out there. Just how much worse do you want their lives to be?"

"I didn't say worse. I said different. The Kornaks need us as a distraction from their tyranny. So, they make us the enemy."

"Everyone has enemies."

"But not everyone *needs* them. The Kornaks see everything as a war. They fight us. They fight the planet with their prosthetics and grafts. But the planet's not an enemy. It's our home, very broken, but still our responsibility."

"You'd turn your back on all technology?"

"*Some* technology," he said. A pause that was a beat too long, and long enough for Lense to wonder what "technology" Saad meant. "Some."

"That seems fairly simplistic, Saad. What if the planet throws a terrible plague your way? You don't want medicine?"

Saad shrugged. "Maybe that's the planet's way of thinning the herd. There must've been a point in this planet's past when everything was in balance."

"So why not work with the Kornaks, instead of against them? My experience, you get more done from the inside."

"We tried that." That too-long pause again. He looked away.

She let the silence spin out. Then: "What about negotiation? Anything's got to be better than living like this."

"What, you mean without prosthetics? In exchange for what? Ration credits for food, water, housing, clothes? Credits for loyalty, so you move up on the transplant list, or get better drugs to fight the cancers? No, thank you. I'm a flesh and blood man, Elizabeth, and I will live and die as one."

There was really nothing to say to that. So she didn't. The day gradually slipped away. The air cooled. A brassy glow to the clouds to the south: the Kornak city or complex or whatever it was. The rest of the sky shaded from a yellowish-brown to a kind of dark beige smudging to a solid brown along the eastern horizon. Odd, but she hadn't stopped to look at the stars since coming here. Were there any to see? She didn't know.

And she was conscious of Saad by her side, and that didn't bother her. She didn't want to speak or do anything to shatter the moment: this small, fragile bubble of peace. So she let her mind drift; she thought of nothing at all. That was all right.

In the end, Saad spoke first. "Rain coming."

She roused herself as if from a trance. "How do you know?"

"I smell it."

"I don't smell anything."

"You have to be here awhile to know. And the clouds have been heavier these last few days. So, maybe, a week. Two at the most." He paused. "I'll be gone in a day or two."

"All right," she said for want of anything else to say. "Where are you going?"

"I am following up on some . . . intelligence."

Whatever *that* meant. "Okay."

"Elizabeth . . ."

"Yes?"

"If things were easier for you, do you think you'd stop hating this place so much?"

"Easier how?"

"Supplies. Equipment."

"Well, yeah, that would make my job easier. But I don't know about the rest."

"Staying here, you mean." He waited a beat. "With us."

Or do you mean, with you? She was surprised that this pleased her, very much. "I already said I don't walk away. But are you giving me a choice?" Saad's face was shadow, and the gathering twilight threw blades of darkness over his hard, lean features. "Am I free to go?"

"If you want. I won't stop you."

She was so stunned, she almost blurted it out: *And go where, exactly?* Instead, she said, "Do you want me to leave?"

"No. I can't promise I can make things better. I'd like to try. But I need time."

"What are you going to do?"

"I need time," he said again.

Her gaze flicked to the horizon behind his shoulder. She couldn't see any stars, but maybe it wasn't dark enough yet. "Okay. Then we've got a deal."

"Good," he said. Then she felt his hands close over hers. She started. "Relax," he said. "I brought something for you."

Her fingers closed around something rough and very cool. Moist. The mug. "Thank you," she said, mystified. Well, she was thirsty. But this water seemed . . . different somehow. It smelled clean. So different from what they called water here: triple filtered but still gray as ash and with a chemical smell.

He must have intuited her bewilderment because he said, "When people bind themselves in a relationship . . ."

"Relationship?"

"Or a partnership, a friendship, whatever you want to call it. It doesn't have to be romantic."

"Of course not," she said, feeling like a complete jackass. Then, wondering why she felt so let down. *You idiot, this is one of those alien culture things.* "So you bind yourselves . . . ?"

"With a gift of something valuable."

"Water."

"A very precious commodity here; this is from someplace deep in the mountains. If you want, I'll take you there. Bathing is quite refreshing."

"Ah," she said. "Well, thank you. But what are we promising?"

"Not you. Me. A month ago, I gave you back your life. You've kept your promise. You work hard. I admire that."

"Could be ego," she drawled. "Could be I'm stupid."

"Well, then I applaud your blind egotism." The glint of a smile. "As you said, doctors are narcissistic. But it seems only fair that I try to level things a bit."

"But what—?"

"Give me time." He cupped her hands with his, a touch that made her pulse stutter. "Now we seal the bargain."

"Okay." There was a startling, wild heat in her thighs, her skin. She was a little out of breath, too, and not from bad air.

He drank first. Then it was her turn. She inhaled that deep fragrance of still green forests and misted ponds, and her heart hurt with longing. She closed her eyes; she drank. The water was very cold and made her teeth ache and tasted very good. She drank it all down. Then she lowered the mug. His hands still cupped hers. "It's all gone," she said.

"No," he said, and then she felt his hand on her cheek, and then his fingers skim her chin, linger over the bounding pulse in her neck. "No, it isn't," he said, and then his mouth closed over hers.

Lense felt some knot deep inside loosen and come undone. It was a kind of letting go. Of restraint and inhibition, yes, but also of her past: her life in Starfleet and on the *da Vinci*. Commander Selden. Julian Bashir. Dobrah. And why not? They were gone. She couldn't change the past, and she had to stop wishing for a better one. So she let it all go. She slipped her arms about Saad's waist and then cupped his shoulders and just . . . let go.

And if there were stars in that sky, Lense didn't see any that night. But she didn't care.

CHAPTER
17

"You think you're the only one with his ass on the line? Julian, I need you to understand just how dangerous things are for you now, and me. Blate's serious. This isn't just an idle threat."

"Oh, believe me, I understand," said Bashir. He stood at a solitary table in a room that was, essentially, a big off-white box: no window, bright overhead fluorescents; a small bathroom off-center along the far wall that contained a toilet, a sink, a shower. A bed he kept neat, the blanket tucked because Bashir knew that morale depended on the little things. A muted vidscreen hung on one wall; Bashir had tuned it to a news station—the only one, government-run—and some newsperson chattered in antic silence through a story that Bashir gathered was about those rebel fighters these people were so obsessed with. There was a straight-back chair and the table strewn with medical texts—anatomy, emergency medicine, physiology, and other books, history principally, that Kahayn had provided at his request, and that he'd devoured and thank the Lord, he could read the language. So he knew about the Cataclysm and what he was up against.

"Let this security man and his people come." He gave his tunic a little tug for emphasis the way he'd seen Captain Picard do once. The long-sleeved tunic fit well but felt odd because it was so loose: some kind of beige cotton with a Nehru neck and a pair of olive trousers. A pair of brown leather shoes with laces. "But I don't know how many times we need to go through this. I'm from another country—"

"But really far away and so, of course, all your people have escaped the Cataclysm and only wish to remain anonymous and, oh and by the way, technologically advanced enough to equip a pressure suit that withstands vacuum and can *fly*." Kahayn snorted. "You think I swallow that? I'm trying to help you. Anything you want, I got. Books, news . . ."

"And guards," said Bashir. "Don't forget my locked door, and just in case I find a way out, my lovely guards at the end of that long corridor and on the other side of a door that's very thick and very locked. Yes, how can one not feel positively pampered?"

"Would you do any differently? In that amazing . . . *country* of yours?"

Of course, the answer to that was *yes*, after a fashion. "Doctor, you've been good to me—more, perhaps, than I could expect, given how I was dropped on your proverbial doorstep."

"Considering your suit . . . yes, that's probably accurate."

And touché, Doctor. Bashir put on his most winning smile. "But I don't know what will convince you that I've told the truth."

"Oh, don't be insulting. Fine, you're a doctor. I believe that. But this fantastic, wonderful country no one's heard of? Please."

"Right. Well, I see your point." Bashir debated, then snapped his fingers. "I know. Let's just say I've told you what I can."

"Uh-huh. Well, I have a better idea. What say we play a game called *Trust*. Here are the rules. You tell me the truth; I tell you the truth. See, in my land, that's what we call trust . . . and don't you say it, Julian, don't you dare. Because I know you don't trust me."

Bashir closed his mouth. He'd been about to say just that. Only it would have been another lie.

"Yah," she said after a pause. "Now let me tell *you* another, very important truth. You remember Blate?"

"Ah. Yes. Very unpleasant fellow. Those goggle-eyes. He really should have them attended to."

"My sentiments, exactly." The ghost of a smile brushed her lips. "But that's the way he likes them, and *you* will have an *excellent* opportunity to study them right up close. He'll be here in about four days."

"Ah." Bashir's stomach churned. "More interrogation? You weren't thorough enough?"

"Not for him. And this time, it won't be just talk. You'll be hooked up to an fMRI. You know the theory?"

Bashir was silent. Oh, he understood it. The machine was something out of the twenty-second . . . no, no, twenty-*first* century. fMRI: Functional Magnetic Resonance Imaging, a primitive system dependent upon alternations in magnetic susceptibility and designed to measure, in the brain at least and very crudely, areas of neural activation.

In humans, oxygenated arterial blood contained oxygenated hemoglobin, which because of its iron matrix was diamagnetic and had, therefore, a small magnetic susceptibility effect. Deoxygenated blood was more highly paramagnetic and, therefore, the machine detected a larger observed magnetic susceptibility effect. In essence, fMRI allowed a window into the brain: a sort of watch-while-you-work.

He wondered how well that technology served this particular species. His gaze skipped over Kahayn's features. That bluish cast to her skin . . . he knew what it was. Her blood, as well as that of everyone native to this world, already possessed huge quantities of methemoglobin: hemoglobin whose iron was ferric, not ferrous, and quite poor at binding oxygen. Still, if they were going to use the fMRI on *him*, the technology must work pretty well on their species, and that was bad because it meant the machine was very sensitive indeed.

"I understand the principle," he said finally. "A lie detector test, right?"

"Yup. Virtually foolproof." She gave him a tight, humorless smile. "Lying causes a very characteristic pattern of brain activation in seven different regions."

"In other words, lying is hard work."

"That's right. By contrast, telling the truth is much easier. Truth only requires *four* neural pathways. Pretty characteristic pattern."

"Ah. So you've concluded that we share enough commonality that my *brain* will tell the truth even if *I* lie."

"You lie? I guarantee that screen will light up."

"Mmmm." Bashir nodded, his neutral expression—the one he'd practiced in that Dominion prison—firmly screwed in place. But a bolt of panic shuddered into his chest. Their just catching him out in a lie probably wasn't the end of it. Maybe they'd take his conscious mind out of the equation. Use truth serum, perhaps, or some other way of cracking his resistance. Or just plain torture.

And—bugger it all—for what? Yes, yes, of course, his *oath*, but was that important now? Elizabeth was dead, and Ezri lost to him before he'd ever set foot on that runabout—and his heart with her. His suit, uniform, and combadge had been confiscated. Picking apart the suit's guts and the combadge would take time, but these people would likely manage. So, if everything he'd ever known was gone; if he were tortured to death or left as some sort of mental vegetable, what did a theoretical abstraction like the Prime Directive, the product of a universe that wasn't perfect but liked to pretend that it was, count for now?

Maybe not very much.

He looked up and met her eyes—*compassion there, sympathy; and sadness, too; why is she helping me, why does she care?*—and said nothing.

She nodded, though, as if he had. "Our world's dying, Julian. We compensate but we can't change things back, not in time to save ourselves."

"What about your children?"

Pain arrowed across her face. "Can't have any. Most of us can't. So we switch out parts; rebuild ourselves. Keep staving off the inevitable as long as possible."

"And then I show up."

"And then you show up. You're the same, sort of. A close match but still very different in some very important ways.

For example, I *know* that you come from a place where there's more oxygen in the air. I know for a *fact* that the amount in silica and copper and arsenicals in your body is only a fraction of what it is in ours and that's because there aren't industrial pollutants in your air or water. Your heart is simpler and still very efficient. You have less surface area in your lungs, and your immunological status is much less reactive than ours. I know because I finally had to give you a transfusion; you'd just lost too much blood."

"Oh," he said, with a dry smile. "I'm sure my system loved *that.*"

"Not to worry; I added a reducing enzyme to convert the iron from ferric to ferrous so you'd bind more oxygen. But the point is you didn't have a transfusion reaction. You didn't go into anaphylactic shock. Your system seems remarkably antigenically neutral, at least to our tissues."

"That's important?"

"As you'd say, quite. Because there's one more thing about you that's very different: your brain. It works really, really well. Is that the way it is with all your people?"

He said nothing. Her lips quirked into a half-smile. "Right. I forgot. You're one of us. But do you know I've never heard an accent like yours either?"

"Oh, *that.* Well, my accent's very common where I come from."

"Then I'm glad I've never visited. I might get a headache. Oh, and there's this other thing that just won't go away: your remarkable suit that resists vacuum and flies." She paused. "You see what I'm driving at."

"Even if your scan says that I'm lying, nothing changes the fact that I can't tell you more than I have already."

"Can't? Or won't?"

"Would you believe *both?*"

"No, because one's predicated on ignorance and the other on will. But that little distinction won't matter, not when this is over."

He tried to be jolly about it, a bit gay, the way he imagined a debonair agent caught in a thorny situation might. "What, torture, Doctor? Thumbscrews? Bamboo under the fingernails?"

"What's bamboo?" Then she waved that away. "Never mind. This isn't a joke, Julian. Because the horrible part is you won't have a choice."

He forced a devil-may-care grin. "I'm sorry. For the life of me, I can't fathom that."

"Yah, for the life of you," she said. "I'd say that's about right."

No idle threat there. His eyes wandered to the room's vidscreen again, and he watched as a soldier—clearly, Kornak—aimed a rifle at the back of a prisoner's head. He turned away. Any fool knew what came next. "So what are my options?"

"I'll show you. And take a good hard look, Julian. Then, you choose."

He took her in: her blue skin and that left eye and her left hand. "What if I still choose my way?"

"Then heaven help you," she said, keying in the code that opened his door. "Because I won't be able to."

CHAPTER
18

When Lense got news that Saad was back, it was midmorning nine days later and she was in the middle of changing bandages. She wasn't prepared for that tug of happy anticipation and the queer fluttery feeling in her stomach.

So this is what it's like to be smitten. She hadn't even felt like that when she and her jackass of an ex-husband started dating back at Starfleet Medical. . . .

She pawned the bandage-changing job off on one of her assistants, then hurried down passages and ducked through corridors. She got some queer looks and bobs of the head in greeting from the others. No secret about her and Saad. *The look on that guard's face when he found us on morning patrol after that first night . . .* But, God, this felt good. Everything looked brighter somehow; she felt better, more acutely aware of textures and smells. She liked exploring his body; she loved the feel of his skin, and his smell was rich and spicy. She liked pleasing him, and receiving pleasure. She just wasn't, well, *depressed,* and she certainly slept better. Her grin broadened. When Saad let her.

Even if it's just infatuation or lust, I don't care because I'm happy. I'm on this godforsaken world and every day is blood and more blood, and still, at least for now, I'm happy. . . .

"Saad," she said, as she rounded the last corner, "I'm so gla—" She stopped. "Mara." Then, awkwardly, to Saad: "I'm sorry. They said you wanted to see me." She edged the way she'd come. "I can come back."

"No." Saad beckoned her forward. "No, no, I want you here. *I* asked Mara to join us. Please, come."

For a fraction of a second, she wasn't sure how to behave. That made her angry, like she was some giggly, gawky adolescent with a crush. "Of course," she said, sliding down to sit cross-legged on a low flat rock. She spotted a lumpy bundle of something heaped a short distance away. Saad sat across from her, but Mara hung back, leaning against the cavern wall.

She looked from one to the other. "Why do I think this has nothing to do with planning some raid for medical supplies?"

Mara just stared. Saad smiled, though only with his lips. "Oh, we still plan a raid. But something else has come up."

"And what's that?"

"I've just gotten word that General Nerrit is on his way to the Kornak complex at the edge of the sea. I think I might pay him a visit."

"And it would be suicide, Saad." Exasperated, Mara pushed off from the wall and paced, the clap of her boots banging off rock. "That you're even thinking of getting anywhere near Nerrit again."

Again? "Who's Nerrit?" asked Lense.

"Supreme Commander for the Kornak Armed Forces," said Saad. "His command center is about five, perhaps six days' travel. But he's on his way, apparently. About four days out at this point."

"Oh. Well, you want to kidnap him, take him out, what?"

"Under other circumstances. But now I have new information that makes me wonder what to do next."

The sound of Mara's pacing was giving Lense a headache. "I'm sorry, but I don't see how I can help here. You want a list of supplies, I'll give you a list. I'll give you ten. But anything tactical, *military . . .*"

"It's not that clear-cut, Elizabeth. Trust me on this."

It was the first time he'd called her by name since she'd entered. Her gaze flicked to Mara, who paced and looked black as a thundercloud, and then to Saad. Something else going on, something to do with *her* . . . But what?

You're being paranoid. It's probably nothing.

She said, "Well, what does this—your source say? How many people do you have on the inside, anyway?"

"We had a few. Three, to be exact. One was discovered, and the other's gone silent. This one . . . the last time we had contact was a little more than a year ago."

Mara cut in, her voice quaking with fury. "I don't care if we've had ten, a hundred sources . . . that you're even thinking of going *back* there—"

"Back. What does she mean, going back?" Lense looked from Mara to Saad, who was staring daggers at Mara. She switched her gaze back to Mara. "What do you mean? Going back to *what?*"

Mara opened her mouth. Clamped it shut. Threw Saad a look so charged that if it had been fire, he'd have burst into flames. She said, "You need to tell her. She needs to know. *You* need to *ask*."

"Ask me what?" Lense said. "What the hell's going on?"

"Mara . . ." Saad's voice thrummed with frustration. "I will ask questions when I . . ." Then he let out his breath, looked at Lense and said, more calmly, "Mara isn't very fond of a particular portion of that base."

Mara was unable to contain herself. "Gee, you *think?*"

Ignoring her, Saad squatted on his haunches beside Lense and drew a wide circle with the tip of his index finger. "Here's the layout. Perimeter security, checkpoints—here, here, and here." He jabbed his finger dead center. "The main hospital's here, at the heart."

Lense's eyes clicked over the rough drawing. "That's a lot to cover, and even if you get in . . . how are you going to do that, anyway?"

Saad's mouth twisted in a wry smile. "Nerrit may have new parts, but he's an old man with ingrained habits. He always travels with a rear guard. We'll ambush the guard, steal their ident tags and then slip into the complex. The beauty is that

Nerrit isn't *going* to the main facility. Once he's in," he sketched a rough square, "my source tells me that he'll peel off *here.*"

"A separate building?" Lense looked over at Mara. Mara just shrugged, looked away. "What is it?"

"A specialized research wing, underground. Totally cut off from the main complex. The only way in or out is a tram tunnel, and a separate foot tunnel."

"Why the special tunnel?"

"They've had to cut power there in the past. And there were . . . disturbances."

"So, is it for a SWAT team?" Lense knew of them, of course; all prisons had them if inmates got loose and cut off power. Underground tunnels ensured speed, stealth, and surprise. "What is it, a stockade?"

"No, I told you. It's a research wing."

"Well, then that level of containment usually means a biohazard."

"Yeah," said Mara. She was holding up the wall again. "What the lady said. Biohazard. Right, Saad?"

"Well, no," said Saad. "I don't think that biohazard really does it justice."

CHAPTER
19

They'd taken a left from his room, away from the guards at the end of the corridor, and then doglegged right. Bashir spotted an adjacent, nearly dark corridor on his left, and he thought he saw some kind of sensor winking like an angry red eye.

But they didn't go there. Instead, they turned right and passed room after silent room through a maze of corridors. They didn't speak. The only sounds were the taps of their shoes and the whoosh of a ventilation system. They finally dead-ended at a thick metal containment door. The door's sheen reminded him of Deep Space 9, all that Cardassian gray. Access required retinal scan and a thumbprint ID. Kahayn submitted to both, and the door slid open with a whine of hydraulics.

The door gave onto another corridor that was much shorter, and now Bashir recognized familiar smells: the sharp bite of fixative mingling with a fuller musk-ripe odor of feces and the wine odor of fermented fruit. The right wall was painted yellow cinder block, he thought. Midway down, the wall was faced with a large rectangle of clear glass. Inside was something that looked like an exhibit in an old-fashioned museum: specimens suspended in jars; a long gurney that gave onto a metal sink and adjoining counter; a ring of metal counters on which stood equipment, analyzers of various sorts. Another metal door, wide enough for a gurney. A freezer, probably. Bashir knew the basic setup of an autopsy suite when he saw it.

But they hadn't entered. Instead, Kahayn went left to another door. She'd pulled it open and a fruity smell pillowed out, one mixed with excrement and hay for bedding.

Animal room. But there was something very wrong here. Bashir turned a slow circle. That strange air, it felt . . . His skin prickled. *Alive, and all edges and sharp angles.*

"Cold, isn't it? But you feel it." Kahayn stirred the air with her index finger. "How *thick* it feels?"

Bashir nodded. "Yes. Crowded. Like I'm being jostled." He did another turn. The room was perhaps six meters square, and bathed in fluorescent glare. Wire cages lined three walls, two to a wall. Each cage held an animal similar to Terran *Pan troglodytes,* chimps, but with orange fur like orangutans and a bit larger.

And they were very strange. For one, they were absolutely silent. Not that this was unusual; Earth chimpanzees hooted only in panic or fear. But these animals were . . . sizing him up, yes. They sat on their haunches, but their heads followed him to and fro, like perfectly behaved spectators to a slow-motion tennis match but in a kind of ripple, like a wave, as if the next picked up where the one before left off.

"You can get closer," said Kahayn. Her voice sounded unnaturally loud in the hush. "They don't initiate."

"That's an odd way of putting it." Cautiously, Bashir sidled up to one cage. The primate inside squatted, watchful. Waiting. But Bashir noticed it right away: a shift in the air. A sense of . . . he frowned. Expectancy?

And that's when he saw an odd bulge tenting the crown of the primate's scalp. The bulge was a rough circle with a diameter of six, maybe eight centimeters. But there was nothing external, no protruding wires or electrodes. A quick glance at the other cages revealed exactly the same bulge in roughly the same place.

He turned back to Kahayn. "It's an implant, right?" When she nodded, he continued, "For what?"

"This." She stirred air again. "What's it remind you of?"

Bashir closed his eyes. Thought. Almost smiled. *Quark's.* "A bar," he said, opening his eyes. "Too many people in a small space and they're all talking at once, so there's only this general buzz but you can't make out the words."

"Do you feel as cold now?"

He blinked. "No, it's gone."

"That's because they're not as worried about you." A pause. "What would you say if I told you there was a conversation going on?"

"You mean the animals? But how—" He stopped. Pulled air in a quick gasp. "My God."

"Yah," she said, softly. "That's right."

"Neural regeneration," said Saad. "The Kornaks are good at developing prosthetic limbs and eyes and ears and a whole host of other appliances. Someday, they'll build a man from scratch; count on it. They'll have to, eventually."

"Why's that?"

"Can't have kids," said Mara. Her expression was bland, and her tone matter-of-fact, as if she were talking about something no more important than the weather. "Kornaks, us. Oh, we get a couple. But usually something's wrong with them. Most of them die."

"The Kornaks have focused their energies on replacing themselves piece by piece," said Saad. "But that only works up to a certain point."

Lense nodded. "The brain's the limiting factor. It doesn't regenerate. You can rebuild a lot of the body, but if you're senile, who cares? It's like a fail-safe device. We're pretty much wired for obsolescence."

The cave was silent. Then Saad said, "Well, not all of us."

The autopsy suite smelled just as primitive as it looked: a strong tang of some disinfectant mingling with the gassy odor of rot. The microscope was also primitive. Binocular eyepiece, adjustable objectives, a slide with a specimen in paraffin mounted on a staging table. But Bashir saw well enough and he didn't like it one little bit.

"Massive rejection. Looks like a battlefield after a war." He exhaled. "Dear God. The tissue's absolutely ravaged. How long did you say the process took?"

"In the primates, within two weeks," said Kahayn. She stood by his right shoulder. "The problem is that with all the damage done to our environment and the weird bugs that developed over time, our immune system is quite reactive to just about everything. To get around that, all our prosthetics are biomimetic and possess a DNA chip that allows for recognition and then integration into the host body. Still, the trick is to make prosthetics as antigenically neutral as possible."

Bashir arched his eyebrows. "Hard to do, with DNA as a template. You produce RNA, which produces proteins, and you'll get rejection. The only way to get around that would be some sort of, I don't know, universal DNA donor. On the other hand, the brain's privileged, relatively antigenically isolated, so it might work. But there's no such thing as a universal DNA donor."

She gave him a strange look. "Well, I tried something different. There were a few records left from before the Cataclysm. I stumbled on some literature about certain species of sea life that regenerated neural tissue."

"I see," said Bashir. Yes, she was on the right track; many Earth species of starfish and amphibians, not to mention Ludian halofish on Lentrex VII, could regenerate entire nerves and whole limbs. "What did you try next?"

In reply, Kahayn switched out slides, peered through the eyepieces, adjusted the focus, then straightened. "Have a look."

Another brain section, but now something in the center . . . When he changed magnifications, he couldn't believe his eyes. Entire neuronal tracks had been reconstructed; the membranes bracketed with an overlay of . . . "That microglia's much too dense, and those axons . . . my God, is that *metal*?"

"A combination of silica and copper. You're looking at what

happens to a primate's brain when it's exposed to MEMs. Microelectromechanical machines, a variant of nanotechnology developed for computer systems. You're familiar with their function?"

"Not really," Bashir lied. Thinking: *Ancient history; computers and hard drives, copper and silica chips, and tungsten for an interconnect.*

"MEMs can rewrite and repair information on nanodrives. So my thought . . . *our* thought, was to replicate this function within a brain. It's one thing to hook up an artificial eye or ear." She touched the corner of her left eye. "Everything works just fine because it's a discrete system, a totally dedicated subunit, you might say. But it's quite another to jury-rig whole tracts of interconnecting neural tissue, or an entire lobe. So my initial idea was to use DNA chips as the programming matrix in a MEM. But in order to facilitate axonal repair, I inserted DNA from a species of diatom. Plankton, actually. Very hardy. Their cell walls are made of silica."

His mind bounced around the problem. Simple biology: there was usually only five to ten grams of silica in the body, either ingested or absorbed from the environment. Silicic acid dissolved in water; silicates in dust. So long as the silicon remained bound as siloxanes, not much of a problem, healthwise. Why, look at any fracture site in bone and the ratio of silica to calcium was nearly double.

On the other hand, these people lived in a kind of pollutant stew: silicates, chromated copper arsenate, copper oxides in the air. So Kahayn looked to rebuild brain by armoring it with a substance that could not be rejected. Ingenious.

"So this would be like encasing your regenerated neurons in an exoskeleton of silica and copper that was antigenically neutral," said Bashir. "Quite elegant, Doctor."

She bobbed her head at the compliment, but her expression was still grim. "Everything went fine. We induced disease in the primates, put in the MEMs, and the primates regained function. It was like a miracle and . . ."

He read the struggle in her face. "And? But?"

"Things we . . . *I* couldn't explain, didn't see coming." She put her hands into the pockets of her white lab coat and shrugged as if suddenly cold. "What is it that a complicated computer does?"

"Information processing. Data storage. Problem solving."

"Plus, the capacity to relay or manufacture commands, tell different parts of a program to run at a certain time or in a certain way, right? But what if a machine wants to share information with another machine?"

"Oh, that's easy enough. Primi—" He caught himself before he could say *primitive.* "Microwave, for example. Beaming messages back and forth; I mean, really, all communications technology relies upon transmission of encoded energy. But a machine can't *decide* things like that. The capability has to be *put* there."

"Yah, you'd think. But that's not the way these implants worked. The MEMs decided . . . they began to rewrite portions of *healthy* brain. The MEMs interpreted normal brain as damaged. And then when I was doing imaging studies, the primates—maybe the MEMs, I don't know—they *decided* to link. I couldn't stop them, and they didn't stop with just one machine. These scanners hooked into more sophisticated systems, and then other systems linked to those computers in a cascade. They were like a virus. But instead of crippling the network, they and the network—our computers—became *dependent* upon one another. They joined forces."

Networking; brains meshing with a computer, behaving like a computer the way a Bynar's must; an amazing discovery . . . "What happened when you tried to disconnect them? Shut down the computers?"

"They just . . . *died.* Like they needed the machines. Or had become them." She looked bleak. "They just died."

"Then what about the animals I just saw? Are they linked to a computer network somewhere?"

"No." She shook her head. "You're in the isolation wing. Our power is self-contained. Our computers are in a separate area. Our communications don't even tie in with the main complex. The animals you saw were never exposed to anything more complicated than a free-standing system that's not on any network."

"But you just said that these MEMs, their natural proclivity is to try to link with another system. So if you—well, I don't know—*starve* them for contact, what do they link with?" Then he remembered that crowded air in the animal room. "To each *other?*"

She nodded. "But, again, limited by distance the way one would see with microwave transmission, or line of sight technology. I keep trying to separate them. Interrupt the MEMs, introduce a lesion, all sorts of things. But I keep failing. I separate them too long or too far, they die."

"Well, then, that would be the end of it, wouldn't it? I mean, you really can't take this any further." But that was a lie. Because Bashir knew that he'd have been tempted to take the next logical step. "What did you do?"

"Isn't it obvious, Julian? If a brain's information could be uploaded or downloaded with another machine . . ."

"Why not manipulate data, yes? Download information into the primates and vice versa?"

"Pretty much," she said, quietly. "It was all so . . . *exciting,* you have to understand that."

"Oh, but I do," he said. "The brain's immense, and there's so much of it we don't use. So I understand the temptation, completely. Honestly."

"No arguments about ethics?"

"Just because I understand temptation doesn't mean there are no ethics involved, Doctor," he said, gently. "I said I *understood.* Here you'd stumbled on a mechanism to put knowledge in or take it out, yes?"

"That's *right,*" she said, her voice thin, intense. "Data is data. That's all we are, really: chemicals and molecules and atoms, and all of it some rearrangement according to a code. All there, just waiting for a compatible system, a way to read it, to edit and to add. It was like being given a key to a locked door. Turn the key and, instantly, you know the thoughts and memories and desires of someone else. Just waiting for me to open that door."

"But some doors are locked for reasons," said Bashir. Thinking: *I'd have been tempted. A window into the mind of an animal, or even another species . . .*

And then it hit him.

She said memories. She said thoughts and memories of some-one else. Not something, not an animal. Someone.

All those isolated empty rooms, each with a bed and a chair and a table and a vidscreen. Just like his. And that angry red eye of a magnetic lock at the end of a silent, dark corridor.

Oh, dear God. Everything came crashing in, and when he looked at her—at that stricken, remorseful face—it was like he saw *her* for the first time. Not just her blue skin or the chocolate cast to her lips, or even her artificial left eye that had no capillaries and a left hand that made a tiny clicking sound when she moved a finger, and held no warmth. For the first time, Bashir saw—really *understood*—what all this meant for him now on this godforsaken waste of a planet.

Because she wore her insignia over her left breast pocket. And there was her rank, bars here instead of pips, tacked to the collars of a uniform shirt.

A scientist who broke barriers, and a soldier who followed orders.

"You said a key to a locked door." His voice was ragged with urgency and hoarse, as if he'd run a great distance, and his mind had only now caught up. "But you didn't have to open it, Kahayn. Not every door *demands* that you open it! And even if someone tried to compel you, if they *ordered* you, you're a doctor, you're a physician! For the love of God, you don't pick people apart! You're a *healer!* You could always *refuse,* you could say *no;* you could say that I am a *person* and a person may only go this far and no *further.* . . ."

"Oh, you could, Julian, you *could,*" she said, and her voice was so full of remorse and compassion and regret he felt like weeping with her. "In a perfect world, you even might. But the thing is . . . I *didn't.*"

CHAPTER
20

Lense felt frozen, like that moment that always came in the transporter just before she dissolved: that tiny hitch in time when things were as crisp and detailed and immutable as if cut into the heart of a rare diamond.

"But who would volunteer?" she said. Yet she already knew the answer: the military. Not different from Earth's sometimes-not-so-distant past at all; in every war, whether with guns or experimental craft or bioweapons, soldiers were fodder. Sometimes they knew what was happening, and why. Many times they didn't.

"They were desperate," said Saad, as if reading her mind. "We're all desperate, Elizabeth, just in different ways. So they did it."

"And?"

"At first, it didn't work. They had the same problem with rejection."

"But that's what's so strange about this whole thing," she said, without really thinking it over first. "I don't understand the violence of this rejection business. The brain's relatively privileged, comparatively well isolated antigenically."

She was only aware when the silence grew that Saad was staring, as was Mara. It occurred to her, too late, that *human* brains were privileged. *But here, their spleen and thymus are so large, probably hyperreactive to stimulus* . . . She thought about trying to backtrack but then figured she'd put her boot in it. "How did they overcome the problem?"

"By finding someone uniquely compatible with everyone else."

"Like a universal donor." Well, it could work. There was blood as a precedent. But DNA? "I take it that's rare."

"Rare. Yes. Likely a mutation, but a very convenient one."

"So they incorporated his . . . her DNA?" she asked. Saad nodded. Mara's eyes had narrowed to slits. "And these people, they linked up and couldn't be separated?"

"Right." Saad held up a finger. "All but one. This universal donor, as you say. He linked, but he could also unlink, still function and think independently. They weren't really prepared for that."

"Why couldn't the others?"

Mara looked at Saad, and Saad stared at a point above Lense's head for a moment, and sighed. "I think they don't really know. But maybe he was what you called privileged."

"But then . . . even if they link, who decides? Which one of them gets to, I don't know, call the shots? What happens to free will?"

"Isn't that obvious?"

Of course, it was. But then she thought again about what he'd just said. "You said *was privileged*. Past tense. What happened to the donor?"

Saad shrugged. "Gone. And no use cloning his DNA without him around to, as you say, call the shots. The rest of the pod was like a computer idling, waiting for a command. So the Kornaks started looking for another, very special person. But now, you see, Nerrit's coming."

"So they think they found someone. Okay. But why are you telling me all this? How is this related to me?"

"Because I have to ask you a very important question, Elizabeth. And I need for you to answer me honestly, truthfully."

"I've never lied to you, Saad," she lied. "What do you want to ask me?"

"When Mara found you, you said you'd come here with friends, on a hike."

"Yes."

"And that you got separated."

"Yes."

"And you had no equipment."

"What is this, Saad?"

"Funny," he said. He pushed up, walked to that lumpy, wrapped bundle she'd noticed earlier, and twitched the cloth free.

Lense went absolutely, perfectly still.

"Because you know?" Saad picked up her helmet and turned it this way and that. "I was just about to ask you the same question."

Bashir's chest was tight. He couldn't breathe. He was burning up, and then freezing cold and the hackles on the back of his neck stood on end, and then he started to shake, uncontrollably. He couldn't help it, couldn't stop it. The beat of blood in his brain was so remorseless he thought his skull would explode. His thoughts raced like rats on a wheel spinning to nowhere: about cogs in a machine and implants and those primates and the air above his head filled with their silent words and images . . . Ah, *God*, if he could just stop his brain from thinking, just for an instant! Just shut his brain off, just shut down!

"Julian."

Got to get out of here. He squeezed his eyes tight, but he was still thinking, thinking, thinking, and he wanted to run to a dark closet and hide and draw his knees up, the way he had when he was small and stupid and couldn't say his name properly; and still he'd laughed with all the other children because he was so lonely and too dull . . .

"Julian."

. . . too simple to understand that they were laughing at him . . .

"Julian."

. . . at poor, simple, dim little Jules, the ninny, the nit no one liked and his parents despised.

"Julian, look at me."

His eyes snapped open. "Why did you show me this?" His voice cut his raw throat like a knife. "Why?"

"Because you needed the facts." That wash of yellow fluorescent glare turned her skin the color of bile and made his look dead. "Truth for truth."

"But *why?*" Hot fury flooded his veins and then before he knew what he was doing—or maybe he just didn't care—he had her by both arms, the way he might with someone he loved and hated in equal measure. She tried to twist away, but now he had her and he hung on tight. "Why have you done this, *why?* To torture me? What do you want? For the love of God, what do you *expect* of me?"

"The *truth.*" Her eyes ticked back and forth, the left lagging a bit; and she'd gone so pale he saw the solitary salt track of her tears dried onto her right cheek. "Where do you come from, Julian? Who are you? *What* are you? If you don't tell me the truth or give me something tangible, I can't help you. Look at it from my perspective. If you have nothing to hide, then why should I interfere? Why show you anything? You would take the fMRI and pass."

"But Blate wouldn't let me go. You know that. Even if I passed, would that *really* stop him? Or you?" He gave her a rough shake. "*Really?* Look at all you've done already! Wouldn't this man Blate simply decide that I'd fooled you in some way? Because, remember, there's the suit, Doctor, there's the *suit.* So would he order you to do this anyway?"

"Yes."

"Then what's the *point?*"

"Because *I* need to know! I need something that tells me this far and no further because there's more at stake here than you can possibly know or understand. So I need to know the *truth.* Before I risk everything, I need to know and I need to know right now, Julian, right *now*—before it's too late."

"Too *late?*" Now he gripped her very hard, harder than he'd ever held Ezri even when she was killing his soul, though he'd wanted to. Oh, God, how he'd wanted to break something in that runabout on that long trip back from Trill to DS9, when she'd let him go. Because it was too late for Julian, always too late: too late with Jadzia and then with Ezri. And yet how delicate he'd been, how so very polite because good, sweet, dear Julian was brought up not to make a scene because it might draw too much attention and then people would start asking the wrong questions. So he'd always been in hiding, all his life. Even in love because the truth was so dangerous. "Too *late?* What does it matter now what I say when Blate's mind is made up?"

"Because it does. Don't you see, Julian? I've been honest with you when I could've lied. Nothing impelled me to choose *against* myself by showing you everything. All my ugliness and all these mistakes, ones I made even when I thought I was doing good rather than harm. But I showed you because you *are* a person, not an animal. I did it of my own free will, and that is the last thing that separates me from the machine, but it is the very . . . *last* . . . *thing!*" She was weeping again, tear upon tear but only along one cheek, one. "A machine can decide, but it can't *think.* Unless it is programmed to do so, it will not choose against itself nor make any other judgment other than what fact *allows* it to see.

"But then there's this." She put the flat of her palm upon his chest and over his galloping heart, and he gasped because that touch burned him like a brand. "There is faith," she said, "and there is hope, and all the emotions that are the truths that bind us in a way that a machine can never know."

"I . . . I . . ." His lips clamped together; despair vised his heart, and then because he knew that he would surely kill her where she stood, he spun away. "No, no, *no, damn* you!"

And then because he couldn't stand any more—because he knew with a sudden, awful clarity what his fate was—he wheeled around, grabbed the microscope and hurled it across the room with all his might. It rocketed straight as a missile and smashed the glass with a tremendous *bang!* The glass exploded in a starburst, shattering with a sound like hard, ancient ice. The sound broke him somewhere inside, like a dam giving way, and he howled. His heart battered his ribs; and he was weeping, too, as much from fury as dread because he was, after all, only a man.

"I *can't!* Please, please, don't you understand? If I could, I would, but I can't! I want to; believe me, you don't know how much. Do you think I want to end up like *them?* Like those *animals* in those *cages?* Ask me something I *can* answer, and I will do it! Because however much I wish I could change this, change *myself,* you've asked for the one thing I just simply cannot do, and precisely *because* of this!" He banged his chest with his fist and then held it there, every beat of his savage heart shuddering through his living flesh because it was still *his* heart; it was *his.* "My faith! *My* heart! *My* hope and my *truth!* And I cannot part paths with *any of that* even to save myself because then I will no longer be a person I . . . *recognize!*"

And then it was like a cord snapped, like he was a marionette whose puppeteer had cut his strings. He broke off, turned away. Stumbled for someplace as far away as he could manage in that awful place.

"And so there's your truth, Doctor," he said, utterly spent. Swaying, he slid down the length of the far wall. His knees folded and he squeezed his roaring head between his hands. "It's the only truth I know."

He didn't know how long he sat there like that. Maybe long enough to turn to stone. (Please, God, he wanted that because a stone can't feel love or agony, or the chilling despair of knowing that there is absolutely nothing left—not even hope.) Certainly he sat long enough for his head to stop roaring and his breathing to quiet.

Then he heard a hesitant step, a crunch of glass. When her hands took hold of his wrists, he started, not only from her touch but because his right wrist was cold and his left was not.

"Julian." Her voice was watery. "Please forgive me, but you must try to understand how very much, how very important this is."

"Why?" His head was still woolly, and he was so tired. "What do you mean?"

"I envy you," and then she swallowed hard. "I envy you your heart. Your faith, your integrity, your passion. So let me ask you a different way." She pulled in a breath. "Julian, will you *fail?*"

"What? Why?"

"Because it's important. It's everything. So in four days, when I have to hook you up to that scanner, will . . . you . . . *fail?*"

And there: He saw what she was doing in that instant—allowing him to tell his truth in the only way he could, and he was more grateful than she could ever know because now, at last, he *could* answer, and it would be no lie.

"Yes," he said.

"I don't know what that is," said Lense. Saad had her EVA suit now and when he shook it, a shower of grit rained upon rock with a sound like rice. "I have no idea."

"It looks to be about your size." Saad hefted the helmet. "Is it yours?"

She said nothing.

"This is a waste," said Mara. "Let's stop this little charade and—"

"Be quiet." Saad hadn't even turned around. His eyes fixed on Lense, and she felt her heart swell with anger. This was so stupid; what did the Prime Directive mean now? More than that, she didn't want to lie to Saad, not anymore.

I care for him, and he cares for me, and that should count for something, shouldn't it? In this whole crazy universe, doesn't love count for anything?

And then her mind snagged on something else: Nerrit, and Saad's source. Nerrit was coming, and that was unusual. Nerrit was coming all the way out here, but not because of *her* suit. Saad *had* her suit. But Nerrit's coming was somehow *about* her, anyway. But that would have to mean that this was about somebody *else*, someone *like* her . . .

Oh, my God, my God!

"Elizabeth?"

"Yes?" She forced herself to focus just on Saad's face and his eyes and everything there was for her in his heart she didn't want to lose.

"Is this suit yours?"

She swallowed. "No."

"Saad," Mara began.

Saad held up a hand, and Mara sank back into silence. He looked like he was weighing something on a mental scale, debating how to ask the next question in a way that she might or could answer. Then he replaced her suit and laid her helmet on top and walked to her and knelt and took her hands in his.

"Well, then," he said, very gently. "Answer me this, my love. Are you the *only* . . . one?"

She knew what he meant. More important, she knew *who*.

"No," she said.

Kahayn still had him by his wrists. Whether she tethered him there, or this was a comfort to both of them, he didn't know. It didn't matter.

Bashir said, "So what now? What happens now?"

"That depends," she said, "on how much you trust me."

"Bashir," Lense said. "His name is Julian Bashir. He's a doctor, like me. We were traveling together and got . . . separated."

"All right," said Saad. He still knelt, still had her hands, but now there was uncertainty in his eyes. "Are you and he, are you . . . ?"

"No. Just . . . we're friends."

His shoulders eased a bit. "Can you tell me where or how you got . . . ?"

"No," she said again. "But Julian's why Nerrit's coming, isn't it?"

He nodded.

"And your contact?"

"Has a plan, a way to get us in by the footpath instead of the tram. It's risky. And we've got to go now. Nerrit will be here in a few days, and it will take us that long just to get within striking distance of his convoy."

"Saad," said Mara. "Please. This isn't wise."

"Really?" he drawled. "I think you've made that abundantly clear."

Lense saw the sudden hurt in Mara's eyes. "Don't dismiss her out of hand. She's your second. She knows your capabilities probably better than you do because your mind's already made up." *And why; why is he so persistent, and how does he know so much if . . . ?*

"I thought you didn't know anything about the military," he said, showing a thin sliver of a smile. "I admit, this isn't exactly the smartest thing I've ever done in my life, but that doesn't matter. If the Kornaks are right about this Bashir, then we've got to stop them. Even if they're wrong, they will take whatever they want from his mind, and then the man you know, Elizabeth, just won't exist anymore. He'll simply *be*. And everything locked in *your* head that you will not say they will *rip* right out of his. So I'm not doing this for *you*, Elizabeth, or even for him. I'm doing it for all of us."

She blurted it out. "No, you're not." She saw the edges of his eyes tighten but pushed on anyway. "Don't kid yourself. You're doing this for you."

"I am?" Saad was very still. "Why?"

"Because," said Lense. She was aware of Mara's eyes on her as well, but she kept hers firmly on Saad. "You've got a grudge."

"About what?"

"You're the donor, Saad. *You're* the one who walked away." Now she looked over at Mara and saw the emotions chasing across the big woman's scarred, ravaged face. "Or did you break him out?"

"Broke him out," said Mara, hoarsely. "We were in the same unit. Saad was my CO. Then Nerrit . . . they tested us. Took Saad. I . . . we figured out what was happening, and then we got him out. We had help on the inside, a few of the scientists."

"Your contacts?" asked Lense. Mara nodded. "What happened to them?"

"One we know for sure was killed. Janel was his name. The other two . . . like Saad said, we've not heard from them for a long time. Until now. But we got Saad out."

"And I've never forgotten it, Mara," said Saad. He'd been staring at Lense but now swiveled his head around to his second. "Your bravery and your loyalty."

And maybe her love, too, Saad, though she'd never say it. "Then you need to listen to her now," said Lense. "Mara's right. You're too emotionally involved."

It was the wrong thing to say. Saad sat up a little straighter, and he withdrew his hands from Lense's—not quickly. But he took them back. "And you're not? You don't care about this Bashir?"

"Yes, of course, I care," she flared. "Don't twist this around to make it my fault. I'm not in command. You are, and you can't lead on emotion. You'll make mistakes."

"Listen to her, Saad," Mara said. "She's right. We were lucky once, but you go back and I feel it down deep, you'll never get out."

Saad's jaw firmed. "And what if you can't get *Bashir* out, Mara? Are you prepared to die for this man? Are you absolutely clear that if the time came, you could kill both Bashir and yourself?"

"Strangers are easy." Mara's face had gone as stony as Saad's, though her cheeks glistened. "My friends, the people I care about, they're hard."

Lense was incensed. "What are you two thinking? You're not going to kill anybody!"

"If we can't get him out, we'll have to," said Mara, flatly. "Otherwise, the Kornaks will still have him."

"Then we'd better be damn sure to get him out," said Lense. "Because you try that, you'll have to kill me, too." She drilled Saad with a look. "We clear on that?"

"You're not going, Elizabeth. I won't allow it."

"Try and stop me. You said I'm my own woman, so I get to choose, and I choose for Julian. You have to take me. Why should he trust you? He doesn't know you. Besides, he might be hurt, and I'm a doctor; I'm the only one who can help him. So, like it or not, you need me, and even if you didn't, I'm sure as hell not staying here. Because let me be crystal clear about this, Saad. I'm not doing this for *you*, either. I'm doing it for *Julian*, and I'm doing it for me because it's the right thing to do. I don't have any other choice." She paused. "He's my *friend*."

Saad looked from her to Mara and then back. "All right then, I guess you're coming. But I'm still going."

"And how are you going to be sure that *you* don't end up as a permanent guest again?" asked Mara.

"By sending them to hell," he said.

Neither woman asked what that meant. They had a pretty good idea.

CHAPTER
21

The rain had started six hours ago: a persistent drumming that was primordial and remorseless. Blate liked the way it lashed his windows, trying to break through, break *him*. Well, come, let it try.

He was strapping on his sidearm when his vidcom chimed. Annoyed, he looked at his screen, noting the time on a desk chronometer with his left eye while scanning the incoming call with his right: Kahayn. He punched his vidcom to life. "Yes, Doctor, what do—Doctor, what's happened?"

Her hair was disheveled; a blotchy purple and brown bruise spilled over her right cheek; her lower lip had swollen, and a dark chocolate rivulet of fresh blood oozed from her mouth. Her collar was torn open at the throat, and Blate saw a livid necklace of fresh bruises. *"Bashir,"* she said.

"Bashir did that?" A very interesting development. He was surprised by the prisoner's ferocity. Ah, but then, four days ago, Kahayn had taken it on herself to give this Bashir what she called a tour. One smashed window and a microscope damaged beyond repair later, she'd conceded defeat. "He attacked you," he said, without inflection. Inside, he was . . . cautious.

"About an hour ago. Stupid, I thought I could still persuade him to cooperate. Anyway, Bashir," she looked away, struggled for control, *"he broke free. Backhanded me across the face, then went for my throat. Screaming something about some woman. A lover, I presume, someone who jilted him. The guards pulled him off."*

"You're lucky he didn't kill you."

"We're just lucky the guards didn't do him any damage. But there's no question now."

"I'd say not. Only a guilty man struggles." Bashir's outburst was interesting, even puzzling. Why now? Because the ax was about to fall? Probably. He supposed even a spaceman could panic. He'd always regarded the fMRI as his trump card against Kahayn, anyway.

Because she'd never have been able to refuse, not in front of Nerrit, because then she'd lose control over the project. That would kill her. Because I know your mind, Colonel, and I have eyes, and they don't miss much.

Aloud, he said only, "So you wish to proceed with the operation instead?"

She gave a curt nod. *"When is General Nerrit due?"*

"Four, five hours, I believe."

"Give me three." Her lips peeled back in a smile. Her teeth were stained light mahogany with blood. *"You and General Nerrit can have ringside seats."*

"Very well, Colonel. But I want Arin there, too."

She seemed to hesitate. *"I don't need an assistant."*

"Arin has always assisted you in the past." Blate fingered up a slim radio from his desk and slipped it into his left trouser pocket. "I should think that past experience with Bashir would've sensitized you to just how . . . different he really is."

"Good point," she said. Her tone was neutral. *"I'll contact him."*

"No, no, I'll do that. Oh, and Colonel . . . do wipe your mouth. You're getting blood on your uniform."

*   *   *

Well. Arin tilted back in his chair, listening to the electric fizzle of his vidcom fade and the lashing of the rain. The wet made his knee ache. *This is a hell of a thing.*

If Kahayn had second thoughts or harbored hopes that Bashir might fail, they had evaporated. Worse, he'd gotten roped in as assistant. And it changed everything.

So how to make this work now? I won't be in place . . .

He debated for a moment, then pulled a bronze hinge affixed to the top drawer of his wooden desk—an antique with an ornately carved lip—and fished around until he found what he was looking for. The spectacles case was very plain and quite old. Some sort of extinct hardwood with a geometric inlay of diamond shapes lacquered purple. He thumbed open the lid. The specs were black-rimmed, a little square. He unfolded the eyepieces. They were quite delicate. He unhinged his steel-rimmed glasses from his ears, and then carefully slid on this second pair. His reflection, ghostly and surreal, stared back from his empty vidcom screen. He hadn't worn these glasses in a long time, more than a year. They made him look bookish. Even better, they didn't slide down his nose.

Then he reached into the drawer again. He found the tiny nub he was looking for. A slight pressure and a small, rectangular panel slid noiselessly from the space between the overhanging lip and drawer.

The radio was very slim and a brushed pewter color, about the size of a largish calling card. It folded, and now he unhinged it, stabbed up the power and then took a moment to decide exactly what he would say.

Everything had changed.

The room was at the end of a far corridor in the research wing. The corridor was always in shadow, the lights on motion sensors that clicked on and off, so that she trailed darkness behind. The room was secured with a magnetic lock that was always armed. It was a corridor she had not shown Bashir. Indeed, few people knew of it. Arin didn't. Neither did Blate, because as he'd pointed out, she commanded this hospital, not

him. So there were nurses, always the same ones and one to
a shift, three times a day. And there was her. She came every
day whether she needed to or not.

The only sounds in the room were the hiss of a ventilator,
the steady atonal blip-blip-blip of a cardiac monitor, and the
tiny chug of an IV pump pushing a yellow nutrient solution
through an indwelling catheter tunneled under the skin of the
patient's chest and into one of the large veins supplying the
heart so he wouldn't starve.

Kahayn sat on a tall stool alongside the bed. Her mouth still
hurt. Bashir had hit her very hard. She hadn't expected that.
But she understood why.

And now there was Arin to worry about, too. She'd still perform the surgery in this wing, of course—had to. She counted
on it. Because the OR was specially refitted, and the computer
didn't tie into the hospital's database. Everything would be
contained. So everything that happened would happen here
and too quickly for anyone to do anything about it. But Arin
was a problem because things had to stop, and Arin would not
understand.

This far. And no further.

Things would only stop if every piece was gone: the technology, her records, the primates. Maybe even her, if she couldn't
get away. She wasn't quite ready for death. Knew, though, that
maybe it wasn't so far distant after all.

And, of course, Julian would have to die. There was no
question. Even he saw that. Hadn't liked it. Who would? But
he saw the logic and knew it was the only way out. The only
recourse left.

*Because there can't be anything, absolutely nothing to work
with. Nothing left.*

She looked down at the bed. She'd managed to rebuild the
skull from where the bullet had blasted away bone and brain.
She'd even managed a nice scar. She stared at the seamless
face—because a man in a coma does not dream and cannot
think. He can only *be*, like an empty glass waiting for something to fill it. And the supreme irony: The machines, these
rudimentary tools with no innards of any interest, kept him
alive even as the machine hidden away in his brain would fill

and transform him from the inside out and only waited for the key—the donor—to turn the lock once more.

This far. She bent and kissed him—the man he'd been—gently, thoroughly, and for the very last time because the man he was would be gone as soon as she flipped the switch. His lips were warm. But she didn't cry. Couldn't. Her tears were all gone, and there was still so much to do.

And no further. Because along every journey through adversity and darkness, a little bit of the self dies. Ego. Dreams. Hope. And love. Sometimes it's right just to let go.

She flipped the switch and sat back to wait.

Bashir was freezing. His skin was prickly with gooseflesh, and he was shivering, like when he was little and came in from the cold. Only he didn't talk very much or very well when he was little and so it always came out: *I'm shibbering.* His parents didn't like it. But his aunt, the one on Earth who hugged him and told him his nose was cold as a brass button and his cheeks little bright apples, always laughed: *Come in now, Jules; no need for shibbering anymore because Auntie loves you. Come now, warm up by the fire and have some nice hot cocoa and biscuits.*

The hand he hit Kahayn with throbbed. Felt like a bomb going off in his hand, like all his bones shattered to dust. Still hurt.

His thoughts kept slewing right and left. Like trying to walk across an endless ice field with thin-soled slippers. His head was airy, too, like the inside of a big balloon, the kind with a thin string that Auntie tied around his wrist when he was very little so he didn't lose it. When he walked, the balloon bobbed up and down and kept tugging to get free.

The cold, maybe, or the sedative. His right hip stung from the needle. How much had they given him? Enough.

The operating theater was very bright. Lights all around. He saw red inside his lids. The smell was sterile and icy, like the edge of a blade stuck in snow. He wanted to get warm. Couldn't. Thin gown. Nothing underneath. Bare feet. The gown tied in back and his neck itched. Couldn't move either. Thick bands around his wrists and upper arms. Legs. Restraints because he'd hit Kahayn and mustn't get away.

Maybe he slept because then there was a buzzing, *brrring* sound. Not bees. Time to get up? Too early. Not time for duty yet. Wanted to sleep. Where was his pillow?

And then there were fingers on his temples, then a hand on his forehead, rolling him right. His head was very heavy. The hands had a sharp, chemical smell. Then, something itchy silting like grass around his ears. He tried to roll his head away, and he must've said something, too, or made a sound. Because the buzzing stopped and someone, a woman, said, "There, there. Just shaving your head. Doctor needs to see what she's doing."

"Buh . . ." His tongue wouldn't work. He tried opening his eyes, but his lids were very heavy, and the light was too bright, and he gave it up. "Coal . . . coal . . ."

"That's the cooling blanket." The buzzing started up again. Something pulling at his scalp, and the hands nudged his head left. "Doctor said she wanted your temperature down. Don't ask me why. She never uses the blanket for these things, but she says you're different and it's to protect you. Something about your system. But not to worry, you won't feel cold in a few more minutes. You just relax and take a nice, long nap."

"Buh . . . nooo," he moaned. But he was starting to drift again. The string knotting the balloon to his wrist was coming undone. "Coal . . ."

"There, there, not to worry," the someone said. "Doctor's good. She'll give you a nice, new scar."

And at that, the string came loose, and there was nothing more he could do.

So Bashir let go.

CHAPTER
22

At first, the rain came hesitantly in big, fat, gray drops, and then picked up speed. Now Lense stood, soaked through to the bone and cold for once, and the rain was still coming, its sound a loud, continuous hiss. The desert was gushing with sudden streams sluicing through gullies.

Saad's men worked fast. From beginning to end, the ambush took, perhaps, ninety seconds. She watched now as one of Saad's men hauled the seventh and last Kornak soldier from the transport, splayed the body out and started stripping off protective, sand-colored armor.

Another soldier stomped up, rifle in hand, the hump of a radio at his left shoulder and now she saw that the mystery of just how anonymous Saad expected they could be was solved. Besides the armor, the soldier wore dark protective eyewear and a helmet with a low brow that flared around his ears. Thick ropes of sodden hair straggled over his shoulders, and water cascaded over the helmet.

"You'll have to put your hair up." She practically had to shout to hear herself over the rain. "Why the glasses? How can you see?"

"Polarized. I see fine," said Saad. "They wear their glasses all the time, though. A good sniper can take out an eye, of course, but the glasses stop shrapnel."

"Seven soldiers. Seven uniforms. But I make eight."

"Change of plans," he shouted over the rain as Mara splashed over, though Lense could only tell it *was* her because of the jaw. "Sorry. There's no other way."

Lense thought something was up. When they'd been crouched atop a flat mesa before the rain, Mara slithered over, a communications device in her hand. She'd whispered into Saad's ear, and Lense watched the color drain from Saad's face and his expression darken. When she asked what was wrong, Saad only shook his head. Then he and Mara moved back in a low crouch from the rim. She couldn't hear what they said, but they were arguing.

Now she said, "But what am I supposed to do?"

At that, Mara palmed her rifle in her right hand and nudged Lense with the barrel. "Exactly what you're told."

First, she went to check on Julian. It was the second time she'd been to the OR that day, but the first that she'd seen Julian since that morning. Julian was asleep atop green surgical sheets; another was draped over his body, and she saw by his bare shoulders that they'd removed his gown. There was a face mask over his nose and mouth to give him more oxygen, one of the things she wanted to make sure the anesthetist hadn't forgotten. Very important.

They were just putting up the drapes to cover his torso and leave his head free. They'd prep his head with antiseptic soap while she scrubbed. When she returned, she'd have them position the remaining drapes in a tent over Julian's face, leaving only the crown of his head exposed. Then she'd make her incision marks with a purple felt-tipped pen and then, well, she'd go to work.

She was sorry Julian was asleep. She didn't want him to feel pain and he must've been worried, maybe frightened when she wasn't there. But maybe it was better this way. He looked very strange without hair, and his scalp was much paler than his normal complexion. For some obscure reason, she cinched up the sheet to cover him just a little more. She didn't know why. But he looked defenseless. Vulnerable.

Everything depends on me now. I'll be as fast as I can, Julian, but I have to be careful, or this has all been for nothing.

The room was chilly. Her primary surgical nurse for this wing, not the hard-ass major, was laying out instruments. The anesthetist was there, checking over his syringes. He complained about the cooling blanket because it made the anesthesia trickier. But she was firm, and he gave up because, she figured, he knew it wasn't his ass on the line.

As she turned to go, her gaze fixed on a glass-enclosed viewing room high on the near wall just behind Julian's head and opposite the door that led from pre-op. There were four chairs in the viewing room, a vidcom on the wall for communications through this wing, and that was all. The room was dim and would stay that way. Like a performer on stage, Kahayn didn't really want to see Blate and Nerrit, not too clearly. But *they* would have an excellent view. Maybe that's why they called it a surgical theater.

In the adjacent scrub room, Arin was already lathering at a large, rectangular, metal basin. They wore identical garb: blue surgical scrubs, blue gauze cap and booties and a surgical mask that hung around their necks, the bottom ties already knotted. Arin's gaze bounced on her and then away. "Filthy weather," he said. He palmed a stiff-bristled brush and scoured his nails with a thick, rust-red antiseptic soap he'd dispensed with a foot pedal. "Surprised Nerrit made it at all."

"Mmmm." Kahayn operated the foot pedal, squirting soap from a dispenser onto her palms and working the scrub into foam. "Nerrit wouldn't miss this." The rules said five minutes for each hand and arm, a minute to every finger, and Kahayn followed this procedure scrupulously. They scrubbed, not talking, the only sound the fits and starts of water splashing against metal and the rasp of bristle brushes. Then Kahayn said, "Sorry you got dragged into this."

Arin hunched his shoulders, let them fall. "Luck of the draw, I guess," he said, passing his now-sterilized hands and arms through a steady stream of hot, gray, filtered water. He shook water from his hands, then crooked his elbows, holding his still-dripping hands and arms up and away from his body, palms turned in. Water dripped from his elbows. "Nothing to be done about it."

"Mmmm," Kahayn said again. "Promise me one thing. No matter what happens, Arin, do exactly what I tell you. Nothing more, nothing less. You understand?"

His eyes narrowed imperceptibly, and she saw the questions there. "All right." He hesitated. "Idit, if you—"

"Don't say any more, Arin. Don't ask questions. Just do what I say, and everything will be fine." She butted open the door. "By the way . . . nice glasses."

"Thanks," said Arin.

The two guards, a PFC and corporal on duty at the entrance into the research wing, didn't like it. More to the point, the corporal hadn't heard anything about it. He eyed the phalanx of dripping wet soldiers, seven in all. "I haven't heard anything about any prisoner."

"Not my problem." The master sergeant, a strapping hulk of a man and obviously SC by the insignia, looked dour enough to eat bullets. "Think we've got nothing better to do than cover your collective asses? You people weren't so sloppy, you'd've picked her up yourself. But now we got her, and we get the credit. General Nerrit's going to want to see this one."

The corporal ran his eyes up and down the prisoner. She was small with a head of limp wet curls plastered to her scalp and clothes that clung in interesting places. Not half bad. But she was also very pale, and what was with those pink lips? She looked scared to death. And cold.

He looked at the PFC. The PFC simply shrugged. "Just a minute," the corporal said, and turned to a vidcom set to the left of the containment door just above a magnetic lock. "I got to check this out with Security Director Blate."

"You do that," said the sergeant. He grinned. "For a prize like this? We got time."

*   *   *

"Describe her again?" Blate listened carefully as the corporal talked. "Just a moment." He muted the audio and turned to Nerrit seated to his right in the surgical theater. "One of your men seems to have apprehended another one of those," he nodded in the general direction of the operating theater where Kahayn was gloving up, "like Bashir there." He described the prisoner, then added, "She was caught outside the complex by your rear guard."

"Yes?" Nerrit was rail-thin and very severe with a hatchet face. His eyes were silver today instead of green. His whisper-thin lips disappeared in a half-moon of a smile. "Do they know how she got here?"

"No. Your sergeant wants to secure her down here." Blate made a face, shrugged. "We could interrogate her together after Kahayn's done."

"Excellent idea."

"Good," said Blate, turning back to the vidcom. "I'll have one of the guards escort her to a holding room."

He'd gowned and just finished gloving when Arin saw the vidcom in the viewing room come to life as a pale blue, electric glow. His eyes flicked to a clock on the right wall and noted the time. Then he stood, patiently, as the nurse reached around and fitted his mask over his nose, pinched it down, and then knotted the upper ties firmly at his crown. He saw Nerrit and Blate lean together, and then Blate turned to the monitor. He couldn't hear what Blate said because of the glass, but it didn't matter.

Kahayn, he saw, was directing the nurses where to place the surgical drapes around the field. "Do me a favor," he said to the nurse. "My glasses need adjusting again, damn things. Would you just give them a good jab, right on the bridge there . . . a little harder, don't be shy . . . that's got it. Thank you," he said, straightening. He wrinkled his nose. "That's so much better."

He heard a sudden gasp and then an exclamation. Startled, he turned just in time to see Kahayn falling in a faint, taking a tray of instruments crashing to the floor with her.

"All right," said the corporal, stepping back from a vidcom. "We'll take it from here."

One of the soldiers, a woman just behind the sergeant, glanced down at something on her wrist, then edged a bit closer to the sergeant. Murmured something. The sergeant half-turned and looked back at the corporal, displeased. "No can do."

"Yeah, well," said the corporal, turning away and tapping out the code that would unlock the door, "those are *my* orders."

"But we have ours." A shuffle of boots over concrete. "They take precedence."

"Give it a rest." The corporal ticked in the last number and just as the door sighed to one side, he heard the PFC say, "Hey, he . . . !" Then, just gurgling, choking noises.

The corporal spun around. He had time to see the PFC's knees buckle and twin arcs of brown blood. But that was all.

In the next instant, the big sergeant had him in an embrace. He tried pulling back but couldn't, and then he felt pain stab the center of his chest, just below the notch of his ribs. His eyes bulged, and he opened his mouth to scream but the sergeant clapped a hand over his mouth.

"Shh, shh, it's all right," and then the sergeant pulled him even closer into a bear hug. "It's all right; shh, now."

That was the last thing the corporal ever heard.

CHAPTER
23

He'd pushed her to one side and now Lense watched Saad step in closer, angling the point of his knife up and jamming its length the rest of the way into the guard's heart. And then the guard just died.

The thing was, Lense wasn't as upset as she thought she'd be. She'd seen a lot of gore the past two months. She watched Saad lower the body to the floor. Mara was wiping her knife clean on her trousers, but her soldier wasn't dead. He gurgled and his fingers scrabbled at the concrete with a sound like mice.

She found her voice. "For God's sake, bad enough you slit his throat. Don't make him suffer."

"Yeah?" Mara gave Lense a hard look, sheathed her knife, and then hunched behind the dying man. Reaching around, she hooked the man's jaw in one hand, palmed the side of his head with her left and then twisted his head right and jerked down. There were crackles, and the mouse noise stopped. "There you go. Happy?"

Lense said nothing.

"The important thing is the door's open and not a shot fired," said Saad. "How's the signal?"

Mara glanced down at her wrist, then back at Saad. "Still there. Damn lucky Arin still had the transponder."

"All right," Saad said again, then took Lense by her right arm. "We'll get Bashir. Mara, you stay here, head off any reinforcements if they get out an alarm. We don't have enough men to secure both this and the footpath. So this is our way out."

"You're not going in there without me."

"I need you here."

"You need me to watch your ass." A jerk of her head at Lense. "She won't be able to."

"Mara's right," said Lense. "I can't tend to Julian and cover you at the same time."

Saad glowered, then gave a curt nod. "One more thing," he said to the remaining men, "if soldiers come and we're not back, you've got to seal this door. Smash the mechanism if you have to, but if you don't hear from us," he tapped the radio at his shoulder, "then nobody else goes in. You need to buy us time to destroy as much as we can."

"I thought you said this wing was self-contained," said Lense.

Saad had taken off the black eyeglasses and his expression was set. "I don't put anything past Blate. He'd be prepared for any contingency even if all he needed to do was take a leak. I swear the man's got eyes in the back of his head."

"No," said Mara, "just on either side."

"Doctor?" Blate had toggled open an intercom. *"Are you all right?"*

"I'm fine," said Kahayn. Arin saw she was embarrassed; her neck was hectic with color. "Just got dizzy. That run-in with Bashir."

"But you'll be able to continue?"

"Of course." She sighed, tugged down her mask. "But I'll have to break scrub; I ripped my glove. Sorry."

It took Arin a minute to let that sink in. If Kahayn broke scrub, that gave Saad more time. It was like some kind of gift.

Kahayn was talking to the anesthetist now, a puckered-looking fellow who didn't look happy. Arin understood the feeling. Lower Bashir's body temperature with a cooling blanket, then throw in anesthesia that would inhibit automatic responses to cold, like shivering, and there'd be hell to pay if things got out of hand. Resuscitating Bashir once was quite enough, thanks. Plus, it would take time to warm him back up.

Come to think of it, getting him alert enough to move will be almost impossible now. . . .

But there was no more time to think about that because Kahayn was breaking scrub and the circulating nurse had scurried off to retrieve another anesthesia tray. "I'll be right back," Kahayn said.

"Take your time," said Arin. His eyes slid to the clock and back. "We sure as hell aren't going anywhere."

Yet.

"How much longer?" Lense whispered. The corridors here seemed endless, and she was thoroughly lost. Worse, Saad had told her why the signal from Arin was coming from an operating room.

And what if they've started? What if they've already made their incisions, made burr holes and taken out bone?

She felt sick just thinking about it. Because it occurred to her that she might not be able to reverse what Kahayn had done quickly enough to get them out.

She was so busy thinking about all kinds of disasters that when Saad pulled up abruptly and ducked left into an adjacent corridor, she tripped over his legs. She would've gone sprawling if he hadn't snagged her arm and reeled her in against him. Mara crowded in a second later.

"We're there," he whispered, then lifted his chin and jerked his head right. "Through that door at the end of the hall. Leads into a central bay for pre-op where they put in the IVs, give the pre-op sedative. The way into the operating room is to the left, through a set of double doors. Very small, just one room. No magnetic lock; they're automatic, touch-plate activated."

"No way to spring a surprise there," Mara said. "Doors will open too slowly. And that still won't take care of Blate and Nerrit."

"Right. So here's how we're going to play it."

"Better now?" asked Arin.

"Much. Thanks." Kahayn turned to the anesthetist. "How's he doing?"

"Pulse and blood pressure are good. A little cardiac irritability. That's the cooling blanket."

"Anything to worry about?"

"No."

"Then push in the contrast dye, will you? I'm going to bring up the iMRI."

"What's happening now?" asked Nerrit. He was leaning forward, his eyes slitted with intense interest.

"Dr. Kahayn's asked for a contrast dye in conjunction with the intraoperative MRI . . . that device there, you see it? She's operating it via a foot pedal, bringing those two large discs up at the head of the table, one to either side of Bashir's head."

"And those are?"

"Magnets. It's a compact MRI, relies on a magnetic field. She explained it once, compared the brain to watery gelatin and said that during procedures, the brain shifts and sloshes, so she likes to be sure she's in the right place. I've only seen her do this when there's some sort of tumor, but this man Bashir is quite unique as you know. She may merely wish to highlight those regions of his brain that are so different from ours."

Nerrit gave him a narrow look. "You're saying the MRI isn't usual?"

"Oh," said Blate, and he told his first lie of the afternoon. "No. Not at all."

*   *   *

Dye and iMRI. What the hell was Kahayn doing?

It had been on the tip of Arin's tongue to say something when she'd asked for the dye. The dye made no sense. They already knew what Bashir's brain looked like, and it wasn't as if they were getting ready to excise a tumor.

But then he remembered: *Do nothing. Say nothing. No matter what happens.* And had he imagined it, or had Kahayn shot him a brief glance just before? He couldn't remember.

Hurry, Saad, hurry. Arin's mouth was so dry, he couldn't swallow.

"Looking good," said Kahayn.

"Yeah," Arin managed. "Great."

"All right." Kahayn depressed the foot pedal once more and the iMRI discs scrolled down with a mechanical whine. Standing at the head of the table, she held out her right hand, and the surgical nurse slapped a scalpel into Kahayn's palm.

Arin went cold. *Too late . . .*

"Hold on!" It was the anesthetist, and when Arin looked over, the man's color was just the near side of ash. "We've got a problem!"

Kahayn turned sharply. "What kind?"

But Arin could hear it: the beeps of Bashir's cardiac monitor, accelerating, going wild. *Oh, dear God . . .*

"Cardiac instability," the anesthetist said. "All of a sudden, I don't understand. I was getting bursts of tachycardia, but now his heart's slowing down, pressure's falling. Looks like heart block, and now there's a PVC . . . there's another! I'm picking up fibrillations . . . !" The anesthetist was standing now, fumbling at his syringes, swearing. "He's crashing; he's gonna crash!"

But Kahayn was already moving in a blur, tearing down the surgical drapes, shouting orders: "Break out the crash cart! Get these drapes off him now, go, go, *go!* I want an amp of dompenephrine, IV push *now!* Start cardiac compressions!"

Cursing, Arin ripped green drape from Bashir's chest and started pumping with all his might. It was all going to hell; it was going to hell! He should have seen this coming; he should've stopped her!

Do nothing, do nothing? His brain was raging. *So you could kill him?* "Idit, what about the cooling blanket?"

But Kahayn didn't answer. The anesthetist was already jabbing a needle into Bashir's IV port, depressing the plunger, sending a drug coursing into Bashir's veins. An instant later: "I don't get it; it's having no effect at all. Worse, it's like the opposite of what . . . Dr. Kahayn, his pressure's *gone!* We're flatline!"

"What? How can that *be?*" Kahayn had torn her mask off, and her eyes were wild. "Are you sure you gave him the right drug?"

"Idit!" Arin shouted. "The *blanket!*"

She rounded on him with a snarl. "Quiet, Arin. Do exactly what I say and not a scrap more, do you understand me?" She whirled back to the anesthetist. "What about my dompenephrine?"

"I'm positive! I labeled these syringes myself!"

"Give him another one!"

"But it only had the opposite . . . !"

"*Damn* you!" Kahayn snatched the syringe from the anesthetist and pushed in the drug herself. "*Do* what I say!"

Opposite. Arin was so stunned, he nearly stopped in midcompression. *The tray, she knocked over the tray . . .* "Idit?"

"Not now, Arin! Don't you stop those compressions, you hear me? Do exactly what you're doing, you understand? Do *exactly* what I say!"

Blate and Nerrit were on their feet. Blate banged open the intercom. "Colonel Kahayn, don't you lose this man, don't you lose him, or I'll . . . !"

A tremendous crash, and then Blate was staggering back against Nerrit as the door into the viewing booth slapped open. A burst of gunfire roared into the air above his head: the distinctive staccato snap-crack of large-caliber rifle fire. Blate ducked as bullets tore a seam into the ceiling. Chunks of tile and plaster rained down on his back and pinged off his arms as he curled up, trying to protect his head. He heard the rifle fire sweep counterclockwise and then hit the glass with a hollow bap-bap-bap! He rolled away from the front of the booth just as there was a solid smack of a boot against the glass and then a thunderous smash as the glass gave way in a jagged shower. The air stank of burnt cordite and hot metal.

"Nobody move!" A woman's voice. Blate looked up to see a giant of a woman: blond, with a scar arcing across a disfigured left jaw and no nose.

I know her; I know her!

Another bang of doors bursting wide open, and Blate jerked his gaze down to the operating room. Two people barreled through the doors leading to the recovery room: a slim, small woman with dark curls—*her skin, so pale, like Bashir*—and a broad, muscular man with a shock of long brown hair whom he recognized instantly.

"Kahayn!" Saad screamed. He leveled his rifle. "I'm here to send you to *hell!*"

"No, Saad, no!" The small woman, by Saad's side and then, my God, yes, Arin, too.

"Saad, *no!*" Arin screamed, lunging for Kahayn who stood to his left, by his side. Kahayn was shocked to immobility, the defibrillator paddles still in her hands. "Saad, you don't understand! Don't shoot her, don't *shoot!*"

But Saad fired.

CHAPTER
24

The rifle was set to three-round bursts, and when Saad pulled the trigger, the bullets screamed from the barrel. The distance was so scant that Lense heard the crack at the precise instant the bullets hit.

The first hit the woman with the defibrillator paddles. A rose of brown blood blossomed on her surgical gown, and she went down without a sound.

The second hit the man with black spectacles who was screaming at Saad to stop—*Arin, that's got to be Arin*—because he'd lunged for the woman to push her aside. Lense saw blood spray erupt from the hump of Arin's shoulder, and then he crashed to the floor.

The third hit no one because everyone had hit the deck, and smashed into the opposite wall.

"No, Saad, stop!" she cried. "What are . . . ?" But then she saw Julian. She sprinted for the table; her gaze jittered over his body: the endotracheal tube, the IV tubes, and his scalp with purple lines to mark incisions, they'd shaved his head. . . .

She spun around and snagged what must be the anesthetist by the collar. "You, what's going on?"

"He's in arrest." The anesthetist was a pruned, wizened man, and when he spoke, his lips quivered. "Looked like heart block, followed by v-fib; Kahayn was just going to defibrillate!"

"No!" A man's voice, hitching with pain. Arin, on the floor, on the opposite side of the table and struggling to his knees. He was panting, and his face was gray. "She put something in the dye and she switched out the drugs!"

"What?" cried the anesthetist.

"What?" Saad said.

"On purpose, she did it on purpose! She knocked over the tray; she must've rigged the other tray, mislabeled the syringes. That's why she put him on the cooling blanket, to protect his brain when she stopped his heart!"

"Oh, no," said Saad. His voice was stricken. "What have I . . . ?"

Of course. Lense's mind raced. *Bring his metabolic rate down; the brain will shut down, but it won't die; like cold water drowning, he can still be revived even after hours; that must've been what she planned. . . .*

"I'm a doctor, but you have to help me," she said to Arin. She threw a frantic, helpless look at all the drugs and machines. "I'm out of my element here; what do I do?"

"Keep calm." Arin's face was twisted with pain as he clambered to his feet and blood sheeted over his fingers from his shoulder. "Just do exactly what I say."

The big woman had made her first mistake: not searching him. Nothing Blate could do to capitalize on that yet. Maybe, though, soon. For now Blate watched, his fury growing with every passing moment: as Arin, that traitor, led the woman—*like Bashir, exactly like him*—through each step. Switching off the cooling blanket, setting it to warm Bashir's body as she administered drugs and then sent electric bolts charging through Bashir's body. Saad roughed the anesthetist back to his feet to monitor Bashir, keep the ventilator going. Five minutes, ten, and then fifteen . . .

And they brought Bashir back to life, an inch at a time.

First the hesitant, irregular blips from the cardiac monitor and then the blips steadied, picked up speed. He heard the anesthetist sing out a blood pressure, and he saw the woman, the one like Bashir, and her wet cheeks and knew she wept with relief.

But Blate had eyes, and so he saw many things at once: not just Bashir but off to his left, the blond woman; out of his right, Nerrit, who'd edged closer.

"How soon can you move Bashir?" The blond woman. She moved closer to the blown-out window. "Saad, we've got to get out of here and—"

She was interrupted by a shout. "My God!" It was Arin, and Blate's right eye saw Arin crouched over Kahayn. "She's still *alive!*"

Saad and the woman with the curls, simultaneously: "What?"

"What?" said the blonde and, out of his left eye, Blate saw her start forward.

That's when the big woman made her second and last mistake. Because he moved into her blind spot. And he had eyes.

Saad watched Lense revive Bashir, and he held his ground, his rifle up, covering the others. But he felt numb. Kahayn had tried to *save* Bashir. . . .

Because she couldn't think of another way, and she didn't tell Arin, or else he'd have let us know. She must've thought I'd never believe her, not after Janel . . .

So when Arin called out that Kahayn lived, his heart squeezed with a sudden spasm of hope. Yes, maybe there was some atonement for this wretched business, some way of letting Kahayn know that her efforts hadn't been in vain, and if they could get out Arin, and Kahayn, *too* . . .

He glanced up when Mara shouted, and then he saw Blate whip around, a pistol in his right hand.

"Mara!" He swung his rifle, trying to catch Blate before he could fire. "Mara, look *out!*"

The viewing booth boomed with a roar like thunder.

 *   *   *

Blate saw Saad out of his right eye. Saw the big man pivot, that rifle come up. Saad's bullets were faster. But Blate had a head start, and he was closer. He lunged for the big woman and pulled the trigger two seconds before Saad fired. His pistol jerked, and there was a spurt of yellow-orange muzzle flash. The bullet bored into the woman's right eye and kept going. Her head exploded in a cloud of fine brown mist and brain and bone.

But Blate was already down, rolling for the door. Something hummed over his head and then there were three sodden *whops* as the bullets slammed into Nerrit.

Blate didn't stop. He banged out of the booth, his left hand already dragging out his radio to raise the alarm.

Lense saw Mara's head blow apart, and then a figure barreled out of the viewing booth. "Saad! He's getting away!"

"You can't catch him!" Arin's teeth were clenched, biting back pain. "Too far from here to the hall! Saad, you've got to clear out, you've got to *go!*"

Saad swayed, turned. He swiped his streaming eyes. "Elizabeth," he said hoarsely, "can you move Bashir?"

She shook her head. Julian was breathing on his own now but still unconscious. "You'd have to carry him. I could cover you, but I don't know . . ."

"No." Saad was in control again. He flicked his rifle at the nurses and anesthetist, who were still cowering. "You, get out." When they didn't move, he said, "I don't ask twice." Then, as they scurried out, Saad turned to Arin. "You, too."

"I'm staying." Arin started wrapping his shoulder. "I die now; I die later. It's all the same to Blate. And Kahayn's still alive. I can't leave her."

"We're not dead yet," said Saad. He shouldered his rifle. "Elizabeth, help me move Bashir to the floor . . . easy now," he said, as they slid Bashir off and eased him down.

It was only then that Lense realized Bashir was totally

naked beneath the sheets. He was starting to shiver now as his body fought off the hypothermia. She swaddled him in sheets and drapes. Then she clutched his chilled hands in hers and put her mouth to his ear. "I'm here, Julian; it's Elizabeth. Don't worry; it's going to be all right." She clamped down on tears. "I'm going to get you out of here." She didn't know if he heard. She didn't know if it were even true.

Saad jerked a metal gurney onto its side, swinging it around between them and the door that led to pre-op. Then he kicked the brakes on the operating room table and clattered it to the operating room doors. Bending at the knees, he wrapped his arms around the single, off-center pedestal, wedged his right shoulder under the table and heaved. The table was blocky and very heavy, but it toppled with a loud, metallic bang. Saad braced it against the door, then scuttled back and began over-turning instrument trays and maneuvering the ventilator to make a barrier.

"I can hold them off for a bit," he said. "Elizabeth, can you help Kahayn?"

Lense bent over the woman. Kahayn was on her back. Her neck veins bulged. Lense ripped open Kahayn's gown, using the surgical scissors again to split the gown in front and then slit her scrubs in two. The wound was centered directly over the lower part of her thick, armorlike sternum: a round ugly hole punched into her flesh. But there was no exit wound.

Suddenly, there was a squall of static and then a frantic voice coming over the radio on Saad's left shoulder. The sound was so loud and so unexpected that Lense's heart nearly jumped out of her mouth. Saad listened, then shouted, "Say again?"

"Soldiers!" A voice scratchy with static. Cracks of gunfire. "There are too many, we can't hold them off, we can't—"

"Doren!" Saad keyed his radio again. Got nothing but static. "Doren, do you read me?" More static.

Lense went cold. *Soldiers on the way. They'll kill Arin but not Saad. They need Saad, and they'll probably keep Bashir and me alive so they can—*

"Pericardial tamponade," said Arin.

"What?" Lense looked at Arin. "What did you say?"

"Her neck veins, the entry wound. She's got pericardial

tamponade; must've hit the heart!" Still clutching his wrapped shoulder, he shuffled closer on his knees. "If you can decompress the pericardial sac, maybe we can fish out the bullet and repair the tear."

"Here? *Now?*"

"There's no time," said Saad.

"I haven't got anything better to do," said Arin. He looked at Lense. "Bashir is stable. Please."

She took a deep breath, nodded. She helped Arin struggle into a right glove, and then snapped on a pair of her own.

"Go for a subxiphoid approach," said Arin. "Just make a window with a scalpel."

"This won't even be close to sterile." Lense felt for the notch at the junction of Kahayn's ribs and drew a scalpel in short vertical. Blood welled up and Arin sponged it away with his good hand. She cut again, and this time she was through skin and into skeletal muscle.

"Easy," said Arin.

She cut again. There was the staccato sputter of gunfire not far now, just down the corridor from the operating room.

"*Hurry.*" Saad, by her side, his body angled, trying to shield her.

"Do what it takes," said Arin. "Don't hurry. We're not going anywhere."

"There's no time!" Saad scuttled closer. "I want you out of here, Elizabeth! Leave Bashir. You and Arin just get out."

"And go where?" asked Lense. She didn't look up. She was through muscle now. Under the smashed xiphoid, she saw the pulse of the bluish-brown pericardial sac, streaked with fat. The sac ballooned with blood being forced out with every beat. She rooted in a clutch of instruments. "I can't stop now, and I won't leave Julian. So we just take our chances."

"Elizabeth." She heard the anguish in his voice. "Don't you understand? I can't let them take you, or Bashir. Or me."

"I know that. So, don't shoot me until I'm done." And now she did look at him. "Deal?"

He looked at her for a long moment, then kissed her hard. "I love you." His voice was ragged. "Hold that in your heart, Elizabeth, and remember."

The pock-pock of sniper fire was so close it made her jump. So she said everything she could with her eyes before turning back to her work—because there was more to do and very little time left.

She fished out a slim pair of surgical scissors. "When I cut through, there's bound to be a clot and a lot of blood, Arin. Better hope it's through and through so I can close. You've got to plug the hole, then tell me which suture to use."

"Don't worry about me," said Arin. "I'm ready."

Hollow thuds, then bangs against the door. Muffled curses and then a grate of metal as whoever was on the other side tried, unsuccessfully, to push open the door.

"They'll come around to the scrub room, or blow that door," said Saad. "You're almost out of time, Elizabeth."

One chance. Lense made first one, then two, then three cuts. A dark brown clot spilled out along with fresh blood, and then Arin had his thumb over the tear in Kahayn's still-beating heart.

"That's got it there." Arin squirmed his index finger around back, searching for another tear. "Got it. Bullet can't be in the heart. Okay, you need suture for—"

But that was the last thing Arin said that Lense ever heard.

Because then, suddenly, she felt a tingling along her skin, one that raised the hackles on her neck. She gasped but knew this was no dream.

The combadge in my pocket; the transporter; they found us; only seconds left!

"No!" she screamed as the air broke apart. Kahayn's blood was warm, but *her* hand was cold because, in another instant, Lense knew she wouldn't be there at all. "No, please, let me *finish!*"

"Elizabeth!" Saad, spinning around, stopping dead, the glow of the transporter reflecting off his skin, turning it white as bone. *"Elizabeth!"*

She saw them all in that last crystalline second and knew she'd never reach or save them all: not Julian *and* Saad *and* Arin. And even Kahayn.

One chance. One choice.

She took it.

EPILOGUE

Well, at least the stars were right again. But so many questions with no answers. A sense of things left undone.

Ship's night now. She prowled the corridors of the *da Vinci*. She was listless, no appetite. She slid into inky shadows splashed in the well of a bulkhead and let the sturdy metal brace her up.

Gomez and her people had rescued them, doping out some kind of alien device that had access to other universes. She didn't understand half of it—and from the sounds of it, neither did anyone else, though Tev seemed to think *he* did—and when they got through and detected gunfire and Bashir's vitals in such poor shape, they beamed them out quickly. Standard procedure.

She hadn't wanted company. After Gold debriefed her, no one pressed. She gathered a lot had happened—phrases like Empok Nor, Rec Station Hidalgo, Artemis IX, Avril Station, and more flew by her ears.

Oddly, it had only been two weeks since they left Deep Space 9, despite how much time they'd spent on that planet. She didn't care. She stayed in sickbay or her quarters, alone. Falcão and Wetzel let her be in the former, and Corsi's shifts kept her out of the cabin for the latter. Often, she asked the replicator for a glass of ice water and then ordered lights out. Then she'd sit in the dark and smell the wet and try conjuring visions of green forests. But imagination failed, and the water tasted sterile.

And then there was Julian. The whole time the *da Vinci* was on its way to rendezvous with the *Defiant* to drop him off, she hadn't been able to face him. All the awful, hurtful, cutting things she'd said and wished she could take back. Once spoken, forever done: That's what they said.

The night before they were to meet the *Defiant*, Bashir came to see her in sickbay. "Julian." Her voice was barely able to say his name.

He came closer. She noticed that his scar was still there, a seam centered on his forehead. For some reason, the EMH never removed it when treating him. "I . . . I wanted to see how you were doing."

"I'm fine," she lied. She forced herself not to look away. "On the runabout, I—"

"It's all right."

"No, I have to say this. Apologizing doesn't feel like enough, but it's all I've got. I was wrong, Julian. Wrong to hold you responsible, wrong to hate you. Just . . . wrong."

"Selden was a bad situation."

"But the Seldens of the universe are to blame, not you. You were right, too. All the people we've lost on the *da Vinci* this year, and on the *Lexington* during the war. A patient I cared about that I couldn't cure. I got mad. Probably my way of not getting depressed. But anger doesn't change anything, and I can get pretty hard to take."

"Yes," he said. "Several hours in a runabout and I was ready to transport you to deep space. Except I'm insufferably polite. But I fail at many things, and I hurt," he said, and bunched his fist over his left breast. "Right here."

She felt like crying. "Do you think she made it?"

"Kahayn? I don't know. I'd like to think so. She wasn't evil, just desperate, and I think there was much more to her story than I'll ever know. She was very sad, a little haunted. I think she struggled to make things right."

"In the end, she chose for you. She might still be alive." *If Saad didn't kill them all, and himself.*

"Perhaps. If she isn't, someone else will pick up her work. The Kornaks are willing to sacrifice a lot to survive. Loss of soul. Loss of self."

"Just like the Borg." The words were out of her mouth before she knew it. "Do you think—?"

He shrugged. "Don't know. This alien device may have slipped us sideways into a parallel timeline. Into the past, the future, or maybe the same moment somewhere else . . . Who knows? For that matter, maybe we got a good look at a past that's happened in *this* timeline on a planet we've never known. Before they *were* the Borg, the Borg were something else. There's got to be a Borg homeworld somewhere. We just haven't found it yet."

"Or maybe we did."

"Maybe." He was silent. "I'm sorry for your loss."

"Saad." Saying his name hurt. Her eyes burned. "I hope he died. I don't want to think of him, hooked up . . ." She cleared her throat. "I just hope he died."

She was surprised when Julian reached out and thumbed away her tears. But she didn't pull away, and he didn't either. "It hurts."

She nodded then bunched a fist over her heart. Mouthed the words because she couldn't speak: *Right here.* Then she released a breath, closed her eyes. This was okay. She cupped his hand with both of hers. Yes, this was all right.

They stood like that for a long time. Then Julian said, "You know, I wonder who won the Bentman. My God, it seems ages, centuries ago that we were boxing around that. I can't imagine either of us won—and something extraordinary: I don't care."

She realized suddenly that she didn't either. "I think the rules say you have to be present to win."

"Well, then we bollixed that up. I don't think the judges'll countenance alien widgets and time-space anomalies. Can you see us explaining? Uh, yes, well, we got sucked into this anomaly and then our runabout disintegrated and then we thought we were both *dead* . . . well, that is, each of us thought the *other'd* kicked it, only we were mistaken and then . . ."

She had to laugh. "God, stop. That's so sick."

"I know; that's the beauty of it. You know something? I want to save this for next time I need an excuse. Do you know that time-space distortions could be blamed for, oh, scads? Like doing your homework, you go to your professor, all hail-fellow-well-met." He dropped his voice an octave and frowned. "Sorry, old boy, can't turn that in. Got sideswiped by a time-space continuum thing, bugger it all. Bloody inconvenience; so sorry, but you understand, don't you, old chap? There's a good fellow."

They laughed until her sides hurt. She knew the joke wasn't *that* funny, but laughter was medicine, too. They finally trailed off; they held hands and looked at each other. It was comfortable. That was all it had to be.

"Your scar," she said, suddenly, "are you going to keep it?"

"What?" Frowning, he fingered the ridge of flesh. "Do you know I forgot it until just now? Like it's a part of me somehow."

She traced his scar with the tip of a forefinger. "I can take that off. I've had practice," and then at his expression, she laughed. "God, no, not with a scalpel."

"Well, thank heaven." He captured her fingers, folded them over his own. "Who could refuse such an offer from a woman . . . I'm sorry, a *colleague?* And let me return the favor. You don't look well, Elizabeth."

She shrugged it off. "Just tired."

"Mmmm. Mind a more professional, unbiased opinion? Or are you one of those doctors who make horrible patients?"

"Which do you think?"

"Mmmm. Right. A positive horror." He tucked her hand into the crook of his elbow. "Shall we?"

"Lead on, Macduff."

"*Ouch.* Didn't Macbeth kill him? Lop off his head or something?"

"Relax, Julian. I'm just getting rid of your scar. Anyway, it's Macduff who kills Macbeth. But the witches were still there at the end. So, the evil wasn't gone. Macduff just couldn't see it, was all."

"Well, then, it seems that things didn't end for the best after all, did they? At least, not for Macduff."

*   *   *

Security Director Blate stood, goggle-eyes whirring as his gaze ticked down the length of scarred metal. The metal was hollowed out and spanned the height of a full-grown man and had a core of honeycombed material he couldn't fathom. The metal was scorched with soot that was sticky, a little oily. Like Bashir's suit . . . He looked back at the soldier. "Is this all?"

"No." The soldier shook his head with the audible click and whirr of a gyro. "There's wreckage strewn over a wide area. Mostly pieces like this, and one big chunk. Some sort of control mechanism."

"Very well, I want a team out there. Bring it all back, and I want it secreted here, in this wing. You are dismissed."

Well, well. Blate walked a corridor of the research wing. The slap of his boots cracked like pistol shots. He entered a room that was the only one occupied for the moment—but only for the moment. *All is not lost, and more gained than I supposed. Pity about Janel, though. I underestimated Kahayn's resourcefulness.*

The room was very noisy: the tick-tick-ticking of IV pumps; the atonal blip of cardiac monitors; and the whoosh and sigh of ventilators. The nurse on duty, a major, stepped smartly to attention and reported that all three patients were doing well.

He ran his fingers along each patient's scalp. Saad's scar was old and firm. But Kahayn's and Arin's were new, the sutures not yet removed, and Arin's new left arm was a wonder: jointed with a thick pincer instead of a hand. None of them dreamed; they were too heavily sedated for that. But he wondered if, when Saad awoke, they would share dreams, too. He knew for sure, though: the man Saad would cease to exist because Blate would break him.

So we're not done for yet. In fact, we've just begun. His lips curled into a smile. *Because no door ever closed that another didn't open.*

*   *   *

"Oh, my God," said Lense. She sat on a biobed in her own sickbay, absolutely stunned. "Julian, that can't be right."

"But it is," said Bashir. The overhead light turned the smooth skin of his forehead a warm bronze. "I can run it again but," he put a hand to her neck, "there's no mistake, Elizabeth."

"But . . ." She hooked her hand onto Julian's arm and just hung on. "I don't know what to do," she said.

"Well, you could give happiness a whirl. Maybe this is good."

"Or maybe it's bad."

"Possibly."

"I don't know what to do," she said again.

"Elizabeth," said Bashir, and he touched his forehead to hers with easy intimacy. "Don't do anything, my dear."

"Do *nothing?*"

"Do nothing. You have time. Give it thought. But above all," he pulled back until their eyes locked, *"be . . . happy.* Because this is rare, and very precious. It's like something out of the ashes. Maybe you won't want it in the end. But maybe you will, because it's a gift of things past and a possible future. It's a gift."

"You think?" And then she said it, out loud, to make it real and because she thought that, maybe, this was a gift she should keep.

"I'm going to have a baby, Julian," she said. "I'm going to have a child."

ABOUT THE AUTHORS

ILSA J. BICK is the author of such prize-winning stories as "A Ribbon for Rosie" in *Star Trek: Strange New Worlds II*, "Shadows, in the Dark" in *Strange New Worlds IV*, and "The Quality of Wetness" in *Writers of the Future* Volume XVI. Her SCIFICTION mystery, "The Key," was given an honorable mention in *The Best American Mystery Stories 2005*, edited by Joyce Carol Oates. Her first published novel, *Star Trek The Lost Era: Well of Souls*, cracked the 2003 Barnes and Noble Bestseller List, and she is the author of several stories that have appeared on/in SCIFICTION, *Challenging Destiny, Talebones, Beyond the Last Star, Star Trek: New Frontier: No Limits,* and *Star Trek: Voyager: Distant Shores,* among many others. She's also the author of another *Corps of Engineers* eBook—*Ghost,* released in 2007—and has written many short stories and novels in the *BattleTech/MechWarrior Dark Age* universe, both in print and on BattleCorps.com. Her latest *MWDA* book, *Dragon Rising,* came out in February 2007. Ilsa is currently at work on an original novel, *Watchers.* Think Stephen King hooks up with Dan Brown and does Kabbalah, and you've got the idea. She lives in Wisconsin with her husband, two children, and two cats. Sometimes, she even cooks for them.

KEITH R.A. DeCANDIDO co-developed *Star Trek: Corps of Engineers* with John J. Ordover in 2000, back when it was called *S.C.E.*, and has written more eBooks in the series than anyone except for Dayton Ward and Kevin Dilmore (for which, of course, they must die). He is also the editor of the *Star Trek* eBook line, having supervised not only this series, but also the miniseries *Mere Anarchy* (for the fortieth anniversary of *Star Trek*) and *Slings and Arrows* (for the twentieth anniversary of *Next Generation*), and has edited several anthologies both *Star Trek* (*No Limits*, *Tales of the Dominion War*, *Tales from the Captain's Table*) and not (*Imaginings: An Anthology of Long Short Fiction*, *Doctor Who: Short Trips: The Quality of Leadership*). As a writer, he's penned tales in many worlds, including fifteen *Star Trek* novels, as well as work in the universes of TV shows (*Buffy the Vampire Slayer*, *Supernatural*, *CSI: NY*, *Gene Roddenberry's Andromeda*, *Farscape*, etc.), videogames (*World of Warcraft*, *StarCraft*, *Command and Conquer*, *Resident Evil*), and comic books (Spider-Man, X-Men, Silver Surfer, Hulk). Find out more at his Web site at www.DeCandido.net or read his inane ramblings at kradical.livejournal.com.

JOHN J. ORDOVER used to be the Executive Editor of the *Star Trek* fiction line for Pocket Books, where he co-developed the *New Frontier* series (with Peter David) and the *Corps of Engineers* series (with Keith R.A. DeCandido), and also brought record-breaking sales to the line. He also used to be the Editor-in-Chief of Phobos Science Fiction and Fantasy. These days, he's a web consultant, and also the happy husband of Carol Greenburg and the happy father of Arren Isaac Ordover.

TERRI OSBORNE has taken several trips aboard the *da Vinci* after *Malefictorum*, which are available in eBook form: *Progress*, which kicked off the six-part *What's Past* miniseries, and the two-part *Remembrance of Things Past*, a crossover with *Star Trek: The Next Generation*. Terri's short fiction has appeared in the *Star Trek* anthologies *Deep Space Nine: Prophecy and Change*, *New Frontier: No Limits*, and *Voyager: Distant Shores* as well as the *Doctor Who: Short Trips* anthology *The Quality of Leadership*. She also wrote *That Sleep of Death*, the fourth part of the six-eBook *Slings and Arrows*, celebrating the twentieth anniversary of *Next Generation*. Terri is currently working on several other projects that will take her to the Ireland of the past, the Mars of the future, and other places both near and far. Find out more at her website at www.terriosborne.com.

CORY RUSHTON is a Canadian living in the United Kingdom with his lovely and patient wife Susan, where he teaches English at the University of Bristol. Having now fulfilled a lifelong ambition to write for *Star Trek*, he feels that retirement from the world is the only rational option.